GEARS OF CHANGE

ANTHONY LAKEN

The Infinity Machine Series

I. One Cog Turning
II. On Dark Horizons
III. Gears of Change

First published by Luna Press Publishing, Edinburgh, 2020

www.lunapresspublishing.com

ISBN-13: 978-1-913387-27-3

For Stephanie and George.

Contents

CHAPTER ONE

Bellina looked up. The sun lounged in the sky like a pregnant cow, lazy, tired. Not a single cloud interrupted the scene. She felt a drop of sweat wriggle free from the nape of her neck and trace a path down her back. *Someone somewhere is enjoying this*, she thought. The idea rolled around inside her skull, conjuring images of a life where a beautiful day could still bring happiness. But for her, she knew those days were gone.

Weeks had passed since they had fled from Victory. The image of the Tremoran flag rising over the Castrian Wall was burned into her skull. So were a lot of other things from that day, but she pushed those aside. The man named Whist had led their escape. He had seemed to have an almost inexhaustible number of connections: people who had given them a night's rest under their roofs, people who had fed them, and a man who had provided them with horses. As such, the most wanted people in the Empire had made it to their destination with little alarm.

You've been lucky, a cold voice in Bellina's head whispered. *You've been more than lucky. But that luck will run out and then …*

With a shake of the head, Bellina silenced her mind. That voice was the voice of doubt, and she had no time for that. She looked round at her companions. Dargo was riding next to a sullen Elvgren, trying to engage him in conversation. Cirona was just ahead staring vacantly into the distance. Holger caught her gaze and smiled. Crenshaw was further back, lost in a world of his own, while Whist and Castros Del Var, the man she now knew was her father, rode side by side, talking.

Her gaze lingered on Castros. She opened her mouth, wanting to call him, to talk with him, but the words collapsed in her throat. That was how it had been the whole journey. Their few chances to speak had faltered into awkward silence, neither knowing quite what to say. Curiosity was growing inside her to damn near bursting point though. But still, the words, the right ones to begin, didn't come.

Bellina forced her eyes back to the road ahead. They were deep in the Sylvantain countryside, making their way towards her grandfather's summer house, the place he had told them to go to with his last breaths.

All around her, steep hills lined with olive groves rose up like shrugging giants. Dust from the path's packed dirt puffed up, making her eyes itch. Bellina rubbed them and silently cursed herself for having made them even more sore. A lizard sat basking on a flat rock by the side of the road, his bulbous eyes meeting her own, seeming alight with reptilian accusation. *What are you going to do?* they seemed to say. *What are you going to do?* She pulled her eyes away, giving herself a shake. *Gods*, she thought, *it's just a bloody lizard; I've been out in the sun too long.*

'Are we there yet!' she heard Dargo cry from behind her.

'It's not far now, Dar,' she replied, repressing a sigh.

Truth be told she had never taken this route to her grandfather's summer residence. Usually, they made the journey from Sipoli — the Sylvantain capital — by carriage, sticking to the main road, and even then, most times she had dozed, lulled to sleep by the clop of horses' hooves and the heat. She was relying on the memories of a few expeditions into the land surrounding the residence, but those memories were old and fuzzed by time. If only she could catch sight of a landmark, something recognisable …

Then she saw it. The white stone walls and the terracotta roofs of the Agrioli family farm. Her mind lit up with memories of the kindly old couple who had taken her on fruit-picking excursions, of her grandfather, his formal self left behind for his holidays, laughing with old man Agrioli in the kitchen over a bottle of wine, of the big tree by the farmhouse where they had all erected a makeshift swing. They were the first pleasant thoughts she'd had in a while, and Bellina could do nothing to stop the wide grin spreading over her face.

'Come on!' she called over her shoulder. 'There are some people I want you to meet.'

She drove her heels into the side of her horse, felt the beast's powerful muscles shift beneath her and was off. The wind slipped through her hair making the dark strands dance. Her heart leapt, and a laugh even escaped her lips. The road disappeared under the horse's thundering hooves, and she was soon at the gate that led into the Agrioli land. Slowing her mount to a trot, she passed through.

As soon she entered, a sickly-sweet aroma assaulted her nose. The path to the farmhouse was lined with orange trees, each branch bent low, barely supporting the weight of the overripe fruit. *This isn't like the old man*, she thought; *he would have hired people to harvest these long ago.*

Something's wrong, the voice in her head whispered. *Something is very wrong.*

Once more, Bellina spurred her horse into life. The orchard whipped past her, the trees smudging into each other as she sped along. Before long, the path ended, the vista opening up to reveal the farmhouse. With a sharp tug, she brought her horse to an abrupt stop. Her eyes grew wide while her mind fought to comprehend what she was looking at. There, hanging from the tree she had played on, were the corpses of the Agriolis. A bloated tongue poked out of the old man's mouth, the rope around his neck still taut. Flies crawled over their faces, and Bellina watched one creep up Mrs Agrioli's nose. Bellina's mouth filled with sour bile, almost choking her.

'By the gods,' she heard someone mutter behind her.

She looked round, seeing the face of her father, his gaze locked on the bodies, lips curled in disgust.

'Who did this?' Holger asked.

'There's your answer,' Cirona said, pointing to the base of the tree.

Bellina's gaze followed the Major's finger. Nailed to the base of the tree was a board, crudely written words daubed across it. *These people refused to pay the duke's army their proper dues*, it read.

'Fucking sickos,' Dargo said, spitting on the ground.

'We … we need to cut them down,' Crenshaw said. 'Give them a proper burial.'

'They've not been dead long,' Whist said, urging his horse close to the tree. 'Maybe three days.'

'Then the duke's men could still be close by,' Castros replied. 'We need to leave. If they were making for the summer house …'

'What do you say, Bellina?' Holger said.

Bellina felt her stomach tighten, solidify into a ball of cold metal.

'We go now,' she said. 'And pray whatever my grandfather left at the house is not already destroyed.'

For a moment, her eyes met Holger's. She watched his brows draw together, a pained expression on his face. Then he nodded and turned his horse around. The others followed suit, and Bellina took her place at the front of the group. As she passed through the orchard once more, she gripped the reins so tight her fists trembled. *They will not have died in vain*, she thought, setting her jaw firm. *Marmossa, Kurkeshi, the duke — they'll pay, they'll all pay.*

***

Scholar Laluc Fontaine sat in the corner of the hidden room, his knees drawn up to his chin, waiting. Though to call the space a "room" was an overstatement of the highest order. In the time he'd spent hidden, he had grown used to the smell of mildew and rot, his eyes accustomed to the dark. If he had been artistically inclined, he would have been able to draw a perfect copy of the space, every crack in the mortar, every spider's web.

He had no idea how long he'd been in the room — days, surely it had been days — as, in his haste, he had forgotten to pick up his pocket watch, a graduation present from his father — no doubt, stolen now. At first, he had tried to reckon the passing seconds by imagining the innards of his timepiece, the steady, comforting regularity of the gears and cogs moving, but the noise from without had shattered his concentration.

All he knew for certain was that the soldiers had arrived at two in the afternoon. He had seen them crest the top of the hill where the gate into the grounds lay, had watched them marshal their horses into single file to enter. He had known they would come, that they must come after the death of the Lord Chancellor — this *was* one of his homes, after all — but he'd thought there would be more time.

How many minutes had he wasted staring like an idiot at the approaching men? How many more treasures could he have gathered together and brought with him into hiding if he had not frozen like a dormouse before a cat? He shook his head. *What's done is done*, he told himself. *At least you saved the book.*

Fontaine licked his dry lips and reached with trembling fingers for his satchel. He undid the clasp and pulled out the book, the *Radiana Magnifica*. It felt as if his whole life had been spent trying to get hold of the tome, thirty-two years begging and pleading to be given access to it, and now, here he sat in the damp corner of a crawlspace with it in his lap. In his mind, he had always imagined studying it in the great library of Hoftstaten University, light streaming through the massive windows, pouring over it like a lover.

The book was the key to it all, the forgotten history of the world, the secrets of the First Ones, captured by the magical process of writing, the words and thoughts of men long since dead transmitted to him through time by the means of pen and ink. In the time he had been in possession of it, he had made some headway ... but the *Radiana* was a puzzle inside a puzzle, page after page of cryptic riddles, and Laluc very much doubted that there had been more than a few men alive at the time it was written who could have solved it. But the writer had done it for a reason. It was a test, a challenge to prove yourself worthy of the knowledge within, and Fontaine was determined to do just that. But how quickly he could do it was another matter, and time was running short.

He hugged the book close to his chest and screwed his eyes shut.

Yes, time really was running out. The words of the prophesy were being proved true, and the only man who had ever believed them as much as Fontaine was now dead. A wave of nausea rolled through his stomach. The Lord Chancellor was gone, shot like a mad dog.

During their years of working together, Laluc had come to view the man as a second father. The differences between his real parent and the Lord Chancellor were few, though he was relying on a handful of memories left at the back of his brain to compare the two men — his father having died when he was just a boy. Both had been stern men, fair men, men who would do anything to protect the people in their care.

The bang of something falling somewhere, brought him back to the present. *What the hells was it? Surely the soldiers had left by now.* He was sure he had heard their feet stamping out of the house ages ago.

Are you sure enough to poke your head from this hole, little mouse? a voice in his head whispered.

Fontaine swallowed hard, his hands clenching and unclenching by his side. Time really was running out, and he was accomplishing nothing stuck in his hiding place. Taking a deep breath, he got to his feet. He was by no means a tall man, but he still had to slouch his shoulders in order to not bang his head. On trembling legs, he crossed the short distance to the exit. From his point of view, it looked like a roughly hewn door, but on the other side, he knew it appeared to be a faultless part of the kitchen wall.

Pressing his ear to the wood, Fontaine listened. The laughter, the cries, the crashing madness of the soldiers were gone. Still his hand hovered above the small handle.

'Come on, you damned coward,' he said to himself.

He took the handle in his sweating palm, twisted it and … nothing. He tried again. Still the door didn't budge. Beads of sweat formed on his upper lip. Was there some kind of lock he didn't know about? No, no, he just needed to be a bit more forceful. Placing his shoulder against the door, he pushed, muscles straining in his back and legs. His eyes narrowed to slits with the effort, and just when he was about to give in, the door moved a fraction.

Wiping the sweat from his brow, he peered through the gap he had created and saw the problem. A cabinet of some description had fallen across the front of the hidden door. Did he have the energy to force his way out? His stomach rumbled as if in answer. He had been living on the rind of cheese and stale crust of bread he had taken in with him. He was a man of learning not action, as his frail frame attested, and he would have been hard pushed to move the cabinet in prime condition. A bitter laugh escaped his lips. *What a farce*, he thought, *the only man alive who truly understands the import of what's happening, the man with the key to stopping this madness is undone by a fallen piece of furniture.*

The laughter turned into hysterical giggles, and he had to pinch his leg to regain control of himself. He took another deep breath and felt his jaw muscles stiffen. No, this was not going to be the end. Taking as many steps back as the small room would allow, Fontaine girded himself then charged the door. He felt it budge a smidge more. Again and again, he threw himself at it. His breath became ragged, sweat drenched his clothes, but still he charged. He paused, panting, his shoulder feeling as if it was stuffed with needles, then threw himself forwards again.

In a cacophony of screeching, the door flew open and Fontaine went sprawling out onto the kitchen's flagstones. His chin jarred upon impact, and he tasted blood on his lips … but he was out. For a moment, he lay chuckling to himself, then with a monumental effort, he heaved his aching body off the floor.

The first thing he did was aim a petulant kick at his tormentor, the cabinet, that left him hopping around the kitchen holding his left foot. When he finally came to a stop, he couldn't believe what he was seeing. The room had been torn apart, literally in some places. Walls had been attacked with hammers, swords. Crude graffiti was splashed over any other clean space. Bottles, plates, glassware had all been smashed in the orgy of destruction. A sack of sprouting potatoes lay upon the table, one tumbling to the floor with a thump as he watched. Fontaine almost laughed; he had been drawn out of hiding by an errant tuber. Turning away, his nose wrinkled when he noticed a shit that had been left by the kitchen door.

Just as he was considering how in the world he was going to sort the mess out, he heard something. He froze, brows furrowed, listening. There it was again. His eyes darted about, searching for an alternative source for the sound … but there was none. What he was hearing was the unmistakable clop of hooves.

Rushing to the window, Fontaine peered through a smashed pane. There he saw them. Riders. He felt the marrow freeze in his bones and was halfway back to the hiding hole when he stopped himself. He shook his head. No, this wasn't how he was going to end, cowering like vermin. He would go down with a bang, taking as many of the bastards as he could with him.

At that moment, the thought of dying seemed a strange, abstract thing. Not something to be feared but embraced. No more worrying about ancient prophesies or cryptic gibberish, just sweet oblivion.

In a manic fever, he looked about him for a weapon. He rattled through drawers, but all the silverware and cutlery had been taken. Then in the corner of a cupboard, he found a large copper pan. His thin arms could barely lift it, but it was the best he could do.

The sound of the horses was growing louder. Fontaine crept towards the front door, crouching low. With the pan in his hands, he waited.

*****

Elvgren sat, shoulders sagged, neck bent, in the saddle. It felt to him as if there was a hollowness in his chest, an aching hole that throbbed deep and dull with every passing second. He would have liked to say that his current mental state was due to the hanging couple he had just seen, but in truth, the sadness that coursed through him was only for himself.

'Are you gonna be like this all day?' Dargo asked, reining his horse back to match the morose tempo of Elvgren's.

'Like what?'

'Like … this,' Dargo said, waving his hands at Elvgren.

Tilting his head to the heavens, Elvgren let out a sigh. 'Can you blame me?' he asked.

'What? For going about with a face like a slapped arse?'

'You little … do you understand what I've lost, Dar? Can you grasp how fucking far I've fallen?' Elvgren said.

'Oh, boo-fucking-hoo,' Dargo replied with a snort. 'You ain't a lord no more. So what? We're alive, ain't we? And that's more than we can say for those poor bastards back at that farm.'

Elvgren rolled his eyes. 'You don't get it, do you? The duke has stripped my family of its assets and doled them out to one of his bootlickers. The Lord Chancellor is dead, and with him, my chance of one day ruling the Empire. I haven't bathed properly in weeks, and to cap it all off, my arse is so sore from riding all day that I doubt I'll ever be able to sit right again,' he said. 'I have lost everything.'

'That was quite the little speech, sounds like something from a bad, half-penny play,' Dargo said. 'Poor old you. What about Bellina, eh? You know, the woman you're engaged to be married to? She's just lost her father, or grandfather, or … well, she's just lost someone she loved. What do you care if your family lost their land? You weren't exactly on the best of terms with 'em; who's to say you would'a got anything outta them anyway after your *last* meeting. As for ruling the Empire … well, I'm yer mate, Gren, and I mean this with all the respect I can find, but I wouldn't trust you to run a piss-up in a brewery; I don't think you were ever going to sit in the big seat.'

Elvgren's eyes grew wide then he slowly shook his head. 'Well, thank you for your tea and sympathy, Dargo,' he exclaimed before spurring his horse into a faster trot.

Drawing away from the boy, he felt his cheeks flush and his nostrils flare. The blood pounded in his temples to the beat of a drum. But he knew deep down that the anger he felt wasn't because of Dargo's words. No, this was something else. *How can I expect Dar to understand?* he thought. *He's never had anything to lose.*

It wasn't the loss of the land, money or prestige that bothered him; it was the loss of the chance to prove himself to either the Lord Chancellor or his parents. For so long, he had itched to show his worth, to make them see the greatness that he knew was inside him, but every chance he'd had had ended in disaster, every opportunity to step out from his brother Jeremias' shadow had imploded.

First the affair in Burkesh had gone so far south it had looped round on itself, then he had been duped by the duke's flattery, revealing all that he knew to the man and gaining nothing in return. Was it all his fault? Was there something fundamentally wrong with him that everything he touched turned to shit?

No.

No, it was everyone else. They were to blame. If he hadn't grown up with the lofty ideal of his brother floating like a spectre over him and his parents, things would have been fine. If the Lord Chancellor hadn't wandered into his life, offering him, and his power-hungry mother and father, a sniff of the power they had craved for so long, things would have gone along quite nicely thank you very much. He would have married some vapid heiress, waited for their respective parents to die, and lived the life of luxury and comfort that was his birthright.

Instead, what had he got? He was now one of the most wanted men in the Empire. His travelling companions consisted of spies, disgraced soldiers, cognopaths and mages. These weren't his people. His people were sitting down somewhere enjoying tea, wearing scandalised faces and whispering with horror about the kind of group he was now part of.

His gaze wandered and rested on Bellina. In what felt like another life, he had stood in front of the assembled great and good of the Estrian Empire and promised himself to her. Elvgren let out a bitter snort of laughter. What did that matter now? There was nothing holding either of them to that promise. Once he'd had time to gather his thoughts and compose himself, it would be time to part ways. He still had a bit of money hidden about his person; he could take that, board a ship and go far, far away, start over. Perhaps he'd ask Dargo to come?

If you really think it's over, his inner voice whispered, *why can't you take your eyes off her?*

Elvgren shook his head, trying to banish the thought, but it echoed around his skull. The next moment, they reached the crest of a hill, and *all* his thoughts departed.

At the bottom of the hill, past a busted gate and a path lined with flowering bushes, rose a white three-storeyd villa, it's blue tiled roof glistening in the sun. It seemed to be calling to him, filling his mind with images of comfortable chairs, soft beds, luxury — things that had been sorely lacking in their travels so far.

'There it is,' he heard Bellina say. 'Let's go.'

'Wait,' Castros said. 'Let's not risk any surprises. The duke's soldiers could be lying in wait for us. Can you sense anyone inside, Bellina?'

Elvgren watched Bellina's brow furrow.

'I'm not sure,' she said. 'I can sense *something* in there … but I can't even tell if it's human.'

Elvgren bit the inside of his cheek. 'I'm not waiting around out here smelling like a docker coming off shift because you think you can sense a dormouse scampering about the wall,' he said.

He geed up his horse and sped towards the mansion.

'Stop, you idiot,' he heard Castros cry. 'There could be men wearing thought suppressors in there!'

'Bah!' Elvgren shouted back at him. He was not going to let such nonsense stand between him and resting his raw arse cheeks on the soft, downy cushion of a good armchair.

The path whizzed by him, and soon, he reached the house. He dismounted in a single leap, his cramped muscles protesting, and strode towards the door. Without a second thought, he pushed it open. The door swung back smoothly to reveal … nothing but a tiled hall.

'You see?' he shouted back to the others, laughter on his lips. 'There's nothing to …'

He was cut off by a rustling sound behind him. Elvgren spun round on his heel and just had time to register the form of a small man brandishing a copper pan before the world went dark.

***

Cirona placed her mug back on the table and let out an appreciative sigh. Despite the ransacking of the summer house by the duke's soldiers, they had managed to make the kitchen look somewhat presentable, even stumbling across a tin of unspoiled coffee. Scholar Fontaine had fussed around like an old maid, fetching water from the well, making the drinks and apologising a thousand times to Elvgren.

Tilting her head to the side, Cirona observed the man. He was of slight build, worry lines etched onto a face too young for them. A frantic energy exuded from him, a contagious sense that time was running out. She bit her lip, brows furrowing; this was the man the Lord Chancellor had told them to find? This was the man who could put all the pieces of the puzzle together?

She closed her eyes and took a deep breath. No. No more questioning. Her mind had done far too much of that lately. What she needed was orders. A job to do that she could focus on and get done. But orders came from leaders, and at that moment, as the group talked over each other around the table, none seemed forthcoming.

'The people need guidance.'

'Why? This is the perfect opportunity to establish a real democracy …'

'Can I just say once more how sorry I am about the whole pan incident …'

'Sorry won't make my head stop aching or this bruise go down. Can't you do anything, Waltus?'

'Yer just got a bump on the head. I ain't gonna waste my time and energy fixing that.'

'I just can't stop thinking about those people back at the farm; we should have done something …'

'Enough!' Bellina cried.

Cirona's eyes, and those of everyone else, turned towards her. She stood, fists resting on the table, glowering. For a moment, it seemed to Cirona as if the spectre of the Lord Chancellor stood behind the girl, a smile on his lips.

'It has been a long trip, and we're all tired, but we don't have time to sit around and chew the cud. We shall each speak in turn,' Bellina said, looking around the room, meeting everyone with her gaze, daring them to oppose her. 'Then we shall plot our course from there. Scholar Fontaine, I would like you to go first. Please tell us what was so important about the scrap of paper my grandfather told us to bring you and fill us in on just what this prophesy is.'

As Bellina took her seat, Cirona switched her attention to Fontaine. His eyes darted about the room, the protrusion in his throat bobbing like a cork.

'Well … um … firstly the … er … piece of paper …' he began.

'For the love of … Spit it out, man!' Elvgren exclaimed.

'Quiet!' Bellina shot at him. Cirona saw Elvgren purse his lips. He looked as if he was about to say something, but instead, he folded his arms and stared at the ground. 'Pray continue, scholar.'

'The piece of "paper" was very important. It has helped to fill in a missing link in my knowledge. Your father …'

'Grandfather.' Bellina corrected him.

'I beg your pardon … *grandfather*, has … I mean, *had* been working on cracking the code to the *Radiana Magnifica*. The Lord Chancellor was one of only a handful of people capable of reading ancient Atvorian. In fact, he made many strides in—'

'May we please have the short version?' Bellina interrupted.

For a second, Fontaine looked, to Cirona, like a ruffled owl. He licked his lips then continued.

'In short, the scrap of paper was a cypher key. With it I should be able to unlock the book's secrets.'

'You mean you haven't already?' Elvgren said. 'We went through the twelve hells to get that bloody thing, and you still can't tell us what it says!'

'The *Radiana Magnifica* is a multi-layered puzzle. It will not simply give up its secrets in one day. It needs to be decoded, teased apart, and even then, the translation is a riddle,' Fontaine replied with a sniff.

Elvgren opened his mouth to add something, but Bellina held up her hand and stopped him.

'Fine. So, the paper was a key to unlocking the book. Now, what is the prophesy?' she said.

Fontaine's eyes took on a faraway look, and he began to recite words like a child repeating back his times tables.

'In the east shall rise a dark sun, terrible to behold. Ageless, deathless, it seeks its kin. Upon its back lays an empire. It shall swallow the eagle whole, lay waste to its nest, calm the churning ocean—'

'Then the City of the Dead shall come to life, and the time of Terrors begin again,' Castros cut in, finishing the scholar's sentence. 'The old man would spout that rubbish to me at any opportunity.'

'It most certainly is not rubbish!' Fontaine cried. 'The dark sun must be Marmossa, the Grand Multan, Burkesh, or possibly, it is all three combined. The eagle—'

'Would be Estria,' Bellina cut in. 'That was the ancient symbol of Amlith's house, if I'm not mistaken.'

'You are quite right, Lady Bellina. Your grandfather taught you well,' Fontaine replied, beaming from ear-to-ear.

'You can't tell me you believe this nonsense?' Castros said, his gaze shifting between Bellina and Fontaine. 'Empires rise and fall. Countries get invaded. It's just the endless cycle of violence and oppression repeating itself. What's happening now was *not* preordained by some mad monk hundreds of years ago.'

'Then do you deny what I saw?' Bellina said, her voice barely a whisper, but each word ringing out like struck steel.

Cirona watched the pair, their eyes locked, the space between them a snow-crusted wasteland.

'I do not deny that you saw … something,' Castros conceded. 'But the duke's daughter was influencing what that *something* was.'

For a second, Cirona saw fury pass across Bellina's face like hot lava. As quick as it appeared it was gone.

'Thank you, Mr Del Var, Scholar Fontaine, for your input. I would now like to add my information to the mix,' she said, ice dripping from every word. 'I heard from Dahlia's own mouth that there was one time when she lost contact with me. That was during my conversation with the Fargazer. During our conversation, I was told that Marmossa is the Thirteenth Terror, that he is searching for things called relics — pieces of the First Ones, from what I can tell.'

'Indeed,' Fontaine cut in. 'The relics are believed to be the source of sortilenergy. Massive deposits of power. With them at his disposal I shudder to think what Marmossa could do.'

'Thank you, scholar,' Bellina said, shooting the man an irritated look. 'The Fargazer also said that around me would gather: a person with newly awakened powers, someone with Amlith's blood, a healer, a warrior, a scholar, a thief, a father, a lover and a fallen king, and that it was my job to lead us. Can you deny that apart from the fallen king and the lover, all those now sit at this table?'

Cirona looked round the table, saw a sceptical frown on Elvgren and Castros' faces, curiosity on Dargo's and Crenshaw's, a look of reluctant acceptance on Waltus', a thoughtful twist upon Whist's lips and unwavering belief on Holger's and Fontaine's. Although Cirona couldn't say she was convinced, she, like everyone else, remained quiet.

'Very well then,' Bellina continued. 'My next question is this — Will you follow me?'

Silence fell across the room.

'Aye. I'll follow you,' Holger said at last.

'Me too,' Dargo answered.

'And I,' Fontaine added.

'Count me in,' Whist replied.

'I'd follow that arse anywhere,' Waltus said with a lecherous smile.

'I would, but my first priority is finding Bar,' Crenshaw said with a sigh.

'I'm … willing to listen,' Castros reluctantly acceded.

'What about you, Major?' Bellina asked.

Cirona met the girl's stare. *No*, she thought. *Not a girl anymore, a woman; and what a woman she's turned into.* A smile spread across Cirona's lips.

'Yes,' she said. 'I will follow you.'

All eyes, including Cirona's, turned to Elvgren. He sat, arms crossed, pouting.

'What?' he said. 'You may all buy this mumbo jumbo, but I don't. If I'd had a dream where some mythical being told me that the world and his butler had to follow me, I'd be laughed out of the room. Much to my surprise, I'm in the same boat as Mr Del Var. None of this is preordained; it's just the natural flow of things. If you ask me, we should thank our lucky stars we've got this far and recede quietly into the background.'

Bellina shook her head. 'After everything we've seen, everything we've been through, you still doubt the danger Marmossa, Kurkeshi and the duke pose? Even if you take out the prophesies and everything else, you still think it's right what they are doing?'

'It's not a case of right or wrong,' Elvgren replied. 'It is merely what has happened. It's over. We lost. We can't come back from this.'

'I know we can,' Bellina said, pushing back her shoulders. 'I have a plan. But first, would you share your information with us, Whist?'

Cirona watched Whist climb to his feet, reach inside his coat and throw a rag-eared copy of the *Estrian Chronicler* on the table. She fixed her gaze upon the headline and had to stifle a gasp.

'I stole this in the last town we stopped in,' Whist said.

'What's it say?' Dargo said.

'It … it says that all the heirs to the throne were found … found to be traitors, and as such, were … were executed,' Elvgren said.

For a second, they all sat in stunned silence.

'Fucking hells! Sorry, Gren,' Dargo said.

'I'm sure Dargo speaks for the whole room,' Bellina said. 'Though it is a personal tragedy for you, Elvgren, it also presents us with an unlooked-for opportunity. With all the other claimants gone, you, Elvgren, are the next in line. As such, I propose we continue our engagement, presenting ourselves as the rightful rulers of Estria and garner support from the people as we make our way to Gortrix. Do you agree to this?'

Cirona watched Elvgren's pale face look up. His gaze was unfocused, his chin trembling.

'What? I … yes … of … of course,' was all he managed to say.

'Good,' Bellina replied with a sharp nod. 'This, though, is only one facet to the plan. Castros, Whist and Holger, I would like you to find Midge and eliminate Khasal. With him out of the picture, the malovors should prove unmanageable for the duke.'

Whist nodded while Holger looked as if he'd just had his insides pulled out and spread in front of him.

'I still believe that the people should govern themselves. Taking down the duke and putting you and Elvgren in his place solves nothing,' Castros said.

'Now is not the time for ideology,' Bellina replied. 'When we manage to gain control, we will be more than happy to listen to your requests. Now, will you help us?'

'I … yes,' Castros replied.

As soon as the words were out of his mouth, she turned to Cirona.

'Major, I would like you to make your way to Narvale. From what Whist has discerned, they, along with Gortrix, have refused to accept the duke's rule. While there, I want you to raise us an army.'

Cirona raised her eyebrows. 'I can't say I'm fully behind this. The Narvglanders are a proud and unpredictable people. What could I offer them to get them onside?'

'If they agree to help, I am willing to allow them to remain part of the Empire but with autonomy over their affairs, including their right to worship their own gods,' Bellina said.

'It'll be a hard sell … but it may work,' Cirona said.

'Excellent,' Bellina replied. 'Waltus shall accompany you; having a White Mage alongside an army will be a massive boon. Waltus, are you happy with this?'

'Fine by me, lass,' Waltus replied, waggling his eyebrows at Cirona.

Cirona felt her skin itch but said nothing.

'Dargo, you will be coming with myself and Elvgren. I would have also liked Mr Crenshaw to travel with us as an adviser, but I fear your path leads elsewhere.'

'I'm afraid it does,' Crenshaw said. 'I know that bastard vooshu took Bar back to Timboko. I'm gonna follow after him, see if I can get him back.'

'Then our interests cross,' Fontaine interjected. 'If I'm correct, one of the relics is located in Timboko. Would you mind me tagging along? If that's alright with you, my lady.'

'I would have had you by my side, scholar but finding the relics is a task you are uniquely equipped for,' Bellina said.

'The more the merrier, I suppose,' Crenshaw replied, but Cirona couldn't help but notice the look of concern on the man's face.

'Then it's settled,' Bellina said. 'We shall go our separate ways in the morning. I suggest we all get a good night's sleep. You can find your own rooms.'

Bellina gestured towards the door. One by one, they left the table. Cirona was the last to go.

'He would have been proud of you,' she said.

For half a heartbeat, she thought she saw indecision flicker on Bellina's face, a tiny crack showing the truth behind the new mask she had put on.

'Thank you, Major. Have a pleasant evening.'

Cirona made her way to the door. She could not help but feel some trickle of sadness for the Bellina who had gone. But somewhere deep inside, she realised it had been inevitable. Perhaps this was what the Lord Chancellor had been doing all along — grooming his granddaughter for this moment. As she opened the door to the kitchen, she shook her head. No, not even Calvin Ressa could plot that far ahead. Bellina was only mimicking what she had learnt at his elbow.

Mimicking or not, Cirona found she didn't care. For the first time in what felt like forever she had her orders. And she was damn well going to follow them … or die trying.

***

'Cass! Are you even listening to me?'

'What? Yes. Yes, of course,' Castros said, pausing mid-stride and shifting his gaze to Whist.

'Alright then, what was I just telling you?' Whist asked.

Castros frowned. What had they been talking about? Everything had been like this of late — a world too loud, full of confusion and uncertainty. He stared blankly around the bedroom as if looking for an answer in the walls.

'I … I can't remember,' he admitted.

Whist let out a long sigh. He stood up and crossed over to Castros, grabbing his shoulders. 'This isn't you, Cass,' he said, looking Del Var in the eye.

Flinching away, Castros pulled himself free of Whist's grasp. 'Oh really?' he replied, a sneer curling his lips. 'This isn't me? Then what about you? I *thought* I knew you. But then it turns out you've been a spy for my father all along, working for the very system we wanted to tear down.'

Blowing out his cheeks, Whist let loose a silent blast of air. He rubbed his hand across his face and sat back down at the table. 'How many times are we going to have to do this?' he said. 'I haven't always been a spy. Your father recruited me after you were exiled. With you gone, Cass, I didn't have too many options. It was work for him or be sent to Raven's Down to bust rocks for the rest of my life.'

'You should have gone to prison. At least then you could've retained your dignity,' Castros replied.

Whist laughed. 'My dignity? My dignity ain't worth squat. The Lord Chancellor saved my life when he signed me up that day. He gave me purpose, drive. I'd trade my dignity in for that any day of the week.'

Castros kneaded his temples, trying to stop a headache coming on. 'The man was nothing but a self-serving liar. He was bloody good at it too. That was his favourite trick — convincing a person they wanted to do something they really didn't. Gods, did he do a number on you.'

'You've made this too personal, Cass. Your father was a great man. I came to learn that, to respect that. He only ever did what he thought was for the best for the people of this Empire. Sometimes that meant he had to make some pretty shitty decisions. But he made them, and he carried the burden of that on his shoulders and never once complained about it. If you could just disentangle your feelings, take a step back—'

'I would see what?' Castros interrupted. 'Saint Calvin up on his lofty throne, gallantly sending people to their deaths "for the good of the Empire".'

Whist tilted his head back and pinched the bridge of his nose. 'This is getting us nowhere,' he said. 'Why don't you just go and speak to her?'

'What?' Castros replied.

'Go and speak to her. Your daughter. It's this family stuff that's got you all muddled up. In the past few weeks, you've lost your father and gained a daughter you didn't know you had. It would make anyone's head spin. But don't make the mistake you did with your dad. Talk to her. Get to know her.'

Castros tapped his foot and shook his head slightly. It drove Del Var mad to think that Whist could still read him so well when his oldest friend was now such a mystery to him.

'I need some space,' Castros said, swatting the air with his hands.

'*Are* you going to speak to her?'

'That's none of your bloody business,' Del Var replied, stepping out of the room and slamming the door behind him.

Once outside, Castros rested his head against the cool wall of the hallway. *Gods, the bastard is right,* he thought, *all of this has spun me round and put me back on my feet again.* The million things he had wanted to ask his father churned inside his head like a storm-whipped sea. He clenched his jaw, his teeth grinding together as he fought to force back a sob. Whist — as much as he hated to admit it — was right. He wouldn't make the same mistake twice. He would talk to Bellina; he would speak with his daughter.

Before he knew it, Castros found himself outside the kitchen door. He stood there looking at it. Listening, he reached out a tentative hand. Was that weeping he could hear? Taking a deep breath, he knocked. He heard rustling from the room beyond then a hoarse voice said, 'Enter.'

With just that one command, he was whisked back to his youth, to the handful of times he had stood before a door waiting to speak with his father on the few occasions each year he saw him. He scrunched his hands into balls. *That's the past*, he thought. *There's nothing you can do about that; focus on what's in front of you.* He closed his eyes, nodded and entered the room.

Night had fallen, and the only light in the kitchen came from a single candle in the centre of the table. Bellina stood with her back to him, looking out of the window.

'I … I thought we should talk,' he said.

For a second, he thought he saw Bellina's body tense. 'Of course,' she said. 'Please have a seat.'

So formal, he thought, *so proper; it's like she's entertaining a distant acquaintance.* But then, they weren't even that. He took his seat and watched as Bellina walked towards the table. She rested her hands on the back of a chair, keeping her face in shadow.

'What is it?' she asked.

Castros opened his mouth, his brain stumbling around trying to find the right words to get things started, to begin building a bridge between them. He had always prided himself on being articulate, of finding the right thing to say, but now, when he needed to most, nothing would come to mind. In the end, it was Bellina who spoke first.

'I hope you are not dissatisfied with today's meeting?' she said.

'Well,' Castros replied, 'I can't say I'm entirely pleased, but there are bigger matters to attend to.'

'Quite,' Bellina agreed.

Silence fell back over them, a silence so thick and heavy it threatened to crush him. Castros licked his lips. *Come on*, he told himself, *talk to her about her mother, her grandfather, you, just say something!*

'It's … er … lovely here this time of the year,' he finally said.

'Apart from the dead farmers and marauding soldiers, you mean?' she replied.

'I, well … yes.'

The silence descended again.

'Well, if that's all,' Bellina said, taking a step back.

'You … you look just like her, you know? Your mother, I mean,' he blurted out.

'I know,' she replied. 'I saw her.'

'Really? Where?'

'While I was in the sleep. Dahlia had twisted some of the memory, but I saw her. Saw her die while I was a babe in her arms.'

'That's … I'm sorry,' Castros said.

'Sorry? Sorry! She was shot in the street like a feral animal. Where were you? Where was the infamous Castros Del Var then?'

Castros felt his neck grow stiff, a pain welling at the back of his throat. 'I was fighting for the cause,' he said, wincing at how small and pathetic his words sounded.

Bellina gave a sharp, bitter laugh. 'The cause. That's what you were doing while the woman you loved — I'm assuming you *did* love her — was murdered? You would place the rights of strangers above those you should have been there for.'

'I … I tried to find her. But …'

'But what? You got waylaid helping some striking labourers gain a penny more an hour? How fucking noble.'

'Please … I …' Castros stammered, his mind reeling.

'Just get out,' Bellina hissed.

'Bellina … listen to me …'

'I said get out!' Bellina said. 'Leave tomorrow and do the job I gave you. Then when I'm in power and there's some bloody order restored, I'll instate the laws you want to see in place; I'll help you win your *cause*.'

Swallowing hard, Castros watched Bellina turn her back on him once more. The corners of his eyes began to sting, and his throat tightened like a noose. Without another word, he left the room.

✳✳✳

Bellina waited for the door to close before she crumpled into the chair, taking her head in her hands. She wanted to cry out, to chase Castros down and tell him to come back, to apologise for acting like a spoilt brat. But she didn't. She couldn't. *Stupid, stupid, stupid,* she thought. *Wasn't that the moment you'd been waiting for? Wasn't that the time to break the ice?*

She sat like that for a while, watching the candle burn down, the wax ooze into the dish, turning from hot and soft to cold and hard. As she stared, three soft raps sounded on the door. Bellina closed her eyes. She didn't want to speak to anyone. The light knocks sounded again. No, she didn't *want* to speak to anyone, but if she'd learnt one thing from her grandfather, it was that what you wanted went out the window when you were in charge. And on top of that, it wasn't as if she'd asked her companions to go out berry picking; they had the right to talk with her. Letting out a long sigh, she said, 'Enter.'

The door swung open, and she saw Holger's head poke round the edge of it. By the gods, this was the last conversation she wanted to have.

'Yes?' she said, climbing to her feet and walking out of the candle's light, desperate to hide the look of horror she knew was plastered across her face.

'I … er … came to see how you are,' Holger replied.

'I'm fine,' she lied.

'No, you're not,' Holger said, stepping forwards. 'You've been through the wringer. What happened with Dahlia, your grandfather, and now, all of this. There is no way you're fine.'

'I don't have time to not be alright,' she said. 'It's my job to lead us from here. To take us gods know where.'

'That's a big burden to carry on your own,' Holger said, closing the distance between them. 'A burden you never asked to carry.'

Bellina let out a bitter bark of laughter. 'What else can I do?' she said.

'Leave,' Holger replied, stroking her cheek with his large hand. 'Both of us, together, right now. We'll find a way to make it work, to be … to be happy. Let the world sort its own bloody problems out. There's nothing holding you here. Your betrothal … well, you're not bound to that anymore.'

'It's not as simple as that. I have an obligation—'

Holger cut Bellina off by kissing her firmly on the mouth. She gave herself over to it, and in that instant, she thought how glorious it would be to do as he said, to run somewhere far, far away and live happily ever after.

Stop it! a voice in her head called out. *You're thinking like a child, and you don't have time for that. End this. End this now.*

It felt like it took every atom of her being to do so, but Bellina pulled away.

'Belle? What's the—'

With a hard slap to his cheek, Bellina cut Holger off.

'How dare you?' she said. 'I am a noblewoman and an engaged one at that. It may be very well for commoners to run off and do as they please, but I have a duty to fulfil. And I might remind you that you have one too. The Lord Chancellor saw value in you, in your abilities. That was the reason he didn't throw you into a power plant. I, like him, expect you to carry out the orders you have been given.'

Holger held a hand to his cheek, eyes wide, chin trembling. 'So that's it?' he said. 'You have the perfect opportunity to be rid of all this madness. To slip away and—'

'Enough!' Bellina cut in. 'I have told you what I want you to do. Either carry out my wishes or go. I won't stop you.'

For a second, Holger's whole body seemed to draw in, shrinking down to nothing. Then he thrust his shoulders back, and looking her straight in the eye, said, 'I will carry out your orders. Even commoners like me want to pay off their debts.'

With that he turned on his heel and marched towards the door. Bellina watched him go, her insides caught in a vice. She struggled to get a breath into her lungs. *Why?* she thought. *Why would anyone want to be in charge? Why do so many fight for this? Why would you want something that hurts so fucking much?*

CHAPTER TWO

A thin band of weak, dawn light stole through the window, glinting on the barrel of the ballistol in Cirona's hand. She held the weapon up to her eye and peered down its length. She gave a crisp nod then tucked the piece into the band of her trousers, satisfied. In one fluid motion, she rose from the chair she was sat in and crossed the room to a cracked mirror.

It had taken her a few hours the previous evening, but eventually, she had found what she was looking for: boot polish and a pressing iron. The effort had been worth it. Her shoes were gleaming and her clothes free of wrinkles. As she gazed at her reflection, she felt, for the first time in a long while, like herself again. No more second guessing, no more whirlwind of confusion ripping up the foundations of her mind. She had her mission.

Cirona lifted her chin high, even allowed herself a smile. Her hands clenched into fists. It was time. She was ready. Turning around, her heels snapping together as if she were on parade, she left the room.

Outside, all was quiet. No one else was up yet. In a few short strides, she reached the top of the stairs. For a second, she paused, glancing back at the row of doors. She breathed deep, in through her nose then out through her mouth. It was better this way, no drawn-out goodbyes or farewells. Taking the steps two at a time, she went down to the ground floor.

She only had one more stop to make — a quick scrounge around the kitchen for supplies. Then she would be off. But as she approached the kitchen doors, she came to a stop, sniffing the air. Coffee. She could smell coffee. Frowning, she grabbed the handle and entered the kitchen.

'Finally up, are yer?' Waltus asked. The old mage was sat by the stove, a steaming mug in his hands.

Cirona rubbed her eyes, hoping the action would make the scene before her disappear. It didn't work. On the table was the meagre mound of supplies that had escaped the duke's soldiers. Castros sat to its side, muttering to himself. Holger was next to him, looking like a man who had just seen his whole life burned to the ground, and Whist was making an inventory.

'You wanna cup of this shit?' Waltus asked. 'Or are yer just gonna stand there gawping?'

'I … what in the …?' Cirona stammered.

'First up is first fed as me old mum used to say,' Waltus replied. 'Did'ya really think you'd be the first one to slink off?'

Cirona pursed her lips. 'Evidently, I won't be,' she said.

'Trying to gimme the slip, weren't yer? Can't shake off old Waltus that easy,' the White Mage said with a cackle.

'I've separated what remains of the food supplies,' Whist said, having to raise his voice over Waltus' laughter. 'The kit bags are by the back door if you're ready to load up and be off.'

Tapping her foot against the floor, Cirona battled to keep her annoyance from showing in her face. She gave Whist a curt nod, grabbed her bag and began filling it.

'Don't you forget those tinned pears!' Waltus cried out.

Cirona took a deep breath, nostrils flaring. 'Why don't you make yourself useful and get the horses ready?' she snapped.

'Oh, I love it when you talk to me like that,' the old mage replied, tipping her a lecherous wink as he left the kitchen.

Uttering a silent curse, she fastened the bag and swung it over her shoulder. Reaching the door, she felt a tug on her sleeve. Turning around, she saw Castros and pulled herself free, recoiling like she had been touched by a plague victim.

'Major … I …' he said.

'What?' she asked.

'It's just … well … I know why you hate me, and … and I'm sorry. If I could go back in time, I would change what happened to your husband … I'd … I'd change a lot of things …'

Rage's icy fire tore through her. How dare he? How fucking dare he … No. No, she was starting again. Cirona scanned his face, seeing the anguish written upon it. Deep down inside, she was glad. Let him hurt. She wasn't going to help him ease his conscience. Without a word, she turned away.

'Please … I don't want to leave things like this between us,' Castros said.

Cirona spun back around, her face tight, mouth pulled into a taut snarl. 'Have you ever lost someone?' she said. 'Someone you care about from the bottom of your soul, someone you truly love?'

Del Var's eyeline fell to the ground. 'More times than I care to remember,' he whispered.

'Then you'll know why "sorry" doesn't cut it,' she said. 'I owe you a debt, Castros, and one day soon, I'll settle it.'

With that she stormed outside into the cold morning air.

***

Running. Bellina was running. Why? Towards something or away? Couldn't tell. Going. Had to keep going. A mountain rose in front of her. No, not a mountain. The walls of a citadel. She made for it, but the ground dissolved beneath her feet. Falling, falling now, spinning end over end, twisting, turning, a leaf caught in the breeze.

'Argh!' she moaned, her body coming to a sharp stop.

She hung in the nothingness, dangling like a puppet waiting for a hand to make it dance, her arms pulled high above her head. A gurgling, giggling laughter erupted all around her, the laughter of a spiteful child about to tear the wings from a fly. A form took shape in front of her. It was a man holding a sword. She recognised him, but from where? The man tilted his head to the side, examining her, his tongue darting out and licking his lips.

'Marmossa,' she hissed.

But how could it be? It was impossible. She remembered the Terror from their meeting in Kurgobad — a fossil, papery skin stretched taut over a skeletal frame. How could this young, vital being be the same person?

Marmossa giggled again. 'Watch,' he said. Then he jabbed the darkness in front of him with the sword. At once. the space began to bubble and blister, a boil filling with the pus of darkness. Then the space began to writhe, stretch. To her horror, Bellina realised something was on the other side, trying to break through. Fear — raw, naked fear — spread through her veins. She didn't want to see.

'Look,' Marmossa commanded.

'No,' she whispered back.

'Look, damn you. Look at the fate that you have doomed them to!'

'No, no, no, no, NO!'

With a gasp, Bellina's eyes tore open. Early morning light flooded through a window. Her brain scrambled, adjusting. She was safe, safe at the summer house. She breathed deep and disentangled herself from the torn curtains she had used as covers. Placing her feet on the floor, she let the soft assurance of the carpet centre her. With each second, each breath, the dream faded. Her heart slowed to its normal pace. She was ready to face the day. Dressing quickly, Bellina left her room and headed for the kitchen. To her surprise, she only found Dargo and Elvgren there.

'The others have already gone,' Dargo said, clearly reading the look of curiosity on her face. 'That Whist fella left some supplies, a note and some gizmo over there.'

'I … see …' Bellina replied, drifting towards the piece of paper and the contraption next to it. It looked like a strange tiara with ugly, rough-cut chunks of stone set on the front and sides. Frowning, she picked up the letter and began to read.

My lady
We have left you some supplies to help you on your travels. They will not last long, but it was the best we could do.
I have also left you a device I acquired from a Tremoran cognopath a while back. It is a headpiece that boosts the distance you can transmit your thoughts. Hopefully, it will serve you well.
Good luck,
Whist.

Bellina placed the note back on the table and picked up the headpiece. She placed it upon her brow and reached out, trying to find Midge.
Nothing.
With a sigh, she removed it, offering a silent prayer that the small boy was somewhere out of its range and not … She left the thought unfinished. Now was not the time to dwell on such things.
'You should have woken me sooner,' she said, turning to face Dargo and Elvgren.
'Didn't wanna disturb yer,' Dargo said. 'And this one's been no bloody use.' He gestured towards Elvgren with his thumb.
Her betrothed sat there, staring into space, glazed, unfocused. She was not without pity for him, could understand the loss he felt, but they had to get moving. With three brisk steps, she crossed the room and slapped him round the face.
'Of all the barefaced …' Elvgren began, his nostrils flaring.
'Good, be angry,' Bellina said to him. 'Hold that anger, store it up and save it for the man who killed the members of our families. Lock it up and keep it waiting. In the meantime, I need your head here, looking ahead instead of navel gazing.'
She watched the rise and fall of his chest steady.
'Fine,' Elvgren replied at last.
Bellina gave a sharp nod. 'Right, let's be off then.'

***

Elvgren swatted at the horde of gnats buzzing round his head, feeling a small sliver of joy as he caught one of the vicious little bastards. Still, its fellow parasites continued to home in on any of his exposed flesh. He let out a sigh. What was the point?

That was exactly the question he had been asking himself over and over as they made their way along half-forgotten trails, slipping across the border between Sylvantain and Gortrix. His parents were gone. The Lord Chancellor was gone. The brother he had only seen in family portraits was gone. He dug deep inside himself, looking for some pain, some anguish at what had happened, but all he found was an empty ache.

He supposed he must have loved his parents, otherwise why had he been so hells bent on impressing them? But whatever that love had been, it had turned into a stifled, repressed emotion, something to tuck out of sight in a back room. Wracking his brain, he searched for a happy memory … but … nothing.

His gaze fell on Bellina's back, his bottom lip pouting a touch. It was alright for her — she understood her feelings, could latch onto anger and let it carry her forwards, take her to somewhere new. But not him. He had lost his centre, his reason for being. There was no one to show off to, no one to impress, no glittering future as one of the Empire's leading lights. Bellina's plan to declare themselves rightful heirs to the throne was folly. Maybe they'd impress a few peasants but never enough to make a realistic grab for power.

'Do you know how much further it is, Belle?' Dargo asked, his voice dragging Elvgren out of his thoughts.

'There should be a village soon,' Bellina answered. 'It's hard to tell as we've taken the long way round.'

'You can say that again,' Elvgren muttered.

'Better the long way than the dead way,' Bellina replied, shooting him a waspish glance. 'You can always take the main roads and try your luck with the duke's soldiers.'

Elvgren narrowed his eyes but kept his mouth shut. Even arguing with his "beloved" had lost its flavour. Instead, he watched the dirt path they were on narrow between a grove of trees before rising gently to the crest of a hill. A wide green valley spread out below them, the last rays of the setting sun kissing the scene with flames. At its heart was a dense cluster of houses, smoke tumbling out of chimneys while the occupants kindled their evening fires.

'This must be it,' Bellina said and led the way towards the houses.

It didn't take them long to reach the outskirts of the village. As they drew close, Elvgren noticed that the inhabitants had been busy creating a makeshift defence consisting of a crudely formed mud embankment that, in his opinion, wouldn't stop a pig escaping its pen.

'Wh-who goes there?' a timorous voice cried.

Tearing his eyes away from the embankment, he noticed a small man, clad in various pieces of rusting armour that were clearly too big for him. He did, though, have a large, sharpened lance that he was pointing towards them.

Elvgren watched Bellina straighten in her saddle and say, 'Lady Ressa, Lord Lovitz and his man.'

The guard's face turned the colour of sun-bleached bone. 'But you're … I mean … What do you want?'

'We wish to speak with the fine people of this village,' Bellina said.

The guard's gaze darted between them. Eventually, he said, 'Alright … I'll … I'll get Bert.'

Elvgren shifted atop his horse. How long was this pointless little game going to continue for? As if in answer, a tall, lean man with thinning hair appeared at the gates, a gaggle of onlookers in his wake.

'That's them, Bert,' the guard said, moving to the man's side.

'I have eyes, do I not, Grell?' Bert replied, fixing Elvgren and the others with his gaze. 'I believe you wish to speak with us?' Bert continued.

Elvgren felt his face flush. No bow? No use of their proper titles when addressing them? Who did this lanky arse think he was? He opened his mouth to say something, but Bellina beat him to it.

'You know who we are, but you do not know why we're here. Clearly you have been expecting other visitors?' she said, pointing at the slipshod embankment.

'Yes,' Bert replied. 'The duke's men have been ravaging the border villages.'

'The duke,' Bellina spat. 'The usurper. As long as his deceitful body sits upon the throne, every citizen of the Empire should be blazing with the indignity of it.'

'Those are pretty words,' Bert said. 'But blazing with indignity or not, the truth of the matter is there is nothing we can do except tend to our own and wait for this madness to pass.'

'There is more,' Bellina replied. 'You could join us, the rightful heirs to the Empire; you could fight.'

A murmuring arose from the crowd.

'How can we trust you? The Lord Chancellor killed the Emperor!'

someone shouted out.

'The Lord Chancellor was not in control of his actions at the time. He was under the influence of a cognopath,' Bellina said.

'What? A mind-melter like you then?' another voice called.

Elvgren watched Bellina bristle, but when she spoke next, she remained calm. 'My father, the Lord Chancellor, worked tirelessly for the good of the Empire. The fact that you've been able to sleep soundly in your beds, bellies full, is a testament to his efforts. How quickly we forget,' she said.

Elvgren watched her with rapt attention. While she had been talking, it had seemed she had grown, now towering over everything else. How could someone who he had smelled the unwashed scent of, a teenage girl in tattered clothes atop a stolen horse, appear so powerful? So regal?

Bert had turned around and was in a hushed conversation with some of the village elders. Finally, he turned back towards them and said, 'We will allow you one night's respite in our village. There is some room in the stables.'

'The stables!' Elvgren couldn't stop himself from blurting out. 'How dare—'

Bellina held up her hand and cut him off. 'We will take it gladly,' she said.

With a nod, Bert turned, the crowd parting to let them through, and led them a short distance into the village to the stables. At the doors, he said, 'I wish you a pleasant night.' With that he left.

Elvgren and the others dismounted and tethered the horses. He could see a ladder that led to the hayloft. 'I suppose we had better go and locate the most comfortable bales we can find,' he said with a sneer.

'Stop moaning,' Bellina said, climbing the ladder.

'Yeah,' Dargo agreed. 'It could be worse.'

At the top, Elvgren looked longingly out of a small window that overlooked the village square at the merry little houses with the snug beds they surely contained. Sighing, he flopped on top of the nearest bale and closed his eyes. More tired than he realised, sleep stole over him.

*

'Gren?' a voice called, pulling him out of the sweet oblivion he had entered. 'Gren! Wake up you lazy, one-eyed git!'

'Leave me be, Dar,' Elvgren murmured.

'Get up. Something's happening,' Dargo said.

Lifting his heavy lids, Elvgren stumbled awake. He saw Bellina and

Dargo by the window. From outside, he could hear shouting and cries for help.

'What is it?' he asked, joining the others.

'The duke's men,' Bellina replied, pointing out the window.

Outside, he could see what looked like the entire population of the village. They were surrounded by about thirty men pointing balliskets at their skulls. A man, his uniform marking him out as a captain, stalked in front of them, his hand on the hilt of his sword.

'There must be more than this,' the captain was saying to Bert. 'There is not nearly enough food here to last you through winter.'

'Please,' Bert said. 'That's all we have.'

'Liar!' the captain screamed. 'Answer me truthfully or people start dying.'

'We need to help them. Get them to fight back,' Bellina said.

'Are you mad, woman?' Elvgren exclaimed. 'What we *need* to do is get the hells out of here.'

'No,' Bellina said, getting to her feet. 'I will confront them.'

'Dargo, surely you don't agree with this guff?' Elvgren said.

'Sorry, Gren, but I think we should help,' Dargo replied, following Bellina down the ladder.

'If you want to get yourselves killed then fine,' Elvgren said as he too reached the ground floor. 'I'm off.'

'Go then,' Bellina said.

'I will, you know,' Elvgren replied.

'Good,' Bellina said, opening the stable doors a fraction to see out.

The sound of the captain's voice travelled into the building. 'Very well, kill—'

'Wait,' Bellina cried, stepping out into the night.

'Good gods, she really is insane,' Elvgren hissed.

Dargo shrugged. 'I'm gonna see if I can take some down from behind,' he said.

'No, Dar,' Elvgren said. 'We can still get out of here. She'll be enough of a distraction to …' but the boy had gone.

Elvgren's mind raced as sweat trickled down his brow. *Got to get out of here,* he thought, *got to get out.* His darting eyes saw a back door to the stables. Whispering a prayer of thanks, he made his way towards it. After a cautious peek, Elvgren stepped outside. He crept to the edge of the building and peered round. *Good, all of the soldiers are facing away from me, now all I have to do is—*

'Oi! Where in the hells do you think you're going?'

Looking up, Elvgren saw one of the duke's men staring down at him.

'Shit.' Elvgren swore as the soldier lowered his ballisket.

In one swift motion, Elvgren drew his sword and plunged it into the man's gut. Startled, the guard pulled the trigger. The bullet sailed harmlessly into the air. As the soldier coughed blood onto his arm, Elvgren turned to see the rest of the men aiming their weapons at him.

'Fire!' the captain roared.

Elvgren flinched, his eye shutting. He heard the drumming of the balliskets being fired, waited for his body to dance to their beat when the shot riddled his body. Nothing. He opened his eye to see the soldiers had all pointed their balliskets into the air. They stood frozen as if giving some bizarre salute. Then he saw Bellina, her face scrunched in concentration.

'I can't hold them for much longer!' she yelled at him.

He glanced at the road. *There's no one stopping me now, I could—*

'Argh!' a soldier cried breaking free of Bellina's control and swinging his bayoneted weapon towards Elvgren.

Bringing his sword round just in time, Elvgren deflected the blow then sliced into the soldier's side. He met the shaken gaze of Bert.

'What are you waiting for, you imbecile? Attack!' Elvgren cried.

Fuelled with adrenaline, Elvgren lunged at another frozen soldier, his blade plunging into the man's spine. A great roar erupted from the villagers, and Elvgren watched them pounce on their paralysed captors. They clawed at faces, stole weapons, stabbed, shot and gouged. The superior numbers of the villagers were too much, and soon, they had won.

Elvgren wiped a hand across his face, smearing it with blood. He gazed around at the villagers. They all stood in wide-eyed disbelief.

'We won!' Bellina bellowed, shaking them out of their daze.

Cries of joy and laughter rang out. Elvgren couldn't help but smile a touch. Then Bert stood and gestured for quiet. The noise died down as he crossed over to Elvgren, a strange look on his face. Elvgren's smile died, and his hand inched towards his sword. Bert met his eye then dropped to one knee.

'I don't know if I'm doing this right,' he said, 'but I pledge myself to you, Emperor, Empress.'

'I …what?' Elvgren stammered.

Bellina crossed to his side and placed a hand on Bert's head. 'Your service is gratefully accepted,' she said.

Soon, all the village was kneeling before them.

'Long may they reign!' Bert screamed.

'Long may they reign,' the crowd chanted back.

Elvgren rocked back on his heels, warmth radiating through his body.

Maybe there *was* a point to all this.

***

Peering up through the branches of the thin, pointed trees that hemmed him in, Castros Del Var saw the night's sky. For a second, the stars winked back at him, sharing a cosmic joke he didn't understand, then they were gone, obscured by cloud. He wondered if his daughter was looking up at this sky, whether she was safe.

Worry twisted in his gut, a serrated blade probing his stomach. It hurt. It hurt how he had left things with Bellina, hurt that he hadn't tried to talk to her sooner, hurt in dim recesses of his soul he hadn't realised existed. But he wasn't the only one hurting.

Holger sat opposite Whist around their small campfire, his body crumpled like a discarded piece of paper. An ache formed at the back of Castros' throat. He wanted to wrap his arms around this honest, earnest young man, a young man who had been punished for his love. *That's all love ever really is, though*, Castros thought, *a bizarre form of punishment.* He wouldn't lie to Holger, wouldn't tell him it would all be okay, that time is the greatest healer or some other pointless banality. He would let the boy grieve. Looking away, Del Var's gaze settled on Whist.

'Do you have any idea where Khasal is?' he asked.

Whist put down a piece of paper he had been studying and turned to face Del Var. 'Well … the last news I received placed him still in Victory,' he said.

'Fantastic,' Castros replied, rubbing his eyes. 'So, we've got to go all the way back to the place we've spent so long getting away from.'

'I'm afraid so,' Whist said with a sigh.

'How in the twelve hells are we going to get back in?' Castros asked.

'I have my ways, Cass,' Whist said. 'There are tunnels and entrances under the city that even you don't know about.'

'I suppose my father taught them to you, did he?' Castros said, his lips curling into a sneer.

Now it was Whist's turn to rub his eyes. 'Don't be so childish,' he said.

For a heartbeat, a sorry trembled on Del Var's lips. He shut his mouth with a snap and said, 'I'm going to draw some power from the manastream.'

'Sounds like a good idea,' Whist replied, blowing out his cheeks and returning his attention to the paper he had been looking at.

With his finger, Castros drew a crude vitaspiral in the dirt. He focused on it, letting his chattering thoughts float away. He closed his eyes and was there, his conscious zipping along the ribbon-like tendrils of the manastream. The thrill of the motion, of being one with the pulsating life of the world filled him with a happiness he hadn't felt in a long while.

Careful, his mind warned him, *many a mage has got lost in here, seeking refuge from life's troubles.*

The thought pinched him, refocused him. He knew it was best only to dip your toe in the manastream, to never let yourself fully submerge. But something pulled him on, a thought … no, a feeling that something was wrong. The streams of sortilenergy were still flowing, the vast reservoirs of magical energy — the gifts of the First Ones — were …

Then he had it: two of the five sources had shifted, bunched together somehow, and there was something else, a large magical signature he had never noticed before. What the hells was going on? *Think*, he told himself, *think*. If the gifts of the First Ones were stored in relics — he had every reason to believe that they were now — and if Marmossa *had* found some of them, that would explain why the massive stores of power had shifted.

The thought chilled him, his consciousness shivering. So much power in one place and at the disposal of one man. The likes of it were unknown. And as far as they all knew, Marmossa was looking for the other three. If he got his hands on them …

The disturbance in his mind ripped him out of the manastream and back to reality. He sat, chest heaving, sweat trickling down his cheeks.

'You alright, Cass?' Whist asked.

Del Var heard the man as if from another world. He had always known they were playing a high-stakes game, but now … now he wasn't sure they had enough in their pot to keep from folding.

CHAPTER THREE

'All clear,' Crenshaw said.

Scholar Fontaine poked his head around the large, wooden container he was hidden behind and said, 'Are you sure?'

'Positive,' Crenshaw replied. 'The train porters are working their way from the front to the back. It'll be hours before they begin to unload this carriage.'

Swallowing hard, Fontaine nodded and lifted his aching body from out of his hiding place. Gods, but it felt good to stretch himself out. They had spent the better part of three days hopping from train to train, keeping themselves out of sight behind the cargo carried in the rear carriages as they made their way to the Sylvantain coastal town of Ravella in the hope of finding a boat to Timboko. There had been a few close calls, but Crenshaw had proved himself a master of deception. When Fontaine had asked him how he had acquired such a skill set Crenshaw had laughed and said, 'When you've spent twenty years with Bar, you get good at escaping.'

Ginko Barboza. Fontaine had had a lot of time to wonder about the man Crenshaw was going so far out of his way to save. Along their journey, his companion had kept Fontaine entertained with stories of Crenshaw's and Barboza's misspent youth, always on the run, lurching from one mad caper to another. Fontaine had enjoyed the tales — he'd even told Crenshaw he should write a book — but he knew the man was telling the tales as much for his own sake as to thrill the scholar, almost as if he was afraid his memories would slip away.

The rest of the time Fontaine had spent puzzling over the *Radiana*. Even with the information from the Lord Chancellor, the book's deepest mysteries still eluded him. He was fairly certain that the five relics had been hidden across the world and thought it safe to assume that the western relic and the eastern relic were in Marmossa's hands. If there was a relic hidden in Timboko, was the Arch Vizier aware of it? And if so, how much manpower had he devoted to acquiring it?

'Are you coming?' Crenshaw hissed from the doorway. 'We've got a clear run here.'

Fontaine shook his head, clearing his mind, and walked over to Crenshaw.

'On three, we leave the carriage,' Crenshaw said. 'And try to act natural.'

The scholar licked his lips and nodded.

'Alright — one, two … three.'

With what he hoped was a nonchalant step, Fontaine followed Crenshaw's lead and walked onto the platform of Ravella station. The station itself was built like an ancient temple. As they mingled with the crowd and entered the main terminal, Fontaine couldn't help but be impressed by the massive marble columns that swept up to support an arched roof studded with glass panels. Light streamed through these rooftop windows, glinting off the golden adornments on statues that stood sentry in little alcoves all over the station.

'Stop gaping like a caught fish,' Crenshaw whispered to him. 'We're trying to act natural, remember?'

'S-sorry,' Fontaine replied.

'Good,' Crenshaw said with a nod. 'Look, when we get out of here, we need to secure our passage on a ship. A passenger one will do us no good. Too many people. But I know a bloke who might be able to get us on a cargo ship. We'd have to work our passage, but no one would be asking any awkward questions.'

'Work our passage?' Fontaine replied.

Crenshaw must have noticed the look of disgusted disbelief on the scholar's face, because he laughed. 'It'll be good for you,' he said. 'Get a bit of muscle on them bones.'

'But I've never engaged in manual labour,' Fontaine said, continuing in his shocked tone. 'My mind is my tool.'

'Then maybe you can *think* your way across the Herridian Sea,' Crenshaw said, rolling his eyes. 'Now come on. We don't have much time.'

Still reeling from the thought of a week's hard labour aboard ship, Fontaine stepped out into the midday sun. The station was atop a hill, and before him, he could see the town of Ravella spread out like an open jewellery box. Multicoloured houses chased each other down to the seafront where a mishmash of ships lay waiting in the harbour. The salt from the sea air tickled his nose, and he sneezed.

'Beautiful place, isn't it?' Crenshaw said. 'But deadly too. Even without the possibility of the duke's men finding us, the gangs here would gut you as quick and easy as they would a fish, so keep your wits about you.'

For a moment, Fontaine stood rooted to the spot. *What kind of world have I stepped into?* he thought. Why had he ever exchanged the cosseted security of the library for this madness?

Get a grip on yourself, man! Fontaine's inner voice cried. *You're the only one who can solve this riddle, so pull yourself together.*

Taking a deep breath, the scholar hurried after Crenshaw.

They made their way through the choked streets, a million balconies overhead, some with washing strung between them, women shouting across to each other and laughing. Soon they were in the market, small shopfronts, their wares spewing onto the cobbled street, battling for attention. Shouted prices carried on air rich with the smell of citrus and spice. A man in a wide-brimmed hat bartered with a vendor. Fontaine would have loved to watch the excited scene, but Crenshaw turned into a back alley. He led them to a nondescript door and knocked upon it. A small eye-slot flew open.

'What?' a gruff voice called from behind it.

'I need to see Satelli,' Crenshaw said.

'So does half of Ravella,' the gruff voice said with a laugh.

'Tell him Crenshaw wants to see him.'

'Fine, fine,' the man behind the door replied. The eye-slot snicked closed. After a few tense minutes, it popped open again. 'Satelli will see you, but your jumpy friend there will have to stay put.'

Crenshaw gave Fontaine a quick look and said, 'Alright.'

'Wait just a minute!' Fontaine said as the door opened.

'You'll be fine,' Crenshaw said. 'Just keep your head down.'

Fontaine was left with his mouth flapping when the door closed again. *Keep calm*, he told himself, *act natural.* He leaned against the wall, trying to adopt a carefree stance, as if lurking in a back alley was as commonplace to him as breathing. His eyes darted between the opposite ends of the alley, watching the flow of people. He caught sight of the man in the wide-brimmed hat again; he seemed to be talking to someone. The man shifted and pointed down the alley. Fontaine felt his heart freeze when he saw two uniformed guards behind him.

Calm, calm, calm, he thought as he turned to the door. He tried a few jaunty knocks. No answer. The guards were making their way down the alley now. Throwing all pretence aside, Fontaine began to hammer on the door.

'What?' the gruff voice exclaimed from behind it.

'G-g-guards,' Fontaine managed to squeak out.

'Fucking hells,' the voice said. 'Get rid of them!'

'Please … I … Let me in!'

'You,' a guard called. 'Stay where you are!'

'For the love of all that's holy, let me in!' Fontaine cried.

'Open that door now!' he heard Crenshaw shout from inside the house.

'Do it,' another voice said.

The door flew open so quickly Fontaine stumbled inside. Before him, the scholar saw Crenshaw and a fat, sweaty man.

'Why do I trust, eh? You bring nothing but trouble to my door,' the fat man said.

'You owe us, Satelli. You owe me,' Crenshaw said.

Satelli mopped his face with a stained handkerchief that may have once been red. 'Fine, take this note to the captain of the *Lavezza*. He'll work you like a dog, but you'll get where you want to go.'

'Good enough,' Crenshaw said, taking the piece of paper and stuffing it in a pocket.

Scholar Fontaine jumped as pounding started on the door behind him.

'Open up, Satelli! We know who you've got in there!'

'Go,' Satelli said, waving towards the back of the house. 'The Lavezza sets sail before long. I'll deal with this.'

'Thanks,' Crenshaw said.

'Don't thank me. We're even now, eh? All squared up. Next time you knock on my door, I'll shoot you for the crazy son of a bitch that you are.'

Crenshaw nodded then turned to Fontaine. 'This way,' he said.

He led the way through the house and out a back door. After a furtive look, he gestured for Fontaine to follow him out.

'What are we going to do?' the scholar asked, his heart racing.

'Hide in plain sight,' Crenshaw answered. 'Mingle into the crowd and make our way to the docks. We've got to hurry though, the *Lavezza* is set to depart soon.'

They slipped into the throng of people. Fontaine's gaze bounced around, searching for more guards. He loosened his collar to alleviate the heat pulsing off his body. *This is intolerable*, he thought.

'Shit,' Crenshaw spat.

Fontaine looked ahead and saw a guard's head bobbing in the sea of people. The guard was trying to battle his way through the people between them. He pulled a whistle from his pocket and blew on it.

'Grab those men,' he shouted, pointing at the scholar and Crenshaw. 'They are wanted by the Emperor.' The crowd looked unimpressed. 'They have a massive bounty on their heads,' the guard added.

Noise erupted all around. Fontaine felt rough hands grab at his clothes, pulling, tearing.

'Let go of him!' Crenshaw cried, taking a ballistol out of his waistband.

The hands holding the scholar relinquished their grip, and Fontaine found himself with some breathing space.

'Follow me.' Crenshaw went tearing off ahead, screaming at the top of his lungs and waving the ballistol at anyone who got close.

They rushed down alleys, streets, all the time fighting the force of gravity as they pelted downhill. Fontaine could hear the ragged gasps of air he was drawing in, felt the muscles in his legs burn like a furnace while a stitch pinched at his insides. *Keepgoingkeepgoingkeepgoing*, he told himself over and over as he chased Crenshaw's back. There was a shout from behind him. He turned to look, saw two guards, caught his foot on a cobblestone and went sprawling to the ground.

'H-h-help me!' he panted.

Crenshaw paused for a moment and fired the ballistol. The shot rang out, bouncing off the street, sending the guards diving for cover.

'Move your arse!' Crenshaw bellowed. 'I'm not stopping again.'

Somehow, Fontaine manged to drag his protesting body to its feet and set off once more. The narrow streets began to widen, and he could see they were nearing the docks.

'Where's the *Lavezza*?' Crenshaw bellowed at a stupefied dockhand, pointing the ballistol at his face. The man pointed towards a large ship just a little way to the left.

Crenshaw tore towards it, the scholar trailing some way behind him. Fontaine heard the sound of his running feet change from the sharp clack they had made on the stone street to an echoing thump as he reached the jetty that lead to the *Lavezza*.

'Gods damn it!' Crenshaw cried.

Fontaine's stomach did an elaborate flip when he saw what the problem was — the *Lavezza* was ready to depart, the boarding plank drawing in. The scholar watched in disbelief as Crenshaw found an extra burst of speed from somewhere. He skidded to a stop, clambering up the retreating board and waving the note from Satelli in the bemused captain's face.

Whistles and shouts chorused around Fontaine. He stole a glance over his shoulder and saw what must have been the entire City Watch at his heels. On the ship, Crenshaw was arguing with the captain, trying to make him leave the board out, but to no avail. Fontaine was beside it now, the ship already moving a touch.

'Jump!' Crenshaw screamed, leaning towards him, arm outstretched.

Never … can't … won't …

Yes, you can, his inner voice yelled. *You can and you will!*

Fontaine dug deep inside himself, pulling on every reserve of strength left in his body. He reached the end of the pier and jumped. Time slowed, all his senses on fire. He saw Crenshaw, crystal clear, in front of him, his own arm reaching, reaching for his … then he was falling, the *Lavezza* slipping through his fingers … a firm grip locked around his wrist. His momentum carried him forwards, his head colliding with the side of the ship, stars flashing in his vision. Then he was being hauled upwards, upwards to the safety of the deck.

'Never seen a jump like it,' Crenshaw said, collapsing beside Fontaine.

'Can't … no …' Fontaine wheezed.

'Save it,' Crenshaw said, slapping him on the back.

'Up. Both of you. Now,' the captain growled behind them. 'There's work to be done.'

Crenshaw offered Fontaine his hand. The scholar took it, allowing the other man to haul him to his feet. Fontaine opened his mouth to say thank you but instead vomited over the side of the ship. As he looked up, he saw the guards standing on the pier, arguing with dockhands and waving at the *Lavezza*. Despite the sour taste of sick in his mouth, the burning air in his lungs and the ache in his calves, Fontaine laughed.

***

The glorious smell of frying bacon filled Bellina's nose, accompanied by stifled yawns and mumbled greetings. She watched the camp come to life in wonderment, a living being moving in languid motion. There had to be over five hundred men, women and children following her and Elvgren now, a number that inspired both satisfaction and fear.

As they had passed through towns and villages, more and more people had left their old lives behind and joined them. The tale of their battle with the duke's men had spread before them, and so they were met with open arms. Not all the citizens decided to join the march towards Hidenbaden, the capital of Gortrix, but most did, pledging their fealty to Bellina and Elvgren.

How do I look out for these people? she thought. *How do I feed them, clothe them, keep them safe and warm?* They had tried their best to gather as many supplies as they could carry — Bert and his men had been invaluable in this, taking inventories, making lists of names — but would it be enough to sustain them? Bellina sighed; only time would tell in the end.

She heard a rustling behind her and turned to see Elvgren emerging, tousle-haired, a yawn parting his mouth, from the tent behind her. He rubbed at his good eye.

'Is there bacon?' he said. 'I can smell bacon.'

'I believe so,' Bellina replied.

'Then where's the bloody man with my food? Dargo? Dargo! Go and see about getting us some grub, eh?'

'Do it yer bloody self,' Dargo replied sleepily from within the tent.

'What a bloody palaver,' Elvgren said, plonking his arse in a travel chair next to Bellina and waving his hands at the huddled mass of tent tops. 'When they said they would follow us, I didn't think they meant it literally. They're filthy, smelly, wretched things. Why won't they just go away?'

'Such compassion for your subjects,' Bellina said, spitting her words at him. 'Being a leader isn't just feasts and anxious maids scampering about to fulfil your every whim. They have followed us to be safe, followed us in the hope we can restore some normality to their world, and I bloody well intend to do just that.'

'Father save me from another one of your sermons,' Elvgren said, rolling his eye. 'Part of being in charge is acting like you're in charge. Watch this.' He put his fingers to his lips and whistled. The followers nearest them turned, and Elvgren pointed at one of them. 'You man, bring us our breakfast.' The man's face split into a grin, obviously thrilled to be of service, and he darted into the thicket of tents.

'Very masterful, Your Majesty,' Bellina drawled, fixing Elvgren with a look of pure ice.

'Majesty,' he said, tilting his head back and grinning. 'It has such a good ring to it. To think I was willing to settle for Lord Chancellor when I could have had so much more.'

Bellina's lip curled, a bitter taste filling her mouth. 'You are an utter pig,' she said, rising to her feet so quickly she toppled her chair.

She strode away from Elvgren, away from the camp, looking for some space to think, to breathe. She looked out across the field they had trudged across yesterday, at the matted grass and shallow grooves where foot and cartwheel had left tokens of their passage.

How did he do it? she thought. *How did my grandfather manage to carry the burden of leadership for so long? How did he manage to take on the hopes and expectations of an empire and—*

Her thoughts were cut off by movement at the far end of the field. She froze. Gods, no. It was a troop of those malovor creatures the duke had in his power led by a few men on horseback.

'We're under attack,' she bellowed. 'To arms. Everyone to arms. Elvgren you—'

But Elvgren was gone.

***

Elvgren could feel the muscles of his horse ripple as he spurred it on. He had caught sight of the malovors a minute or so before Bellina had, and his body had moved of its own accord leaping onto his mount and geeing it into life. Del Var had filled them in about the creatures … but seeing them in the flesh was another matter. He heard Bellina's rallying cry but noticed with perverse satisfaction that no one was responding.

He led his horse on a mad dash through the camp, trampling over belongings, colliding into the sides of tents. Around him, he could feel the gazes of the people upon him, people who had sworn their life to him, who had abandoned their homes to follow in the hope he could lead them to a better tomorrow.

Coward, a voice in his head whispered. *What kind of a king … no, what kind of a man are you?*

Better a live coward than a dead hero, he thought in response.

And what could he possibly do? He was king in name only. He had no real power, had no real army to fight the war he found himself in. As a matter of fact, wasn't it more selfish of these people to lay the burden of their expectations around his neck like a noose? How was he supposed to fight a war, take back an empire, with nothing but a gaggle of half-starved peasants?

A shrill cry split the air in front of him and Elvgren pulled back on the reins. He looked down to see a girl of five or six, a straw doll clasped to her chest, the toes of her bare feet digging into the soft dirt. Behind her, a woman he assumed was the girl's mother wrapped an arm around the child defensively.

'Where is the Emperor going, Mummy?' the girl asked.

The woman looked up at Elvgren, accusation burning in her eyes and said, 'I don't know, love. I don't know.'

Gods, Elvgren thought, *it's like a scene from a bad play*. He pulled on the reins, manoeuvring the horse towards a path through the trees. His gaze darted between the advancing malovors and the path, his chest tightening.

'Damn it all to the Void,' he muttered. 'To me men!' he roared. 'To me!'

Digging his heels into the flank of his horse, Elvgren charged towards the approaching malovors. Behind him, he heard the mismatched war cry of his followers split the air, a ragged tapestry of sound, an incoherent roar laced with fear. He drew his sword, waving it madly over his head. As the distance between Elvgren and his opponents closed, he saw that there was a handful of the duke's men leading the malovors.

One of them, reacting a touch quicker than his comrades, lowered his ballisket, ready to fire. Time slowed, Elvgren saw the man cock his weapon, line up his bloodshot eye with the sight and move a dirt-grimed finger to the trigger. He was closing the ground between them but not fast enough. Fear ripped through him, sharp and cold as he waited for the shot to ring out. He watched the man's face spread into a grin, lips pulled back, revealing a cluster of misshapen teeth.

Then the man's head snapped back. For a moment, Elvgren wondered what the hells was wrong with him. Then he saw it — the shaft of a crossbow bolt sticking out of the man's forehead like a bizarre pimple. Stealing a glimpse behind him, Elvgren saw Bert, crossbow still raised, the rest of the men surging forwards around him, and nodded. Concern clouded Bert's face, and he shouted something.

'What?' Elvgren bellowed back. 'I can't—'

Next thing he knew, he was on the ground. Above him stood one of the malovors, the knuckles of its hands scraping the ground, flat nose quivering beneath a protruding brow. Revulsion and terror squirmed through Elvgren's body, wrapping themselves together like mating worms. The malovor knitted its hands together and lifted them above its head, ready to strike. Elvgren scrabbled backwards in the dirt. His hand brushed against something. For a moment, he stared at it in mute confusion.

It's a sword, you fucking moron! a voice in his head screamed. *Use it!*

Letting out a strangled yelp, Elvgren swung the sword, its edge biting into the creature's calf with a meaty thunk. The malovor let out a braying sound and sunk to its knees. Wasting no time, Elvgren yanked his sword free and buried it in the malovor's neck. Hot blood, the colour of a day-old bruise vomited over him. Elvgren gagged, ejecting a mouthful of sour spit to his side.

There's no time for this, his inner voice raged; *get on your feet and fight!*

Not needing to be told twice, Elvgren lurched to a standing position. Around him, he could see hoes, trowels and sickles, instruments for farming not fighting, flash in the early morning light, could see the faces of men contorted into battle scowls. *And to think you were going to abandon these people*, he thought, body shuddering with disgust.

He saw a man pulled to the ground by three slavering malovors.

Elvgren charged at them, his blade sinking into the grey-green flesh of one of the creatures. Yanking his sword loose, he brought it down in a shimmering arc, slicing off the top of another malovor's head before plunging it into the chest of the third. Elvgren reached out to the fallen man.

'Th-thank you, Your Majesty,' the man stammered.

The only thing Elvgren could think to say in response was, 'Fight!'

For the next twenty minutes — minutes that felt like a lifetime — Elvgren was a human blur, the sword a glittering extension of his arm, dealing death to any who came within reach.

With an almighty swing, he took the head clean off the shoulders of the nearest creature and turned to find his next opponent. Covered in blood and gore, he spun on the spot, unblinking eyes searching for one of the malovors. All he saw was a corpse-strewn field, men — *his* men — standing triumphant.

'We won,' he muttered to himself in amazement. 'WE WON!' he roared.

The men howled in response, and before he knew it, he was being borne atop their shoulders. For a moment, Elvgren thought it was probably most unbefitting for an emperor to be treated in such a way by his subjects. Then he wondered when the last time had been that an emperor had led his men into battle, the last time one had stood by their side, willing to spill his blood as well as theirs and decided to just enjoy it.

Cheering, they carried him all the way back to camp.

***

Eyes. Eyes everywhere, loaded with suspicion, boring into her from all angles, following her footsteps, each one driving her closer to insanity. With every mile they travelled, Cirona had grown more and more paranoid, a situation made worse by the fact that their journey had been unnervingly simple. Although the route they had taken was sparsely populated, she found herself casting frequent glances over her shoulder, convinced she would catch a glimpse of a group of soldiers bearing down on them with swords aloft.

The town they were in now was in the shadow of the Yammeroff mountain range, a sight she refused to take in. *If I can't see it, it's not there,* she thought. *Gods, I sound like a child. You'll have to look at it eventually, you've got to go up that, you've got to—*

'I'll cross that bridge when I come to it,' she murmured to herself, forcing her thoughts aside.

It was by far the largest place they had passed through. Up till now, Cirona had led her and Waltus around such townships. Whenever they'd had to interact with people, Cirona had hidden her face in the shadow of her hood and affected a deep voice. It wasn't much of a change, but in doing so, she could pass for a man … a fact Waltus found hilarious.

Unfortunately, there was no other way to reach the mountain base, and the pressure of being surrounded by so many people was getting to her. Around them, wooden houses she would normally have considered quaint took on leering sneers as she passed them.

Despite the cold, people were bustling about in the streets. A pair of giggling girls passed, their laughter seeming knowing to Cirona. She ached to turn her head, to see if they were looking.

You will NOT turn round! her inner voice cried. *You're being ridiculous. No one is following you. Now, think about something else!*

Unbidden, the face of her daughter swam into her mind. *Anna*, she thought, *her name is Anna.* She wondered how Anna was doing under the duke's new regime. Was she happy, free … safe? Such questions would have seemed laughable in the recent past, but after the duke's homicidal purge of the nobility, Cirona wasn't so sure.

The wind picked up, whipping her cloak around her with a sharp snap, the cold air pulling her out of her introspection. *You've got your mission soldier*, she thought, a shiver passing over her. *No time for all the crap in your head, not if you're going to do it right.* Gritting her teeth, she forced her freezing body forwards.

'Shop over there,' Waltus said.

'We're not stopping,' Cirona replied. 'We have enough food to get us over the mountains and into Narvale, and I refuse to make any unnecessary stops.'

'Well, the thing is, you see, the other night I got a touch peckish and …'

Coming to a sudden stop, Cirona looked into Waltus' face, scanning for a lie. She felt her shoulder muscles tense as fear bit into her. Swinging the kit bag off her back, Cirona opened it. She clenched her jaws together, fighting back the scream that was building inside her.

'You idiotic old fart,' she hissed, gripping the front of his coat and pulling him close. 'You knew we were rationing that food. How could you be so fucking irresponsible?'

'In my defence, I didn't realise we were running that low on food,' Waltus said. 'Look let's just stock up over there and be on our way.'

'The risk is too great,' Cirona said, letting him go.

'Come off it! We've been alright so far. And who's gonna recognise you in this place? We're in the arse end of nowhere here.'

Cirona felt her hands clench and unclench at her side. Two young mothers, babes at their chests, kept flicking their eyes towards them. *We're making a scene*, Cirona thought; *let's just get the supplies and get out of here as soon as possible.* Without another word to Waltus, she headed towards the shop. Stopping by the door, Cirona snapped her head left and right. The mothers were still yakking behind them, but so far, no one else had appeared.

'Don't forget me pears,' Waltus said.

Shooting him a look of pure acid, Cirona entered the shop. The bell above the door made a soft jingling sound overhead. A man popped out of a back door, as if by magic, wiping his hands on the apron around his waist.

'Can I help you, sir?' the shopkeeper asked.

Pulling her hood tighter, Cirona said, 'Yes. I would like a wheel of cheese, some tack bread and some cured beef strips.'

The shopkeeper cocked his head to the side, listening to her order, a smile on his face despite the furrowing of his brow. Cirona felt her skin begin to prickle under his gaze.

'Do you have these items?' she said.

The man's face cleared. 'Of course, sir,' he said.

The shopkeeper turned his back to her, gathering the order. Cirona felt sweat trickle to the base of her neck, tracing a path down her spine. *Come on*, she thought, watching the man's back. *Come ON!* She felt the urge to bite her nails, but she forced her hands to stay where they were. Her breath was coming in ragged snatches now. The overstuffed shelves twisting and skewing themselves till they seemed to reach the heavens.

'That'll be six harvings, please,' the shopkeeper said.

Cirona looked at the man, and for a moment, he looked like a toad, bulbous eyes staring, long tongue flicking at the air as if tasting her lies. Closing her eyes, she took a deep breath. When she opened them again, everything was back to normal. Taking out a moneybag, she counted out the coins and handed them over.

'Many thanks,' the shopkeeper said.

Giving him a nod, Cirona headed towards the door.

'Hang on a minute!'

Cirona felt her pulse speed up, the blood thrashing in her ears. She moved her hand to the ballistol she had in the waistband of her trousers. It seemed to take her forever to turn back around, like the air was filled with hundreds of groping, prying hands.

He'll have a ballistol, and he'll shoot me, or I'll shoot him, and this is going to be terrible. I don't want to kill him, but I will, and it'll be—

'I forgot your tack bread,' the man said.

It took Cirona a long moment to process what was happening. She reached out and snatched the bread from the man's hand.

'Are you alright, sir?' the shopkeeper asked.

'Yes,' Cirona replied in her normal voice. She coughed then said in a deeper tone. 'Yes, I'm fine.'

She hurried out of the shop and took a great gasp of air, telling herself the worst was over.

'Let's go,' she said, thrusting the shopping towards Waltus.

'Weren't there no tinned pears?' he asked.

Cirona barely heard him as she raced off. Mind whirring, she looked up, and for the first time, took in the Yammeroff mountain range. It soared towards the heavens, snow-covered from halfway up. Huge needles of jagged black stone pierced the sky like the teeth of some hungry god. Cirona rocked back, her hands trembling. She had been so desperate to ignore the mountain, to not acknowledge what lay ahead of them … and now it was staring her in the face. She swallowed hard.

Maybe the worst *was* yet to come.

CHAPTER FOUR

The good thing about the sewers of Victory was that they extended out like veins far into the suburbs of the city, allowing Castros, Whist and Holger to enter them far from the city walls. Unfortunately, that was the bad thing too. It seemed to Del Var that they had been stuck in this reeking subterranean hell for a lifetime.

Mile after mile of curved brick tunnel had passed by with the promise of miles more to come. The dank, cold air had seeped into Castros' clothes, making them cling to his body in a chilling embrace. The sound of dripping water, almost pleasant at first, was now grating against his sanity, filing away at his nerves. And then there were the rats. Del Var could have sworn he had seen one as big as a dog.

'Is it much further, Whist?' Castros called, removing the perfumed rag from his face so he could be heard.

'It shouldn't be,' Whist replied, the light from the lantern he held bobbing as he walked. 'We're deep into Victory now. My man should be just around the next … ah.'

'Ah what?' Holger said as he and Castros followed Whist round a turn in the tunnel.

'He's not here,' Whist replied, his brow furrowed.

'Brilliant,' Castros said. 'What do we do now?'

'Hang on, hang on!' Whist said, setting down his lantern and inspecting the sweating sewer wall. He ran his fingers with practised precision between the grooves in the brickwork. 'Aha!' he said when one of the bricks came loose.

'What is it?' Holger asked.

'A note from the man we were supposed to be meeting,' Whist answered, his eyes scanning the scrap of paper.

Castros tapped his foot against the ground. 'Well? What's it say?'

'Something about more purges. Masses of people being rounded up and taken off somewhere. It's hard to make out; he must have written this in a hurry.'

Pinching the bridge of his nose, Castros said, 'What does it say about Khasal?'

'Oh. Right. It says he's staying at the Lord Chancellor's palace.'

'Can we get there from the sewers?' Holger asked.

'No,' Whist replied. 'We get to travel through something a lot more fancy than that.'

Whist took off, leaving Castros and Holger trailing in his wake. They travelled on for another hour, twisting and turning through the labyrinthine tunnels, till finally, Whist came to a stop before a stretch of wall. He placed his lantern on the ground and began knocking on the brickwork. After a minute or so, he rapped on a spot that echoed with a hollow bang.

'Do I know these tunnels, or do I know these tunnels?' Whist said, turning towards Del Var with a smile.

'Yes, yes, you're fabulous, but what in the world are you up to?' Castros said.

Whist waggled his eyebrows and said, 'Watch.'

He pushed one of the bricks, and there was a dull clicking sound. To Castros' amazement, a portion of the wall began to slide backwards in a shower of dust.

'A secret entrance!' Holger said.

Del Var marvelled at the boy's ability to state the obvious. 'But what's it for? And why here?' he said.

'It was a secret entrance for the workers who made what's below us,' Whist replied.

'And what exactly is below us?' Del Var asked.

'You'll see,' Whist answered, entering the now gaping hole in the wall.

With a sigh, Castros followed Whist through the gap. Behind the wall, he found an elaborate wrought-iron staircase spiralling downwards. Round and down they went, the constant turning giving Del Var a spinning bout of vertigo. Just when he thought he was going to puke they came to the bottom.

Castros felt his breath catch. After the squalor of the sewers, the sight that was before him felt like a mirage. Overhead, an arched ceiling covered in mosaic tile glinted and shifted in the light of Whist's lantern, stretching off as far as the eye could see. The walls were covered in an epic mural, characters from myth and fable depicted, larger than life, playing out their roles. Along the floor ran a set of tracks, deep grooves wide enough for carriage wheels to fit into.

'What is this place?' Castros whispered

'A secret escape route for the Emperor and the top government officials,' Whist said. 'It was built over a hundred years ago; that's why the tracks are designed for horses rather than a locomotron. The Lord

Chancellor thought about updating it, but he never had the time … or the money.'

'And no one knows about this place?' Holger asked.

'Not many, no,' Whist answered. 'And the few that do want to keep it quiet. That's why there are no guards. If you sent a patrol down here, the men would be blabbing about it as soon as they got down the pub. Anyway, we better get going; it's still a bit of a trot to the Olphant Hill.'

On they travelled, each step revealing more of the ornate tunnel. After another hour of trudging, Whist once more came to a stop. He began to caress the right wall's brickwork as he had done before, and soon, another hidden door slid back.

'If I'm right,' Whist said, 'the stairs behind here should take us to the Lord Chancellor's palace.'

'Lead on,' Castros said.

They climbed another iron staircase and were greeted at the top by what looked like a trapdoor in the ceiling overhead. It took all three of them pushing against it to get the thing open, the hinges grating so loudly Castros thought that surely someone would hear them. The trio emerged like overgrown moles into the night air. When Whist had helped Castros to clamber out, Del Var saw that they were on the outer edges of the front garden, the gravel drive just visible in the distance, the palace looming beyond that.

'We'll make our way to the house using the trees for cover,' Whist said. 'Stay low and try to keep to the shadows.'

'This isn't my first clandestine infiltration,' Castros hissed.

'I was speaking for the benefit of our young friend,' Whist said, gesturing towards Holger. 'Gods, what are you so touchy about?'

'Nothing,' Del Var said. 'Just shut up and move.'

Running in a hobbled crouch, Castros led the way towards the palace. He came to a stop in the shadow of a tree that grew a stone's throw from the drive. He waited for the others to catch up.

'Not many lights on,' Whist said.

'Perhaps no one is home?' Holger asked.

'Even if the master of the house is away, in a home this size the servants would have the lights on,' Castros said, biting his lip. 'What the hells is going on here?'

'Hang on … there's someone coming up the drive,' Whist said.

Castros turned his attention to the drive and saw a carriage pull up to the front door. The driver brought the horses to rest and out popped Khasal flanked by two soldiers. Del Var's eyes narrowed to slits, his hand curling into a fist while he watched his fellow mage saunter into the building.

'Makes you sick to think that he's living here, doesn't it?' Whist said, reading Castros' mind.

'It doesn't matter,' Del Var lied. 'Lot of arseholes have lived in that palace, what's one more to add to the tally.'

Silence fell over them as they watched some of the galvanic lights come on inside the building. The last one to burst into life was on the second floor.

'That's the study, isn't it?' Whist said, pointing at the newly illuminated window.

'You tell me,' Del Var said with a sniff. 'You've clearly been here more often than I have. In fact, I'm surprised you haven't got a set of keys!'

Whist cocked his head to the side. 'Is that why you're so tetchy? More of your flaming daddy issues? Poor little Castros didn't get to play at papa's mansion. Not like you were raised in some tenement with ten to a room is it though? Your childhood wasn't exactly that of some poor Bottom Barrow bastard.'

'You want to watch yourself, old friend, you're walking a very thin fucking line!' Castros said, leaning towards Whist, eyes flashing.

'Stop it, the pair of you!' Holger cut in. 'We have a job to do. Let's get it done and get out of here; this whole place is making my teeth itch.'

Del Var took a deep breath and closed his eyes. 'You're right,' he said. 'Let's just get this over and done with.'

Still keeping low to the ground, they sneaked round the back of the palace. One of the only other lights on was shining from a ground-floor window. Cautiously, Castros made his way towards it and peered in. He saw the two soldiers. One was sitting at a table with a steaming mug in his hand. The other was placing a hunk of bread next to a few meagre strips of cheese on a plate. The one with the plate said something to the one at the table then left the room.

Castros scratched his chin. 'It looks like there's only two of them,' he said.

'What? Two men looking after this whole place?' Whist asked.

'I know, seems weird, doesn't it? But then Khasal always was confident in his abilities.'

'How about we thank our lucky stars?' Holger said. 'Having to deal with just a couple of blokes is much better than having to deal with twenty.'

'Certainly cuts through the crap, don't he?' Whist said with a smile.

'That he does,' Del Var replied. 'Let's go.' They soon reached the servants' entrance. Castros grasped the handle. 'Locked. I can bust it open though.'

'Might be too noisy. Can't know for certain there's only two of them in there,' Whist said, taking out a large set of keys.

'I thought I was kidding about him giving you the keys to the place!' Castros said with a frown.

'Don't be dense,' Whist replied, trying different ones in the door. 'These are skeleton keys. Nicked them off a locksmith years ago. Aha! There we go.'

The servants' door swung inwards with the smallest of sighs. Castros went to go in first, but Whist pushed him back.

'I know the layout of this place better than you,' he said. 'No hard feelings.'

Castros felt his skin bristle but gave his friend a nod. They made their way inside — Castros in the middle of their single-file line — down a tight corridor that ended at a narrow flight of steps.

'Servants' stairs,' Whist said, nodding his head towards them. 'Should get us up to the second floor unseen.'

Rising onto the balls of their feet, they began to climb the stairs. Castros held his breath every time a creak or groan came from the wood beneath him, but no guards descended upon them. They paused at the top while Whist stuck his head out of the doorway.

'All clear,' he said.

They crept along the hallway, Castros glad for the thick, footstep-muffling carpet beneath their feet. A feeble smear of light escaped from one of the doors, and they came to a stop before it.

'Right,' Castros whispered, 'Whist, prime your ballistol. Holger, ready your spark sticks. Khasal will be a tough opponent, but we have the element of surprise in our favour.'

'Hang on,' Whist said his brows furrowed. 'We're just gonna burst in there? Not much of a plan, Cass.'

'What's wrong with it? If all goes well, we should be able to kill him with one short, sharp shock,' Castros replied.

'Kill him? Why would we do that? We should at least interrogate him first,' Whist said.

'Is this really the place or time to be having this conversation?' Holger said. 'We have no idea where that guard—'

Castros held up a hand to cut him off, never taking his eyes off Whist. 'Look, I know Khasal, and the best chance we have is to blast him into nothing before he knows what's going on.'

'No. We should—'

At that moment, the door swung open. Castros snapped his head round and looked into a guard's face. For a long, drawn-out second, they stared into each other's eyes, their mouths agape. In some remote corner of his mind, Castros realised that the scene would probably look hilarious to an outside party. The muscles round the guard's jaw began to mobilise in a chewing motion, as if he was trying to remember how to talk.

'What the—' was all he managed to say before Holger leapt forwards and landed a blow squarely on the guard's chin. His head whipped back, then he crumpled in a heap.

Castros, Holger and Whist froze, their eyes darting between each other, waiting to see if the other guard had heard the commotion.

'Stop gawping at each other, you morons, and drag him in here!' a voice hissed at them from inside the room.

Following the voice, Castros looked into the room for the first time. His eyes blinked rapidly, trying to deny what was in front of them. There, in the middle of what should have been a study, was a large cage. Even from his position by the door, Del Var could see it was made out of tharg's bane. Behind the bars, sat on a stool with his arms folded and a look of high amusement on his face, was Khasal.

'It's entirely up to you though,' the mage continued. 'Keep standing there like that, and I'm sure the other one will be along to throw you in here with me.'

'What do we—' Holger began.

'Just grab his other arm and get him inside,' Castros said. Holger nodded and did as he was asked. The carpet beneath the guard hissed like a sackful of snakes, but Castros was sure the other guard wouldn't hear it … almost sure

'Oh, and I'd close the door too,' Khasal said to Whist who, looking rather dazed, did as he was told. 'Good man. Well, Castros, this is a surprise. I don't suppose you're the prince come to rescue me from my tower?'

'Um … what … wait … no,' Castros stammered, his mind reeling. 'I actually … er … came to—'

But before he could finish, Khasal broke into a grin and laughed. 'By the gods,' Khasal said, 'you came here to kill me, didn't you?'

'Well … yes,' Castros said. His reply was met with another wave of laughter.

'And I suppose you think that will make the malovors uncontrollable? You do, don't you? I can tell by the look on your face. Well, unfortunately for you, they don't listen to me now, if they ever did for that matter. No, they are held in check by the Heir to Excellus. He doesn't have to be near them anymore either. They can sense his presence. In fact, the only reason I'm alive is because I have them convinced that a few hundred of the malovors are still loyal to me.'

'Well, this certainly changes things,' Whist said, scratching his cheek.

'Yes, it's quite the anti-climax,' Del Var replied.

'You mean we came all this way,' Holger said, 'through those … those fucking sewers for nothing!'

'It seems like it,' Castros said.

'It needn't be,' Khasal said, standing up so fast his stool toppled over. 'I know where they've got him … the Heir to Excellus that is.'

It was Castros' turn to laugh now. 'And I suppose, if we set you free, you'll help us reach him? Excuse me if I don't trust you, old friend, but I still have the scars on my body from that little boat cruise we took together.'

'Oh for heaven's sake, Castros! You certainly know how to hold a grudge. Look at it like this — you left me for dead, I almost killed you. But neither one of us has passed through the Shimmering Veil, so we're even, aren't we? I have no love for the duke. Look what he's done to me. He's fucked me, and I'd love the chance to fuck him back. Come on, what do you say?'

'I say goodbye, Khasal,' Del Var replied.

'Wait!' Khasal said, rattling his bars. 'Look at this. I even have an execution collar on. The duke slipped it round me when I tried to melt his face. That guard there has the control for it. With that you could bump me off at the press of a button.'

Castros paused between the door and the cage.

'Cass, tell me you aren't seriously considering this?' Whist said. 'I know you spent time with him during your exile, but I've read his file — this guy's a psychopath!'

Del Var went to the guard and began to rifle through his pockets. Behind him, he heard Whist let out an exasperated sigh. He soon found the controls to the execution collar and the key to the cage.

'Don't make me regret this,' Castros said, sliding the key into the lock.

'I won't. I'll behave, I promise,' Khasal replied, a hungry glint in his eye.

The same second as the lock slipped open, the door to the room swung in.

'What the hells has been keeping you so long?' the second guard said. He registered the scene in the room and added, 'Ah, shit.' The man spun on his heel and bolted.

'Stop him,' Khasal cried. 'There's an alarm down there that will bring the whole army down on our … too late.'

Castros turned on the spot as a klaxon let out a stream of bone-shaking wails.

'Follow me!' Khasal roared, struggling to make his voice heard, before disappearing from the room.

Holger and Whist looked at Castros who shrugged and said, 'Let's go.'

They chased after Khasal who was already at the top of the stairs. There was no sign of the other guard as they raced through the house, but Castros could hear the angry cries of the guard's colleagues arriving at the front door.

'This way,' Khasal said, leading them out through the back door and to the stable. Inside were a pair of disinterested horses and a lumpy mass obscured by a piece of tarpaulin. With one swift motion, Khasal ripped the fabric away.

'What do you think?' Khasal said.

'I knew you wouldn't be able to give it up,' Castros replied.

'What is it?' Whist said.

'An aerolyte,' Castros said.

'What does it do?' Whist asked.

'Just get on and I'll show you,' Khasal said from the controls.

They all clambered aboard, and the next thing Castros knew, they were shooting through the air. Shots rang out from below them pinging off the aerolyte. Khasal sent the ship upwards, out of range of the bullets.

'Where are we going?' Del Var said, noticing they were heading further up the Olphant Hill instead of away from it. 'The Castrian Wall is that way!'

'We're going to help out another one of your old friends,' Khasal said, a grin splitting his face.

***

Fontaine watched Crenshaw grip the calloused hand of the ship's captain.

'I shall be sorry to see you go,' the captain said. 'I worked you hard, but you were a match to it. Even your mousy friend got there eventually.'

The words "I worked you hard" were perhaps the most understated Fontaine had ever heard. He was sure there were a few pack horses somewhere who had been pushed harder than he had … but he was equally sure there weren't that many. He'd puked because of the work, fainted because of the work, even *cried* because of the work, and the ship's crew had always been right there to cheer him up with a chorus of hysterical laughter. But he had stuck with it and was proud of that. He was also proud of the muscles that had developed on his usually stick-thin arms and legs.

'Be safe,' the captain said, taking Fontaine's hand and pumping it like a piston. 'And good luck with your journey. I hope you find what you're looking for.' He let go of the scholar's hand and let out an ear-splitting roar in response to one of his crew dropping a barrel they were unloading, then he was gone.

'You ready?' Crenshaw asked.

Although he wasn't, Fontaine nodded his head. Crenshaw led the way down the ship's boarding plank, and within a handful of minutes, they were out of the docks and into the throes of a market.

The explosion of life and colour around him was staggering. Men and women dressed in fabrics of vibrant colours and patterns sat beneath awnings of equally vibrant hues, their goods set out in front of them. Sounds bulged, rippled, merged. The cry of a vendor turned into the babble of someone haggling. Powerful scents mingled: spice, roasting meat, tobacco, sweat. For a moment, Fontaine stood there, stunned, convinced that any second his overloaded senses would shut down, burned out from overstimulation.

'Come on,' Crenshaw said. 'Someone here must've seen Bar and the vooshu come through. You take the left side of the market. I'll take the right. We'll meet in an hour by that big tree.' Fontaine opened his mouth to protest, but Crenshaw was already slipping into the current of the crowd.

As he asked around, a similar pattern emerged. To begin with the stallholders greeted him with smiles and brought out their most expensive pieces, but as soon as he mentioned Barboza's name, the smiles disappeared, replaced by angry sneers and signs to ward off evil. One man had even threatened him with a ballistol.

It was a thoroughly deflating and unnerving hour. He was glad to be waiting under the shade of the tree. After a further fifteen minutes, Crenshaw appeared, looking as perturbed as Fontaine felt.

'Any luck?' Crenshaw asked.

'I'm afraid not,' Fontaine replied.

'Shit,' Crenshaw swore, sinking to the ground beneath the tree. 'Alright, we'll move out into the town and—'

'You,' a voice said, cutting Crenshaw off. Fontaine looked up to see an old woman, faded tribal scars pocking the sagging flesh of her cheeks. 'I know the man you seek. More to the point, I know where dey went.'

'Really?' Crenshaw said, climbing back to his feet, eyes lighting up.

The woman nodded. 'His father be a great man. Young Ginko maybe not da same, but he got a kind heart. I never did believe dem stories none.'

'Thanks for your kind words, madam, but we're in a bit of a hurry,' Fontaine said.

'Mmm-hmm. I'm sure you are if the look on dat vooshu's face was anything to go by,' she said. 'I heard him talking, said he was taking Ginko to Bambezi for a trial.'

'The old capital?' Crenshaw said. 'But why?'

'Said there was going to be a gathering. All de tribes will be there.'

'How long ago was this?' Fontaine asked.

'Over a month now,' the woman answered.

Fontaine bit his lip. 'If they are following the ancient Timbokan ritual of Hansi then the trial would be—'

'Tomorrow,' Crenshaw finished for him. 'And Bambezi is two days' ride away.'

'I never said my news would be good,' the woman said.

'No … it's fine … thank you, grandmother,' Crenshaw said, fishing a coin from his pocket.

The old woman shook her head. 'Keep your money. I gotta feeling you'll be needing it more than me.' She shuffled around them then set off with surprising speed through the crowd.

'That's it then,' Fontaine said, leaning back against the tree. 'There's no way we'll make it in time.'

'Don't lose heart just yet,' Crenshaw said, staring off at something in the market. 'We might just have a way to get there.'

***

Castros covered his eyes, the glare from a spotlight dazzling him. It seemed like there were hundreds of them shining on the Olphant Hill now, like someone had stuck matches into the side of an anthill.

'Wahoo!' Khasal yelled as he pitched the aerolyte into a stomach-spinning dive. 'Freedom sure is sweet. A starry night, the wind in your hair, a magically powered flying machine at your fingertips; what more could any man want?'

'To stay alive for the next thirty seconds which seems highly unlikely with your flying skills!' Castros replied.

'Stop worrying, Cass. Hang on, how about we give this lot a scare?'

Without waiting for a reply, Khasal plunged the aerolyte down until it was a mere six feet from the ground. Castros felt his heart shoot into his throat and stick there like a fish bone. With mounting horror, he realised what Khasal was doing. In front of them was a gaggle of five soldiers their helmets lined up with the front of the flying machine. *He's going to knock their bloody heads off,* Castros thought. *This is too much.* Del Var's perception of the world slowed to a crawl, the heads of the men and the vehicle inching closer and closer.

At that moment, he noticed a curious thing. The guards stood in front of them, swaying side to side, seemingly unaware of their impending deaths. Then at the very last second, they all drew there ballistols and fired as one, like they were performing some lethal dance routine. *Now that's weird,* Del Var thought. Khasal made a violent right turn to avoid the bullets, and all Del Var could think about was clinging on for dear life.

'Where exactly are we going?' Whist asked when Khasal began to fly level once more.

'We are going to the tallest tower of the Imperial Palace,' Khasal called over his shoulder.

'Are you insane?' Holger cried.

'Of course he's insane,' Del Var said. 'But he's not stupid. What's up there that you want?'

'Like I said, Cass, an old friend of yours. One even the spymaster here doesn't know about. Someone who will be very useful in our now joint efforts to fuck the duke up his warty arse,' Khasal said.

'Gods, do you love the sound of your own voice!' Castros said. 'Who the hells is it?'

'Melek,' Khasal replied.

'You're joking,' Whist said. 'My men haven't been able to find hide nor hair of him for months. Are you telling me the duke's had him all this time?'

'I am. You don't believe me? You'll see soon enough. As long as he hasn't worked himself to death first. Duke's been giving him drugs. Loves drugs does our dukey-poo, can't stop popping them himself, has a whole fleet of chemisticians cooking up new ones all the time. It's how he's got the Heir to Excellus under control. Anyway, get ready, Cass, we're almost there. Everyone else, hold on.'

'What do you mean, get ready?' Castros asked.

He was answered by Khasal swinging the aerolyte in a sharp arc. Castros lost his balance and went flying off the back of the vehicle. He spun through the air like a child rolling down a hill. Then he collided with a window, crashing into the room beyond, surrounded by a million glistening fragments. He hit the floor hard and skidded into a bedpost.

Castros pushed himself up, a discarded piece of paper with a design on it crumpling beneath his hands. He lifted his spinning head and looked around the room. Every available surface was piled with books, papers and glass bottles. On one side of the room, a purple liquid dripped through a filtration device. On the other side sat a complicated bit of machinery, cogs and gears gleaming in the light.

Melek sat at a table, hunched over as he furiously scribbled in a book. He seemed completely unaware of what had just happened, even though Castros could see tiny flecks of glass shimmering in his hair.

'Melek?' Castros said, climbing to his feet. 'Melek!'

The inventor paused, scratched at his ear then resumed his writing.

Del Var gripped the man's shoulder and said, 'Melek! It's me, Castros.'

'Yes, yes, hello, Castros. What do you want? As you can see, I'm extremely busy,' Melek said.

'Well …I've … I've come to rescue you,' Del Var said.

'Rescue? Me? I don't need rescuing! I'm having the most fruitful period of my entire working life. My mind is alive with the light of understanding!'

'It's alive with the light of something alright,' Castros said.

'I have no idea what you mean,' Melek said with a sniff, his hand reaching out for what looked like a jar full of red sweets.

'No more of that rubbish, I think,' Del Var said, snatching the jar.

Melek hissed like a cat then pounced towards Castros who only just managed to sidestep the attack.

'It's for your own good,' Del Var said.

'Give me them, Castros. I won't be held accountable for my actions if you don't.'

'These are poison, old friend. I'm saving you from yourself.'

With a guttural growl, Melek launched himself at Del Var again. This time, he connected with Del Var's left leg, and they both tumbled to the floor. The jar came free of Castros' grip and rolled away. Melek let out a giggle of delight and made a grab for it. His fingertips brushed the glass just before Del Var sent him flying backwards with a blast from his screamer.

'Monster!' Melek howled. 'Devil! Guards! Guards!'

Castros heard banging against the, thankfully, locked door. 'Time to leave, I think,' he said. He walked up to Melek and added, 'I'm sorry.'

'For what?' Melek asked.

'This,' Castros answered, landing a punch on the man's chin.

'What did you do that for?' Melek yelled.

'I … well … it was supposed to knock you out.'

'Didn't work, did it?'

'Apparently not. Hang on.'

This time, Melek's head snapped back, banging against the leg of a table, rendering him unconscious. Castros bent down and picked the inventor up, swinging him over his shoulder, marvelling at how light he was. Making his way towards the shattered window, he noticed a satchel filled with papers and gadgets and picked that up too.

'We're coming out!' Castros bellowed.

'I'll try and straighten her up,' Khasal cried back.

'Don't take too long,' Del Var said, looking towards the shuddering door.

'Right, we're ready,' Khasal said.

At the same moment the door flew open.

Once again, Castros was struck by the vacant look on the guard's face. Did he look a bit green as well? The guard cut his pondering short by pulling out his ballistol and pointing it at Castros' head. Castros took his screamer in hand once more and sent a blast of magically infused air towards the guard, using the same momentum to carry himself out the window and onto the aerolyte.

'Nice exit!' Khasal cried.

'I know,' Castros said. 'Now get us out of here!'

***

Bellina sat upon her horse at the head of the great train of people who now called her Empress. They said summer never came to the northern countries of the Empire — a fact some attributed to those lands being closer to the damned air given off by the Scorched Earth — and Bellina was now getting to experience that truth first-hand. A chill fog crept along the ground like an assassin, leaving freezing blades in any exposed flesh. But it wasn't just the fog that was chilling her that morning.

'Are you sure this is all that's left?' Bellina asked, looking into Bert's solemn face.

'I'm afraid so, Your Majesty. After those five bags of grain are gone, we're down to nothing but the jars of preserves, and those will do nothing to calm a person's hunger,' Bert said.

'Can we put everyone on rations?' Bellina replied.

'I already have, Your Majesty, but if we don't reach Hidenbaden soon, we're going to start to lose people.'

'What do you suggest I do?' Bellina said. 'I can't magically make the capital of Gortrix move closer to us, can I?'

'No, Your Majesty,' Bert said, 'but there is a shortcut. One which many would avoid, myself included. Perhaps it's best I don't mention it.'

Bellina took a deep breath. 'Tell me,' she commanded.

Bert swallowed, the protrusioin in his throat bobbing. He licked his lips and said, 'About an hour's ride, we'll reach a fork in the road. One path is the main thoroughfare to Hidenbaden. The other … well, the other leads to Walderforst Forest. You see, the main road skirts around it for miles, adds roughly five days to the trip. But if we go straight through Walderforst, it should only take two.'

'Why does it go around?' Bellina asked. 'The model for road building in the Empire is straight lines, taking the shortest route possible. I find it hard to believe they would have created such a needless detour.'

Bert cleared his throat. 'They wanted to go through … but … er … things started to happen — men disappearing in the night, measurements and calculations going awry, not to mention the wolves and the bears. People think there are bad spirits in there.'

'That sounds like a load of superstitious twaddle. If it's the quickest route, we'll take it,' Bellina said with a snort.

'I'm not a superstitious man, Your Majesty, I wouldn't have mentioned it if I were. But a lot of the people here are. They're already telling each other ghost stories about the place round the campfire. They'll follow you in there … at least, I think they will. But don't make the decision lightly.'

the decision lightly.'

'I won't. Thank you, Bert,' Bellina said.

He nodded his head and slipped back into the throng of people trudging along behind Bellina. "Don't take the decision lightly"! She couldn't remember the last light decision she'd had to make. Her recent past had been a long list of choices that ranged from not good to complete madness; what was one more to add to the mix?

She looked around for Elvgren and found him with Dargo, some twenty feet behind her, surrounded by a group of boys in their late teens regaling them with some tale. There was a burst of too loud laughter from them, the laughter of people on the edge. No, she was not going to find any help from her betrothed. Bellina pursed her lips. *It's alright for some*, she thought.

The idea of bad spirits was ludicrous, and she dismissed it out of hand. But wolves and bears … that was another story. The smell of so many people was sure to draw them out, especially when that smell would be laced with fear. How long had Bert said it would take to get through? Two days. But was that the best-case scenario? If they went through, they could lose people to animal attacks. If they went round, she wondered how many of her half-starved followers would have the energy to reach Hidenbaden? Any way she looked at it, people were going to suffer.

The thoughts raged inside her head like duelling dragons, sucking her into a world of her own. It wasn't until she heard the cries of those around her that she realised they were at the fork in the road. Looking up, Bellina saw the two paths. To the right was the straight stone of the Imperial highway. To the left was a snaking path of rutted dirt and, at its end, the shadowy mass that was the Walderforst Forest.

Feeling the weight of the crowd's eyes upon her, Bellina turned round. It was clear word had spread of the choice Bert had left her with. Men and women with the startled eyes of trapped mice whispered hurried conversations to each other. Even with her cognopathic powers dimmed to their lowest, she could feel in her mind the waves of fear that were washing off them.

Bert made his way through the crowd, hushing and calming those he passed. 'Your subjects would like to know which road we take, Your Majesty?' he said.

'Hang on one second!' Elvgren said, leading his horse up to Bellina's. 'I will have my say in this too.'

The thought occurred to her, as she looked at the man she was engaged to all puffed up like some ludicrous owl, that she could simply press a button on her power controls and pop his head like a rotten tomato.

Something in her face must have conveyed this idea, because Elvgren quickly added, 'Of course, I stand by any decision my beloved should … er … make.'

Bellina looked at the faces of the people in front of her, haggard, weary, half-starved faces, and she made her decision.

'We go through Walderforst.'

***

Heavy clouds hung low over the mountain peaks, a bitter wind howling out of them, whipping a fine flurry of snow into Cirona's face. Underfoot, the scree crunched in time with the laboured breaths escaping her throat, a throat raw from the thin air. Despite the fact she had covered all of her face except for a small gap so she could see, the skin on her head still felt chapped, raw. *Who would have thought climbing a mountain would be this hard?* she thought, stifling a bitter chuckle.

There was a sound behind her, and Cirona spun to see what it was, ballistol drawn, heart crashing in her chest like thunder. All her air left her in one whooping sigh when she saw it was only an eagle. It was perched on a rock, head cocked to one side with a mouse dangling from its bloodstained beak. For a heartbeat, it regarded her with button-bright eyes then began to devour its meal.

You're jumping at shadows, woman. No one is following you. If you keep this up, you'll be crazy as a starved dog by the time you get to Narvale.

'You sure you know the bloody way?' Waltus asked, coming to a stop beside her. Even though the mage was hundreds of years older than her, he still seemed to be faring better.

'Of course I do,' she snapped. 'Someone I knew was from these parts.'

Not just someone. Trafford. Trafford told you the way. Gods, how many times had he bored her close to weeping with tales of his goat-herding ancestors and the trail only they knew over the Yammeroff mountains? Gods, what would she give to hear them again, to watch his face light up as he jabbered on and on about people even he only had a dim recollection of? She shook her head. *None of that.*

'Come on,' she said. 'We're wasting time.'

After another hour's worth of battling onward, they came to a stop. Cirona felt her mouth go dry — very, very dry — when she observed what was in front of her. A large gap yawned open before them, like the mouth of a waiting giant. Covering the gap was a monumental plank of wood, two large pins at either end of it supporting an age-worn length of rope.

'What are we waiting for?' Waltus asked.

'I … um … don't … like heights,' she answered.

'Shouldn't 'ave decided to climb a mountain then,' Waltus replied.

'Shut up, you rotten old git.'

Waltus sighed and lifted the woolly hat he was wearing to scratch at his scalp. 'How about I go first then? Show yer there's nothing to worry about?'

'Alright then.'

With a brisk nod, Waltus walked to the beginning of the plank and stepped on. Just over a minute later, he was on the other side.

'There yer go, nothing to it!' he called back from the other side.

'That's easy for you to say,' she muttered.

'What was that?'

'Nothing. Just shut up and let me concentrate.'

She covered the distance to the board with the shuffling, unsure steps of an infant and placed a juddering foot at its start. *Father bless me, that creak just then was as loud as thunder. This is ridiculous. There's no way this is safe. I don't care if Waltus has just done it; he probably used some magic trick and—*

Get a bloody hold of yourself woman and get across this gap.

'Who's wasting time now?' Waltus called across at her chuckling.

'I told you to shut it.'

Peeling her gloves off to get a better grip, Cirona took hold of the rope like a lover. Beneath her fingers, she could feel the cool, heavy dampness of the hemp, its frayed edges somehow calming her. *Easy does it. Move one foot a bit, then the other. You can do this.* The sound of her left boot scraping across the boards to meet the right one made her chest ache.

She looked over to see how far was left to go. The other side seemed to stretch away from her till Waltus was just a dot. She squeezed her eyes shut, trying to regain a fragment of composure. *Now, that was a bad idea,* she thought.

'Has it not occurred to you yet,' Waltus called, 'that the longer you stay on that plank the more likely it is to break?'

'You're not helping, old man!'

After a deep breath, she set off again, sweat pouring off her head so fast she had to remove her hat and scarf. The sound of her steps took on a rhythmical quality — step, creak, scrape, step, creak, scrape. *Gotta be close now. Just keep going, and any second now, you'll step onto the other side.*

'Come on, girl,' Waltus was cheering. 'Not much further and … bloody hells! Look out!'

At first, all Cirona felt was her hair ripple, then a stinging by her ear. She reached up to it with her left hand and felt the hot ooze of her own blood seeping from where the top of her ear had been. A screech tore the air over to her left. Snapping her head towards the noise, she saw an eagle. *No,* she thought, *it couldn't be the same one.* But somewhere inside, she knew that it was.

Then the bird was nothing but a blur of movement. It tore and gouged at the top of her head. Cirona tried to grab hold of it, completely forgetting where she was. It was quick though, far too quick for her groping hands, and managed to make a swipe at her exposed face, missing out on the prize of an eyeball by the smallest of margins.

'Fuck off!' Cirona bellowed, making one last grab for the bird before tumbling backwards into the gap.

CHAPTER FIVE

The shifting, ephemeral light that had managed to elude the grasping canopy above them was now slipping into near total darkness. Elvgren guessed that somewhere outside of these blasted woods the sun was setting. Lanterns were lit casting weak bubbles of light around them, coating the massive tree trunks in a sickly yellow, the burning garwhale oil merging with the over-sweet smell of resin and decaying foliage in a horrific perfume.

All in all, the day's journey through the Walderforst Forest had passed without any major incidents — a few trips and scrapes, the worst resulting in a sprained ankle — but the air of foreboding hung above the travellers like a thick, dark cloak. It seemed to slink along somewhere above their heads, every now and then smothering them in its folds.

This atmosphere hadn't been helped by the detritus left by the roadbuilders. They had found chunks of stone, hammers, chisels and other tools, all in the exact position they had been left in, some looking new despite the years which had passed since they were lain aside. That was worse than finding them rotted and weatherworn.

There's a stillness here, Elvgren thought, *a patient watching that tugs on the nerves, toying with them like a cruel child might with a trapped fly*. Gods, but the place was making him gloomy. He should have tried harder to have his say, to make sure they took the path around the forest. Having a few of the sickly fade away would have been a small price to pay to avoid this … place.

He looked at Bellina who was riding her horse at the front of the massed people next to him. Her shoulders were tense, her eyes bright and alert, twitching at the slightest noise. *I guess she's thinking twice about this place as well*, he thought.

'I don't like this place, Gren,' Dargo said, from his other side. 'Back when I was a kid, I had this book of fairy tales. I couldn't read the words, but it had pictures in it. One of 'em looked just like this place, but there were these … things with massive, round eyes that shone out like flames.'

'If I see any flaming eyeballs, I'll let you know,' Elvgren replied.

'Yeah, yeah, laugh it up. But you'll be the only one smiling in 'ere.'

'Your Majesties,' a voice called from behind them. 'Your Majesties, we must stop!'

Elvgren pulled his horse to a stop and turned his one good eye upon Bert. The man was holding a lantern on the end of a pole, the light dancing over his face in great jumping shadows.

'We can't go any further in this dark, sooner or later someone will trip and break their neck,' Bert continued.

'And that would be a crying shame,' Elvgren said, trying to keep the sarcasm from his voice. He realised he had failed by the look Bellina shot him. 'I mean to say, make sure we make camp in as tight a circle as possible. Find the least tired men and set up a guard perimeter around us. Dargo and I will take part in the first watch as well.'

'Thanks for including me, Gren; I feel all warm and fuzzy now.'

'Shut up, Dargo.'

'Very well, Your Majesty, I'll see to it right away,' Bert said.

Elvgren turned around and saw Bellina staring at him, her head cocked to one side.

'What?' Elvgren asked.

'I suppose you do have some uses,' she said.

'My uses are many and varied, my love; it is you who chooses not to appreciate them,' he replied. Bellina let out a snort of laughter.

Deciding to ignore her, Elvgren dismounted and watched as the servants — Bellina liked to call them helpers — scurried about setting up their tents. The royal couple had a large tent each, a luxury considering as many as ten people were somehow cramming into ones of the same size. Elvgren's mouth twisted into a pout when he looked at the tent he shared with Dargo. He had thought about sabotaging it in an attempt to get into Bellina's, but he was confident that he knew the response he would receive from his wife-to-be.

His good eye fell upon her now. She had her arms wrapped tight around herself despite the heavy cloak she wore, her creamy skin pocked with goosebumps. *There's no doubting she's always attractive*, Elvgren thought, *but this is one of those times when she looks truly beautiful.* He had bedded what he reckoned was a considerable number of women, his first time being when his fellow officers took him to a whorehouse for his eighteenth birthday. The handful of other women had also been whores, the couplings short, urgent affairs that had left him with an echoing hollowness in his gut. *What would it be like*, he wondered, *to run my fingers over her skin, to feel it shiver with excitement instead of the cold, to feel—*

'Are you going to stand there like an idiot all night, my love,' she asked, ripping Elvgren out of his fantasy.

'What would you have me do, my beloved?' Elvgren replied through gritted teeth.

'I don't know! Find firewood, get some water … anything but what you're doing right now!' she said, her chin quivering before she collapsed onto a stool one of the servants had set up.

'Dargo, get some firewood,' Elvgren said.

'Why should I? Belle told you to—'

'Just get it, you lazy little git,' Elvgren snapped.

'Yes, Your *Majesty*, anything you like, Your *Majesty*,' Dargo said, giving an exaggerated bow with each "Majesty" before stomping off.

Elvgren flopped onto his own stool beside Bellina's and said, 'Are … are you … alright?'

'Since when have you been concerned if I'm alright?' she said, lamplight flickering in her large eyes.

'Well … I just … I just wanted to tell you … it'll be alright.'

'Alright?' she hissed, leaning in close. 'Alright? We are leading thousands of people through a supposedly haunted forest towards a capital city that might not take them in. We have no food left, and if we don't find a stream in this place, we'll run out of drinkable water as well. Now tell me, my love, what part of that seems alright?'

'I didn't say it was alright. I said it *will* be alright. We'll get through this. We've been attacked by reanimated corpses, airlifted out of a city as the gates were stormed, burned down the most holy place in the Empire, and we're still here.'

Bellina sighed and stared at him. 'Why can't you be like this all time?'

'Like what?'

'Exactly.'

Silence crept over them, and Elvgren stared out over the tents that were being erected. 'Do you really think these woods are haunted?' he asked.

'Of course not,' Bellina replied.

'Only … Dargo was telling me this story about creatures with giant—'

'Flaming eyes.'

'That's right. Did he tell you as well?'

'No, I *mean*,' Bellina said, her mouth hanging open. 'over there. Flaming eyes.'

For a breath, he saw a pair of huge eyeballs among the trees, shining with a blue flame, then they flickered out. A single howl, a howl that made the valves in his heart slam shut, tore through the night. Then the screaming began. Elvgren drew his sword and ballistol, his head snapping towards each new cry. There was a flash of silver before his eye. It took his adrenaline-addled brain a second to work out what it was, and even then, he wasn't sure he believed what he saw.

In front of him stood a wolf the size of a small horse. The shimmering silver of its fur was flecked with blood and gore. Its mouth and snout were dyed crimson and from its jaws dangled a grown man, neck snapped and twisted at an impossible angle. The beast padded forwards on paws the size of sewer hatches. With a casual flick of its head it tossed the man aside as if he were made of paper and settled the blue-fire of its eyes upon Elvgren.

Raising his sword and ballistol, Elvgren put himself between the wolf and Bellina. He swallowed a mouthful of sour spit, his chest tightening, crushed by an invisible snake. *It's just a dog*, he told himself, *just a big, killer dog with flaming eyeballs*. The creature let out a low guttural growl and inched forwards, its head bent low.

Shoot it! Shoot it now, Elvgren's inner voice screamed, *before it can get any closer!*

His ballistol gave a hoarse cough as Elvgren pulled the trigger. The bullet soared through the air, tearing a bloody clump of flesh from the wolf's flank. The creature didn't even acknowledge the wound. Instead, it leapt. The beast's massive bulk hit Elvgren like a cannon shot. He felt the air driven out of him in one great whooping sigh.

The wolf had him pinned to the ground, its hot, rank breath assaulting his nose. It drew back its head, jaws stretching wide, the livid pink of its tongue clashing with the white pointy teeth. Elvgren flinched, waiting for the bite to come. When it didn't, he opened his eye and saw the wolf dangling in mid-air, jaws snapping, body flailing. It shot upwards like an escaped balloon. He clambered to his feet and turned to see Bellina breathing deeply, one of the gems on her power restraint glowing.

'You're welcome,' she said.

'I … er … thank you,' he stammered.

At that moment, Dargo came running up to them. 'Wolves, Gren. Bloody great wolves are on us,' he said.

'If there was a cash prize for stating the obvious, Dargo, you would have just won it,' Elvgren replied.

Elvgren looked around and realised they were now at the centre of a huddling mass of people. The wolves were circling them, herding them like sheep.

'They'll pick us off one by one at this rate,' Dargo said.

'Bellina, can you use your powers to shield us?' Elvgren asked.

'I'd never make a shield large enough to cover everyone,' Bellina answered.

'Then cover those you can,' Elvgren said.

'You can't seriously be asking me to sacrifice any of these people?'

'It's lose some or lose everyone,' Elvgren replied.

'I won't do it, I won't!' Bellina screamed.

A piercing whistle cut through the air like an executioner's axe. Elvgren clapped his hands to his ears to block out the sound; he noticed he wasn't the only one. If the sound was causing him pain, it was nothing compared to the effect it had on the wolves who lay writhing in agony. From out of darkness of the trees, men in uniform appeared carrying balliskets. They opened fire, slaughtering the beasts where they lay. *We're saved*, Elvgren thought. *Praise the Father, we're saved!*

The whistle stopped, and Elvgren watched the crowd part before him. Soldiers jostled the people aside, forming a path towards him, Bellina and Dargo. A man, epaulettes and medals hanging from his chest marking him out from his colleagues, strode up the newly created walkway. He stopped before them.

'Lord Elvgren, Lady Bellina,' he said. 'You are both under arrest.'

***

'Are you sure about this, Cass?' Whist asked.

'Yes,' Castros lied.

Sighing, Whist took a length of rope and tied Holger's hands behind his back. Then he moved towards Khasal.

'You are not tying me up!' the mage said, spitting his words. 'I haven't even agreed to go into that fucking place.'

Castros felt his eyes drawn towards the place Khasal's finger was pointing – the Ravensdown Institute. The institute lay among low, rolling hills, a stone giant squatting in the landscape. The institute was a purpose-built prison-cum-sortilenergy plant, the first and most infamous ever constructed. No one had ever escaped Ravensdown, and here he was preparing to walk into the heart of it.

'Khasal, we spoke about this,' Castros said. 'We decided that entering as prisoners under Melek's supervision was the only way we could get to the Heir of Excellus.'

'You decided, Castros, you!' Khasal said, moving in so close to Del Var their noses almost touched.

'We voted on it,' Castros calmly replied.

'And I voted against it.'

'Look, I know how you feel—' Del Var began.

'No, you don't,' Khasal said. 'You didn't grow up in one of these state-sanctioned hells. You could never imagine the horrors that are suffered within places like these.'

'I thought you wanted to, and these are your words — "fuck the duke up the arse". I personally can't think of a better way to do that than walking into the largest sortilenergy plant in Estria and liberating it.'

Khasal stared into Castros' eyes, his nostrils quivering, brow furrowed. 'Fine,' he said at last. 'But once we've got the Heir, I'm going to tear this place down brick by sodding brick.'

'That's the spirit,' Del Var said.

While Whist tied Khasal's hands, Castros turned round to face the crumpled form of Melek. The inventor sat huddled in a ball on the aerolyte. He hadn't stopped shivering since they had rescued him. Sweat was pouring down a face the colour of curdled milk. *Great*, Castros thought, the most integral part of our plan is a smoffhead shaking like an anxious hummingbird.

'Melek?' Del Var said, kneeling down to look into the other man's eyes. 'Melek, it's time.'

'I ... can't, Castros ... I ... I can't,' Melek replied.

'I'm afraid that wasn't a request.'

'I am ill, Castros, very, very ill. I cannot do what you want. I simply can't. And as a side note, I would like to ask why I should? Come on, tell me that? I've already suffered due to you. If I hadn't been associated with you, I never would have been forced into the army. Do you realise how many years that episode set my studies back by? I owe you nothing, Del Var, and I will not be party to this ... this madness.'

Castros let out a long theatrical sigh. 'That's a shame. You see, when I was rooting around in my pocket the other day, I found this,' he said, holding out a small blue pill. 'If you don't want it, I suppose I'll just have to throw it—'

'Give it to me!' Melek squealed, lunging towards the pill.

'Uh-uh-uh,' Del Var said, waggling a finger back and forth. 'After you've done what I need, then you can have it.'

'You are a rotten, suppurating boil, Castros Del Var,' Melek said, climbing unsteadily to his feet. 'And one of these days someone is going to lance you.'

'I'm sure they will.' Castros turned towards the others and said, 'Let's do this.'

They left the aerolyte in a thicket of bushes and set off on foot towards Ravensdown, following the path of loose rock that cut through the moorland like a sliver of moonlight. The massive black stone walls that encircled the institute grew with each step, until they soared above like a sheer cliff face made from onyx. Poking out from above the walls were smokestacks with purple-black smog, the colour of a fresh bruise, belching out of them. *Nowhere near as dense as it should be though,* Castros thought. *The sortilenergy must really be running low.*

Before he had any more time to dwell on his thoughts, Del Var realised they had reached the gatehouse. In front of him sat a broad building with a portcullis grinning from its centre. Two thin towers flanked it, arrow-slits at regular intervals running down their walls. Standing watch in front of it all was a solitary guard, his ballisket aimed at them.

'Halt,' he said. 'Who goes there?'

This is it, Castros thought. *You can do this, Melek.*

The inventor closed the gap between him and the guard, producing a badge with the duke's seal on it. 'I am Melek,' he said. 'The duke has sent me with these prisoners. They are all people of magical capabilities.'

The guard took the badge and licked his lips. 'Thank the Father you're here, sir,' he said. 'Things have been mental round here since we got our orders this morning. Some of the lads are taking them a bit too far.'

'Yes,' Melek said, not missing a beat. 'That was why the duke ordered me here to impose some kind of order.'

The guard nodded then shouted, 'Open her up, Varlos.'

A second later, the portcullis shuddered into life with a rusted screech. *Don't look at our hands,* Castros thought, *if they see we're not bound in tharg's bane handcuffs the jig will really be up.* Melek led them past the first portcullis and into the gatehouse proper. Del Var focused his attention on the second portcullis, forcing himself to not look up at the murder hole above their heads from which he expected hot death to cascade any minute. *Please, just let us through,* Castros thought, *please just let us through, please just let us through—*

'Hang on a minute,' the guard called from behind them.

Del Var closed his eyes, stomach writhing like a barrelful of eels. It was over. The man had spotted the rope that tied their hands and was going to give the order for Varlos to pour down whatever vat of hot awfulness he had up above them.

'Is something the matter?' Melek asked, a tiny tremor in his voice.

'You forgot your badge,' the guard said. 'You'll need that on the other side.'

'Thank you,' Melek replied, taking the badge in his shaking fingers.

'Open the next one, Varlos,' the guard yelled.

The second portcullis groaned into action and they all stepped through. Castros turned to the others and said, 'We're in.'

Cirona's eyelids slowly opened, each one feeling as if a ten-tonne weight had been tied to it. Above her head, stalactites dangled from a roof of rock like teeth in need of pulling. *I'm in a cave*, her groggy mind thought. The smell of fire drifted to her, and she tried to turn towards it. It was a move she instantly regretted. Sickening waves of pain rolled over her body, threatening to shove her back into unconsciousness. A groan escaped her lips.

'Stop moving,' Waltus called.

With some effort, she was able to turn her head towards the sound of his voice. Waltus was sitting near the mouth of the cave tending to a small fire.

'Where are we?' she managed to croak, the words making her cracked lips ache.

'We are almost exactly where you fell to,' Waltus said. He pointed an age-warped finger at a large, jagged rock just outside the cave entrance. 'You were about an inch away from smashing yer brains out on that. That was lucky, about the only bit you've had an' all.'

'Wh-what do you mean?' she asked.

'Well, you were bashed up pretty bad. All yer ribs were pretty much broken. Loads of internal bleeding as well. It was close, but I just about managed to save yer. Took all the juice I had stored up to do it, mind.'

'Thank you,' Cirona said.

'If you really wanna thank me ...'

'Shut up, Waltus.'

'Alright, alright.'

With a deep breath, Cirona tried to haul herself into a sitting position.

'Will you just lay still, woman!' Waltus cried.

'No,' Cirona said. She bit back a scream and succeeded in getting into a seated posture. 'We need to get moving.'

'You need to rest.'

Looking the old mage dead in the eye, Cirona said, 'How long was I out?'

'Just over a day,' Waltus replied.

'All the more reason to get going again.'

'That fall must've rattled your brain more than I thought,' Waltus bellowed, climbing to his feet. 'You ain't nothing more than a giant, walking bruise at the minute, girl. One more night, and you'll be as right as rain.'

'Fine, I'll go without you,' Cirona said. Using the cave wall for support, she managed to drag herself upright. 'There. I told you I was ...' Grey spread from the corners of her eyes. The ground seemed to leap up at her. She fell against the wall.

Waltus hurried to her side and helped her back onto the floor. 'Look what yer went and did, yer daft cow!' he said. 'Rest. For the love of the gods, rest. It's not like Narvale is going anywhere, is it? There's no rush.'

'Wanna ... wanna get it over with,' Cirona said, through heaving breaths. 'Gotta get ... get back to Bellina.'

'She's fine. Got the one-eyed lad and that little street rat to look after her.'

'She ... she needs me.'

'Does she? Or do you need her?' Waltus said, looking deep into her eyes. 'There was a reason I wanted to come with you, yer know? I've seen what loss does to people, seen it up close. They all get the same look in their eyes that you've got, kinda lost and confused. They were searching, see, searching just like you are now, looking to find something they could put their faith into, something that would give 'em a reason to live. You, just like them, need saving from yerself.'

'I don't want you to save me, Waltus. I'm a grown woman,' Cirona replied, pushing herself away from him, making her body cramp all over.

'I don't give a tin shit about what you want,' Waltus said. 'I'm going to save you. Maybe then I can ...' He turned away.

Silence fell upon them. Cirona saw the old mage take out a dirty handkerchief and mop at his eyes. *This man has saved your life*, she thought, *brought you back from the edge of the Shimmering Veil, healed you better than a shipload of medificers could, and you're giving him grief over it?* She rested her head back and let the silence stretch out, content to listen to the howling of the wind outside the cave.

'Sorry about that,' Waltus said as he resumed his seat by the fire. 'It's just that you remind me of someone is all. At least back home when I got all emotional, there weren't no one to see me.'

Cirona's brow furrowed — gods even that hurt — and said, 'How long were you on your own for, Waltus?'

''Bout fifty years, I reckon.'

'I'm ... I'm going to go to sleep now.'

'You do that, luv. I'll be right 'ere.'

*

The next day dawned, bright and crisp as a fresh apple. Much to her surprise, Cirona found Waltus had been telling the truth — she did feel better. After a hasty breakfast, they set off. It was a hard climb back up to where she had fallen from, but they made it. The old mage needed to take a minute to catch his breath, so they took an early lunch. Soon after, they started out once more. Cirona soon noticed that they were going downwards, and the hike got much easier. *Things are going well,* she thought, *too well.* That was when they reached the cavern.

Cirona eyed the wide opening with suspicion. A mere pebble's throw in from the entrance, things got dark, very, very dark.

'Gonna have to take our time with this one, Waltus. Could be …' She turned and saw the mage perched on the edge of a flat rock, sweat pouring from his brow. 'Are you alright?'

'Yeah, yeah, just not as young as I used to be. Healing you took a bit more out of me than I expected. Gimme a minute, and I'll be alright again.'

Gaze shifting from Waltus to the cavern entrance, Cirona said, 'How about I go on ahead, make sure the way's clear?'

'Okay, luv, I'll … I'll just sit 'ere and catch me breath.'

With a nod, Cirona moved towards the cavern. She broke the branch off a scraggy-looking tree, tore a piece of cloth from a spare shirt, soaked it in oil from her pack then wrapped it around the branch and lit it. Makeshift torch in hand, she went into the darkness. The narrow cavern seemed to go on forever, the flame off her torch making the wet walls glisten. In reality, it only took twenty minutes before she saw daylight again.

She rushed towards the opening and felt her heart sink. It was half full with boulders from a rockslide. *Shit,* she thought, *how's Waltus going to get up this?* Maybe if she just cleared a few of the stones away?

No. She would go back, and they would deal with it later. Surely, Waltus would have got his wind back by now? She set off back through the cavern, boots crunching on the loose stone, each step accompanied by the incessant dripping all around her. When she reached the other side, Waltus was nowhere to be seen. She paused, nostrils quivering as if they could smell out the danger.

'Waltus? Waltus! Where are you?' she cried. 'If this is one of your jokes, it's not funny.' She drew her sword and stepped out of the cavern. 'Waltu—'

Pain exploded in the back of her head. Then everything went black.

***

A yellowy-green ocean of grass spread out before Scholar Fontaine. Every so often, the vast, flat landscape was punctuated by a forlorn umbrella tree, hidden roots keeping the thing alive in the dry wilderness. A sun the colour of amber blazed in a cloudless sky, and Fontaine could feel the sting where it had burned his face and neck.

Beneath him, he could feel the lengi tiring. The short hair of the massive antelope was lathered in sweat, the soft graceful motion of its legs losing their rhythm. Crenshaw had said that the creatures were the fastest in Timboko, but they had still managed to ride two of them into the ground already. Fontaine reckoned they had been in the saddle for well over sixteen hours now; his arse had gone numb and his legs were following.

He was just about to ask Crenshaw how much longer the journey would last when he saw the city of Bambezi. Large conical towers the colour of bone rose up from behind a huge encircling wall. In contrast to the bleached whiteness of the city, a swarm of multicoloured tents hummed around the walls like bees. *It would seem*, the scholar thought, *that all the tribes really have shown up for the Hansi.*

'One last push, eh?' Crenshaw said to his left.

Fontaine nodded, and they both dug their heels into the lengi, coaxing out the last of their respective beast's strength. They sped across the plain towards the city, past the dazzling tents, before coming to a stop by the city's gate. Two giant guards, their bodies covered in animal hides, barred the way with spears. The scholar began to rein his lengi in, but to his amazement, Crenshaw kept going at the same pace. The guards shouted warnings, but on he went. Fontaine watched their faces turn from anger to confusion then finally fear. A second later, they both jumped aside.

The lengi's hooves beat out a crazed tattoo as they sped along the narrow stone streets of Bambezi. Crenshaw was now brandishing a ballistol and screaming at the top of his lungs at any unfortunate who got in their way. The path through the city led them in concentric circles till at last they arrived in a large clearing at the centre.

The large, circular space was choked with people, light glinting off the coloured beads around their necks. Some wore animal hides like the guards, others were wrapped in loose cloth garments. A few, here and there, bore elaborate headdresses, the feathers of different exotic birds waving in the slight breeze, burly spearmen by their sides. *Those must be the chiefs*, Fontaine thought. *Surely, Crenshaw will slow down now?*

Despite the multitude of armed men at the gathering, Crenshaw showed no sign of stopping. Without warning, he fired his ballistol. The scholar looked on in horror as the crowd began to turn towards them. A few flinched, trying to get away, but the chiefs were made from sterner stuff. They ordered their spearmen forwards, the men forming a line, weapons angled outwards, creating a wall of death.

To Fontaine's eternal amazement, he saw Crenshaw actually try to gee his lengi on. Fortunately for him, his mount had more sense than his master and came to a skittering stop in front of the line of spears. The scholar brought his beast to a stop next to his companion. The whole crowd was now looking at them like they were bugs under a microscope.

'I ... er ... hello?' Fontaine stammered.

'Let us through, you bastards!' Crenshaw bellowed.

There was a brief pocket of silence, then the chiefs ordered their spearmen forwards. The men advanced as one. Fontaine felt many hands grab at him, pulling and tearing at his hair and clothes. He fell to the floor, landing hard on his shoulder. Someone kicked him between the shoulder blades, pain knifing down his back. Another caught his elbow when he covered his face. Words were being cried in Timbokan, harsh, barked words that had to be bad.

At last, his attackers reached down and hauled him roughly to his feet. Someone behind him pinned his arms to his back, another grabbed his collar, and he was marched forwards. The pool of people in front of him parted, their dark faces jeering at him as he was led through. He was shoved through the last people and went stumbling into a clear area.

In front of him, he saw an old man standing before a lectern covered in animal hide. To his right was a man sat upon a throne of carved ivory, a golden necklace covering his shoulders and chest. Beside him stood another man in the traditional costume of a vooshu, his face and body covered in white paint. Behind them was a line of warriors standing guard in front of a massive Timbokan in chains. *That must be Ginko Barboza*, Fontaine thought.

'Bolwa! Bolwa! Let me go, dammit!' Crenshaw said.

Fontaine turned to see his companion thrust forwards in the same manner he had been. Barboza's face first smiled then frowned.

'Why did you come, El?' he said to Crenshaw.

'As if I'd leave you to these bastards,' Crenshaw replied, moving towards the man.

'Stay where you are!' the old man at the lectern cried. 'What is the meaning of this? Outsiders are forbidden during the Hansi.'

'This man,' Barboza said in a deep, rich voice. 'Is Elton Crenshaw. He is my khofu.'

There was an excited buzz from the surrounding crowd. *Khofu*, Fontaine thought, *I know that word, it means ... no, that can't be right.* The scholar flicked his eyes to Crenshaw who was standing with his chest puffed out, jaw set firm. The old man held up his hand for silence.

'Is this true?' he asked Crenshaw. 'Are you the accused's soulmate?'

'I am,' Crenshaw replied, retrieving a small metal token from his pocket.

'Has your partnership been consummated?' the old man continued.

'It has,' Crenshaw said.

More murmured wonder from the crowd. Fontaine stood, mouth agape. *They're lovers*, he thought. *Crenshaw and Barboza are lovers.* The idea of it pinged around his head, refusing to settle. If this was to be known in Estria they would be hanged for sodomy.

'Elder Fahim!' the vooshu said, stepping forwards. 'This is most unusual.'

'Unusual,' Fahim said. 'But not unprecedented, Kana Vooshu. The man named Crenshaw may stay. As for this other—'

'Excuse me, Elder Fahim, but I have brought this man to act as Ginko Barboza's counsel,' Crenshaw said.

'You have?' Barboza said.

'Do you accept this man as your counsel? Would you accept this … Estrian over those others you have refused?' Fahim said.

'I would,' Barboza replied after sharing a look with Crenshaw.

At this the crowd broke into uproar. Fontaine looked around at the baying faces, heart galloping in his chest. From the corner of his eye, he saw the man on the ivory throne stand. He held up his hand, the gold upon his body jangling, and brought the people to silence.

'I, King Ayotunde, allow this,' he said. The vooshu at his side began to speak hurriedly into his ear, but he waved him away. 'It matters not where his counsel is from. The outcome of the Hansi will be the same, and he will die.'

'Well,' Elder Fahim said as the king returned to his throne. 'I call this Hansi back to order. Ginko Barboza, you stand accused of the murder of your grandfather, Chidiki Barboza. How do you plead?'

'Not guilty,' Barboza replied.

'We have already heard testimony from ten people that you were seen on the night of the late king's death running from his tent covered in blood.'

'I did not murder my grandfather. I … I found him dead. The real culprit sits on the throne, a throne not just drenched in my grandfather's blood but my father's also. He should be on trial. He should stand accused. Instead, he sits there as your king!' Barboza bellowed.

'Be that as it may,' the elder continued, 'you have brought forth no witnesses for your defence or anyone to substantiate you other claims. I'm afraid that in this light …'

'Do something,' Crenshaw hissed at Fontaine.

'What?'

'Something! Anything! I thought you were supposed to be clever.'

'E … Elder Fahim!' Fontaine called. He felt the eyes of the hundreds assembled fall upon him. Sweat began to trickle down his brow. What could he do? There had to be something? He licked his lips and continued. 'I … I request the … er … right my … um … client has to … er …'

'Attempt the trial of the first king,' Barboza cut in.

If Fontaine had thought the crowd had gone wild before, it was nothing compared to their reaction now. The warriors from behind the king had to fan out to keep the protesting mob from falling upon the trial. Once more, the king stepped forwards, but this time, drums had to be used to restore order.

'This is a desperate ploy by a desperate man,' the king said. 'No one has passed the trial in a thousand years. If he wishes to take it, let him.'

'The king has spoken,' Fahim said, quieting down a few raised voices. 'The trial shall begin at sundown.'

CHAPTER SIX

Castros stared across the wide drawbridge at the squat, ugly collection of buildings. Long rectangular windows punctuated the walls, gormless eyes betraying nothing of the horror contained within. Now he was closer, Del Var could see that the magically infused smog coming from the smokestacks had a lot of black in it, something he had never seen before. Other blocks of buildings spread out from the sortilenergy plant like infected tendrils trailing from the main abscess.

'So this is Ravensdown,' Whist said.

'I don't like this place,' Holger added.

'You're not supposed to,' Castros said. 'Melek, Whist, undo our bonds.'

With a sigh Melek stepped behind Del Var and undid the rope binding them. Castros rubbed his wrists and flexed his fingers.

'Castros, old friend, do you think it may be possible …' Melek began.

'You'll get the pill when we've concluded our business here and not a second before,' Del Var said with a wave of his hand.

'But—' Melek said, starting to argue.

'No,' Castros interrupted. 'The last thing we need is you bouncing around this place like a popped balloon. Now, where is the Heir being held?'

'He's on the bottom level of the institute, in the dungeons where the most dangerous prisoners are kept.'

'Alright then, shall we get going?' Castros said.

They crossed the bridge, a slight humming sound — which Castros assumed was coming from some contraption inside the plant — growing not just louder, but fuller, tangible almost, as they got closer to the building. Power throbbed from within, radiating out of the brickwork and making the air fizz and crackle.

'Hold up,' a solitary guard said, stepping away from the entrance. 'Who the hells are—'

He was cut off mid-sentence when both Castros and Khasal unleashed a blast from their screamers. The man flew backwards, colliding into the huge iron door with a sickening thump.

'What the hells did you do that for?' Castros cried.

'I was following your lead, o fearless leader,' Khasal said.

'I only loosed enough power to knock him out, not turn him into a human flatbread!'

'And?' Khasal asked. 'What do we care what happens to the scum guarding this place?'

'They're just men doing their jobs; they don't deserve to die for it.'

'You can't be serious?' Khasal said.

'I am. No killing — that's an order. Melek, see if he's alive,' Castros said.

The inventor walked over to the crumpled body and felt for a pulse. 'He lives.'

'Good. Take his key and open that door,' Castros said.

'Does no one else finds this odd?' Holger asked as Melek found the keys.

'What's odd?' Castros said.

'Well, for an imposing prison-cum-power plant there aren't many guards.'

'It's arrogance,' Khasal said. 'They have complete faith that none of the mages they've bred would dare try to escape, and that no one in the Empire would want to see them free.'

'Still …' Holger said.

'I've opened it,' Melek called.

'Look, let's just worry about finding the Heir, eh?' Castros said, placing a hand on Holger's shoulder. 'We've got enough on our plates without questioning our good fortune.'

Inside, the first level of the institute was a bewildering array of pipes, dials and churning turbines, all devoted to the business of converting the collected sortilenergy and sending it out to the various towns and cities of Estria. In the centre of the space, a handful of men stood checking the output of the machines and adjusting levers. Above all this was a metal walkway where everything could be observed from.

'What now?' Castros said to Khasal.

'There's an elevator back there,' the mage said, pointing towards the opposite end of the room. 'It should take us down to the next level.'

'Not all the way to the dungeon?' Castros asked.

'No,' Melek said. 'The institute is designed so that if a mage were to escape, they would have to pass through each floor, slowing them down and providing greater opportunity for their capture.'

'How the hells did you ever escape a place like this?' Holger said to Khasal.

'It's a long story, one we don't have time for now. Castros, you take the men on the right. I'll go left, and the boy will provide backup. Melek, Whist, you keep out of sight.'

'Whoa, whoa, whoa,' Del Var said, holding up his hands. 'We're going to take that walkway, and quietly too.'

'Balls to that!' Khasal said and dashed ahead.

'For the love of … get back here!' Castros hissed, but it was too late.

Two of the men had fallen from Khasal's aqua bullets before the others had time to turn around. Khasal ran towards them cackling. *Thrice-damned, irresponsible fuckwit*, Castros thought, drawing his screamer and charging after him. The remaining workers were running towards the elevator, slipping and stumbling as they went. Khasal chased after them, sending wild shots of magically infused water towards them. The shots found their marks, and Castros could only watch the workers' heads snap forwards before the men collapsed to the floor.

'See?' Khasal said, dusting off his hands. 'Job done.'

'You absolute—' Castros began, stalking towards Khasal and grabbing the front of his shirt.

'Don't worry your poor bleeding heart, Castros; they're not dead.'

'They better not be,' Del Var said, letting go.

'Anyway, as fun as that was, hadn't we better get going?' Khasal said, pushing a button beside the elevator. A second later, the elevator arrived, and he pulled the metal gate aside.

'They better not be dead,' Castros said as they all got inside.

'They're not,' Khasal replied and pushed another button, this one with an arrow pointing down on it.

Castros felt the elevator shudder and groan into life. The five of them could barely squeeze into the cramped space. Del Var became acutely aware of the others' body odour. It didn't take long for them to come to a stop. Castros drew out his screamers.

'Alright, everyone,' he said, gripping the elevator's sliding door. 'Be ready for a fight. It's not beyond the realms of possibility that someone has found the … mess upstairs and alerted this level. We go on the count of three. One, two … three!'

Throwing back the door, Castros leapt forwards. His eyes flicked left and right. *This can't be right*, he thought. *Where the hells is everyone?* They were now on the generator level, the space given over to the forced harvesting of sortilenergy from the captive mages. Lining the walls were the giant glass spheres which contained the mages, a multitude of tubes designed to pump ether into them ran into the tops.

Halfway along the rows, the spheres gave way to giant brass cauldrons with lids clamped on top. In one space, Castros could see where the old spheres were being taken out and the cauldrons fitted. Tools lay scattered around as if the workers had just left.

'It seems our reputation has preceded us, eh, Cass?' Khasal said. 'Cowardly bastards have already scampered.'

'This is wrong,' Holger said. 'Where is everybody?'

'What do you want me to do?' Castros snapped. 'Go back and say to the guards, "Sorry, but we found this a little too easy; could you please ensure you have a battalion of automatons for us to take down?"'

'I don't know *what* I want you to—' Holger began.

'I ... I think I designed these,' Melek said. He was standing next to one of the cauldrons, staring into a circular window.

'What are they for?' Castros said, glad for the distraction from his argument with Holger. He walked up to Melek and stared into the window. Inside, he could see a thick black fluid pulsing and spinning wildly.

'They are ... yaksit converters,' Melek said. 'I remember the duke ... he came to me and ... wanted me to improve their design ... and ...' The inventor let out a howl and sank to the floor. He grabbed his knees and began to rock gently.

'Melek? Melek! What's wrong?' Castros said.

'I ... I can't remember ... I can't remember, Castros! Don't you see? I can't remember!'

'Alright, alright. But you've been drugged up the whole time you were with the duke; it's not surprising you don't remember some things.'

'But if I've forgotten this, what else have I forgotten?' Melek said, grabbing the front of Del Var's shirt. 'I can feel something ... something in the back of my brain, something important ... but I just can't remember.'

'It's alright,' Castros said, gently taking Melek's hands and removing them from his shirt. 'I'm sure it will come back to you. Gotta get all of that muck out of your system and you'll be right as rain, eh?'

Melek gave a sniff then nodded. 'He's ... he's a bastard, Castros. I think I hate him,' he said.

'Who?'

'The duke.'

'That makes two of us then,' Castros said with a smile. He reached out his hand and helped the inventor to his feet.

'We've found the next elevator,' Khasal called. 'If Melek has finished having his breakdown that is.'

'We're coming,' Castros called. 'You ready?' he said to Melek.

'Yes, I think I can go on.'

Castros gave a nod, and they walked over to the elevator. Down they went to the next floor. Khasal opened the door this time. Del Var stepped out onto a cold, shining floor. Overhead, galvanic lights stuttered and spat light. There was a medicinal smell to the air mixed with something Castros couldn't put his finger on at first … then he had it — blood.

A gutter ran down the centre of the room, studded with circular drainage gratings. To one side of the gutter were a series of cubicles. Each one contained a bed, straps dangling from their sides like tongues. On the other side were worktables stacked with books and vials of strange coloured liquids.

'What is this place?' Holger asked.

'Research and development,' Khasal answered. 'Where the scientists of our great and wondrous empire chop up the bodies of mages in an effort to rip more energy from them.'

Castros walked through the space, stomach rolling, a sour taste at the back of his throat. He could see the stains now, dark reddish-brown stains that looked like over-sized ink blots. In a daze, he stumbled towards one of the tables. A piece of paper sat on top of it. He picked it up.

Dear Bruens,

Thanks to your harebrained scheme we have lost a total of five infants! I don't know how many times I told you that exposing the cattle's young to ether would be disastrous, but you had to know for sure. Five potential sources gone in the blink of an eye, enough power to fuel a large town. I hope you reflect on, and remember, this incident the next time you get one of your bright ideas.

On a side note, Emperor Vontanza has ordered the speeding up of Operation New World, so make sure you and the guards are ready when the time comes.

Yours,

Dr Hawthorne.

'This is the worst place in the world,' Castros hissed, crumpling the paper in his hand.

'Oh … fuck … I think I'm gonna …' Holger said before running to retch in a corner.

Led by a perverse sense of curiosity, Castros walked towards the cubicle Holger had been staring into. Del Var felt bile rise up in his throat, and he had to battle to keep it down. There, in front of him, was a woman's body. It had been left mid-dissection, the skin of the stomach cut open and pinned down by her arms like sails. Inside the mess of her gut was a host of writhing maggots. Flies swarmed over her face, chitinous legs stalking across open, unseeing eyes.

'Why … why is she strapped down?' Holger asked, a hand wiping across his mouth.

'Because she was conscious when they did this to her,' Khasal said, looking at the body, a muscle twitching at the corner of his eye.

'I think we should move on,' Melek said from where he stood by the next elevator.

Castros began to move, but Khasal stood still. 'Come on,' Del Var said. 'There's no use wallowing in the horror of this place.'

Khasal ignored him and went into the cubicle. He shooed the flies away then closed the woman's eyes. He kissed her forehead and said, 'Sleep now, sister, sleep.'

When they were all inside the elevator, Melek pressed the button and down they went, a heavy silence cast over them, each lost in their own thoughts. *Cattle*, Castros thought. *That was what they had written in the note. Cattle — that's what they think of these mages, these people.* The final elevator took longer than the others, but it eventually came to a halt.

'Last stop,' Khasal said, pulling back the door. 'Gods, I hope there's someone to hurt down here.'

Castros grabbed Khasal's sleeve as the other mage went to step out. 'I know it's hard after seeing that,' Del Var said, 'but try to show some restraint.'

'I'll try,' Khasal replied. 'But I make you no promises.'

Outside of the elevator, they were confronted by a thick stone wall slick with damp. A single galvanic light illuminated the rusted bars of a door. To one side of that was a low stool and table, a pipe smoking gently upon it.

'Someone must be close,' Castros said. 'Happy now, Holger?'

'As a matter of fact, I am and—'

'Father save us!' Del Var interrupted. 'I was joking. Now let's see what I can do about this lock, eh?'

He took out his waterskins — filled with liquid he had magically infused — and was just about to squirt some into the lock when Melek grabbed his arm.

'Hang on,' the inventor said, rummaging in the satchel hanging from his shoulder. 'I've got something in here that should do the job and considerably more quietly than what you have in mind. Now where is the blasted … aha! Here we go.'

From his bag, he produced a small object that looked like a brass cricket. Melek wound it up then moved his hand towards the keyhole. The cricket walked off his palm and into the lock. There was a faint whirring sound followed by a series of clicks, then the door swung open.

'What do you think? Good, isn't it?' Melek asked.

'It's alright, I suppose,' Castros replied, disappointed he hadn't got to blow the lock apart.

One by one, they edged round the door, Del Var feeling his gut tighten with every creak and groan. They now found themselves in a wide corridor. The walls were pitted with large iron doors, thin puddles of light spilling from lamps set between them. The cell doors had peepholes for the guards to keep an eye on the prisoners. Castros was just about to peer into the first one when he heard a voice echoing down the corridor. He turned towards it and could just make out the back of a man, an audiphone receiver in his hands.

'Yes, sir,' the man was saying. 'You want me to bring up the Burkeshi and the nutter, sir. Very good, sir. Are you almost finished, sir? Only I was worried we might miss the boat, sir. I see, sir. Excellent, sir. Thank you, sir.'

'He's mine,' Khasal said, taking out his screamer.

'Restraint!' Castros cried, watching the mage use his device to blast himself to the other end of the corridor in the blink of an eye.

'Come on!' Del Var said, racing towards Khasal who now had the guard pinned to the floor.

'Tell me why I shouldn't?' he was saying, a stream of sortilaqua swirling around his fingers. 'Go on, tell me. Weep, whimper, beg. Tell me about your beautiful wife and your sweet little kiddies at home and how they'd miss their father so very much.'

'Please,' the man panted. 'Please!'

'Let him up, Khasal,' Castros said, steel in his voice.

'What if I don't, Cass? What then? Would you press the controls for my execution collar and kill me? Kill me for this piece of filth!'

'Our quarrel isn't with this one man, Sal. Killing him changes nothing.'

'You,' Khasal said, placing a finger on the man's nose, 'are a very lucky man.'

The mage got off and the guard clambered to his feet. 'Thank you, sir, thank you,' he said, extending a hand towards Del Var. Castros slapped it away.

'Keys,' he said. The guard unhooked them from his belt and placed them in Castros' outstretched palm. Immediately, Castros landed a punch on the man's jaw. The guard's head snapped back, and he fell to the floor like a bag of wet cement.

'You get to have all the fun,' Khasal said with a sniff.

'Are you sure that was wise?' Holger asked. 'He could have told us where the Heir is?'

'Ah,' Castros said. 'Er … not to worry, eh? We're going to open all the cells anyway, so no harm no foul. Let's start with this one, shall we?'

Del Var moved to the closest door and, after going through several keys, managed to get it open. The room inside was gloomy, and it took a while for his eyes to get used to it. When they did, he wasn't sure he believed them. There, in the centre of the room, was a statue sitting cross-legged. Seeing things, old boy, he thought. But then the statue opened its eyes.

'You've finally come, eh?' it said, getting to its feet.

'I … what …?' Castros stammered.

'About bloody time an' all,' a new voice said, its owner dropping down from a cot on the wall.

As the men drew closer to the door, Castros got a better look at them. One was an ancient Burkeshi, his taut brown skin covering a mass of stringy muscle. The other man was an emaciated Estrian, wild eyes blazing beneath a thicket of tangled and matted hair.

'In the name of … it can't be!' Holger said.

'You know these people?' Castros asked.

'Aye, he does,' the one with the mad eyes said. 'I'm Torkwill MacLoud, Master Cognopath, at your service.'

'And I am Yevad,' the Burkeshi said. 'A kaffar.'

For a moment, they all stood looking at each other in silence. Castros' mind struggled to come to terms with the men who stood in front of him and why they were locked in the bowels of the Ravensdown Institute.

'Right,' Torkwill said. 'Ain't no sodding point us standing around gawping at each other. Bung us the keys an' I'll get the rest o' us out, eh?'

'Wait, what?' Castros said.

'The rest o' us,' Torkwill replied as if he was talking to a simpleton. 'The other cognopaths and kaffars — the ones who didnae want to work for the duke or Kurkeshi. Dinnae worry, we're on the same side youse an' us. Now gimme the keys.'

'Alright, but we're looking for—' Castros began, handing the keys over.

'I know what you're looking for, but he has already gone. Taken by the duke's men,' Yevad said.

'Gone? What …. who … how do you know so much about us and what we're here for?'

The old Burkeshi looked at him, his eyes sparkling and said, 'Kaffars draw their magic from the Void. We look into that space between worlds, sometimes calling forth the creatures that lie there to do our bidding. But in there, we also see the others. We call them djinns, but I believe you call them Fargazers. One of them spoke to me, the first time they ever have, and it told me I would meet you and stop an act of great evil. Yes, the boy may be gone, but it might not be too late.'

'What in the twelve hells are you talking about?' Castros said 'Too late for what?'

'To stop the executions'

*

Castros yanked back the metal grate that served as the elevator door, not waiting for his companions, and sprinted ahead. He darted past the prone bodies of the unconscious workers on the first floor without a second look and pelted towards a set of large doors at the back. *The old man can't be right*, he thought, *he just can't be*. Del Var collided with the iron doors and bounced back. Not bothering to look for a handle, he took out his screamer and blew them from their hinges.

'By the gods,' he whispered, stepping through the opening.

He found himself in a large courtyard at the back of the institute. The acrid smell of ballisket powder hung in the air. In the distance, he could see a line of ragged mages standing back to back on the lip of a trench. In front of them was a formation of guards. The guards lifted their balliskets. Castros lifted his arm, trying to make his jaw move to cry "stop", but it was like his body was paralysed. In hideous slow motion, the balliskets fired, the small metal balls exploding from the backs of the mages' heads in a shower of bone and brain. The bodies crumpled and fell into the trench. A guard went along, making sure no limbs were left sticking out.

'Next!' he roared.

From the far left-hand side, ten more mages were marched forwards, leaving behind a line of hundreds. A woman fell shrieking to the ground, an outstretched arm pointing back at her howling child still waiting in the line. One guard smashed the butt of his ballisket into the face of the child while another hauled the woman up by her hair, a knife at her throat. The men waiting by the trench laughed.

Behind him, Castros heard the sound of running feet. Khasal said, 'What in … this is a hell made real.' He moved forwards and Castros caught his arm. 'Are you seriously going to tell me not to kill these men?'

'No,' Castros said. 'Make sure you do it slowly and painfully.'

A crazed smile lit up Khasal's face. 'Now that's more like the Castros Del Var who I know.'

Khasal sprinted towards the guards screaming. They turned to look at him. The mage ignited a spark stick, took control of the magically infused fire and sent it roaring into three of the men's faces.

As the flesh began to melt from their skulls Del Var drew out his screamer and made his way forwards.

***

Despite herself, Bellina watched in mute wonder while the great clockwork gate of Hidenbaden clicked and whirred into life. Sunlight gleamed off the wild, spinning cogs and gears, dazzling her eyes, making her raise a hand to protect them. Without so much as a squeak, the gate slid open, allowing them access through the city wall.

Bellina was seated on the driver's platform of a cart with the soldier who had arrested them between herself and Elvgren. Despite the arrest, neither herself nor Elvgren had been restrained in any way — a mark of good faith, apparently, from the ministers in the Gortrixian capital who had ordered their capture in the first place. *If they think a mere trifle like that will win my favour, they've got another bloody thing coming*, she thought.

Casting a glance behind her, Bellina glimpsed the frayed mass of followers they had acquired. The Gortrixian soldiers had led them safely and quickly through the forest, but Bellina wondered, would they be welcome here? A large city like Hidenbaden should be *able* to find the resources to feed, clothe and shelter a thousand or so extra souls … there was a big difference between being able and being *willing* though.

'Say, old chap, we're almost there now — how about you fill us in on what this is all about, eh?' Elvgren said.

'My orders are to—' the soldier began.

'Bring us to the First Minister, yes, yes, we know,' Elvgren finished for him before letting out a sigh and leaning back in his seat.

Bellina looked across at him and frowned. Back in the forest, when the monstrous wolves had been upon them, he had put himself between them and her. He hadn't mentioned it, and she couldn't be sure if he even realised what he had done. The idea that Elvgren thought she needed protecting annoyed her, but at the same time, she couldn't help feeling a little touched. If anyone had told her a year ago that Lord Elvgren Lovitz would put someone else's life before his own, even for a second, she would have laughed them out of the building. *He's changing*, she thought, a smile playing at the corners of her mouth. *It may only be by fractions, but he's changing.*

The cart rolled on into the city where they were confronted by amassed ranks of guards. Their vehicle was let through the wall of grim-faced men. Bellina looked back over her shoulder and was dismayed to see them close ranks again. *Father help me*, she thought, *what have I led these people into.*

Soon, the people were out of sight. Their cart moved along wide cobbled streets flanked by tall timber-framed buildings painted white and topped with high, sloping roofs. People went about their business as usual, unaware of the theft and villainy their fellow Estrians, those living outside the protection of city walls, were suffering.

They entered a large square, a fountain bubbling at its centre. Each of the shops crammed around it had automaton signs: a brass blacksmith hammering at an anvil, a tailor endlessly working on the stitching of a coat … The signs were testament to the advanced engineering prowess of Gortrix, the heart of the Empire's scholarship. Further testament were the four academies that sat brooding on the far edges of the city, each in competition to produce the brightest and the best students.

Their cart turned down a street to their left, trundling out of the square and onto a stone bridge. On the other side was the Gofthaus, seat of Gortrixian power. It completely covered the small island it was built on, hundreds of brilliantly white towers soaring upwards, their turrets disappearing within the clouds. Bellina heard movement behind her and saw Dargo stick his head out.

'Bloody hells, that looks like a wedding cake with windows,' he said.

Bellina felt the soldier bristle beside her. 'It most certainly does not …' he began before composing himself. 'Silence!'

Clamping her jaw shut, Bellina fought hard against the gale of laughter threatening to escape her lips.

'For the Father's sake, Dargo, get back inside. You have no idea of diplomacy,' Elvgren hissed.

'And you do, do you?' Dargo spat back.

'Just sit down!'

Dargo retreated, muttering under his breath as they passed into the grounds of the Gofthaus. The clack of the horses' hooves changed tone when they moved from the cobbled bridge to the smooth stone of the courtyard. Two more soldiers, bearing long, vicious-looking pikes, stood at the bottom of a set of sweeping stairs that led to the building's entrance. The man driving the cart gestured for Bellina and Elvgren to get down then followed suit, offering a crisp salute to his comrades. They returned the greeting.

'Lord Elvgren, Lady Bellina,' one of the soldiers said, stepping forwards, 'we are to lead you to First Minister Gestaffen.'

Bellina felt her stomach twist and churn. *This is it*, she thought, *so much depends on this meeting; we've got to get Gestaffen onside.* She took a deep, steadying breath, forcing her expression into one of icy command.

'I think you meant to address us as Your Majesties,' she said.

The soldier's face twitched, his mouth moving without sound. 'I … er … this way, please,' he said finally.

He led them up the stairs to where the large wooden doors were opened by servants. They walked through a marble hallway, and to the accompaniment of Dargo's artificial leg thumping out a regular beat, into a vast hall. The tops of the walls were decorated with a mural depicting Gortrix's most notable thinkers and inventions: the creation of the tharg engine, the first vorotorium cell, the opening of the first sortilenergy plant and the founding of the city's universities among them. Above it all, dominating the ceiling, was a painting of the legendary inventor Lokos Vistas carrying the torch of knowledge. Behind him was a depiction of the giant's tomb, the place where he had hidden the weapons created to defeat the Old Terrors, locking them away for fear that future generations would use them to tear the world apart — a place no one had managed to enter in a thousand years, a place that would only open for the chosen ones.

Within seconds, they had swept through the hallway and were stood before a set of double doors which were again whisked open by servants. Just as she stepped forwards, Bellina heard a scuffle behind her. One of the soldiers had hold of the back of Dargo's shirt. The lad was hissing and spitting like a cat, trying to get free.

'Your servant will wait here,' the man said.

'I ain't no bloody servant! Let me go!' Dargo yelled.

'Just do as he says, Dar,' Bellina said.

Dargo's face broke into a pout, but he stopped squirming. 'Alright,' he said. 'But I'll be right 'ere if there's any trouble.'

Despite herself, Bellina smiled. 'Thank you, Dargo.'

'Can we bally well get on with this?' Elvgren said.

Bellina turned and looked him square in the eye. 'Yes. Let's,' she said. Then added in a whisper, 'Let me do the talking.'

The doors closed behind them with a definite click. The room was decorated like a simple study. At the far end of it, beneath a large window, was an over-sized desk, behind which three men sat.

'Please, be seated,' the man in the middle said, gesturing to a pair of chairs in front of the desk. 'I am First Minister Gestaffen. To my left is Second Minister Roltz; on the right is Third Minister Brestag.'

Be calm, Bellina told herself, *be calm*. 'Is this any way to treat the rightful Emperor and his wife-to-be?' she said.

Gestaffen laughed as he sat back down. 'No,' he said. 'But I think it is more than generous for a pair of fugitives.'

Bellina arched an eyebrow, her nostrils flaring.

'You can stand there looking indignant, my lady, or you can take a seat; the choice is yours.'

Bellina's gaze bore into Gestaffen. With great reluctance, she took a seat.

'My first question is — what madness possessed you to go through with all of this?' Gestaffen said.

'I do not believe that what we have done is even close to madness,' Bellina said. 'In fact, I think sitting back and doing nothing as the throne is stolen, as murder is committed, as our territories on the Eastern Continent are handed to our enemies is what many would consider madness.

'But despite all these atrocities, we face a greater threat. Marmossa is the Thirteenth Terror. As we speak, he is gathering the relics, making himself more powerful than anything we have faced before.'

Gestaffen sighed. 'And where, pray tell, did you come by this information?'

Bellina licked her lips. 'I … I met with a Fargazer. With the information she passed to me, combined with the prophesy, my father believed—'

'Your father's belief in that nonsense was one of his few faults,' Gestaffen said. 'You really don't expect us to believe it too?'

'I believe that my destiny and a those of a few others is—'

'And you would claim that our soldiers being in the forest that night is also part of this preordained destiny?'

'I would,' Bellina replied.

'This is nonsense, Miss Ressa. But perhaps, we should focus on the truths. We were out in that forest after obtaining intelligence informing us that you had gathered a large following and were heading towards Hidenbaden. Many of this following are Sylvatians from border towns with no right to asylum in Gortrix. There are now hundreds of homeless, hungry foreign nationals in our capital. These are the facts, Miss Ressa, and they are not very happy ones.'

'Firstly, Minister Gestaffen, stop interrupting me,' Bellina said.

'Sylvatians or not, the people who followed me here did so out of fear for their lives. While you have sat safe and secure in your ivory tower, pondering whether or not to accept the Duke of Tremore as the Emperor, he has allowed his soldiers free rein in the country, your country, as well as Sylvantain.'

'Premier, these claims are false. The duke assures us the men in question are brigands who have stolen uniforms and are using the confusion the Empire finds itself in to "fill their boots" as it were,' the Second Minister said.

'These are not lies. I have seen these men—' Bellina began.

'Enough,' Gestaffen said, cutting her off. He rubbed his eyes then pinched the bridge of his nose. 'What would you have me do, Miss Ressa? Hmm? Declare you Empress and send you to Victory with our army at your back?'

'Yes. Yes, I would.'

Gestaffen laughed. 'You are as blunt as your father. And it is out of my respect for him that I have met you today. But I can see you are as crazy as I've heard.'

'Premier, please,' Bellina said.

Gestaffen shook his head and got up from the table. His fellow ministers hurried after him.

'Let me go to the giant's tomb,' Bellina cried.

Gestaffen paused. 'And why would I do that?'

'Is it not believed that in the time of our greatest need the tomb will open for the chosen hero.'

'This is superstitious garbage of the highest order. We have had our best men, scientists and thinkers of the highest calibre, attempt to open that tomb many times. All have failed. What do you propose to do — magic it open? I have had enough of your time-wasting; I bid you good day, Miss Ressa.'

'If we fail, we will relinquish our claim to the throne and publicly accept the duke as Emperor.'

'Hold on a—' Elvgren began.

Bellina held up a hand to silence him before continuing. 'I'm sure that the man who managed to get us to do this would be thought of most highly by the duke.'

The First Minister cocked his head to the side and looked at her. It was a cold stare, the kind a butcher might give a pig, sizing up, working out where the best cut would lie.

'And you will make this statement publicly? Keep those who have joined you under control?' he asked.

'We would, yes.'

'First Minister, you can't seriously be—' the third minister began.

Gestaffen held up a hand for silence. 'We accept your offer. You will be an excellent bargaining chip. The servants will show you to your quarters.'

With that the ministers stalked from the room, Roltz and Brestag whispering and gesticulating to Gestaffen. As soon as they were out of the room, Elvgren placed his head in his hands.

'What have you done? What the fuck have you done?' he wailed.

'Get a hold of yourself, man,' she said.

'Get a hold of myself? Get a hold of myself! You've just written our death warrants! What in the twelve hells do you think will happen once the duke gets hold of us? Perhaps you think he'll throw a grand ball in our honour? Oh gods, help me, help me!'

Bellina slapped him round the back of the head. 'Stop it this instant!' she said. 'The tomb will open for us; I know it will.'

'Are you certain?' Elvgren asked.

'Yes,' she lied.

CHAPTER SEVEN

As an acid burp escaped Scholar Fontaine's lips, he rubbed at his eyes like he could make what was in front of them disappear. He was standing by the side of Barboza and Crenshaw at the head of a massive crowd of Timbokans. Before them was the entrance to a mist-shrouded swamp. Its perimeter marked with wooden stakes bleached white by the sun; its length only breached by a small gap flanked by two thin trees. A piece of string had been draped between the trees, a myriad of charms and wards against evil dangled from it making small, hollow knocking sounds as they banged together in the breeze. Between the trees, he could see the first few paces of a narrow, muddy path before it too was gobbled up by the mist. Fontaine licked his lips and shivered, telling himself it was the night chill and not his frayed nerves that had made his body ripple.

King Ayotunde, Kana Vooshu and elder Fahim stepped forwards, their faces lit with the dancing light from torches held aloft by servants. Fontaine's gaze ricocheted between each man, waiting for something to happen. At last, Fahim spoke.

'Blood friends, honoured sisters and brothers, the accused, Ginko Barboza, has requested the trial of the first king. He will attempt to find the sacred spear left by that most glorious monarch. Should he succeed, where hundreds of others have failed, we will have a new king, a king destined to lead us to glory. Beside him stand his chosen sword and shield.'

Fontaine looked down at the hide covered disc resting against his shins. *This is utter madness*, he thought. *What am I doing here?* He'd come with Crenshaw to find a lead on the Timbokan relic and now …

'Ginko Barboza,' Fahim continued, 'we will wait a day and night for your return. After that, we will assume you are dead. Are you ready to proceed?'

'Yes,' Barboza replied, pulling himself up to his full, impressive height.

'Do you have any last words?' Fahim asked.

'I'll be back by daybreak.'

With that he turned on his heel and strode towards the swamp's entrance, closing the distance to it in long graceful strides. Fontaine grabbed at the shield and hurried after him and Crenshaw. *How can they be so composed,* he thought, *when we're marching into certain death?*

The mud path was so narrow they had to walk in single file. Almost instantly, the sound of the outside vanished as if someone had drawn a heavy curtain behind them. He could just make out the trunks of black trees rising out of the scummy water, forming forbidding, haunted shapes. No frogs croaked; no flies buzzed round their faces. This was a place of death and nature knew it. Fontaine felt the shield tremble against his arm.

'Don't worry,' Crenshaw called back to him, his voice flat and dead in the still air. 'We've been through worse than this and come out the other side of it, ain't we, Bar?'

'What? Oh, yes, much worse,' Barboza replied.

Silence fell, and Fontaine's world shrank to a small island of mud directly in front of him. On they went for what seemed like hours, the path snaking and twisting. Every so often they had to climb over some deadfall, but other than that, the monotony continued until the scholar crashed into the back of Crenshaw.

'Er ... is ... is something the matter?' he asked.

'The path has stopped,' Barboza replied. 'Look.'

Fontaine moved forwards and saw the problem — the path really had ended, and in front of it was the start of a body of water.

'No way to tell how far it is to the other side in this mist,' Crenshaw said.

'Perhaps we could ... er ... wade across?' Fontaine suggested. 'We could use one of those logs in the water to help us.'

'Those aren't logs,' Barboza said.

Squinting, Fontaine stared at the log he had pointed out. One of the holes he had taken for a knot blinked. 'Gracious Father,' he exclaimed. 'They're—'

'Armodiles,' Barboza finished for him.

'Well, it looks like swimming is out,' Crenshaw said.

'Perhaps ... if we ... walk round the edge? We might find something?' Fontaine said.

'An excellent idea, scholar; lead on,' Barboza said, pointing in the wrong direction.

'I couldn't possibly ... I mean ...' Fontaine mumbled.

'Please, I insist,' Barboza replied.

'Oh, for the love of ... I'll go first,' Crenshaw said, pushing his way to the front.

'Be careful,' Barboza said.

'Yeah, yeah, I'll give you … aargh!'

Crenshaw went sprawling forwards, hitting the ground with a dull thump. Fontaine winced as a stream of expletives flowed from the fallen man's lips.

'Are you alright, El?' Barboza asked.

'No,' Crenshaw replied. 'I think I've twisted my bloody ankle.'

'What happened?' Fontaine said.

'Me foot got caught on a damned stone or something,' Crenshaw said, pointing to something hidden in the mud.

Fontaine knelt down to examine the stone. He realised that it wasn't an odd-shaped sphere like he had been expecting but level and smooth. Reaching out, he touched it. He rocked back, startled. It extended out beneath the mud. The next thing he knew, he was scraping away the muck and grime covering it. When he was done, he felt his breath catch. In front of him was a flat stone engraved with strange, swirling symbols; symbols he could read.

'What's that nonsense?' Crenshaw said.

'This is not "nonsense",' Fontaine replied. 'It's ancient Atvorian, the language of the first civilisation, ancestor to the common tongue.'

'Can you read it?' Barboza asked.

'Yes, just give me a minute … hmm … some of the letters have faded over the years, but I think it reads "Speak my name and I shall come to you".'

Barboza let out a heavy sigh and crossed his arms. 'Well that's not very specific,' he said.

Fontaine frowned at the stone and pulled absently at his ear. 'Hang on,' he said. 'Let's just think about this for a moment. Whose trail is this?'

'The first king of Timboko,' Crenshaw said.

'And his name was?' Fontaine asked, a gleam in his eye.

'Jabja Oboya,' Barboza answered.

A strange, low humming sound, almost a throb, filled the air. It was coming from a spot five paces to their left. Fontaine turned towards it, his eyes growing as wide as cartwheels. Stood there was a life-size image of a man. He was constructed out of a shimmering blue light, parts of his body flickering and distorting. A thick, spotted animal pelt was draped across his shoulders, upon his head sat a crown and one hand held a massive spear.

'Sweet merciful Mother!' Barboza cried, clutching a hand to his chest. 'It's the ghost of the first king. Forgive us, oh mighty king, for disturbing your slumber.'

The ghost of King Jabja paid no attention to them whatsoever. Instead, he stepped out onto the water.

'What the hells is he doing?' Crenshaw said.

'I … I think we need to follow him,' Fontaine said.

'Quick,' Barboza added, 'before we lose sight of him.'

The trio hurried after the advancing ghost. Fontaine expected his foot to plunge into the water as he took his first step, but to his surprise, there was solid ground just a few inches beneath the surface. The king's ghost led them on a twisting, serpentine path that, at some points, looped back on itself, but everywhere he went, it was safe to follow. At one point, an armodile cruised past to their left, and the scholar felt his knees buckle. It looked at them with one lazy eye then floated on.

Fontaine breathed an audible sigh of relief when they reached the far shore. As he steadied himself, he realised that the mist was gone. Without it obscuring his view, he was able to see a massive tree in front of him. Its monumental trunk was swollen as if it were pregnant. Great wrinkled branches, like suspended elephant legs, spread up and out, reaching for a circle of clear sky directly above.

'What's he doing now?' Crenshaw said, drawing Fontaine's attention back to King Jabja's ghost.

The ghost of the ancient king was now standing in front of the tree on top of a stone disc. He moved the spear he was carrying and dragged its edge across his palm. Holding out the cut hand, he let a dribble of phantom blood fall to his feet. With that done he strode into the tree.

'He certainly has a flair for the dramatic!' Barboza said.

'So that's where you get it from,' Crenshaw replied.

'You wound me, El. Why, I'm—'Barboza began.

'Er … I'm sorry to … er … interrupt, but I think you're supposed to copy him,' Fontaine said.

Barboza took a step backwards, raising his arms. 'You mean I have to go over there and cut myself … on purpose?' he said.

'I'm afraid so,' Fontaine replied.

'But why me?' Barboza whined.

'Because you are the only one here descended from King Jabja,' Fontaine said.

'Crenshaw, El, my knight in shining armour! You wouldn't mind shedding a tiny drop of blood for me, would you?'

'Sorry, Bar, I think the scholar's right – this one's on you,' Crenshaw said.

Barboza looked between Fontaine and Crenshaw with narrowed eyes.

'Fine,' he said at last, throwing up his hand. He walked over to the stone disc and stood upon it. 'El, give me your sword.'

'A please wouldn't go amiss,' Crenshaw said, handing over his weapon.

Licking his lips, Barboza inched the point of the sword closer to the index finger of his right hand. 'I'm really going to do it!' he called out.

'Yeah, yeah, just get on with it,' Crenshaw said.

Eyes scrunched tight, Barboza jabbed the tip of his finger with the sword. A small bead of blood blossomed on the end of it. For a second, it hung there, defying gravity, then dropped. As soon as the blood hit the stone it began to glow. A beam of light shot out from it and hit the centre of the bulbous trunk. With a groaning creak the wood in the middle of the tree began to rearrange itself, pulling itself back like lips over bared teeth until an arched doorway was formed.

'Well, that's certainly … something,' Barboza said.

Fontaine crept towards the tree. The light from the disc had filled the doorway with a strange, rippling illumination. For a heartbeat, he stood there gazing at it intently. Then he extended a finger and prodded the door of light. He was unable to stop the gasp that escaped his lips when the top of his finger disappeared. Startled, he pulled it back and watched the light shimmy like a lake disturbed by a thrown stone.

As he caught his breath, he could hear Barboza and Crenshaw arguing behind him about the safety of the door. Fontaine himself had no such fears. His whole being was filled with a mad passion, the kind he felt when he made a breakthrough on the *Radiana Magnifica*. There was no doubt in his mind that this was first civilisation technology, and who knew what riches lay beyond the strange door.

With a lick of his lips he stepped towards the tree once more. He could feel his heart thrashing in his chest, his breath coming in short snatches. *What's the matter with you?* he thought. *Just go for it.* Taking a deep lungful of air, he stuck his arm into the light.

'See, that wasn't so bad, was it?' he mumbled to himself.

Suddenly, he was yanked forwards. His shoes scuffled in the dirt as he tried to stop himself from being pulled through the door. Sweat beaded on his upper lip. He tried to call out to the others, but his voice died. His mind was spinning, looking for a way out. The pressure on his stolen arm was immense. He was convinced, at any second, it would be torn off, and he'd go flying onto the ground, a bleeding stump where his limb had once been.

'What in the …? Scholar!' Crenshaw cried, finally noticing what was happening.

'See, I told you that door was unsafe,' Barboza said.

'Not now, Bar! Come and give me a hand!'

Fontaine stretched his free arm out towards them, felt Crenshaw's fingers brush his own, then he went flying backwards through the door. He felt the air whoosh past him, ruffling his hair and clothes, felt his body spin and jerk at strange angles, felt his back collide with something cold and solid as he came to a stop. For a while, he lay, eyes squeezed shut. His chest rose and fell, rose and fell, while he tried to get himself under control.

At last, he forced his eyelids apart and found he was staring at a grey ceiling, a strip of light in its centre illuminating the area. He hauled himself to his feet and was just about to investigate further when something crashed into his back. He went sprawling to the floor once again, cracking his chin on the unforgiving surface.

'Sorry about that, scholar,' Crenshaw said.

Rolling onto his back, Fontaine looked up into the man's face. Crenshaw offered a hand and the scholar took it.

'Bar should be through any second … Ah! There he is.'

The giant form of Barboza came spinning out of the doorway, rolling a few paces before coming to a stop. 'What infernal lunatic,' he said, clambering to his feet, 'decided that was a good way to travel?'

'The first civilisation,' Fontaine said, taking in his surroundings — the dark grey walls punctuated by bands of swirling metal, the floor of polished black stone. 'We are standing in an undamaged structure built by the first civilisation before the second fall. This is the archaeological find of the century!'

'As happy as I am for you, scholar, I think we should head back and plan our next move,' Barboza said.

'Never!' Fontaine yelled. 'I need to study this, make notes. Oh my goodness, there is so much to do. You go back if you want, but I'm staying.'

'No one's going back anywhere,' Crenshaw said. 'Door's disappeared.'

'There you go, Mr Barboza — we have to go forwards,' Fontaine said, skipping ahead.

Barboza muttered darkly behind him, but he couldn't have cared less. He had always dreamed of finding such a place, and now, here he was, walking down the same hall people of the first civilisation had used. His head spun with questions. What was the purpose of this place? How did it tie in with the royal line of Timboko? What was powering the lights overhead? There were just so many mysteries.

At the end of the hall, the scholar came to a V-shaped door. As the others approached, there was a hiss of air, and it rose upwards in one smooth motion. Fontaine shared a glance with Barboza and Crenshaw then crossed into the room beyond. Once they were through, it came shooting back down, the motion followed by a dull thunking sound.

'Locked,' Crenshaw said, rapping his knuckles against the door.

Fontaine's gaze swept around them. The room they found themselves in was large and perfectly square. The walls, ceiling, floor all shone, as if they were trapped in a box of light. In the middle of the space were, what appeared to be, four statues covered in garments. Past them was another V-shaped door with more Atvorian writing above it.

'What does it say?' Barboza asked.

'It says "Only the one who bears the garments of a king shall pass",' Fontaine answered.

'So, Bar needs to dress up in one of these outfits, and we can get out of here?' Crenshaw said.

'That seems to be the gist of it,' Fontaine said.

'Which one though,' Barboza mused as he walked past the statues.

Following him, Fontaine began to take in the different costumes. One was a full suit of dark grey armour, the second was a tunic of purple silk and a cape of finely woven gold, the third was a traditional Timbokan witch doctor outfit complete with a wooden mask and the fourth was a cloak made out of wrought-iron chains. As the scholar peered closer at this last one he saw that each link was a stylised petal. He heard laughing behind him, and he turned to see Barboza in the cloak of gold.

'Well, I think this is the one that suits me best,' he said.

'We're not looking for the one that is most flattering, Bar,' Crenshaw said, wiping his eyes.

'Nonsense,' Barboza replied. 'Surely, a king wears what he wants to wear.' With that he strode towards the door.

'Wait!' Fontaine exclaimed, but it was too late.

A faint beam of light shone out of an almost invisible hole at the top of the door. It scanned Barboza from head-to-toe. Then a klaxon sounded, and the room flashed red. There was a grinding noise, and Fontaine saw with dismay that the room was shrinking. He threw his hands over his head and crumpled to the ground, waiting to be crushed alive. Then, just as sudden as it had started, the walls stopped moving, the klaxon fell silent, and the room became white once more.

'Clearly, that was wrong,' Crenshaw said, looking around the now smaller space.

'I shall try them out one by one,' Barboza said. 'That way we're sure to find the right garment.'

'I ... um ... well, I think that ...' Fontaine muttered.

'Confidence, scholar, confidence,' Barboza bellowed.

Fontaine took a deep breath and said, 'I think that we need to concentrate on the wording. Why does it say "bears" and not "wears"? Maybe we need to work out what a king bears along with his title.'

They all fell silent, thinking.

'I suppose a king bears a lot of responsibility,' Crenshaw said.

'And the hopes and expectations of his subjects,' Barboza added.

'Hopes and expectations …'Fontaine muttered to himself. Then he clapped a hand to his forehead and ran towards the iron cloak. 'Of course, this is right! Why didn't I think of it sooner?'

'What is it?' Barboza asked.

'These links have been fashioned into these stylised petals. I was sure I had seen them before, but now I know,' Fontaine said, holding the metalwork up so they could see.

Barboza gasped. 'The petals of the rekurra flower,' he said. 'Symbols of hope.'

'Reckon we've found your coronation outfit, Bar,' Crenshaw said. 'Slip it on and get back over to the door.'

With a nod, Barboza lifted the cloak off the statue and draped it across his shoulders. Despite his powerful build, Fontaine saw the would-be-king's body sag under the weight of it. He walked towards the door, his footsteps visibly slower than usual. The scholar saw the light begin to scan Barboza again. *Please be right*, Fontaine thought. There was a soft dinging sound, then the V-shaped door shot upwards.

'It … worked,' Barboza said.

'Shall we?' Crenshaw asked, gesturing at the door.

Nodding, Fontaine walked over to Barboza, and they exited the room in single file. On the other side, the scholar's eyes grew wide. For a breath, his heart froze then began pounding harder than ever. They stood on a thin, metal platform that seemed to float out over an abyss. Around them, the walls were covered with large squares, each one had a hole in the centre, glowing with a crimson fire.

As they began to walk forwards Fontaine could feel his muscles tense. On either side of him was a drop fathoms deep. *Don't look down*, he told himself, *don't look down*. After a few heart-stopping minutes the platform widened into a circle. In the centre of it was a massive metal longbow and three arrows. Next to it was another Atvorian inscription.

'What's this one say?' Crenshaw asked.

'It … er … says "Judge your shot well and seek forgiveness".'

'What am I supposed to shoot?' Barboza said, waving his hands in the air. 'And can I take this ludicrous cloak off?'

'I … er … think it best you keep the cloak on,' Fontaine said, looking nervously around at the walls. 'And, if I may be so bold, perhaps your target will become clear once you pick up the bow?'

Barboza rubbed at his ear, frowning, then heaved the metal bow out of its supports. There were two sharp clicks followed by the sound of air being whooshed forwards at speed. From below, another circular platform came into view. Stopping some fifty feet across from them, Fontaine could see an exquisite silver replica of the tree they had entered through. Leaves made from jade protruded from the branches, the creases in the bark created using flowing, molten gold, making the whole thing seem to shift and move. In the trunk was another V-shaped door. Just above it, a small glowing hole.

'Well, there's your target, Bar,' Crenshaw said.

'It's … so far away,' Fontaine added.

'Ha! That's nothing,' Barboza said. 'I spent my youth hunting small birds; this should be easy.'

He picked up an arrow and notched it to the bowstring. Pulling back on the bow, Barboza's muscles grew taut and quivered. Fontaine heard the man take a deep breath then release it slowly, letting the arrow fly at the same time. It shot straight and true. *He's going to do it*, the scholar thought. *He's really going to do it*. Then the arrow veered wildly to the left and began to plummet.

'What in the … This is nonsense!' Barboza cried. 'That arrow must have been broken!'

Fontaine was about to agree when a high-pitched whine filled the air. He turned round to see streams of red light shoot out of the squares on the walls. The streams hit the platform behind them. It glowed white-hot then exploded in shards of molten metal.

'Fucking hells,' Crenshaw whispered.

Fontaine thought he couldn't have put it better himself.

'This is hopeless!' Barboza said, throwing up his hands and sinking to the floor. 'We're stuck in the middle of nowhere with arrows that have a mind of their own and death beams blowing up our way back. I'm beginning to think my ancestor was a bit of an arse.'

'No,' Fontaine murmured.

'What was that, scholar?' Barboza asked.

'I … I said no! We've come this far. Further than anyone else who's attempted this trial, and we're going to succeed.'

'That's the spirit, scholar,' Crenshaw said, clapping him on the back.

'All the enthusiasm in the world can't make those arrows fly true,' Barboza said, pouting.

'But if we take the error into account and use maths to guide us, you should be able to do it! Just give me a few moments,' Fontaine said.

He sat down and began to draw signs and equations in the dust. After a handful of minutes, he jumped up and motioned for Barboza to pick up the next arrow. Then he moved the big man backwards, tilting his arm so the arrow pointed upwards.

'There,' Fontaine said. 'Try it now.'

Once more, Barboza took a deep breath then loosed the arrow. Fontaine bit his lip. *Come on*, he thought, *come on*. The arrow was flying through the air in a majestic arc, pulling itself around to meet the target. Then, at the last moment, it simply stopped and fell to the ground.

'No,' Fontaine said. 'I … I used maths!'

He didn't have to long to worry over his failure, because once more, the streams of light blew away another part of the platform. Fontaine looked at the smouldering, twisted lip of metal not five paces away.

'This is nothing but a low-down dirty trick!' Barboza bellowed, throwing the bow to the floor.

'There's got to be something we're missing here,' Crenshaw said.

'Judge your shot …' Fontaine mumbled. 'Seek forgiveness …'

'What about it?' Crenshaw asked.

'Well, what if it means Mr Barboza is literally meant to judge his shot as in good or bad. We keep blaming the arrows, but what if you're supposed to seek the arrow's forgiveness for being a bad shot.'

'But I'm not a bad shot,' Barboza said.

'I think it's an exercise in humility, Bar,' Crenshaw said.

'It's worth a try,' Fontaine added.

'Oh, alright,' Barboza said. Picking up the bow and the last arrow, he readied his shot. 'Please forgive me for being a poor shot. I humbly ask you help me hit the target.' Before he could even loose the arrow, a walkway spread from the tree platform to their own.

'Looks like you passed,' Crenshaw said, placing a hand on Barboza's arm.

'Yes, it … it seems I did,' Barboza said. 'Thank you both. I would never have done it without you.'

'Don't thank us just yet. Gods know what's in that fancy tree,' Crenshaw replied. 'Better get over there and see, I suppose. Everyone ready?'

Fontaine voiced his assent along with Barboza. They crossed over to the tree and went inside. It was dark, and it took a moment for Fontaine's eyes to adjust to the gloom. When they did, he saw a simple wooden throne in front of him. Across its arms rested a giant spear carved out of bone. The scholar blinked and the ghost of King Jabja appeared in the seat.

'You have done well, blood of my blood, distant kin. You have passed the trials of faith, temptation and humility. If you have come here seeking my power, it must be a time of grave need.

'The spear you see before you is a relic of enormous power, carved from the thigh bone of a god. With this relic and others like it we banished the Rinmati to other realities, but such relics also have the power to bring them back and to wreak great evil. I entrust it to you. Use it wisely.'

The ghost of Jabja faded, and Barboza picked up the spear. ''Twas a fine speech but how the hells are we supposed to get out of here?' he said.

As if in answer to his question, a light began to glow around the three of them. A thrumming sound filled Fontaine's ears, growing in insistence. The room, the floor, everything vanished from around him, and he began to tumble through darkness. He tried to scream but nothing came out. Then with a joint-crunching thump he came to a stop.

Rolling onto his front Fontaine pushed himself up. Around him, he could hear hushed, excited voices whispering. His vision wavered, slipping in and out of focus. He saw that they were back in the camp on the outskirts of the swamp. As his brain scrabbled to work out what was happening, he heard an order barked, and he was grabbed under his arms and yanked to his feet. There was a commotion to his left, and he could make out Barboza swinging the spear in a great arc, keeping the guards from restraining him too.

'Enough!' Elder Fahim cried, stepping forwards. 'Have you no respect? They have returned successful from the trial, and you try to restrain them? Shame on you all. You should be bowing to the chosen king!'

'He is no chosen king,' Ayotunde spat, stalking towards Barboza. 'I have no idea what witchery he used to accomplish this, but he is still a—'

'Silence!' Barboza bellowed.

He pointed the spear at Ayotunde, the tip just touching the former king's shoulder. Ayotunde collapsed to the floor, clutching his skull. Fontaine stared at Barboza. It was like looking at a sculpture of a legendary ruler, as if he had stepped from the page of a history book to walk among them.

'Speak,' Barboza commanded, his eyes blazing.

Ayotunde's body went rigid. Then he spoke in a flat, lifeless tone. 'I was the one who killed King Chidiki, my father, and my brother Halwi. With the help of Kana Vooshu, I achieved this. With his help too, I was able to place the blame on my nephew, Ginko.'

There was uproar in the crowd. Ayotunde and Kana Vooshu were grabbed by guards and civilians alike. Elder Fahim was spinning in the middle of the heaving mass of people, trying to restore order. Just when Fontaine thought the whole thing was about to descend into pandemonium, Barboza stepped forwards.

'Cease this madness!' he bellowed, his voice carrying loud and clear over the tumult. The eyes of all assembled turned to him. 'As my first act as king, I order that Kana Vooshu and the former king, Ayotunde, be placed under arrest. Their trial will take place one week hence. As my second act, I order the wine casks opened and a mighty feast prepared. All shall eat and drink their fill on this momentous day!'

A ground-trembling cheer erupted from the people. Fontaine staggered through the crowd towards Barboza and Crenshaw. He smiled up at them and they beamed back. Then the crowd began to take up a chant. The scholar couldn't make it out.

'What are they saying?' he cried into Crenshaw's ear.

'Swalsi mufiti,' Crenshaw replied. 'The fallen king has risen.'

***

Cirona could feel rough hands under her arms, pinching, bruising, as they dragged her along. She could hear her feet scraping on the floor, though they were a distant problem, as if her body was a hundred paces long. Her chin was resting against her chest, her consciousness bobbing and weaving while she tried to come to terms with what was going on.

Where was she? What was happening? For a heart-halting moment, she thought she was in the dungeons of the palace in Kurgobad, that she was being taken to one of the cells to watch Reveeker be mutilated and killed. A soft moan escaped her lips, and she tried to break free. One of the men dragging her landed a blow between her shoulder blades, pain lancing outward, filling her body with galvanic fire.

No, this wasn't Kurgobad. Snatches of memory came back to her: hiking up a mountain, being attacked by a bird, falling, a cave, someone tending to her wounds. Waltus. The name came to her like a shot through the brain. The old mage had disappeared. She had looked for him and then … everything after that was darkness. Until now.

Her head was beginning to clear, and she saw that she was being pulled down a flame-lit corridor towards a pair of dark wooden doors. Without stopping, the men pushed the doors open and led her inside. She found herself in a long hall. Above her, hammerlock beams with wrestling dragons carved into them supported the ceiling. Wooden pillars descended down from them, carved in intricate swirling patterns. A blazing fire burned in the middle of the room, the smoke twisting up to a small opening above.

Cirona was dragged past all of this towards a golden throne with arms shaped like snarling wolves. Upon the throne sat a thickset man with a drooping blonde moustache. Somehow, he had managed to cram at least two rings on to all of his chunky fingers. *Einar*, Cirona thought, *Einar Egilson, Narvale's delegate to the quorum.*

To the left of Einar stood a stout woman in her late forties. A pair of sharp eyes glinted out of an oval face crowned with salt-and-pepper frizzy hair. Her shoulders were draped in a variety of shawls and scarves, hundreds of metal charms and wards against evil attached to their edges. In one delicate hand, she held a wooden staff topped with a small skull, bangles and bells shimmering along its length.

Einar waved a hand and Cirona was dropped to the floor. She struggled to her feet, the footsteps of the men as they retreated to the back of the room echoing in her head.

'So, the great Cirona Bouchard is stood before me. I can't tell yer how much I longed to see yer in a state like this whenever I got a look at yer guarding the Emperor,' Egilson said. 'First through the breech when you invaded here, weren't yer? First to get killing?'

Cirona tried to move her mouth, but it felt like her teeth had been covered in glue.

'No, no,' Einar said. 'Don't feel the need to explain yerself. Yer a warrior, and if there's anything us Narvglanders like it's a warrior. All water under the bridge. The problem I've got is why you've come 'ere now.'

'Y-you doan know why I'm here,' Cirona said thickly.

'Don't I?' Egilson said, tilting his head to the side. 'I'm afraid I do, lass. See this 'ere is Maver Dalla. We've got many names for what she is up 'ere: wise woman, soothsayer, even witch, but your lot would call her a person of magical capabilities.'

'No … no, we rounded them all up,' Cirona said, grimacing as she remembered the horror of the purges on Narvale.

'I'm afraid you didn't. We hid them, see, hid them nice and deep in places only we know. And now she stands by my side, an aide to the king,' Einar said.

'You're … the king of Narvale?' Cirona asked, her brow furrowing.

'I am indeed, lass, I am indeed. Voted in by all the clan chiefs. But we're getting off track 'ere,' Einar said. 'Now, Maver Dalla saw you when she was casting her bones. Saw that you were coming to ask us a favour.

We tried to stop you reaching 'ere — that was Maver Dalla that was, in the bird that attacked yer. But you survived thanks to that old mage you've got in tow. So, we sent some boys out to intercept you and 'ere you are.'

'I don't understand,' Cirona said. 'Why not just kill me?'

Einar stroked his moustache then reached for a goblet at his side. He drank deep then said, 'You've left a bit of a mark, see, Major. What's a fancy way to put it? Ah, a scar on our collective psyche. Not just you personally, but the whole farcical Empire you represent. I was going to kill yer, but then I had an idea.

'We have a tradition up 'ere, you see. When someone wants to lead our troops as you do, we have them battle the other generals. Everyone turns up to watch it. And if the challenger wins, they get to be a leader. I thought it would be good for my men to see you lose. Thought it would be … what's the word I'm looking for? Oh, symbolic, that's the one.'

'Fine,' Cirona said. 'I'll look forward to it.'

'I wouldn't be so sure, lass, I wouldn't be so sure,' Einar replied.

He gestured to the men at the back of the room, and they came forwards to grab Cirona. She shook herself free from their grasp and stormed towards the doors. *I'll give the fat prick a battle,* she thought. *I'll rip his men to fucking shreds then tear out his throat with my bare, bloody hands.*

CHAPTER EIGHT

A shaft of sunlight slipped through a break in the heavy clouds and warmed Elvgren's face; it lasted all of a second. He heard the wind swishing through the knee-high grass he stood in, saw it tremble the petals of a cluster of wildflowers then snake its way towards the giant's tomb.

The tomb rose out of the ground like a green beer gut. Its bottom was ringed with giant standing stones their faces pitted and worn by age. Directly in front of Elvgren was a doorway made from the same monumental stones. From where he stood, he could see that entry into the tomb was blocked by yet another massive chunk of rock.

So, this is what we've gambled on, is it? he thought. *If we can't get into this godsforsaken, jumped-up grave then we'll be handed over to the duke.* It was so crazed he had to stifle a burp of laughter. The whole thing was madness, pure and utter madness. He cursed himself for getting swept along with Bellina's bizarre schemes. Why hadn't he run?

In his heart of hearts, he knew the answer for that too — it had been fun playing Emperor. The awed respect from the horde of people that had followed them to Hidenbaden had clouded his mind, blinkered his judgement. Gods, there were so many holes in Bellina's plan it resembled a sunken ship. Even if they did somehow convince the Gortrixians to lend their support, they would only have a fraction of the army the duke possessed and nowhere near the number of weapons required to retake Victory. In short, they had no chance.

With a turn of his head, he looked towards Bellina. She stood staring at the entrance to the tomb, her brow furrowed, hands balled into fists at her side. It looked as if she was getting ready to try and physically smash the door.

Dargo, on the other hand, was staring at the burial mound in mute wonderment. Elvgren had tried to get him to stay in Hidenbaden, to flee should the inevitable happen, but he had insisted on coming. Now he was here, Elvgren found he was glad to have him.

'Well,' Gestaffen called out from behind them. Elvgren turned to face the minister and the gaggle of scholars and government bigwigs he had brought along to witness their failure. 'We have tried every means possible to open that tomb: digging, flashpowder, hammers, chisels, even firing our biggest cannon at it; nothing worked. In fact, we didn't even put a scratch on the door. So, you can see why these other fine gentlemen are fascinated to see what will happen here today.'

'I heard you were going to magic it open, ya?' one of the scholars shouted out, his comment met with a wave of laughter.

Dargo went to shout something back, but Bellina put a hand on his shoulder and shook her head. 'Ignore them,' she said. 'We'll be the ones laughing when we get into that tomb.'

'Oh, will we?' Elvgren said. 'I'm glad you have so much faith that the unbreakable door will somehow open up for us.'

'It will open,' Bellina hissed at him. 'Now let's get going. I think we've provided them with enough things to laugh at this morning.'

Elvgren turned back round to face the stones. From behind him, he could hear the murmur of the ministers' conversation. Every so often, someone would let out a bark of laughter. A flush stole its way across Elvgren's cheeks, and he felt his toes curl. *How can this be happening?* Before he could dwell anymore on his embarrassment, he saw Bellina striding towards the tomb. He hurried to catch up, feeling like a man running towards the gallows.

Soon they stood in the shadowed recess of the doorway. In front of them, the massive stone blocking the entrance barred the way, a mute, immovable guardian.

'Now what?' he asked.

'I …I don't know,' Bellina answered.

'Really?' Elvgren said in mock surprise. 'No more premonitions? No mythical beings to guide us?'

'Well, I'm sure being sarcastic is just the ticket to opening it so carry on!' Bellina said.

'I have the right to be sarcastic or any other damn way I—'

'Shut it the pair of you,' Dargo interrupted. 'Come and have a look at this.'

With reluctance, Elvgren stopped talking and moved to where Dargo stood running his hands over the entrance stone.

'What is it, Dar?' Bellina asked.

'Not sure really,' Dargo replied. 'But does that look like an eye to you?'

'What the hells are you talking about?' Elvgren said, kneeling down to look at what Dargo had found. Fresh laughter from the ministers reached his hearing.

'That there, look!' Dargo said, pointing at the stone.

Leaning in close, Elvgren examined the spot Dargo was pointing at. 'It's just a pattern in the—' he began to say. As he spoke a cone of turquoise light beamed out of the pattern, scanning his eye. Jerking back, Elvgren fell on his arse, much to the amusement of the watching ministers. Their laughter was soon cut short when the entry stone ground into life.

Elvgren watched in amazement as the huge rock that had seemed impenetrable only a few seconds ago now slid neatly into the ground. Clambering back to his feet, Elvgren moved towards the tomb's entrance. Squinting, he tried to make out what was inside, but it was too dark.

'Told yer there was something there, didn't I?' Dargo said.

Bellina let out a shaky laugh. 'Great work, Dar,' she said, placing a hand on the boy's shoulder. A hand, Elvgren noticed, that was trembling ever so.

'Let's go!' Dargo said, running inside.

'Hang on!' Elvgren called after him, but it was too late.

'I suppose we'd better follow him,' Bellina said.

'What? We said we'd get the tomb open, and by some miracle, we have. Our job is done, and I'm not going in there. Gods only know how many booby traps and whatnot we'd run into. Better to leave that to the scholars and whoever.'

'But Dargo!' Bellina said.

'He'll be fine,' Elvgren replied. 'Little bugger shouldn't have run in there in the first place. One of Gestaffen's men will find him and send him back.'

'Well I'm going after him,' Bellina said, fixing Elvgren with a look filled with venom.

'Bellina would you just … and she's gone!' Elvgren cried, throwing up his hands.

'By the Father!' Gestaffen cried as he and the other ministers ran to the tomb's entrance. 'You did it, Lovitz, you actually did it!'

'Was there ever any doubt?' Elvgren said. 'And you'll address me as Your Majesty.'

'Of course, Your … Majesty,' Gestaffen said. 'Klein get in there.' This last was addressed towards a man at his side.

Klein nodded and walked towards the entrance. As soon as his foot crossed the threshold though, he was blasted backwards.

'What the in the world are you doing, man?' Gestaffen asked.

'I-it wasn't my fault, First Minister. The door it … it repulsed me,' Klein said.

'Really?' Elvgren asked, stepping into the tomb. 'I don't seem to have—'

He was cut short when the entry stone once more sprang to life. Elvgren watched in stunned horror as the rock rose up to bar the way.

'Well, I didn't think that would happen,' Elvgren whispered to himself.

He turned around and banged his head against something hard. Staggering back, Elvgren rubbed at his forehead. Stretching out his hands, he felt the cold wet of grime-covered stone. Tracing his fingers downwards, he found an entrance. Doubled over, he stumbled forwards, the smell of mildew and damp infesting his nostrils.

After what felt like an age the tunnel ended, and he came into a large circular room lit by torches burning with a blue flame. Its walls were made of intricate layers of rock, each piece fitting perfectly with its neighbour. Bellina and Dargo were studying the room, peering at the stones, looking for a way forwards.

'Decided to join us, eh, Gren?' Dargo said.

'Didn't have much choice — bloody door shut behind me,' Elvgren replied.

'You let the door close?' Bellina said, turning towards Elvgren, a horrified look on her face.

'There wasn't anything I could do about it. As soon as I came in, it just … shut. Blasted rock has a mind of its own.'

'You irresponsible—' Bellina began.

'Oh, stop it, would yer?' Dargo said. 'Ain't no point arguing. Gotta be another way to get out, so let's get looking.'

With a sigh, Elvgren nodded and set about examining the room. He gazed round at the walls and ceiling, his eye searching for some clue. When he reached the centre of the room, his foot snagged on something, and he went sprawling to the floor.

'Great bollocking piles of shit!' he swore.

'What's the matter with you now?' Bellina said.

'I'm fine, my love, please restrain yourself; your overflowing concern for my health is embarrassing,' Elvgren said as he rubbed his toes.

'Looks like you tripped over this raised bit o' stone,' Dargo said. 'Hold up … it 'as an edge.'

Elvgren got back to his feet and hobbled back to see what Dargo was on about. *He's right — there really is an edge.* It was clear as day now that he looked at it; the stone was even a different colour from the floor surrounding it. Taking another step back, Elvgren could take it in fully. There, in the middle of floor, was a large, round plinth raised up by an inch or so.

'What do you think it does?' Dargo asked.

'It's probably just decoration,' Elvgren replied.

'I'm not so sure,' Bellina said. She was kneeling at the heart of the platform peering at the rock. 'Looks like that eye pattern Dargo—'

Before she could finish, Elvgren saw a cone of light, exactly like the one that had scanned his eye, shoot out at Bellina's. The platform began to spiral downward, great clouds of dust showering on them as the piece of floor moved for the first time in what must have been a thousand years.

When it came to a stop, Elvgren removed his hands from his head and took a tentative look about. The space they were now in had the feel of being gigantic, though he could see no further than the platform because the only light was coming from the hole above them. He climbed to his feet, brushing off the dust and debris, and saw Dargo place one foot outside the platform. The boy grimaced as he did so, but when nothing happened, he stepped off completely.

There was a deep clunking followed by a whirring sound, then all around them, light began to flood the room. Elvgren felt himself flinch at the brightness of the room being illuminated with a harsh white that seared his eye. Once his vision adjusted, he could see they were in a cavernous rectangular room, the walls and floor made from gleaming, polished rock.

'What is this place?' Bellina said, spinning around to take it all in.

'Looks to me like a warehouse or storeroom,' Elvgren replied. 'Don't quite know why nothing's in it though.'

'You don't think someone's already been in here and took what Lokos left behind?' Bellina asked.

'I think we would have heard if a group of people got hold of magical weapons from the past, don't you?' Elvgren answered.

'Oh, shut up,' Bellina snapped back.

Before Elvgren could reply, Dargo shouted, 'Oi, lovebirds! Over here.'

Bellina gave Elvgren a haughty snort of derision and stalked towards Dargo, leaving Lovitz to follow in her wake. They didn't have to go far to see what Dargo had found. He was sat, legs crossed, by another eye in the floor.

'D'ya think it would work if I looked into it?' he said.

'Only one way to find out, Dar,' Elvgren replied.

Dargo's face lit up, and he leaned forwards to gaze at the pattern. Once again, the cone of light appeared and this time scanned Dargo's eye. Then something weird happened. The small circle of floor that contained the eye began to unfurl like a flower. Out of this opening poured the same blue light that had been scanning them. The light swirled and danced, catching dust motes and turning them into tiny sapphires, before finally, it formed itself into the figure of a man.

Elvgren went to draw his sword, but Dargo, who was closer, already had his dagger out and pounced. To Elvgren's amazement, the boy flew right through.

'What the hells?' Dargo said.

Stepping forwards until he was face-to-face with the man, Elvgren waved his arm through the figure. 'He's transparent or intangible or … something,' he said.

'Maybe he's a ghost?' Dargo hissed, backing away like a shocked cat.

'Don't be ridiculous—' Bellina began.

'Greetings, Variables,' the figure said, cutting Bellina off. 'I am Lokos Vistas.'

'Don't look much like them paintings of him,' Dargo said.

Taking in the pot-bellied, dishevelled man that stood before him, Elvgren found he had to agree but said, 'Oh mighty, Lord Vistas, please forgive our—'

'If you are here then my worst fears have proved true and the world is once more facing the threat of the Deivars, though what you are calling them in your own time I can only guess,' Vistas said, stopping Elvgren short.

'Bloody rude, isn't he?' Elvgren said. 'Won't let one of us finish a blasted sentence.'

'I don't think it's that,' Bellina replied. 'It's as if he can't hear us. Like he's an echo of the past or something.'

Before anybody could say anything else, Lokos continued. 'I am sure you have many questions, but unfortunately, my time is short, though I shall endeavour to surmise what this place is and why you are here.

'After my companions and I succeeded in sealing the Deivars, we led what remained of the population from the now inhospitable Atvoria and out into the wider world. I followed Amlith Castria to whom I owed my life, while others sought their destiny upon different soil

'Amlith was a great man, but his biggest flaw was his naivety. He believed that by banishing what remained of the technology we had created in Atvoria he could lead the people in a return to a simple way of living. As such, he ordered me to destroy all the arms and devices we had used to wage our war against the Deivars. I could not do this.

'It was my belief that a threat would rise again, and I had heard tales of a thirteenth Deivar in a land to the east. I set out to destroy it. If you are watching this, I failed. But I had set up a contingency plan: the nexus hubs. The hubs are vast computational devices designed to trace the bloodlines of the men and women who helped seal the Deivars. You, standing there now, are those descendants.

'I designed the hubs to lead you to this weapons store and the relics of the creators. With these items and some luck, you should be able to accomplish what I and my fellows did.

'With that I leave you,' Vistas said. Then he furrowed his brows and continued. 'But one last word of warning: the metropolis of the dead must not rise again.' There were a series of plinks, like someone flicking a wine glass, and he was gone.

'Well that was something, eh?' Dargo said, letting out a low whistle.

'Yes, yes, that's all very well and good, but where are the weapons?' Elvgren said.

As if in answer, there was a loud clanking noise and parts of the floor began to move. From out of the ground rose row upon row of metal cabinets lined with weapons. Stunned, Elvgren walked towards one of them and took what he could only assume was a ballisket. It was a touch smaller than any he had seen before. It had a definite barrel with a muzzle, but it was made of gleaming copper and brass, and at the end, just above the grip, sat four vials of glowing liquid that fed into the weapon. Intrigued, he lifted the weapon closer to his eye … and accidentally pulled the trigger. A jet of blue light erupted from the weapon's muzzle and blasted into the far wall.

'You moron!' Bellina cried. 'That's part of the arsenal needed to beat a Terror; it's not some plaything!'

'I know that,' Elvgren snapped. 'It was a sodding accident.'

'Whoa!' Dargo cried. 'Look what it did!'

Elvgren walked to the far wall and felt the breath catch in his throat. Where the jet of light had hit there was now a smouldering crater, three feet wide and several inches deep. *By the gods! What would that do to a man?* He looked down at the weapon in his hands, felt the thrum of power that exuded from it. He had started the day convinced they were on a fool's errand, that there was no hope of taking Victory and bringing the duke to justice.

But now, he wasn't so sure.

***

Cirona hefted a sword from the rack and frowned. A long crack ran from the hilt to the middle of the blade. *Useless*, she thought, *one good hit and it'll shatter like a cheap mirror*. Disgusted, she tossed it away and looked around the rest of the room. All around her were stacks of swords and shields, heaps of armour. So far, every piece she had looked at was rubbish.

'Is there one decent weapon in here?' she asked the guard assigned to watch her.

'There … um … probably isn't, ma'am, I mean, Major,' he said.

Pausing for a moment, Cirona looked him up and down. He was young, not more than twenty-five she reckoned, possessing the hulking frame common to the majority of Narvale's men. His face was square and hard, but his eyes were large, blue, fringed with long, thick lashes that seemed almost feminine. Feeling Cirona's gaze upon him, the man blushed and looked at the ground.

'What's your name, boy?' she asked.

'Dofri,' the guard replied.

'Well, *Dofri*, can you tell me why everything in here is a piece of shit?'

The guard swallowed hard and shifted from side to side on his feet. 'This is the old stuff we keep for training the young'uns,' he said.

A bitter laugh leapt from Cirona's lips. 'Your "king" really does intend me to lose,' she said. 'I'd be better fighting bare-handed than using this shit.'

With a lick of his lips, Dofri took a tentative step towards Cirona. He drew his sword and held it out to her.

'Here,' he said.

'What are you doing?'

'Trying to help,' he said. 'Take this too.' He took what looked like a dried-out piece of old boot leather from a pouch and offered that as well.

Cirona narrowed her eyes and tilted her head to the side. 'And why would you be so willing to help me?' she asked.

'The king ain't being fair. This is not the same as what the other generals have gone through,' he answered. Dofri lowered his gaze and blushed before continuing, 'Plus me da' saw yer fight, said it was the most beautiful thing he'd ever seen — apart from me mam, o'course — and I … I wanted to see it too.'

'And what is that?' she asked, pointing to the red, wrinkled lump in his hand.

'It's a lingl berry. Our ravagers use it to give them energy,' the guard said.

Despite herself, Cirona felt a smile crease her lips. 'Thank you, Dofri,' she said, taking the sword and the berry.

The young man blushed harder than ever and replied, 'S'alright.'

'Now, if we can find a halfway decent shield, I may last longer than a few minutes,' Cirona said.

Dofri nodded and, after a thorough search, she managed to find a shield and a sword to replace the one the guard had lent her. When she had arranged her battle tools just right, Cirona nodded to Dofri, and he led her out of the room.

They made their way along a narrow stone passage, flickering torches emanating a yellow light. Ahead, she could see the end of the tunnel, the bubbling sound of many people talking washing out of it. Dofri gave her a concerned look when they reached it, his eyes seeming to ask if she really wanted to go through with this. In that moment, she knew this man would help her escape if she wanted, get her away from the madness befallen her. For a treacherous second, her heart wanted that more than anything else. But then she thought of Waltus locked away gods only knew where, thought of failing the mission Bellina had given her, and knew she had to finish this.

Placing a hand on Dofri's chest, she gently pushed him aside and stalked through the entrance. Cirona found herself in massive cavern. Rows of seating ran around the space in a circle, framing a fighting pit at their centre. In one place, the wall of seating was broken by a huge statue of a man resting his hands on a sword. Above that sat the royal box. Even from that distance, she could see the smirking face of Einar.

A hush fell over the crowd when they spotted Cirona, then they exploded into a chorus of hissing, boos and catcalls. Ignoring them, she lifted her head and walked out onto the arena floor. Her mind filled with memories of walking into the coliseum in Varash, and the mad, hallucinogenic fight that had followed. She shook her head. *It won't be like that … this is different.*

Over by the statue, Cirona saw the crowd part like a river round a rock. Through the newly made gap, she saw Einar and Maver Dalla walk onto the arena floor. The king held up his hand and an almost total silence descended.

'We are 'ere,' Einar boomed, his voice echoing round the space. 'To see if Major Cirona Bouchard can win the right to lead our men in battle.' This announcement was met with another round of booing. The king gestured once more for silence before continuing. 'It is usual for the king to choose a champion to represent him, and I'm pleased to say I have many fine men to call upon.' More raucous approval from the crowd. 'But I have decided that someone so notorious deserves a special challenge. Maver Dalla, if you would.'

The woman nodded and walked towards the statue. Reaching for the middle of the massive stone sword, she inserted a bronze disc which she turned twice in a clockwise direction. There was a grinding squeal, and the bottom of the statue opened. Inside, Cirona could see a suit of armour. *What in the twelve hells are they doing?*

'You need to run,' a voice whispered in her ear.

She turned to see that Dofri had brought himself alongside her. 'What's going on?' she asked.

'A Beckoning, something that ain't happened in hundreds of years,' Dofri said.

'And what's a "Beckoning"?' Cirona replied.

Dofri bit his lip. 'It's … it's a type of magic. Only the most powerful Mavers can do it right. They summon back a spirit from beyond the Veil, call it back to an item they were particularly attached to. That there armour belonged to Raknar.'

Cirona gave a slight shake of her head. 'Raknar Rageblade?' she said. 'The warrior you Narvglanders have all those ballads and songs about?'

'Like I said — you need to run. I thought King Einar wanted you dead, but now I think he wants you massacred. If you go now, I can say you overpowered me and—'

'I won't run,' Cirona interrupted. 'Don't think I'd get too far anyway. All I've ever been good at is fighting, and I'm not backing out of this one.'

Dofri opened his mouth to try and argue, but Cirona gave him a look that quieted him. She looked away to watch the ritual unfolding at the base of the statue. Maver Dalla was kneeling over a small fire she had created. The woman was chanting and, every so often, throwing some kind of dust into the flames. Then she took out a long, charred bone and placed this in the fire as well.

At this, the smoke that had been rising upwards was drawn to the armour as if pulled in by one huge breath, filling the gaps between the joints, drifting menacingly out from behind the face plate. An otherworldly roar escaped from the armour, and Cirona felt the small hairs on her body stand up. There was no doubting that the spirit of Raknar Rageblade had been summoned.

'And now,' King Einar announced to the baying crowd, 'let battle commence!'

Before the king and his Maver even had the chance to leave the arena floor, Raknar picked up a sword left by Einar and charged. A frontal assault was a staple of a Narvale ravager, and Cirona was expecting it, leaving it to the last second to pivot out of the spirit's way. If she had been facing a normal opponent, this move would have bought her a few seconds, but Raknar corrected his charge in a heartbeat and was upon her once more.

Steel smashed into steel; the music of swords meeting rang out in the massive space, the crowd releasing an appreciative "ooh". Cirona was only vaguely aware of this, her attention focused fully on the spirit in front of her. She tried to push back with her blade but Raknar was stronger. He bore down on her, pushing the swords to within an inch of Cirona's face.

Then she twisted, her weapon scraping against the resurrected warrior's as she ducked down and thrust her shield into his gut. The armour gave just enough for her to roll away. She needed time. She needed to think. But Rageblade was not allowing her either. He attacked again and again, Cirona just managing to avoid being impaled. Sweat ran down her face in rivers, flowing into her eyes, making them sting. The sword now felt heavy as a cannon, and her muscles ached and burned.

It was then that she remembered the berry Dofri had given her. In the space of a sigh, she had pulled it loose and stuffed it in her mouth. Instantly, she began to feel her heart pump harder, her limbs filling with an insane pulsing power.

She surged forwards, parrying Raknar's blade and driving the point of her own through the bottom of his faceplate. With a grunting heave she ripped the protective plate and the entire helmet from his head. Cirona looked round to see coiling streams of smoke pouring out of the armour's head, and she could have sworn it looked somehow shocked.

If Raknar was shocked that was nothing compared to the crowd. Most had assumed the fight would be quick and decisive, but now they realised they had a true battle on their hands. The mood of those watching changed too, and it seemed now some were even rooting for Cirona. *Well, if nothing else, Narvglanders love a fight.*

Raknar's spirit recovered from its shock by sending a vicious swing at Cirona's head. Her now electrified muscles met the stroke, turned it aside and punched a hole into Rageblade's breastplate. Smoke began to billow out of this opening too, and Bouchard danced back laughing. By the gods, she felt amazing, everything felt possible, all was—

There was crunching sound as one of Raknar's gauntlets connected with her nose. Pain flared in her face, bright white, then receded to a shuddering throb. Cirona raised her head, blood pouring down her chin, to see the gauntlet returning to the armour via a tendril of smoke. *Obviously has more tricks than I thought.* Bouchard cuffed some of the blood, spat, then charged with grin spread across her face.

When she drew near, the armour unleashed a gout of jet-black smoke. Her vision obscured, Cirona stumbled forwards and felt a blade bite into her calf. She fell, spinning to take the impending blow on her shoulder. Managing to roll onto her back, she was just in time to deflect another hideously powerful sword swing. But her power was ebbing now, whatever unnatural energy the lingl berry had given her fading just as quickly as it had come.

Trying one more feeble slash, Cirona felt her wrist break as the blade was kicked out of her hand by Raknar. Chest heaving, breath whistling out of her demolished nose, she looked up into the face of her executioner. *At least I gave him a couple of new holes.* She tried to laugh but all that came out was a hoarse braying sound. *So, this is how it all ends, eh? Sorry, Bellina.* Cirona closed her eyes.

Then she heard a strange sound almost like … sniffing? The Major reopened her eyes to see the plume of smoke emanating from Raknar's neck leaning over her, and it was indeed sniffing. A halloing whoop came out of the spirit, and it grabbed Cirona by her unbroken wrist and hauled her to her feet.

'Blood of my blood!' Raknar's spirit howled. 'Kin of my kin. Honour her!'

In one whooshing rush the smoke exited the armour and left Cirona looking at a crowd of kneeling, reverent Narvglanders.

***

The sun was low on the horizon, the last of its glow casting an amber fire over the hedge-lined road they traipsed along. Castros, at the head of the column, turned round to see the faces of those they had saved shining in dusk's last light. Instead of making them look healthy, the light deepened the shadows under their eyes and cheeks, making the whole company look like marching skeletons.

A bird flew out of a hedgerow whistling a song and the freed mages nearest it shrank back in fear. *It wasn't supposed to be like this*, Castros thought. In his youth he had planned to liberate the sortilenergy plants, and he had always imagined the escapees with smiling faces, full of wonder at the world around them. What he had was a hundred or so terrified, starving people to take care of.

Not all of the group were mages though. There were at least ten cognopaths who had been locked up for refusing to accept the duke's daughter as their leader, seven old kaffars and an admiral who had disobeyed orders. *The very definition of a motley crew.*

Back at Raven's Down, Castros had managed, among the carnage Khasal was creating, to interrogate a guard. The man had begged and pleaded, babbling something about a boat and the chosen people before Del Var had managed to get him to answer his questions. Maggots of disgust had writhed in his stomach as the guard had told him the same genocide was happening at all the sortilenergy plants, only healthy young men escaping the process.

A surge of nausea rose in his stomach, and he balled his hands into fists. He had failed them. He had failed all of them. Castros wanted to rip at his skin, tear away the failure that seemed to coat him.

No. A clear, rational voice spoke inside his head. *This is not failure. Not while those people back there draw breath. They need you.*

The words echoing around his brain acted like a slap to the face. He had to find food and shelter for everyone soon, a few of the older mages, in particular, looking close to collapse. Khasal had gone on ahead in the aerolyte to scout out any place they might find rest. Castros prayed he returned soon.

'It's gonna be a dark night,' a voice said behind Castros.

Del Var turned and saw the wild-eyed cognopath. 'It's Torkwill, right?' Del Var asked.

'Aye, that's me alright. And you're the mysterious renegade, Castros Del Var. Always wanted to meet you, see what all the fuss was about,' Torkwill said.

'And?' Del Var replied.

'You look like a lanky streak o' piss. But yer got a kindness about ye. Maybe that's what she liked.'

'What who liked?' Castros asked.

'Nairne o' course, you great lummox.'

'How do you know … By the gods! Are you … no … but … Are you Uncle Tor?'

'Aye, that's what she called me.'

'You helped her escape.'

'Me and a few others. We couldnae all get out, but Nairne was young and beautiful, and I was not gonna let Alcastus get his hands on her. She had a laugh like tinkling glass.'

'She did, yes,' Castros said, a lump forming in his throat.

'The world's a more rotten place without her an' that's a fact. But there's a lot left of her in yer daughter, eh?'

'Thankfully, yes,' Del Var said with a smile.

'Have ye told her about her ma yet?'

'Well—'

Before Castros could answer, Khasal came zooming back, bringing the aerolyte to a stop overhead.

'Did you find anything?' Castros called up to him.

'There's a village. About half an hour's walk from here,' Khasal replied.

'A village? What bloody good is that going to do us? They're not likely to welcome an assortment of cognopaths and mages with open arms, are they?'

'Well, there's the thing,' Khasal said. 'The village is deserted.'

*

Due to the slow crawl that some of the party were moving at, they didn't reach the village for about an hour. Full dark had settled by then, and it made the lightless windows forbidding. An almost total silence hung over the place, and everyone seemed too frightened to break it. It was as if some unspeakable horror had occurred, leaving no witness to tell the tale.

Ever practical, Whist took charge, sorting people into the empty homes and sending others out to gather any food that had been left behind. Castros stood by while this took place, numb, mind racing, desperate to discern some reason for what had happened. Once done, Whist guided Del Var into a large house and into its kitchen. Holger got a fire started in the hearth while Melek, Khasal, Yevad and Torkwill joined them.

'Just what the hells happened here?' Castros asked aloud, his hands resting on a large table. 'A whole village of people doesn't just vanish into mid-air!'

'We have seen similar occurrences in Burkesh,' Yevad said.

'Aye, we have too!' Torkwill added.

'But where the people go,' the kaffar continued, 'your guess would be as good as mine.'

From the corner of his eye, Castros saw Whist go rigid. A series of strange expressions passed across his face as though he was reacting to some silent story.

'Is he having some kind of fit?' Khasal asked.

'I don't know,' Castros said, moving towards Whist. He gazed straight into his friend's eyes and clicked his fingers. Then, with a jerk, Whist was back. With a sigh of relief, Castros asked, 'What just happened?'

'I have just received word from your daughter, Her Majesty the Empress, she says we are to meet at Hidenbaden. We are ready to go to war.'

***

The world swayed in front of Elvgren while he followed Bellina staggering out of the banqueting hall. A magnificent feast had been put on in honour of their accomplishments, and they had celebrated. In a dim recess of Elvgren's mind, he thought perhaps they had celebrated too hard. His knee hit the door frame, and he went sprawling into a wall. Giggling, he slid to the floor where he sat listening to Bellina's laughter. Dargo stood in the doorway, hands on hips, shaking his head.

'I told you two to go easy on that firewater. Bloody stuff is lethal,' he said.

'Oh, stop being an old fart, Dargo,' Elvgren replied.

'Yes — stop being a f-f-fart,' Bellina added, bursting into fresh gales of laughter. Elvgren joined her.

'Come on, let's get yer to your rooms,' Dargo said.

'Y-you're not our bloody nanny. We … we can get there on our own, can't we, Your Majesty?' Elvgren said, climbing to his unsteady feet and bowing to Bellina.

'Why of course we can, Your Majesty,' she replied, dropping a curtsy that almost put her on her arse.

'Fine then. If you two want to stumble about the palace like a couple of drunken idiots, be my guest,' Dargo said before storming off.

'Dargo? Dargo! Don't be like that you big … big spoilsport,' Elvgren called after him.

'D'ya think we … hic … upset him?' Bellina asked, leaning on Elvgren's shoulder.

'Oh, h-he'll be fine in the mornin'. Jus' having one of his ickle tantrums is all,' he replied.

They stayed that way for a moment — Bellina leaning on his shoulder. He could smell the clean scent of her even through the alcohol on her breath, could feel the warmth of her body and slight weight pushing against him. A fierce longing pierced through his own drunkenness, a fire swirling through his chest, filling him with desire.

'Come on,' she said finally. 'I've got something to show you.'

'What?' Elvgren asked.

'Just follow me.'

Taking his hand, Bellina led Elvgren through the palace corridors towards their rooms, the pair of them giggling the whole way. Soon they reached her door, and Bellina pushed him through it. Elvgren stood — not a little dazed — by the foot of the bed. He watched as Bellina closed the door and leaned against it, breathless, her pale cheeks flushed.

Elvgren licked his lips and swallowed. 'What is it you want to show me?' he all but whispered.

'It's under here,' Bellina said, pointing at her dress.

Hands trembling at his sides, stomach fluttering, Elvgren saw Bellina begin to lift up her dress. He watched, skin tingling, as it rose past her thighs. There she stopped.

'Ta-da!' she said, whipping out a bottle of firewater. 'I stole it from the table. Didn't think anyone would miss it.'

Bellina pulled out the cork and took a huge swig. Elvgren's head dropped and he let out a bark of laughter.

'Wassa matter with you?' Bellina asked.

'It's nothing. I-I just thought …'

Understanding dawned on Bellina's face. She let out a snort of laughter and fell onto the bed. She lay on her side cupping her chin with her palm.

'You thought I was trying to seduce you?' she said.

'I … well … no … maybe,' he murmured.

'Who knows,' she said, 'maybe I am?' She rose to her feet and crossed the room towards him. 'Kish me.'

'You're drunk,' he said.

'So are you,' she replied.

Their lips met, and for a moment, Elvgren could have sworn his heart paused mid-beat. Then they were laughing, kissing, removing each other's clothes. Both stripped to their underwear, Bellina leapt back into the bed.

'Are you coming?' she said.

Elvgren didn't need to be asked twice.

CHAPTER NINE

Bellina stood in front of a full-length mirror fussing over the sleeve of her gown. The dress had been specially made for her by the finest seamstress in Hidenbaden and was, she had to say herself, the most gorgeous garment she had ever owned. It was black in colour with vivid slashes of red here and there. She had wanted the gown to be powerful, bold, and it most certainly was; now Bellina just hoped she could live up to it.

Her head was thumping like a tribal drum while her eyes and throat were both sore and dry. *My first proper hangover*, she thought, annoyed at herself for letting it happen. That wasn't the only thing she was annoyed at letting happen — there was the small matter of her night with Elvgren to consider. *No doubt, he'd want to talk about it and—*

There was a knock at the door.

'Come in,' she said.

The door opened and Elvgren and Dargo entered. They too wore brand new clothes. Elvgren wore a smart uniform, a gleaming officer's sword dangling from his hip. Dargo was in a finely cut suit, his tie already pulled loose. The young man had also been fitted with a top-of-the-line automaton leg which he had decided to show off by cutting one leg of his trousers short.

'You look beautiful, Belle,' Dargo said before letting out a whistle.

'Thank you, Dar. You're looking very smart yourself,' she replied.

'He doesn't scrub up too badly,' Elvgren said, giving Dargo a playful punch on the shoulder. He then bowed deeply to Bellina. 'You look divine, my love.'

'Thank you, beloved,' she said.

Miming being sick, Dargo said, 'Aargh, leave it out will yer? Think I prefer it when you're at each other's throats.'

'Today is not for petty squabbles,' Bellina said. 'We must show a united front.'

'Quite right, my love. Dargo, would you mind leaving us for a moment?' Elvgren said, gesturing to the door.

Dargo arched an eyebrow. 'Can't keep yer hands off each other, eh?'

Bellina heard a nervous titter escape her lips while Elvgren inspected the ground, his cheeks flushed. Dargo frowned.

'Alright,' he said. 'I'm going.' With one last inquisitive look, he left the room and closed the door.

Still looking at the floor, Elvgren said, 'I … um—'

'Yes?' Bellina interrupted. If they *had* to discuss this, she wanted it over quickly.

'Well … I … Are you alright?' he said.

'Of course I am. Why wouldn't I be?'

'I just thought … after last night …'

'Last night was last night. We were drunk and we … we did what we did. Please don't read too much into it. I think it best we put it behind us and move on.' she said.

For half a heartbeat, she could've sworn she saw a look of hurt flash across Elvgren's face. Then he tossed back his head and laughed.

'Quite right, quite right. Shall we set off?' he said.

Taking one last look in the mirror, Bellina nodded, joined arms with Elvgren and left the room. They swept through the elegant rooms of the Gofthaus, each step making her heart pound ever faster. Reaching the sweeping staircase to the ground floor, Bellina hitched up her skirt, desperate not to fall in her new and extremely uncomfortable shoes. With that disaster averted, the trio clacked their way across the marble floor and towards the doors of the Grand Assembly room.

'Are you ready?' Elvgren asked her.

Taking a deep breath, Bellina said, 'Yes.'

'Well, I'm glad you are, because I'm nigh on defecating myself.'

In spite of herself, she let out a snort of laughter, some of her nerves escaping with it. She then stood to her fullest height, thrust back her shoulders and nodded for the servants to open the door. The room beyond was huge. In its centre was the largest table Bellina had ever seen, each side crammed with people. The foremost were their friends, each returned from their own adventures, while even more people stood behind them. Silence fell when the occupants of the room noticed Bellina and Elvgren, then everyone scrambled up from their seats and bowed.

'Your Majesties,' Gestaffen called from the head of the table. 'If you would like to take your places.' He gestured at the chairs beside him.

Bellina opened her mouth to speak, but no words came out. Suddenly, the enormity of it all was crushing her, smothering her, the walls sliding forwards to capture her. She couldn't do this; it was too much. All of them were looking at her with expectation. What if she couldn't deliver?

'Thank you kindly, First Minister. Esteemed guests, honoured friends, please, be seated,' Elvgren said. The gathering bowed once more then retook their seats.

'Thank you,' Bellina said.

'For what?' Elvgren replied.

'Just then. I ... I don't know what came over me.'

'I know. Usually can't shut you up,' he said, squeezing her arm gently.

She reached up and pressed the back of her hand against Elvgren's forehead.

'What in the world are you doing?' he asked with a startled laugh.

'Well, you haven't got a temperature,' Bellina answered. 'I thought maybe you weren't feeling yourself; you're acting almost ... pleasant.'

Elvgren let out another laugh and said, 'I don't know what's come over me to be honest. Wouldn't worry — I'm sure I'll be back to normal tomorrow.'

Bellina smiled. *By the gods*, she thought, *I must really be nervous if Elvgren is making me feel better.* Then she caught the eye of Holger seated next to her father, the pain and sorrow etched deep into his face, and she looked away.

Reaching their seats, Bellina could finally see everyone else clearly. Cirona was next to the king of Narvale, an old soothsayer stood behind them. Her father sat with Whist, Holger and Yevad. It had been an unlooked-for joy to be reacquainted with the kaffar and Torkwill again, the pair reclined in chairs at the back of the room. *Plus, the cognopaths will be more than useful in what's to come.* Barboza, Crenshaw and Fontaine were further back and she found the sight of a wigless Barboza somehow wrong. But the newly crowned king had brought with him a thousand of his finest warriors. Yes. Everyone was there. Everyone had survived and succeeded against all the odds. Now, she had to lead them.

'Friends, new and old,' Bellina said, 'thank you for heeding our call and lending your strength to our cause. Our enemies, no, the enemies of all those who would live free are planning a great evil. What form that evil will take is unknown to us. The rightful Emperor and I wish to cut this evil off before it can take root, to stop it before more lives are destroyed. As such, we have decided to fight, and today, we form the first free army of the world's people.'

At this there was a large whoop and cheer from the Narvale camp, while all others voiced their assent.

'Using my powers, I have been in contact with my advisers, and we have come up with a plan. A plan we believe will take back Victory and bring the duke and his conspirators to justice.

'Our first wave of attack will be led by Castros Del Var and—'

'Our men won't be led by a mage and a traitor!' one minister bellowed.

'Quite right!' another chimed in.

'Man can't be trusted—'

Bellina slammed her fist on the table. 'Everyone here is fighting for a better tomorrow,' she said. 'If you do not like our decisions than there's the door.'

She waited with bated breath. *Please don't let anyone call my bluff. Please.* No one made a move.

'Good. Now, as I was saying, Castros Del Var shall lead the first wave of attackers through …'

***

The sewers, back in the damnable sewers, Castros thought. He'd spent so much time in them recently that they felt like a second home. Behind him, he could hear the shuffle of boots; it was the only sound the sixty men he was leading made. Dank stone wall followed dank stone wall. The rushing gurgle of sewage a constant companion. To his left was Khasal and Whist, on his right Holger and Melek. He was glad to have them. The gods only knew what they would find topside. They turned a corner, and Whist held up his hand. Everyone came to a stop.

'What is it?' Castros asked.

'We're here,' Whist replied. 'The opening above us should lead into a backstreet in Skelm's Den. Hopefully, any guard presence there will be light.'

'*Hopefully*, you're right,' Castros said, looking up at the sewer covering. 'Suppose I have to go first then, eh?'

'Just one of the perks of being our fearless leader,' Khasal said with a wicked grin.

'Be careful, Castros,' Holger said, his jaw set firm. 'We'll be right behind you.'

With a nod, Del Var turned and walked towards the ladder that led from the sewer to the outside world. He gripped the first slime-slick rung in his hands and began to haul himself up. It was a difficult climb, his boots slipping, missing rungs; at some point, one even came out in his hand. Eventually, he made it. He closed his eyes and took a deep breath, then he placed a hand on the bottom of the covering and lifted it gently aside.

Cautious of any onlookers, Castros poked his head from the hole. He found himself looking at one of Skelm's Den's many narrow, squalid backstreets. Thankfully, it was deserted. Ducking back down, Del Var gave the all clear signal then climbed out. He edged towards the end of the street and stole a quick glance around the corner of a building. The next street was deserted too. *This isn't right*, he thought.

Curiosity overcoming him, Del Var walked down the next street. He gazed side to side at the silent buildings, windows shuttered blind, doors shut tight. *I have never seen the Den this quiet. Something is seriously wrong here.* As he turned another corner, Castros froze. There in the middle of the street, with his back to him, was a child, no more than four or five. He was completely alone.

'Hello?' Castros called, walking towards the boy. 'Are you alright? Where are your parents? Where's anyone for that matter?'

The child began to turn his head towards Del Var … and didn't stop till it was twisted all the way round at a grotesque angle. The child stood up as if pulled by invisible strings and moved towards him. Castros backed away, his mouth hanging open like a trapdoor. His mind fizzed, desperate to make sense of what he was seeing. Then the doors to either side of him flew open and people began to pour out, moving in the same puppet-like way as the boy. The street was now choked with bodies all stumbling after him.

'Gods, no!'

Del Var turned and saw Holger and the others had caught up. 'Do you know what these … things are?' Castros asked.

'Nekrolytes,' Holger answered in a whisper. 'Corpses controlled by a kaffar.'

'The darkest of all magic,' Khasal said. 'It's certainly impressive.'

'Impressive? Impressive! Those are people over there. By the father, they must have slaughtered all of Skelm's Den!' Whist cried.

'Everybody, calm down!' Castros bellowed. 'We still have a job to do. We need to get through here and open …'

***

'… the north gate will be our focal point. Once Del Var and his men have opened the way, General Bouchard will lead our main force into the city,' Bellina said, gazing round the room. She checked each face in turn to make sure there were no objections to Cirona's promotion. There were none.

'Emperor Elvgren will be …'

***

… bored. There was no other word for it. Elvgren was bored. He sat atop his horse at the head of the meagre cavalry unit they had managed to cobble together, staring at the north gate. The mounts snorted and pawed at the ground, as impatient as their riders for something to happen. But so far, there had been nothing.

This isn't right, he thought. *It's not exactly hard to miss a horde of eight thousand sitting on your front doorstep; why aren't they firing?* Elvgren stared up at the massive gate sitting snugly in the magically bonded stone of the Castrian Wall. He had never looked at the city as an attacker before, and he had to say it was an impressive sight. Could it be that they had such faith in the defensive battlements that the duke's men weren't even bothering to attack? Were they content to wait for Elvgren and the Free Army to make a move?

'Argh,' he said, running a hand through his hair. 'Dargo, you stay here and watch the gate. I'm going to speak with the General.'

'That mean I'm in charge, Gren?'

'Yes, yes, whatever.'

Touching his spurs to the horse's flanks, Elvgren set off. He leaned forwards, racing his mount through the ranks of infantry to where Cirona stood, spyglass in hand, gazing at their intended entry point.

'What do you make of things, General?' he asked.

'I think we should have sent someone else to open the gate,' Cirona replied, snapping the glass shut.

'I'm inclined to agree, and would you please address me as Your Majesty. I know we've grown … close, but it sets a bad example.'

'Excuse me, Your *Majesty*,' she said with a bow that just stopped short of being insolent.

'You think Del Var's run into trouble?' Elvgren said.

'I wouldn't be surprised — trouble follows that boy around like the stink of shit,' this was Waltus, appearing from behind Cirona. The White Mage was puffing on a hand-rolled cigarette, his jaw moving in a cow-like chewing motion.

'Why don't we just attack the gate head on?' Elvgren asked.

'With all due respect, Your Majesty, that would be insane,' a large, fresh-faced Narvglander to Cirona's left said.

'Dofri's right,' the General added. 'We would crash against those gates and break like water upon a rock.'

'So, what are we supposed to do?' Elvgren said.

'We wait,' she replied.

With a barely suppressed grunt, Elvgren turned his horse and rode back to his station.

'What's the word?' Dargo asked as Elvgren came to a stop.

'Apparently, we wait,' Elvgren replied. 'You know, you would think that being Emperor would give your opinion importance.'

'Ah, don't pout, Gren, Rona knows what's she's doing.'

'I suppose.'

Time crawled past like a fly with plucked wings. A murmured chatter broke out in the cavalry ranks, and Elvgren couldn't be bothered to stop it. Letting out a deep sigh, he began to drum his hand against the side of his leg. This was intolerable! Here they were, ready to sweep in and retake his city, and instead, all they were doing was waiting for some half-baked mage to get the doors open. No. This was ridiculous, and he was going to do something about it.

'Troops,' he cried to the rest of the cavalry, raising his sword aloft. 'To me!'

With a whooping cry, Elvgren dug in his spurs, the horse responding with a burst of speed. Soon, he was racing across the plain, wind whipping against his face, the sound of his soldiers close behind. As he closed in on the gate, he kept his eye on the wall above. He had expected to be met with ballisket fire, maybe even cannons, but there was nothing.

He reined his horse in just before the gate, knowing that defenders would be waiting above it ready to pour boiling hot oil and other nastiness upon his head. Straining his ears, Elvgren listened. Silence. Not a cough, sneeze or fart could be heard. Puzzled, he edged his beast closer to the gate, the horse fighting every inch. Patting his mount's neck, he tried to calm it. But to no avail.

'What's the matter, eh boy?' Elvgren whispered in its ear.

A thunderous splintering sound ripped through the air. Elvgren watched in stunned horror as the massive gate disintegrated in a shower of needle-like splinters that, by some miracle, only grazed him and his steed. His heart froze in his chest as he watched a gigantic black hand the size of a wagon appear through the storm of wood.

'Shit!' Elvgren said as the hand grabbed him round the middle and pulled him into the …

***

'… city will undoubtedly be heavily defended,' Bellina said. 'As such I will lead an attack up the …'

*

… Tollfaith river churned in great grey-green bubbles as the prow of the boat sliced through the water. Bellina watched it roil from the deck, *thinking* it looked how her stomach *felt*. She wondered how everyone else was doing, even contemplated making contact with the cognopaths attached to each group but decided against it; they were busy doing their duty, and she needed to do hers.

A call went up among the crew, and she turned to see what was going on. And there was the imposing Castrian Wall and the giant iron portcullis of the Tollfaith Gate, the entrance into the city that all the trading ships took. But it was no trading ship sailing towards the gate now. This ship, along with its two sister ships, was state-of-the-art, iron-plated, stuffed with men and fitted out with three of the ancient weapons at the prow.

The weapons themselves were long, brass cylinders and roughly resembled cannons, though they were a lot thinner. Attached to their sides were the same blue vials as the smaller weapons had, though these were a lot bigger.

Standing next to Bellina on the bridge were Barboza, Crenshaw and Scholar Fontaine. The newly crowned Barboza looked resplendent in his battle armour, the spear-relic clasped firmly in his hand, a look of imperious command on his face. Barboza had brought a thousand of his finest warriors to join the Free Army and Bellina thought of the promises that had been made to acquire that help.

It wasn't just the Timbokans who had been promised their freedom. Gortrix had also asked for greater autonomy, and Narvale wished to keep ties with Estria but return to having their own king. She had promised her father that she would institute a constitutional monarchy with a democratically elected parliament. And for Khasal, she had offered the Shattered Land to re-home the mages who had survived the purging of the power plants. It would be a very different Empire indeed should they achieve victory, but Bellina was unworried — she would happily concede all she had and much more to stop Marmossa and bring the duke to justice.

'Not much further now, Your Majesty,' Barboza said.

'No, Your Majesty,' Bellina replied.

'Perhaps we should drop the formalities; all these "your majesties" are making my head hurt,' Barboza said with a smile.

'Perhaps we should,' Bellina replied with a smile of her own.

Silence fell once more before Barboza said, 'Why do they not fire? We're well within range.'

'Might be waiting for us to get as close as possible,' Crenshaw said, scratching his chin. 'Make sure they blast us into the Void.'

'Well, we'll certainly have a surprise waiting for them,' Bellina said, nodding at the ancient cannons.

Why weren't they firing though? Bellina couldn't understand. No. It didn't matter. There was no point trying to second guess their enemies' designs. They had their own plans, and they would stick to them.

'Captain, make ready the cannons,' Bellina called.

The captain nodded then began to bark orders at his crew. Each cannon was controlled by three men, though this was unnecessary to fire them. The iron portcullis was dominating her view now. All around, the deck bristled with anticipation — Barboza's warriors tapping their spears against shields, the sailors with ballistols in one hand and swords in the other. Everyone was tense.

'Fire!' Bellina cried.

One of the cannon operators at each weapon yanked down a lever and scurried out of the way. A strange humming filled the air, vibrating bones and making the air crackle. A deep pressure fell over the boat, like the second before a lightning strike, then the cannons belched out a vivid blue ball that shot through the air, hitting the iron portcullis with a horrific shriek of grinding metal. Bellina watched, wide-eyed at the impact. There was no smoke, no lethal fragments ricocheting outwards — it was as if the ball ate the bars. The gate there one second and not there the next.

'By the gods,' Barboza exclaimed. 'How can any stand against us with weapons such as these?'

'Don't get too excited,' Bellina said. 'We still have an entire city to conquer.'

The boat ploughed on through the gap created by the cannons, the bars still glowing white-hot from the blast, and came to stop at the first available dock. The gangplank was deployed, and Bellina was in the first wave of people off the ship. There was still no sign of any defenders. In fact, Bellina realised, she couldn't even see a rat scurrying about or a bird careening in the sky. It wasn't simply that the place was deserted; it was almost as if life, in all its varying forms, had abandoned the place.

'Where is everyone?' Barboza hissed at Bellina, afraid to break the otherworldly silence.

'I … I don't know,' was the only answer she could give.

'Look!' someone suddenly shouted, his voice carrying true on the still air.

All heads turned towards what the soldier was pointing at. Lifting her arm to block out the sun, Bellina gazed down the length of the docks towards the massive warehouses where the vast produce of the Empire was stored. The large doors on each were pulling apart. That was when she saw them. People, hundreds of them, no, thousands upon thousands streaming out, some falling and being trampled by those behind, all stumbling and scrabbling towards them. It only took her one look into the lifeless faces to know what she was dealing with: nekrolytes.

***

Elvgren heard the air whistle past as he was pulled through the tattered remnants of the gate. The giant hand had him in a grip like steel, all the breath crushed from his lungs. Panic coursing through his body, Elvgren wriggled and squirmed in a desperate attempt to gain freedom, but it was no good — nothing could dislodge the fingers grasping him.

With horror, he gazed down the length of the arm to see what had grabbed him. The limb was attached to a giant body at least fifty feet tall and as dark as the hand. It was made out of what seemed to be thick, rope-like cords that swirled and twisted in a constant sinuous motion. The creature's head was tiny in comparison to the rest of it, nothing more than a round lump with glowing eyes. He also noticed with horror that there were two more of these monstrosities on the other side of gate.

By all that is holy, Elvgren thought, *how am I going to get out of this? Think. Think!* But no brilliant escape plan leapt to his rescue, his brain too suffused with terror to function in any kind of useful way. The giant lifted him higher, and the twisting cords beneath its eyes and down into its chest snapped outward revealing a vivid pink maw with triangular teeth. Elvgren closed his eye.

The waiting mouth, instead of devouring him, gave a shrill shriek. Forcing his eye back open, Elvgren looked down to see Dargo jabbing his dagger into the giant's leg again and again. And he wasn't alone, the rest of the cavalry had arrived and were attacking. Feeling the grip around him loosen, Elvgren reached into his pocket and pulled out the ancient ballistol he had taken from the tomb. Hoping he was pointing it far enough away from his own body, he squeezed the trigger.

In a blast of pale blue, the hand blew apart, covering Elvgren in a thick black ooze. His brain had just enough time to register that it maybe wasn't the best of ideas to blow up the hand that was holding him so high up, before he began to fall. On instinct, he stuck out a hand, his fingers closing round a tendril of flesh.

His descent halted, Elvgren tried to figure out what to do next. At that moment, the giant began to thrash and twist as more of the cavalry's attacks landed. With shaking fingers, Elvgren stuffed the ballistol back into the band of his trousers and drew his sword. With one hand still grasping the rope-like flesh, he used the other to drive the point of his weapon into the beast's side.

A howl that threatened to burst Elvgren's eardrums erupted from the giant. Down below him, he could see riders weaving around the creature's legs, darting in every so often to deliver powerful slashes to its shins. Returning his attention to the job at hand, Elvgren swung himself round and gripped another part of the giant's body. Once his hold was secure, he brought his sword round and drove it into the monstrosity's flesh for extra purchase.

Working like this, Elvgren made his way onto the giant's back. With a vicious thrust, he forced his blade deep into a spot just below the thing's neck. Ululating in pain, the creature reared up. At this point, Elvgren took hold of the weapon's hilt with both hands and used his own weight and gravity to pull him downward. The ground rushed up to meet him as his razor-sharp sword cut through the giant's flesh. Around its hip area, the sword jammed and Elvgren was jerked loose.

With a choked scream, he plummeted the last ten feet to the ground. He hit the cobbled street hard, pain sweeping through his body, almost sending him into unconsciousness. Then he felt hands pulling at him, shimmying him out of the way as a colossal fist slammed into the ground, sending chunks of stone flying in all directions.

'Dargo,' Elvgren said, looking up into the face of his saviour.

'Come on, Gren, let's get you back on a horse and out of that thing's range,' Dargo said.

Following Dargo, Elvgren came to a rearing pair of horses, their eyes mad with fear. In one of the stirrups was a bloodstained boot, all that was left of the previous owner. Stifling the urge to retch, Elvgren pushed the boot away and climbed onto the horse's back.

For the first time, he got a good look at the carnage unfolding around them. The cavalry had now been joined by ranks of infantry. Some were firing regular balliskets, the tiny lead balls disappearing into the giants undulating flesh with a series of faint plops, like stones thrown in a pond. The soldiers armed with the ancient weapons were causing more damage, but to Elvgren's horror, he could see the gaping holes created by the ancient weapons were healing, the back tendrils knitting themselves back together. *How in the twelve hells do you stop something like this,* he thought. Heart hammering in his chest, mouth dry, all he wanted to do was turn his horse around and run. It was the only sensible course of action really.

No, a voice called out in his head. *We haven't come this far to run now. We've been through worse than this and survived. Just one more battle, and you will be Emperor.* Emperor! *This is our destiny!*

In that instant, two soldiers loosed shots from their ancient weapons, the blasts blowing open a huge cavity in one of the giant's chest. For a moment, Elvgren saw a flash of red where the creature's heart should be, and then another blast bounced off it before the monster healed itself. *Maybe if you attacked it from a bit closer…*

'Dargo, you go and find the General. Let her know what's going on,' Elvgren said.

'But I should be with you!' Dargo protested.

'Listen, Dar, I have a plan but it's a bit risky. I don't want you nearby when I put it into action.'

'But—'

'Please, Dargo,' Elvgren said.

'Oh, alright. Just don't go and get yourself squashed or something,' Dargo replied before turning his horse towards the gate.

Spurring his horse into motion, Elvgren rode over to a group of soldiers each equipped with Lokos Vistas' weapons. The men stood to attention.

'At ease,' Elvgren said, looking down at them. 'Alright, chaps, here's what I want you to do. You two concentrate your fire on that one's legs. Once it falls to the ground, you two blast open its chest, then I'll do the rest.'

'Sir,' the men said with another sharp salute.

'Oh, and would one of you be kind enough to lend me a sword? I … I seem to have misplaced mine,' Elvgren asked.

'It would be my honour, sir,' one of the men replied, offering up a wicked-looking blade.

'My thanks. Right then, fire on my command,' he told them then positioned his horse so as to be parallel to the shots. 'Now!' he bellowed.

Elvgren nudged his horse into a canter as the first soldiers fired. He watched the giant in front of him collapse down on one knee, turning a group of soldiers into a bloody puddle. Then the next shots came whizzing past him, cannoning into the monster's chest and ripping it open. Fascinated, he saw that what he had thought was a heart was a large red gem.

Horse at a gallop now, Elvgren fired his own ancient pistol at the exposed heart. The blast hit the gem headon but only caused a splinter of damage. *Damn it*, Elvgren thought. *Ah well, suppose it's time for my backup plan.* Riding his horse in close to the giant, Elvgren waited till he was directly beneath it. He drew his sword then leapt.

His leap, coupled with the horse's momentum, helped him soar through the air. Time seemed to slow to a trickle as Elvgren's focus stayed solely on the gem. It grew in his vision till it blocked out everything else, then with one almighty swing, he smashed his sword into the fracture line he had caused. The gem shattered, and half a heartbeat later, the giant disintegrated in a shower of black gore.

Elvgren once more crashed into the ground, covered in the liquidised body of the slain giant. He coughed and wiped the worst of it from his face. Looking up, he saw the battle still raged. *One down*, he thought, *two to go*.

***

Bellina found herself being pushed back like a feather caught in the breeze as the soldiers around her rushed forwards to meet the nekrolytes. She heard a dull, meaty thump when the undead threw themselves against the shields of Barboza's warriors. The king of Timboko stood in front of her along with Crenshaw and Fontaine, the three men fanning out around her in a protective semicircle.

She stood there, hands clammy, shoulder muscles tight, the sound of battle filtering back to her. Everything had taken on a surreal tinge, and Bellina fought to keep her mind clear. *Calm down*, she told herself, *these things can be beaten. We must aim for their heads*. The head, that was right. Now she just had to pass the message along, but how would anyone hear her voice over the carnage?

'Stupid, stupid!' she muttered, slapping a hand against her forehead.

Then, with a few clicks on her control conduit, she began to broadcast her message cognopathically. *Soldiers of the Free Army, this is Empress Bellina Ressa.* In front of her, she saw heads twitch and look around for the source of the voice. *Do not be alarmed, I am using my powers to communicate with you. These creatures are known as nekrolytes and can only be stopped by destroying their brains. This is kaffar magic and* … That was it! Kaffar magic. She had been so stunned it hadn't occurred to her before, but if she could stop the kaffar controlling the nekrolytes … *Everyone keep fighting. Aim for the heads. I will seek out the kaffar and bring these abominations to an end.*

'What do you intend to do?' Fontaine asked.

'Battle the kaffar and destroy his psychic core. I've done it before, and I can do it again,' she said.

'Is there anything we can do to help?' Barboza asked.

'Just … just keep me safe,' she said.

With a nod, Bellina sat down on the floor and tried to block out the screeching clamour of the battle raging ahead of her. Her mouth was dry, and she swallowed sour spit. *You can do this*, she thought; *you took out Varl Faisook*. A nasty voice at the back of her head added, *You almost died too*. Breathing deep, she pushed all other thoughts aside and conjured the image of a candle's flame in her mind's eye. The sounds around her began to melt away, and she pushed her consciousness towards the orange flicker.

Then she was free, looking down on the fight. The soldiers, *her* soldiers, appeared as dancing balls of white, struggling to fight back the vast black mass of the nekrolytes. Hard as it was, she forced herself to ignore this and focus on the purple strands that flowed from the heads of the reanimated corpses. Following them, Bellina came to a bubbling scab of green that undulated like poison loosed from a vial. Despite the sickness that rose within her, she forced her will down into it.

***

Fontaine looked down at the frail young woman sitting on the ground to his side. The strength of the girl was something that continued to astonish him. Despite all her trials and her losses, here she was leading an army she had assembled, using her powers, powers that had seen her shunned, for the greater good. *You would have been proud, Lord Ressa,* he thought; *you would have been so proud.*

A high gurgling scream brought him back to the present. Turning his attention to the men fighting in front of him, Fontaine was pleased to find it impossible to locate whoever had made the noise. Due to the limited space at the docks, the battle was being waged on a small spit of walkway, dozens of the nekrolytes falling into the water as they mindlessly slammed forwards in attack.

'I should be in the front lines,' Barboza said, his voice a brooding rumble. 'What's the point of a magic stick if I can't use it?'

'We have discussed this, Your Majesty,' Fontaine said. 'If you should, by some chance, fall, and if the only relic we possess was captured by the enemy—'

'Yes, yes, I know,' Barboza interrupted. 'It's just hard to stand here and do nothing.'

'I think you might be called into action after all,' Crenshaw said. 'Look over there.'

Fontaine turned, following Crenshaw's outstretched finger. There, behind them, he saw nekrolytes appearing out of the water like malevolent spirits, using each other to clamber up onto the dockside.

They must have fallen in the water and walked along the riverbed behind us, he thought. *This … this has to be a nightmare.*

But as the first of them staggered towards him, shrunken lips drawn back in a hate-filled snarl, he knew it was real. So, so real.

***

Bellina quickly established her preferred psychic landscape — a well-manicured garden — expecting to encounter resistance. She met none. Instead, what met her gaze was a huge black sphere, its surface boiling and rippling like storm clouds. She took a hesitant step towards it, unsure what to do. Deep down in her, gut she knew that whoever was controlling the nekrolytes was hidden inside it. Focusing on the ball, she forced an opening. For a heartbeat, she paused, then strode inside.

Behind her, the opening closed with a wet slopping sound like an old man gumming food. She was astonished by what she saw. A vast desert of black sand stretched ahead of her, a light wind sweeping across the dunes whipping the grains into a mad jig. Above her yawned a violet sky, stars wheeling across it so fast they were nothing more than yellow smears. Scanning the landscape, she saw a flash of white. She flew towards it.

Coming to a stop some twenty paces from her target, she could see what she was up against. There before her, sitting in straight-backed chairs were three young women. They were covered from head-to-toe in billowing white cloth, only their faces exposed. Chest heaving, Bellina stepped forwards. The women made no move to stop her.

Then Bellina saw why. The eyes gazing out at her were covered over in a milky film. The women were blind. Bellina studied their faces for any hint of consciousness, and she realised that their lips were moving, as if reciting some sort of prayer. Closing the gap, she stood before them and listened.

'The rabid man's dog was killed shot in his place cold light colour of truth poured from the heavens and darkness sent her son to us the son the sun master of shadows he leads them and brings them and makes them grow …'

'Gods, what have they done to you,' Bellina said, reaching out her pale hand to one of the girls' brown one.

At her touch, the girl's eyes lost their milkiness. They were frightened eyes, desperate eyes. A tear rolled from the corner of one of them.

'Kill me,' she said.

***

Fontaine took a faltering step backwards, and the walking corpse rushed towards him. Everything slowed. Heart pummelling against his chest, he tried to free the ancient weapon in the band of his trousers. Hands that felt like bloated slabs of meat grabbed for the device, but his new sausage-like fingers were betraying him.

At last, he managed to free the weapon, but still, it seemed as if his body was covered in treacle, unable to perform at a regular speed. He pointed the weapon, his brain blank. If truth be told, the scholar had been much more interested in *studying* the weapon than its practical applications, and he cursed himself for not learning how to use it properly.

With a snap, time not only returned to normal but sped up. The nekrolyte in front of him covered the ground between them in what felt like the blink of an eye. Fontaine's finger jerked on the trigger, but his shot went wide. The corpse lunged forwards. With a cringing shriek, the scholar collapsed into a ball. There was a whooshing noise, and something sped past his neck making the small hairs upon it bristle.

'Get up, scholar,' a voice called. 'This isn't over yet.'

Looking up, Fontaine saw Crenshaw above him, hand outstretched. He took the hand, allowing the other man to take most of the burden in getting him upright. Over Crenshaw's shoulder, he could see Barboza hacking away at the nekrolytes with his spear-relic. Its blade was sweeping through flesh like a sabre through silk. The sight of decapitated corpses collapsing to the ground turned Fontaine's stomach, and he cringed away once more. Then he felt a stinging slap.

'No more of that,' Crenshaw said. 'We've gotta protect Belle. I don't know what she's doing, but she's the only one who has half a clue how to stop these things. So, we make sure they don't get to her. Do you understand me?'

'Y-yes,' Fontaine stammered. Crenshaw slapped him again.

'Do you understand me?'

'Yes!' Fontaine cried, anger flushing his cheeks.

'Good. Now come and help me blow these things apart.'

***

'Kill me,' the girl repeated. 'Kill *us*. Marmossa, he made us drink yaksit, gave us these powers. Then the killing started. I … *we* didn't want this. Please …'

She stopped talking as her eyes filmed over. Her lips began to move again in a dull rhythm, spouting gibberish. Bellina looked deep into her face and those of the two other young women. *They're my age*, she thought. *No, no; they're younger.* From the brief lucid words spoken to her, she knew the trio of girls had been made to become naffirs — people granted the temporary power of kaffars by drinking yaksit.

Biting her bottom lip, Bellina wondered where the three unwilling naffirs' psychic cores were. Then she noticed what looked like thick black cords coming from the base of the girls' necks. The cords resembled vines twined together to make rope. As they left the back of each naffir's head they coiled around each other in a thick pillar that rose to the heavens.

Instinct told Bellina that this was the way to stop them. *No*, she thought, *I'm not stopping them … I'm murdering them.* Her arms broke out in goosebumps. She had fought before, fought with the intention of killing, but in those cases, she had been defending herself. Here, looking at the blank faces of the three girls, she found herself scared and confused.

She took a deep breath and shook her head, trying to get her thoughts under control. With a pop, a sword materialised in her hand, and she walked towards the spiralling black column that was the naffir's psychic cores. With a heave, Bellina lifted the blade. She thought of the soldiers — *her soldiers* — in the real world, fighting, dying. *You can do this*, she told herself. *You can do this.* The sword and her hand began to tremble violently, and she felt the corners of her eyes grow hot and wet.

'I can't do this,' she whispered.

***

At least thirty of the nekrolytes had crawled out of the water and were bearing down upon Fontaine and the others. Lifting a trembling arm that felt as if it weighed the same as a cannon ball, the scholar aimed his weapon and squeezed the trigger. Not meaning to, he closed his eyes when the ancient weapon let loose a blast of blue light. When he opened them, he saw that the bottom half of the walking corpse he had been aiming at had disappeared. This hadn't stopped it though. It crawled towards him, entrails streaming out.

Another blast sounded to his right and the nekrolyte's skull disintegrated. 'Aim for the head, scholar,' Crenshaw said, placing a hand on his shoulder. 'Aim for the head.'

Fontaine nodded. Once more, he hauled up his ancient weapon. *They're not people anymore*, he told himself, *they're not people*. With that he pulled the trigger and watched in amazement as his shot struck home, blowing the head from the nearest nekrolyte. Part of him was amazed at what he had done, another part was sickened, but mostly, he was buzzing with adrenaline.

He did not have long to dwell on this though. More and more of the reanimated bodies were leaving the river and shambling closer. Fontaine heard a cry then saw that some of the soldiers had come to help them. Adrenaline pulsing through his body, the scholar rushed forwards to help, sending a series of blasts before him.

His shots landed true, and he let out a high, warbling laugh that sounded nothing like his own. *So, this is what battle lust feels like*, he thought. Still emitting his new high, hysterical laugh, Fontaine darted forwards. Someone bellowed a word of warning to him, but the call barely registered. Eyes large and unblinking, he rushed into the heart of the nekrolytes and let loose.

The laugh escaping his lips was nothing more than a high-pitched whine now, the sound a dog makes when it's been kicked. To Fontaine's glee, the corpses were falling around him, crumpling to the ground like scarecrows cut loose from their poles. Why did people pretend soldiering was difficult? You just had to point and squeeze, point and squeezepointandsqueeze …

A rough hand grasped him by the collar, and he fell. He hit the ground hard, the air ripped from his lungs. A halo of snarling, pallid faces filled his vision. Probing fingers wrapped themselves around his limbs, and the nekrolytes began to pull. He felt his ligaments and tendons stretched to their limits, knew that in a few seconds they would go beyond that and tear. And what then? His whole body would be torn apart.

Fontaine screamed, a high, keening sound very similar to his earlier laughter. And while he screamed, he prayed that whatever lady Bellina was doing she would do it quickly.

***

Bellina blinked back the tears in her eyes. *They aren't human anymore,* she told herself. *Marmossa has robbed them of that, just like he's done to those shambling corpses in the real world.* She knew all of that, understood it perfectly, but still, she could not swing the sword.

Get a hold of yourself, a cold voice at the back of her mind cried. *Did you think you could wage war with no casualties? Or did you just think that you would never be the one wielding the blade? You're not killing these girls; you're freeing them.*

Setting her jaw firm and her shoulders wide, Bellina drew back her sword.

***

The gnashing teeth of one of the nekrolytes dove at Fontaine's face. At the last second, he turned his face to the side. Pain erupted from the side of his head, and he felt a warm gush of blood pour down his neck. His left arm was ripped out of its socket, and he let out a shriek of pain. This was it — he was going to die. And for the first time in his adult life, he began to pray.

What he saw became a kaleidoscope of horror. He saw the nekrolyte that had bitten him, the bloody lobe of his right ear dangling from its mouth. He saw hands clawing, grabbing. He saw the maddened faces of the corpses who were fighting to get at him. Once more, the biting nekrolyte lowered his chomping jaws towards Fontaine's face. This time, the scholar couldn't move, his mind and body frozen in terror.

Then the reanimated bodies stopped. The scholar watched the eyes of the one that had bit him roll back. The nekrolyte spasmed for a handful of seconds then collapsed on top of him. Fontaine smelled the stink of the tomb. With his right arm he tried to push the bodies off, but he couldn't do it, all strength had left him.

'Scholar? Scholar!' he heard someone shout. It was the sweetest sound he had ever heard.

'I … I'm here!' he howled. 'I'm here!'

He felt the pressure on his body begin to lessen as the bodies were hauled off him. Three faces appeared above him, two soldiers and Crenshaw. Before long, they had cleared enough of the corpses to get to him. Fontaine let out a cry when one of the men took him by his dislocated left arm. Back on legs that felt like trembling stalks, he surveyed the scene, swallowing hard at the sight of the corpse-strewn dockside. *By the father*, he thought, *there are enough bodies here to fill a city block.*

'Are you alright, scholar?' Crenshaw asked.

'Yes … yes, I'm fine,' he replied, feeling like a man trapped in a nightmare. 'Where is the Empress?'

'This way,' Crenshaw said.

Barboza was stood with his arm around her shoulders. As Fontaine and Crenshaw approached, she gently moved it away. She looked unsteady, and for a heartbeat, the scholar thought she was going to be sick. Instead, she drew a deep breath and straightened up.

'Bring me the cognopaths in our group,' she said. 'If the others are facing the same thing, I must pass on how to defeat those controlling the nekrolytes.'

Her voice came out true and clear, commanding. She seemed stable enough as she spoke to the other cognopaths, but there was a coldness to her eyes, like they were gazing into the fathoms of a deep iced-over lake. *She may have won her battle*, he thought, *but what has it cost her?*

CHAPTER TEN

Castros snapped his wrists back, triggering his screamers and unleashing two blasts of magically infused air. They hit the moaning nekrolyte, sending the thing barrelling back into its counterparts, creating a temporary gap. It was soon filled. It seemed for every one of the walking bodies they destroyed, two more took its place.

Holger had told Del Var to attack the heads of the nekrolytes, that this stopped them by severing the link to the kaffar or naffir controlling them. He'd also said that Bellina had fought a kaffar manipulating the undead, but how she did it and triumphed, he did not know. Once this information had been passed through his squad, the young Narvglander had led the charge. Khasal wasn't far behind him and, much to Castros' disgust, seemed to be revelling in the chaos. Their combined magical assault was having an impact, but still, the monsters streamed forwards.

Castros pulled back from the front line to catch his breath, and two Gortrixian soldiers moved in front of him. One of the men brushed against Del Var, and he felt the soldier shiver in disgust. *It's going to take a long while to change that attitude, even if we win the day,* he thought. And with the trouble they were having, he wasn't so sure their attack would yield a glorious victory. *What if they've killed every person in Victory? What do we do then?*

Feeling a tap on his shoulder, Del Var's mind slid back into the present. He turned around to see a young man, short even for his age, giving him a stiff salute. Castros returned it with the ghost of a smile tugging at the corners of his lips.

'At ease,' he said. The man relaxed a fraction of an inch.

'Avrick Briant, sir,' he said, 'Cognopath Third Class. I've received word from one of my colleagues working with the General. They have entered the city and are doing battle against … against what they could only describe as giants. They said—'

His sentence was left to hang in the air as a look of confused serenity clouded his eyes. Castros knew that look — it was the look Nairne always got when she was using her powers; the man was receiving another message. The look blew away like morning mist, and Avrick, blinking rapidly, looked up at Castros.

'That … that was a report from the Empress, the lady Bellina herself,' he said, his face glowing as if he had just shaken hands with the gods. 'She has explained what we must do to beat these … things. Permission to gather the two other cognopaths with us, captain?

'Granted,' he replied.

Avrick made a gesture with his hand and his comrades hustled over to join him. One was as thin as a whip, the other was rather portly. They went into a tense huddle, their heads nodding as the message was relayed. Once this was done, Briant returned to Castros.

'We have a way to locate the people in control of the … the nekrolytes. From what I've been told, we should have little trouble defeating said people in psychic battle,' he said. 'All you need to do is keep us safe.'

'You can count on us,' Castros replied.

Giving a quick nod, Avrick returned to his colleagues. They sat on the ground and the dreamy look Castros had seen on Avrick's face was now on all of them. Despite the sound of the battle raging behind him, Del Var found himself transfixed. More memories of Nairne rustled in his mind; as usual, they filled him with the sepia glow of nostalgia. Minutes ticked by then Skinny and Portly opened their eyes. There was a huge cheer from the soldiers, and Castros knew they must have been successful.

'We've done it, sir,' Skinny said, staggering to his feet, face the colour of curdled milk. 'How long were we gone? It felt like an age.'

'Fifteen minutes tops,' Castros replied then pointed at Avrick. 'What about him?'

Skinny frowned. 'I don't know, sir. The task wasn't hard just … unpleasant. We encountered what the Empress termed as "naffirs" — people given temporary powers by drinking that black stuff the Burkeshis brought with them. I would have thought defeating them a simple task for Avrick.'

Portly gave a stifled scream. It didn't take Castros long to work out what had caused it. Avrick had now began to convulse, his body twitching and shuddering as if a galvanic current had been applied to him. Kneeling down, Del Var was just in time to snake an arm around the man's back and save him from dashing his brains out on the street. His mouth was a perfect "O", tongue flat, as he voiced a soundless scream.

'What's doing this?' Castros cried. 'What's happening?'

'I … he …' Portly stammered.

'Gods damn it, man — spit it out!'

'He … he can't break the psychic connection. I've heard about it in theory but—'

'Never mind that. How do we save—'

But as Del Var spoke, Avrick's body began to twist in his arms. He looked on in mute horror, the man's elbow twisting left while his wrist turned right. There was a series of cracks, the sound of dry twigs snapping, then jagged shards of bone tore through the cognopath's skin. Castros was forced to let go as Avrick's hips, shoulders and neck began to follow the same gruesome path of his arm. Then Briant's neck broke, a bizarre black tear rolling down his cheek; at that moment, it was all Castros could do not to vomit.

'Oh gods, oh gods, oh godsoh …' a voice called behind him.

Castros looked round to see Skinny wide-eyed and backing away. Portly was throwing up. *What happened?* Castros thought. *Why did Avrick die and not the others?* Then it came to him — Avrick must have run into the big boss, the ringmaster, the string puller; in short, he had run into a real kaffar.

Del Var grabbed Skinny by the shoulders and shook him. 'Where is the person Avrick fought?'

'O-over th-there,' Skinny said, pointing at a window high up on a tumbledown tenement.

'Good,' Del Var said. 'Now, sit down and get yourself together.' Turning back around, Castros almost crashed into Whist.

'Only a few of them left now,' Whist said, smiling from ear-to-ear. 'Whatever you lot did it worked.'

'It's not over yet. Those last few are being controlled by a kaffar, and I intend to stop him,' Castros replied. 'Whist, you're in charge till I get back.'

'Aye, aye, captain,' Whist said, giving a quick salute.

'Especially, keep an eye on Khasal, restraint is not a word he understands.'

With that Castros used his screamers to launch himself onto the nearest roof. His feet landed on loose tiles, a few skittering away and falling to the street below with a sharp tinkle. Ignoring this, he sprinted across the roof towards the tenement the cognopath had identified for him. Aided by another blast of sortilaero, Del Var flew over to the building and crashed through the window. He slid to a stop, puffs of dust billowing around him.

'Mr Del Var,' a voice said. 'I am Tashid. I was hoping to run into you.'

Castros saw a stocky man of medium height, a coat of raven feathers trailing from his shoulders to the floor. His head was round and perfectly smooth. Some kind of black paint was streaked down his cheeks beneath a pair of hooded eyes that glinted like crushed sapphires.

'Sorry to disappoint you, Tashid, but I'm not quite as impressive as the tales make out,' Castros said.

'Really?' Tashid said with a smile.

'But I'm still more than enough to kill a two-bit conjurer like you.'

Snapping his wrists, he shot a huge gust of magically infused air at the kaffar. Castros enjoyed a second of satisfaction when Tashid was hurled across the floor and into a window. The feeling was short-lived. With a manic cackle, the kaffar seemed to shrink in on himself, turning into a swirling mass of darkness and emerging transformed into a raven. Glass breaking into a thousand sparkling pieces, the raven flew out into the street.

Not missing a step, Castros ran to the broken window and looked out. He saw the raven circling in the alley below. Jumping onto the windowsill, Del Var ignored the shards of glass stabbing into his hands and through his boots and leapt out. At the last second, he used his screamers to break his fall and spun on the spot looking for his foe.

He saw him at the end of the alley. The kaffar had returned to his human form, now standing with his hands behind his back. 'I'm glad for this opportunity, Mr Del Var. Indeed, I praise Varl Dressera and Arch Vizier Marmossa for allowing our paths to cross — I've always wanted to battle a mage. You're only half a one, but it will do I suppose,' he said.

'Let me know if you are still grateful when you're nothing but a squealing ball of pain,' Castros replied.

Pressing a button on the gauntlet, he switched from his store of sortilaero to sortilaqua. With a twist of his wrist, he sent two balls of water, manipulated magically to the hardness of lead, flying at Tashid. The aqua bullets found their mark, ripping through the kaffars left eye. Instead of hearing a howl of pain, Castros heard the maniacal laugh again as the struck kaffar turned to smoke and flew away on the breeze.

'Not quite, Castros. I can call you Castros, can't I?'

Del Var whirled around and saw Tashid sitting on a roof above him, his legs dangling over the gutter making him look like a malevolent schoolboy. 'How long are you going to keep running,' Castros said. 'I thought you wanted to fight me?'

'Oh, but I am fighting you, Castros. Fighting you with the powers of a kaffar. No, not just a kaffar, but a kaffar enhanced by consuming yaksit. A kaffar—'

Not allowing him time to finish, Castros sent another pair of water bullets towards Tashid. Again, they found their mark. Again, the kaffar disintegrated into smoke.

'How very rude.'

Spinning to his right, Del Var saw Tashid leaning against a doorpost. 'I hadn't finished speaking. You know where a kaffar draws his power from?'

Two more balls of water left Del Var's wrists, once more smashing into Tashid and turning him into a swirling ball. Breath coming in ragged bursts, Castros turned on the spot, eyes narrowed as he searched. *He has to be here somewhere*, he thought, *he has to be.*

'A kaffar draws his power from the Void,' Tashid said, his voice seeming to come from everywhere at once. 'He steals strength not from life but the space between worlds. Summoning, shape-shifting, even illusions like this are the gifts we draw from the darkness.'

There was a scuffling sound behind him, and Castros whipped around in time to see what looked like two decomposing rabbits bounding towards him. Their fur was jet-black and matted. Two over-sized and discoloured teeth protruded from their top lips. They were moving at a ridiculous speed and were on Del Var before he knew it. He felt the sting of their bites sink into his calf and thigh, felt his blood, hot and warm, flow down his legs. With a squawk of pain, Castros fell to his knees and grabbed the creatures, his stomach squirming in revulsion as he touched the lank greasy fur. Tossing them to the side he finished them off with a couple of aqua bullets, the bodies dissolving into puddles of black liquid. Then laughter filled the air again.

'Did that hurt, Castros? I do hope so.' Tashid tittered.

Think, man, think — where could he be hiding. Del Var took a deep breath and looked, screwing up his eyes, focusing hard. Then he saw something, a slight shimmer by the wall at the end of the alley. He ignored it. *Keep him thinking you don't know, keep him feeling safe …* Then with a sharp jerk of his hand, he shot a water bullet at the kaffar. Hearing a satisfying yelp of pain, Castros snapped round to see Tashid, left arm dangling, blood pouring from his elbow and mixing with a black pool at his feet.

'That wasn't nice, Castros. And here I was thinking we'd built up a rapport,' he said.

In answer, Del Var fired twice more at him. The black substance leapt from the floor as if it was alive and formed a shield, deflecting the shots. *Gods damn it! He's got a solution for everything I do. I need to get in close, but how?* The idea came to him in an instant. Dashing forwards, he unleashed more shots, each one swatted away with an ease that bordered on arrogance.

'A suicidal last try, eh? Rather cliché … I must say, I applaud your tenacity if nothing else.'

Shut up, Castros thought, *shut up, shut up, shut upshutupshutup.* The black ooze now morphed into a series of jabbing spears and Del Var just nudged them off course with a blast from his screamer. Tashid's eyes were wary now, and he looked as if he was about to bolt. *Oh no you don't.* Deliberately tripping over his own feet, the demi-mage went sprawling onto his back.

The kaffar laughed. 'Goodness me, the legendary Castros Del Var brought down by his own bootlace.'

Keep laughing, keep thinking you've won … just move closer.

As if in response, Tashid's shadow fell over him. 'I must thank you for a most diverting afternoon,' he said. 'A last quip before you die?'

'Look up,' Castros said.

As the kaffar looked up, the self-satisfied smirk died on his lips and turned into one of confused horror. There, dangling above, was a shard of diamond-hard ice formed by the aqua bullets he'd deflected. Castros had kept them airborne, manipulating them for this moment. With a gesture that looked like he was beckoning his favourite hound, Del Var brought the shard down. Tashid shrieked and tried to form his shield again, but the glittering splinter was too fast, ripping through his neck in a shower of blood. He collapsed forwards, a choked gurgle escaping his lips. Then he was silent.

Castros pushed himself up, pain throbbing in his legs, wondering to himself just what kind of germs the rabbit things might have had on their fangs. Then he heard the tramp of boots. He looked up and saw Whist leading the squad round the corner.

'Gods, Cass, are you alright?' he asked.

'Just a couple of bites,' Del Var replied.

'Bites?' Whist said.

'Don't ask.'

'Killed a kaffar, eh?' Khasal said, nudging Tashid with his boot. 'You get all the fun.'

'Next one's yours, how about that?'

'Deal.'

'Tell him about the message,' Holger said, his brow creased in frustration.

'Empress says we're to all meet at Dullet's Square,' Whist said. 'As soon as we can.'

'Let's head out then,' Del Var replied.

Whist offered Castros his arm, but he waved it away. He took one last look at Tashid's blood-smeared face then set off.

CHAPTER ELEVEN

Cirona put the spyglass to her eye and pointed it towards the gate. Inside the city walls, she could see the soldiers concentrating their fire to bring down the last of the giants. After a moment's searching, she found Elvgren. He was covered in black gloop but otherwise unharmed. She could see him ordering the troops, calm and collected, and was amazed. Some people sank beneath the weight of responsibility, but it seemed that Lord Elvgren, no, *Emperor* Elvgren, was rising above it. Part of her longed to be beside him, leading the charge, but her responsibilities were different now. It was her job to keep the soldiers in order, to plan, to see the bigger picture of the battle. In short, it was her job to stop the whole thing turning into a sprawling mess.

The bark of ballisket fire melded with the humming blasts of the ancient weapons. Landing true, the shots blew open the giant's chest and revealed not a gem this time but a person. With a small twist of her spyglass, Cirona brought the face of the figure into sharp focus. Her breath caught in her throat at what she saw. It was a woman's face but that was only just discernible. Her mouth was stretched out in a rictus scream, eyes white and bulging. Her skin was raised up like unseen rivers flowed beneath it. *Make it quick*, Cirona thought as the troops readied their next wave of shots.

They did.

Collapsing the spyglass against her clammy palm, Cirona was surprised to discover she was shaking. *Deep breaths*, she told herself, *deep breaths*.

'How goes it, General?' Dofri asked, handing her the reins to her horse.

'Those … things are dead. The way forwards is clear. Ready the troops to move in,' she said.

'Sir,' Dofri replied with a crisp salute as she climbed into the saddle.

Putting spurs to her horse, she entered the city. The soldiers who had fought the battle against the giants were sitting on their packs, some were sharing canteens that Cirona knew were *not* filled with water. To her left lay the wounded and the dying. She could see Waltus administering to them. She rode her horse over and looked down into the gasping face of a man whose body looked like it had been run over by a locomotron.

'Will he make it?' she asked.

'Nah,' Waltus said, pressing a bloodstained rag against the soldier's forehead. 'He's got a shattered pelvis, his ribcage is smashed to shit and, to top it off, both his lungs are punctured. Poor bastard's way beyond my help.'

Cirona nodded. 'Give him some morphium. Make him … comfortable.'

'Already have, love,' Waltus replied.

She tightened her grip on the reins, oblivious to the pain of her nails digging into the flesh of her palms. *Just what the fuck have we walked into?* With a jerk, she manoeuvred her horse over to where Yevad was crouched. His hands were clasped in prayer above the woman who had been trapped inside the giant.

'What were those things?' she asked him.

'We call them the uresh. They are creatures from the darkest realms a kaffar can summon from,' he replied.

'Was … was she controlling them?'

'Control is too strong a word. I fear this girl was forced to consume a large amount of yaksit then summon the uresh. As long as she lived, they were bonded to her. She would have felt every blow the three received.'

Cirona looked down into the woman's face. Her almond eyes were closed, and her mouth had relaxed, parting slightly. The cords Cirona had seen bulging under her skin had faded almost to nothing. She looked at peace, and Cirona found herself glad of this. The Burkeshi woman had been as much a victim of the strange and disturbing war they all found themselves fighting as anyone else.

'Lass, I mean, General!' a voice called from behind her.

With a gentle tug, she turned her horse to see who it was. She saw Torkwill running over to her. The cognopath came to a stop in front of her and bent over trying to catch his breath.

'Bloody hells, I'm not as young as I used to be. Could jog round the city walls with nary a stitch a few years ago,' he said.

'You have a message, Master Torkwill?'

'Aye. The Empress wants us all to regroup in Dullet's Square. Said she's been dealing with nekrolytes, but they got the bastards whipped.'

'Thank you, Master Torkwill. Dismissed.'

Offering her a clumsy salute, the cognopath walked away to make himself useful elsewhere. *Or find the nearest flask of booze*, she thought.

Watching Torkwill move away, she got a panoramic view of the aftermath of the battle. She saw the wounded on one side and could have sworn she could smell the acrid tang of blood on the air. She saw the faces of the battle's victors, some trying their hardest to smile, to pass it off as no big deal, while others sat stunned, vacant eyes looking but not seeing, like they could find some answer to the madness they had experienced somewhere in the middle distance. Finally, she saw the troops who had been unable to get through the gates, the troops who had been with her. They were licking dry lips and taking uncertain steps forwards, unsure what to make of any of it.

In summary, they were lost.

You need to do something about this, she told herself, *but what?* What would the leaders she had fought under do now? Gabbinhurst, the first general she had known, would probably be dishing out floggings to the soldiers for lallygagging. Fadér would be dishing out booze and treats. She shook her head — that was them and she was her. *What do these people need?* Then it came to her — order.

'Companies!' she bellowed, surprised how loud and true her voice was when she had been sure all that would come out was a hoarse croak. 'Form up.'

The troops snapped to life as she had hoped they would. A soldier's worst enemy could be his mind, but a body, trained and drilled, could always overcome it — somehow the instructions ingrained in the muscles just took control.

'Cavalry. Form up,' she said, and Elvgren, Dargo and the rest got themselves into order. She waited a beat then cried, 'March!'

She led the way in a calm trot. After ten minutes, they came to Dullet's Square, the soldeirs coming to a neat halt. Across from her, she could see Bellina and her forces, to the left, Castros' small squad. Just as Cirona was about to move over to the Empress, a voice sliced through the air.

'Greetings, my young pretenders to the throne. I do hope you enjoyed the diversions we put in place for you.'

Wheeling her horse about, Cirona saw the voice was coming from a cognovision screen, the smug face of the duke plastered all over it. An urge, so strong and clear it felt like a sea squall in her veins, to blast the device with one of the ancient weapons came over her, and she only just managed to control herself.

'We have judged this country, no, this world and have found it wanting. Soon, an airship will carry us away to the Scorched Earth where we shall start anew, where we will become more than men. As a parting gift, we have left you this.' At his words, the picture shifted and showed what looked like a cauldron. 'This bomb has the capacity to level the whole of Victory, including the few surviving members of its populace. If you don't believe me ask dear Melek; he was the one who designed it.

'With that we bid you farewell. Come to the throne room. If you're quick enough, perhaps you can stop us … perhaps.'

The screen went dead and a nervous babble began. Cirona bit her lip. Was the duke telling the truth? She could see that Melek and Castros were making their way rapidly towards Bellina. Spurring her horse, she followed them.

'Do you remember making it?' she heard Castros ask.

'I … no. It must be one of the things I cooked up when they had me on the drugs,' Melek answered.

'Fan-fucking-tastic,' Castros said.

'General!' a voice called. Cirona turned to see Elvgren catching up. 'What in the hells do you make of all this?'

'I don't know,' she replied as they reached Bellina who was already in conversation with Castros.

'No,' she was saying. 'I don't care if it's a trap. If there is any chance of catching that bastard, then I'm going.' Del Var opened his mouth, but before he could talk, Bellina held up a hand. 'Elvgren,' she continued. 'Help me onto your horse. General, give yours to Castros and Melek.'

'Your Majesty, I really don't think this is a good—' Cirona began, dismounting.

'There's no time to debate this. We need to move now,' Bellina interrupted. 'General you stay with the troops in case there's any more trouble. We'll go and see what we can do about this bomb.'

Before Cirona could say another word, Bellina smacked the rump of Elvgren's horse and was off. As she watched them go, Bouchard's hands seemed to freeze and began to tremble. Inside, her stomach rolled like a ship caught in a storm. She squeezed her eyes shut and tried to shake the feeling that Bellina and the others were riding into death.

***

'Can't you make this thing go any faster?' Bellina bellowed in Elvgren's ear.

'Oh yes, silly me, I forgot to press the button that makes it grow wings,' Elvgren replied.

She had her arms clasped firmly around him, hair whipping about her face. With no idea if the duke was telling truth, she only had her instincts go on, and they said this was the right path. Her mind filled with images of capturing the duke at the Imperial Palace and using her powers to make his head pop like an overripe grape.

The coppery scent of adrenaline filled her nose. Whether it was hers, Elvgren's or a combination of the two, she couldn't be sure. Around them, the streets flashed by and soon she could see the Olphant Hill. It soared up like a blister, the mansions of Victory's nobility clinging to its side, marble limpets on the hull of some strange green ship.

Elevation Street was the name of the road they were now thundering along. It was named after the carriages that were in the middle of it, sat waiting to climb up the hill and bear them home. Both sets of riders made for the first carriage.

'Quickly, inside that one. We don't know how much time we have,' Bellina said.

They entered the compartment, and Elvgren grabbed the lever to make it move. 'It's not working,' he said, pumping it furiously.

'Well, wrenching it about like a maniac is sure to fix it,' Bellina said.

'Enough, both of you,' Castros cried. 'Melek, can you get it going again?'

The inventor was already kneeling by the front of the carriage. He had removed a panel and was staring intently at a bed of wires.

'I think so,' he said, taking two of the wires in his hands.

He took a pair of pliers from a tool belt round his middle and skinned the outer coating from the cables with the precision of an expert hunter preparing a kill for dinner. Then he cut both wires and, tongue dangling from his mouth like an overexcited dog, touched them together. There was a flash between his hands and the carriage got moving.

Moving is an understatement, Bellina thought. They were rocketing up the hill faster than she had ever known the elevated cars to move. Looking out the window, she saw sparks dancing through the air, generated as the harness holding the carriage to the steel cables overhead protested at the speed they were being forced to move at. Her breath caught in her throat, and she expected at any minute to hear a loud twang, something like a string breaking on a violin only a thousand times louder. From the front window, Bellina could see the Imperial Palace rearing up at them, the last stop for the cable car.

'Slow down!' she cried at Melek.

'I'm trying, I'm trying!' he yelled back, sweat marching down his brow like an army of ants as he tried to stop the carriage.

'Everybody, get down!' Castros bellowed, grabbing Bellina's hand and pulling her to the floor.

Even though she was covering her ears, Bellina was still close to deafened when the racing carriage smashed into the post which was supposed to bring it gently to rest. Glass showered down on them as the front-end caved in. The car bounced and swung like a hammock caught in a strong breeze, then it was still.

Bellina's arms stung in a thousand different places where the glass had landed, one cut just below her left elbow looked like it would need stitches. *No time for that*, she thought, *no time*. She felt arms around her, and she was lifted from the floor. It was Castros. Once she was standing, he began to brush any other shards from her hair and clothes.

'I'm alright, I'm alright! Stop fussing!' she said, pushing him gently away. He stood looking at her, a smile playing on his lips. 'What?'

'That's exactly what you mother used to say when I tried to help her.'

A rush of warmth went to her cheeks, and she found herself both annoyed and thrilled.

'I hate to disrupt the familial bonding, but we do have a bomb and a homicidal lunatic to stop,' Elvgren said, opening the carriage door.

'This in one of the rare occasions when I agree with you,' she replied.

They bustled out, and Bellina looked up at the Palace. The massive building looked to her like a tomb, and she shivered with foreboding. *Don't go in there!* a quaking voice shouted in her head. She fought it off and made her way towards the gate. Elvgren who had been by her side suddenly paused.

'For the Father's sake — what's wrong now?' she said.

Elvgren was pointing a trembling finger up at the rails. 'My … those are my parents,' he whispered.

Looking up, she saw Lord and Lady Lovitz dangling from spikes. Their bodies seemed to have been tanned, their skin the colour of old leather. Bellina felt her stomach lurch, and she ordered it to be still. She stepped towards Elvgren and took his still pointing finger in her hand.

'I know this is horrible. But if we don't move, we'll lose our chance to catch the bastards who did this,' she said.

Eyes losing their glazed quality, Elvgren nodded. 'Yes,' he said, voice thick with emotion. 'Let's get this fucker.'

Running now, they dashed up the steps and into the Palace, through the Hall of Remembrance with its painted ceiling depicting the history of the Estrian Empire and towards the doors to the throne room. Reaching them, Bellina and the others skidded to a stop. To left of the doors, the body of a man was slumped. For a heartbeat, her brain couldn't process who she was looking at. Then realisation clicked into place.

It was the Grand Multan. It was Kurkeshi.

Blood had leaked out of a wound in his chest and pooled around him like a crimson sea. His jewelled turban had been lost and a rolling sheet of raven black hair obscured his face. *Dead*, Bellina thought. Then he drew in a shuddering breath that forced a fresh gout of blood from his wound. He looked up and recognition dawned on his face.

'I'm sorry. I … I tried to stop them,' he wheezed. 'When I found out … I …I tried … s-sorry, so sorry.'

'What's happening here?' Bellina said, kneeling beside him. 'Where is the duke and Marmossa?'

'G-gone. They're gone … wanted to … to trap … you, make sure you … you died in the blast. He … he thought you were … nothing … insignificant … a tiny cog … but now … now he fears you,' Kurkeshi said then fell back into unconsciousness.

'Damn it to the Void,' Elvgren spat. 'So, it was a trap all along.'

'Forget it,' Castros said. 'We still need to do something about that bomb. Melek, let's go.'

Bellina hurried after them. 'Elvgren keep an eye on him. He could have a lot of valuable information.'

'What am I supposed to do? I'm not a medificer.'

'Just watch him!' Bellina shot back.

Her father and Melek had already entered the throne room. She rushed through the open doors and scanned the space beyond. Lit from behind by a massive glass window, Bellina took in the magnificent floor mosaic of the Empire, the platinum walls etched with swirls filled with tinted mercury and, finally, the throne.

The witch oak chair with its back carved in the shape of a soaring eagle looked old and weary. 'I've seen too many troubles,' it seemed to be saying. 'Let this bloody bomb on my lap go off, so I can get some peace.' Melek had rushed over to the bomb sitting upon the throne and was checking it over. On top of the cauldron-shaped explosive was an elegant clock piece steadily counting down. Bellina's pulse began to gallop like a racehorse. They only had a minute left.

'Surely, you can stop it,' Castros was saying.

'I … I don't know. I remember designing it to be powerful, mixing sortilenergy and yaksit, but nothing else,' the inventor whimpered.

'What if we threw it out the window?' Castros said.

'No good. You would have to take it hundreds of feet into the air to negate the force of the blast.'

Castros took a deep breath. 'Then that's what I'll do,' he said.

'What are you talking about?' Bellina said, her stomach solidifying into a lead weight. 'You can't do that. No, no, nonononono.'

Del Var crossed the room and took her by the shoulders. 'There's no time. I have to,' he said.

Bellina's lip trembled and a tear leaked from the corner of her eye. 'No,' she said. 'Please no.'

'I have to,' Castros repeated and walked towards the bomb. 'Stand back, Melek.'

'I'm sorry, Cass … I … I just …'

'Don't worry, old friend. This isn't your fault.'

Her legs gave way beneath her, and Bellina collapsed to the floor. What she was seeing took on the surreal quality of a dream. Castros lifting the bomb, moving to the window.

'You are a remarkable woman, just like your mother,' he said, tears glistening on his cheeks now. 'I'm so glad I got to know you both. Even if it was only for a little while. Keep your promises to everyone, Bellina. Make this world a better one, or there's no point in you saving it.'

'I will,' she whispered.

'Good girl.'

***

Castros took one last look at his daughter and gave a blast with his screamers. He went flying backwards out through the window. Almost immediately, the weight of the bomb tried to pull him downwards, and he let loose another gust of magically infused air. On and on he pumped until the device was emptied.

Have to start forcing it now, he thought and began to draw in huge, lung-swelling gulps of air which he quickly fused with his own life force to make sortilaero. Unleashing the air in one breath, he went higher and higher. Still, he kept going, wanting to be sure he was high enough. The veins in his body began to glow like amber lit by a sunbeam, and still, he kept going.

He cast a look at the bomb's timer. Three seconds left. Gods, he hoped he was high enough. In those last moments as he stood on threshold of death's door, he wished he'd had just a bit more time. Time to say all the things unsaid. Time to finish the unfinished plans. But it wasn't a bad way to go he supposed, saving his daughter … and a whole city.

'You would have been proud, Nairne,' he whispered.

And there she was beckoning him, the woman he had loved, the woman he had been too proud to chase after. She stood before a veil of shimmering stars, their light turning her hair into silver thread. She reached out her hand to him.

He took it.

***

In Dullet's Square, Cirona witnessed Castros' sacrifice by accident. She had been sweeping her gaze, keeping a general watch, when high above the Olphant Hill a ball of intense white light bloomed like the cap of a toadstool. It expanded till it seemed the size of a moon then collapsed in on itself faster than a bolt of lightning, making the sky ripple like a suspended pond.

Then everything went back to normal.

'What the fuck happened up there?' she murmured.

CHAPTER TWELVE

Cirona watched the rain pour down on a city that had almost been destroyed. No one was sure if the weather was because of the magical nature of the bomb, but one thing was for sure — the rain had fallen non-stop for the past two weeks. Sometimes it died down to a mournful drizzle, other times it whipped itself into a fury and fell in freezing, hammering sheets. Today it was somewhere in the middle.

The Free Army was still billeted in the city, and Cirona was in charge of them all. Deterring looting had been an impossible task, but she *had* stationed soldiers by every alehouse; the last thing they needed was liquored up troops fighting in the streets.

To keep them busy, she had put the soldiers to work removing the corpses, and the gods knew there were enough of them. The death count was growing every day, but it currently stood at around thirty thousand. Not all had been turned into nekrolytes, many were found, their throats neatly slit, in bed. The three tiny corpses Cirona had helped to move out of one house had caused her to take a moment to brush away her tears and curse the duke and Marmossa. Just the memory was enough to make her throat close up. She became dimly aware that someone was talking to her.

'What was that?' Cirona asked, turning to look at Dofri. He was standing next to her, close enough for her to feel the comfortable heat radiating off him. It was a sensation that made her heart flap like a moth's wings against a lampshade.

'I was just saying,' Dofri began, 'that it doesn't feel like we won.'

Cirona turned her gaze onto the street. They were approaching the market district, a place she associated with life and vitality, where wagons laden with goods would trundle along chased by dogs and small children hoping to snatch anything that fell off. Now the cobbled road, turned a shiny black by the rain, only bore carts of the dead. The hunger-bright eyes of a half-starved stray gleamed at her from an alley.

'No,' she finally replied. 'This isn't victory.'

With a quick flick of her wrists, she pulled the hood of her cloak

over her head. She nodded up the street towards their destination —
the market square. As they set off, the wind picked up and drove fat
raindrops into her face, stinging as they slapped against her chapped
skin. Leaning against what was fast becoming a gale they traipsed along
to the huge black tent in the square's centre.

The tent had been erected to home those soldiers who couldn't be
saved. Emperor Elvgren had insisted that the sick be housed in a wing
of the Imperial Palace, but the troops in the black tent were the ones
who were dying hard and distressing the others. Many had picked up
untreatable infections from being bitten by nekrolytes, a condition the
medificers had already named the widow's kiss. It began with the area
around the bite turning black and raised. After that, evil-looking black
tendrils spread out from the bite and began to strangle the major organs.
Then the screaming started, though screaming was too dull a word —
the men and women howled, wailed, tore chunks from their parched
lips. In the end, they choked on their own blackened blood.

As the hammered-down flaps of the tent grew closer, Cirona began
to feel lightheaded. *Don't go in there!* A hysterical voice raged in her head.
For the love of the gods, don't go in there! She paused, trying to catch the
breath that wanted to sprint from her body.

'You don't have to do this, General,' Dofri said, placing a hand upon
her arm. 'I can do the rounds today.'

She liked his hand there. It was large and scarred, calloused over the
tips of its fingers, but the touch was gentle, reassuring. 'I think I'll be
alright now,' she said, standing up straight. 'And how many times have I
told you to call me Cirona, Rona, even.'

'I just thought … around the other soldiers it might seem …odd.'

'You could be right,' Cirona said. 'Just do it in private then.' She
turned to look at Dofri who had turned a violent shade of red. 'I … oh
gods … I didn't mean,' she stammered, blushing herself now.

'Maybe we should, uh, just go inside,' Dofri said, still red but with a
smile raising the corners of his mouth. Cirona found she was smiling too.

As they opened the flap of the tent, any hints of those smiles were
evicted from their faces. Cirona was no stranger to death and its
accompanying stench, but nothing had prepared her for this. The stench
on the air was beyond rotten, putrid and mouldering; it resembled a
living thing creeping by the bedsides of the sick and stealing their life
away.

Looking at the dying men and women, Cirona began to reach for
Dofri's hand. She caught herself just in time. *Generals don't hold people's
hands*, she thought; *get a grip on yourself.* The medificer was at the far end

of the tent, a beaked mask — the nose stuffed with perfumed herbs — attached to his face. In the gloomy light, he seemed a spectre of death, a black-robed understudy doing the work the big man was too busy for. *Just what can he do for them when they're beyond even Waltus' skills?* she wondered. Pushing the thought aside, she made her way towards the man.

'How are things, medic?' Cirona asked.

'More are dying every day. There seems to be no set time limit on how long each will survive. I am beginning to think death would be a mercy,' he said.

'Keep trying, eh? Maybe some will pull through,' Dofri said.

'Perhaps … perhaps,' the medic replied, though his eyes said he knew the truth — none would make it.

'Is … is there anything I can do?' Cirona said.

'More morphium, that seems to ease their pain.'

'I'll see what I can do.'

Suddenly, she had to get out, out and away. Turning on her heel, it was all she could do to stop herself from running out of the tent. *All that pain and suffering and death*, she thought, *all of it bottled up in one place.* It felt to her then that if they were to chuck the sick out and throw away the tent, they would discover that the ground beneath it had turned black and maggot-ridden. Unable to hold it in, she turned to the side and threw up her breakfast.

'That all of it?' Dofri asked, placing a hand on her back.

'Yeah … yeah, I think so,' she replied.

'You look like you could do with a drink. Half an ale and a shot of firewater, isn't it?'

'It is,' Cirona said, a light crease in her brow. 'How did you know that?'

Dofri tugged at his ear. 'Must've heard you order it, I s'pose,' he said.

There's no way he heard me order a drink. He must've asked one of the others. The idea that he had been asking about her, about the things she liked, filled Cirona with a beautiful warmth.

Stop acting like a schoolgirl! a loud, scolding voice in the back of her head cried. *He's almost half your age — there's no way he's interested in you!*

I think he is, though, I really think he is, she thought.

'Let's go and get that drink then,' Cirona said, setting off.

Dofri nodded, and for a while, they walked in comfortable silence. Then he said, 'It … er … it would be good if I could stay on here as your aid. You know, not have to go back to Narvale.'

'Yes,' Cirona said, her grin growing wider. 'Yes, it would be good.'

The upper hall of the Imperial Palace was filled with a watery light, the only kind that could trickle through the clouds outside. *If only we'd kept some of the mages in the power plants*, Elvgren thought, *then we could have had a bloody bit of illumination around here*. Of course, that was an impossibility — Bellina and himself had signed the paper granting them freedom before the battle, and there was no turning back on it now — so he was forced to stalk the corridors of his new home, carrying a lantern filled with stinking garwhale oil.

Damn it. Damn it all! This wasn't what being an emperor was supposed to be like — stumbling about by the light of a dead sea creature, trying to find a corkscrew. There were supposed to be servants to fulfil his every whim, courtesans to flatter and praise him, and of course, a bevy of curvaceous mistresses. The problem was there were no people.

Marmossa and the duke had somehow spirited away over five hundred thousand of Victory's inhabitants, and reports from around the major cities of the Empire spoke of similar depopulation. The scholar had said the number of citizens taken could be as high as five million, though the purpose for this mass kidnapping remained a mystery to them all.

A smaller mystery — though it took up more of his thoughts — was Bellina's brushing aside of their drunken engagement. She had told him to forget it, and seeing as he remembered so little of it, this wasn't too hard. But for some reason, his mind kept drifting back to that night, the heat from their bodies, the tangled sheets. A lump formed in his throat. To hells with it, if that was how she wanted things, so be it — what did he care?

'Argh,' Elvgren cried.

He had stubbed his toe on the cast-iron leg of a small table that held a vase. While he hopped about, the vase rocked in ever increasing circles, paused for a beat as if it was unsure what to do, then tipped over, spilling water into Elvgren's left boot. Freezing, the water sent icy fingers up his ankle. Letting out a choked cry, the Emperor fell on his arse.

'Damn it,' he hissed. 'Damn it all to the fucking Void.'

This was supposed to be his crowning glory, a Lovitz at the top of the pile, and not just any Lovitz — him. Not one of his ancestors whose disapproving faces had stared down at him from the walls of his family home, not his mother, his father, or his brother, the grand and exalted Jeremias. He felt a sob choke his throat. Why? Why had they all had to go and die?

Forcing himself to his feet, Elvgren dried the tears that had sprung unbidden from his eyes. This was no way to be behaving. He would go down to the kitchen, find that blasted corkscrew and drink till he couldn't feel his face. Picking up his lantern, he walked down the servants' stairs.

The narrow, winding steps brought him to a dusty corridor. He shuffled along, wary now of any more mishaps in the gloom, looking at the name plaques on the door to either side of him. At last, his small sphere of light picked out the fading gilt letters that spelled out 'Kitchen'. Elvgren took the brass knob in his hand and turned.

Nothing happened.

His first instinct was to kick the blasted thing, but the dull throb coming from his toes talked him out of it. Now he was locked out of a room in his own palace! Well, didn't that just sum up the entire farce.

You're angry and acting like a child, a voice that sounded strangely like his mother's spoke up in his head. *If you weren't feeling so sorry for yourself, you might have remembered the key.*

The key, the master key. Of course! Why hadn't he thought of that earlier? The voice of his mother was about to chime in with her opinion on that, but he shut her down. He rummaged through his pockets, fingers tracing the shapes of everything but a key. Just when he was becoming convinced he had lost it, in a flash of inspiration, he remembered where he had put it — on a chain around his neck. With a sigh, he slipped it off and opened the door.

It swung back without so much as a creak. He entered the room and paused, letting his lantern illuminate his surroundings. Elvgren saw cupboards, ovens and all manner of strange utensils hanging overhead, but nothing that looked like a corkscrew. It struck him then that he could count the amount of times he had been in a kitchen on one hand, and he had no idea where to begin his search. Picking a counter with a drawer beneath it, he wandered over and opened it.

'Try the one to your left,' a voice called from behind him. Spinning round, pulse pounding, he saw Waltus lit up by the small light of his pipe, save for that he was cloaked in darkness. The old mage was sitting at the end of a huge table. Before him was a wedge of cheese and a flagon of ale. 'Go on,' Waltus continued, 'try the left one.'

Elvgren did as he was told and soon felt his fingers curl around the corkscrew. 'How did you know—' he began.

'Because you pinched that bottle of Pevontess red I had my eye on, so I hid all the corkscrews but that one. Knew you'd have to come looking for it sooner or later,' Waltus said, his eyes twinkling.

There was something about the White Mage that Elvgren found disconcerting. It was time to beat a hasty retreat. 'Great prank, old chap, first class. Well, I've … er … got what I came for, so I'll leave you to … whatever it is you're doing.'

'Bugger that,' Waltus said. 'Grab a cup and sit down. I've done enough drinking alone to last two lifetimes.'

Elvgren's eyes flicked from the door he had just come through to the mage. His stomach sank; the last thing he wanted to do was waste his evening talking to the old fart, but he supposed it was best to keep him onside. With thoughts of the exquisitely comfortable couch in his room and the Pevontess red banished from his mind, Elvgren took a cup and a chair and sat down.

For a long while Waltus just stared at him, the bowl of his pipe glowing amber. Elvgren licked his lips. 'Is … er … something the matter?'

'For the longest time, I've been trying to work out who you remind me of and now I've got it — Excellus. He had the same mix of brilliance, stupidity and narcissism.'

Choking on the sip of ale he'd just taken, Elvgren cleared his throat and said, 'You knew Excellus? But the mage wars were over five hundred years ago! Just how old are you?'

Waltus gave a dry chuckle. 'I'm old, boy, very old. I remember when he made himself Emperor. It was like the ground was welling up with energy, an energy he was summoning, and I felt, if we just tagged along for the ride, we'd arrive at something wonderful.'

'That didn't work out too well for your lot, did it?' Elvgren said.

'Nah, nah it didn't. I was with him when we had this city under siege. Back then it seemed like it was only a matter of time till we won. Then it turned. Magic has no effect on the walls of this city. A clever bastard by the name of Astus Colt realised it was because of a mineral in the stone, what's now called tharg's bane. With that your warriors could fight back, even capture us. And once you'd captured some of us, we all know where that led. We set out to enslave the world and wound up in chains, how's that for irony?' Waltus took a huge swig from his mug. 'Seen a lotta bad shit in my time, but the dead used as weapons, creatures pulled outta the fucking Void and a sickness even my magic can't touch, that's something else, that's some dark, dark power at work.'

A shiver ran through Elvgren and his fingers trembled against the cup he held. It wasn't just Waltus' words, no, it was something in the mage's eyes — fear. And if he was scared …

'Ah, enough of this old man's prattling,' the old mage said, draining his mug and getting to his feet. 'I'll leave yer to enjoy the last of the ale and that wine.'

Before he could go, the door swung open and a soldier barrelled in.

'Sorry, Your Majesty, thank the gods I found you, there's … there's …'

'Spit it out man,' Elvgren commanded.

'There's someone at the gate. He wants to speak—'

The soldier was cut off as a rangy-looking man pushed past him. Elvgren's eye grew wide, his jaw hanging open like a broken gate. Despite the thick beard and haggard lines, he knew that face. It was the face that had stared down at him from a portrait in the study of his home all his life.

'Brother?' he whispered.

***

Bellina looked down at the documents spread before her. Each one was heavy with doom and death. She bit her lip then stared across the table at Whist. She couldn't help but marvel at how fast he had dispatched agents to the other countries in the Empire, and it was the reports from those men and women that lay before her now. She looked at him for a long time, trying to figure out what to say, his face a study in calm, his eyes assessing.

'Are … are you sure these reports aren't … exaggerations?' Bellina asked.

'Quite sure, Your Majesty,' Whist replied.

She slammed a fist on the table. 'Those bastards,' she spat, 'those utter bastards. They'll pay for this.'

Whist leaned forwards. 'With all due respect, Your Majesty, threats of vengeance will not help anyone. The capital cities of Tremore, Escambria and Sylvantain have been stripped of people and resources. Pevontess, Narvale and Gortrix escaped the worst of the plundering, but many of their food stores have been tainted or destroyed.' He paused and took a deep breath, as if what he was about to say pained him to the core. 'Revenge for the dead will not feed the living.'

'What would you have me do?' she said, a hint of pleading in her voice.

'I would have you do what your father would have done — lead.'

Leaning back in her chair, Bellina rubbed at her temples, the blood rushing through them so fast it sounded like a gale was raging in her skull. And wasn't that what was happening? The fury inside her had evolved into a living thing that prowled her body, pawing at her heart and mind, stirring her thoughts into a maelstrom of incoherent nonsense.

She took a deep breath. *Think of the people*, a voice whispered to her, a voice that sounded like Castros, *think of your people*. But when she did, all she could see were the nekrolytes rushing towards her and her father shrinking to a dot as he gave his life to save the city. *I didn't save this city so you could sit about angst-ridden. Remember what I asked you to do — make this world better.*

Sitting up straight, Bellina said, 'I want emergency centres set up in every town and city. Use the army to gather all food into a central trust, and we'll distribute it from there. I also want administrators from the least affected countries to lead councils in the worst — the people must see that order prevails.'

Whist leaned back and a smile played across his lips. It was the smile of a teacher who has been waiting for their student to learn a correct spelling. 'Very well, Your Majesty,' he said. 'It shall be done.' He stood up and crossed to the door, as he reached for the handle, he added, 'He … they were great men. I'm sorry you didn't get to know Cass better.'

Bellina nodded. As soon as she saw the door had shut, she laid her head upon the table. From the corner of her eye she could make out the word "dead" underlined on one of the documents. She stared at it, willing it to say something different, for the letters to swirl together then change.

It didn't.

The rage-driven beast inside her began to wake up from the temporary sedation she had given it and shot her to her feet so quickly the chair she was sat on fell to the floor with a sharp rattle. She looked around the room, the room she had taken over as her private study for the past two weeks, with hate-filled eyes. The table, the bookcase, the rug, even the bed she'd put in because she fell asleep there so often — it all had the look of a tomb to it.

She walked over to the rain-smeared window and placed her cheek against the glass. Gods but she was sick of death, sick of people saying how sorry they were for her, sick of the pitying stares. Part of her wanted to climb onto the Palace roof and scream that she was still here, that she was alive and that counted for something too, to perform an act of defiance, an act of living, in this city choked by death.

There was a knock at the door and her heart sank.

'Come in,' she said with a sigh, turning to see Holger come through the door.

'Evening, Belle,' he said. 'Waltus sent me to tell you that Kurkeshi is going to make it. He reckons we'll be able to talk to him soon.'

'Good,' Bellina replied.

Holger stood in the door, chewing his lip. 'I—' he began.

'Stop,' Bellina interrupted. 'If you're about to offer your condolences or any such blather, please don't.'

'I wasn't,' Holger protested. 'I was just going to say you're looking well … all things considered.'

For a moment, Bellina just gawped at him. Then she threw back her head and laughed for the first time in weeks. *Looking good,* she thought. *I look like a complete wreck.* And this was true — dark circles the colour of overripe plums sat beneath her eyes, her hair was a tangled mess and she had lost several pounds, taking her from thin to gaunt. A wave of dizziness struck her, and she grabbed for the table.

'Are you alright,' Holger asked, rushing to her side.

He placed his hand over hers, and Bellina felt a jolt sear up her arm making her skin break out in goosebumps. The jolt didn't seem to stop there. It coursed into her body making every atom of her being dance, making her heart hum like a bee's wings, making her feel … alive.

Without warning, she reached out, grabbed Holger's face and planted a kiss on his lips. He tried to pull back, but she wouldn't let him. It only took a second for him to give in, to return the kiss with the same amount of passion, no, even more. Her hands had taken on a mind of their own and were now pulling up his shirt, stroking his neck and chest.

'Belle, I—'

'No,' she hissed. 'Don't say anything.'

With that she led him to the bed.

***

Scholar Fontaine put down his pen and stared out the window. The massive panes in the Palace library offered a glimpse at a sliver of moon giving a bashful peek from behind a rain-bloated cloud. The unseen hand of the wind gave a gentle tug at the cloud's wispy edge and it was gone. He rubbed at his eyes and left smears of ink on his cheeks.

He looked down at the *Radiana*, open on the desk, and it seemed that a chuckle rose from the cracked and ancient spine of the book. *You won't solve me.* It laughed. *Uh-uh not you, not in a million years. And you don't have that kind of time do you, scholar? No. For you, the grains in the hourglass are rushing to the bottom.* Fontaine almost hit the book. Swallowing his anger, he had to content himself with just pushing it away.

A groan escaped his lips, and he shook his head like a dog getting out of a river. He knew that the secret to Marmossa's plans was locked away in the book, knew he was close to prying out the information like pulling a limpet from its shell, but the final answers kept slipping through his fingers. *Pull yourself together, Laluc!* The voice of his mother sounded in his mind. *I didn't work my fingers to the bone to pay for your schooling so you could give up when you're needed the most.*

'I'm not giving up, Ma-ma.' He sighed into the dusty room. 'Giving up in this situation is not an option.'

And wasn't that the truth, Father be praised. Surrender before the *Radiana* was unthinkable, but what was he supposed to do? Sit staring at it and hope the solutions reached out and slapped him round the face? Maybe there would be some forgotten tome that could help him hidden in the library. Gods knew the place was big enough.

Climbing to his feet he felt his knees pop and a sullen flare of pain rush from his arse and lower back. *Good grief,* he thought, *I've got the ailments of an old man!* Though he supposed this was the physical toll for a lifetime spent poring over the dry, crackling pages of obscure books. *Whoever said men of learning had it easy?* Taking his lantern, he set off into the corridors of bookcases.

He hadn't got far when he heard footsteps. Stopping, he looked around, shining his light around him as his ears strained to detect any new sound. Silence. *Must be the floorboards coming to rest or some such thing,* he thought, *nothing to worry about.* His brain scanned this idea and decided that, yes, that was the most sensible answer, but still, his heart pounded in his chest like a piston.

Licking his lips, he took a tentative step forwards. He froze … there it was again, and this time hadn't he seen a shadow scuttle past out of the corner of his eye. Goosebumps broke out on his skin then began to throb. *You've been through worse than this,* he told himself; *you survived the trial in Timboko!*

Mustering his courage, he called, 'Wh-who's there?'

The question didn't receive an answer, the words just hanging in the still, musty air like the cry of a phantom. Then from behind him, he heard the dull thump of something falling to the floor and a curse. While his nerve still held, he rushed round the corner. And saw the progenitor of the footsteps.

'It's you!' he cried. 'Daigo, isn't it?'

'It's Dargo,' the boy said, rubbing his foot. Then he murmured, 'Why couldn't it have fell on me automaton leg?'

Fontaine ignored this last bit and said, 'What the in the twelve hells are you doing here?'

'What d'ya think?' Dargo replied in the tones of someone talking to a simpleton. 'I'm looking for a sodding book to read.'

'You can read?' Fontaine said. 'I didn't think your … people like—'

'A street rat? A gutter dweller? Is that what you mean? And yes, I can read thank you very fucking much! Maybe not as fast as most people, but I can get by.'

Fontaine ran a hand through his hair. 'I'm sorry. I didn't mean to insult you. But it is unusual, isn't it?'

'Dunno. S'pose so. Just kinda picked it up as I went along.'

Picked it up as he went along? Fontaine thought. *Why, that's close to a miracle.* He looked Dargo up and down then, really seeing him for the first time, saw the boy's hungry face and the shrewd, assessing eyes. Street rat or no, the young man before him was a clever operator and no mistake, just what would he have become if he'd had the opportunity to study?

'What you looking at me like that for?' Dargo said. 'You a pervert or something?'

'What? Ah, no … I was just thinking that teaching yourself to read is a remarkable achievement.'

'Yeah, I'm pretty damned amazing,' Dargo replied, giving his first smile. 'You're an egghead, ain't ya? You must know a good book to read.'

The scholar smiled back. 'Story books are in the fiction section across there,' he said, pointing to a row of shelves past his table. 'I recommend *Haltrop's Peril*. It's a first-rate adventure.'

'Is there lots of battles in it?' Dargo asked with a sniff.

'Tonnes of them,' Fontaine answered.

'Good stuff.'

Dargo set off towards the fiction books, and Fontaine watched him wistfully. *Ah, to be a boy again*, he thought, then turned away and began scanning the titles of the books in front of him.

'This that *Radiana* thing you working on?' Dargo called.

'Yes,' Fontaine replied, still looking at the spines of the books. 'Please don't touch it.'

'How come the writing on the page is all over the place?'

The scholar sighed. 'The *Radiana* is a riddle. Some of it is written in prose, some like poetry. Now would you please leave it be?'

'Alright, alright keep yer hair on. Just that some of it looks like a pattern.'

'A pattern?' Fontaine said, straightening up. 'How do you mean?'

'Well, say you tore this page out an put it …'

A dry rasping sound like the skin of a mummy cracking filled the air. Fontaine felt as if a block of lead had fallen on his chest. *No*, he thought, *he couldn't have done. No one in their right mind would …* But there was Dargo, two torn pages from the *Radiana* in his hands. The boy was twisting and turning them.

'What have you done!' the scholar shrieked, running towards Dargo.

'They do form a pattern,' Dargo said, ignoring the insane squeaks Fontaine was emitting. 'Just look will yer?'

Then he saw it. The boy was right. The torn-out pages really did form a new set of text if you placed them in the right position. 'Do you have a knife?' he asked.

'Here ye go,' Dargo said, handing him a spiteful-looking dagger.

Tongue poking from the corner of his mouth, Fontaine carefully began to free the pages from the books binding. They came away with an easy sigh, as if they knew they'd finally be taking on their true form.

Once all the pages were free, he looked up and said, 'Don't just stand there — help me, boy!'

'Oh, now I'm allowed to touch your precious book, am I? Well, it's a good job I'm the forgiving sort.'

They worked quickly. A fever of understanding was coursing through the scholar's veins, setting alight his mind and body as it all came together. How much time passed, Fontaine would not have been able to say, but eventually, they stood looking down at the *Radiana Magnifica* in its complete glory.

'Will this be able to help us?' Dargo asked.

Fontaine pulled him into a bear hug. 'Help? Help! This is the key to it all! You're a genius, boy. You cracked the last riddle, a riddle the makers of the book knew no scholar would ever think to do!'

'Really?' Dargo said. 'What was that then?'

'Tear it apart!'

<h1 style="text-align:center">CHAPTER THIRTEEN</h1>

Bellina awoke with the tentative light of another rain-soaked morning creeping through her window. She looked across expecting to see Holger, but he was gone. Much to her surprise, she felt relief flood through her. What had she been thinking? Thank the gods he'd had the good sense to leave — what if someone had found him here?

She sat up, feeling sore and sticky down below. Last night's act of lovemaking flashed through her mind. Hadn't it felt good while he was inside her? Hadn't it felt right? It had, so why did she now feel so hollow and alone? After they were done, Holger had held her and, his eyes shining with unwept tears, told Bellina he loved her. She had searched her feelings and found she could not say it back — as her grandfather had said, a half-truth was a lie in the making. Instead, she had kissed his lips, as much to stifle a horrified moan that was building in her throat than anything else.

What now? she thought. *Do I pretend it never happened? Do I make him my lover, luring him to my bed whenever I'm feeling out of sorts? Could I keep using him like that?* Because using was what it had been. Oh, he had been more than willing, that wasn't in doubt, but she had instigated it. The rage, fury and bitterness that had pushed her to the act was gone. All she felt now was confused … confused and a little ashamed.

There was a knock on her door, and Bellina was pulled out of her thoughts.

'Yes?' she cried, trying her best to sound regal.

'I bring news, Your Majesty,' a guard's voice called. 'The mage known as Waltus says the Burkeshi is awake.'

'I shall be down shortly,' she said.

'Very good, Your Majesty.'

Dressing quickly, she took one look in the mirror on her table. Her hair had grown long. Lately, she had taken to pinning it up and out of her way, but today, she let it hang loose. If Bellina had been able she would have liked to cover he face with it, certain as she was that something in her eyes would betray her night of passion. Satisfied as she could be, she left the room.

Approaching the sweeping staircase to the ground floor, she saw Elvgren. He smiled at her, and she felt icy fingers curl round her heart, forbidding it to beat. *He knows*, she thought with horror. *I don't know how but he knows.* She waited with bated breath for the accusations to fly from his mouth like black arrows aimed at her chest. Instead, he offered her his arm.

'My beloved,' he said, the smile growing larger on his lips.

Stunned, she was about to take the offered arm when a small voice in her head said, *Act normal!*

'I am more than capable of walking down the stairs on my own,' she said.

Despite the reproach, he laughed. 'Very well, *darling*,' he drawled, and they began to descend. 'You look better,' he continued. 'More alive somehow.'

Bellina flushed. 'And since when have you cared for my wellbeing?'

Elvgren stopped then and took hold of her elbow. 'Maybe I didn't at first,' he said, his one good eye flaming. 'But after everything we've been through, everything we've endured, I wouldn't be human if I hadn't grown to lo— if I hadn't grown to care for you deeply.'

The flush in her cheeks deepened till it felt like she was hiding two smouldering coals in them. 'Fine,' she said at last. 'It was a quip and nothing more. Now, would you please let go of my arm?'

He did, and they carried on down the rest of the stairs in silence, a silence that grew and grew, ballooning out, catching them in a frigid bubble.

'Where's Dargo?' she asked, desperate to pop their trap.

'I've given him the run of the Palace. Apparently, he's a genius now, a rare one-in-a-million type according to the scholar … Are we sure Fontaine is sound of mind?'

Unable to stop herself, she smiled. 'If he *were*, do you think he would have got involved in all this madness?'

'Perhaps you're right.'

'I hear your brother has come back from the dead?'

'Yes,' was all he said in response.

'Where has he been?'

'Not the foggiest. He asked for a room, went to bed and then holed himself up in the library with Fontaine and Whist.' Elvgren paused, brows furrowed, jaw clenched tight. 'The Lovitz family are not known for grand emotional displays, but by the Father, he hasn't seen me since I was three years old, a small chat wouldn't have been too much to ask, would it?'

'No,' she said softly, 'no it wouldn't.'

Silence fell over them again, and Bellina watched Elvgren withdraw into himself like frost retreating before the morning light. She felt a strong urge to comfort him, to hold him. He had suffered, they both had, and shouldn't that be something to pull them together? *You don't deserve to hold him*, a voice hissed in her head. *Were you thinking of his suffering last night when you took another man into your bed?* She bit her cheek using the pain to banish the voice from her head. Then she slipped her arm in his.

Elvgren looked shocked, then his face broke into a grin again. 'And what is this in aid of?' he said.

'We are about to entertain our first foreign leader as Emperor and Empress. I think we should show a united front, don't you?'

Laughing, Elvgren said, 'He might find our hospitality a bit wanting. I wonder how he feels about turnip soup for dinner? Though, I'm sure we can find a piece of salted meat the rats haven't got at too badly.'

Bellina began to laugh too. 'What a ditz I've been! I've forgotten to sort out any entertainment,' she said.

'Don't worry, my love,' Elvgren replied. 'We can always get Barboza to perform one of his infamous one-man plays.'

At this, she roared with laughter, they both did, bent double, tears streaming down their faces. When she finally managed to control herself, Bellina wiped her eyes and saw a guard staring at them.

'Carry on,' she said, giving him a curt nod. As soon as he was gone, another fit of giggles struck her.

'Gods!' she said. 'Are we evil to be laughing in times like these?'

'No,' Elvgren replied. 'To laugh is to live, and I'll be damned if I'll apologise for that.'

Bellina smiled. 'That was almost poetic.'

'I am poetic,' Elvgren said, puffing out his chest. 'You've just never noticed.'

'Come on then, oh great bard, we'd better get moving or Waltus will have kittens.'

They carried on through the corridors of the Palace, and by the time they had reached the room Kurkeshi was being treated in, they had managed to control themselves. The guard at the door gave a salute then opened it.

The first thing that struck Bellina as she entered was the smell. It wasn't the smell of decay, though that was faintly present, but a strong, acrid scent, as if someone had managed to set fire to the very air. It was the smell she remembered from when Waltus had healed her. Bellina fought the urge to cover her mouth and nose … and only just won. The room itself was lit by a thin sliver of light stealing through the gap in some heavy curtains, illuminating a large bed and an even larger man upon it.

Grand Multan Kurkeshi, ruler of almost half the Eastern Continent, looked as if he had been through all twelve hells and back again. His broad face was covered in a thicket of beard that was rapidly turning to grey, his hair, loose from its turban and flowing over his shoulders, was following suit. Around him, the covers had bunched at his middle, revealing his upper body and the masses of bandages applied to his wounds. *Gods*, Bellina thought, *he looks like he's aged fifty years since we saw him last.* To his side was Waltus, the old mage sprinkling loose tobacco into a rolling paper.

'Is he ready to talk?' Elvgren asked.

'You can try,' Waltus replied, licking and sealing his cigarette.

Elvgren nodded and said, 'Grand Multan, we would speak with you.'

At this, Kurkeshi's eyes flickered open. For a moment, he regarded them, his eyes fever bright and staring from cavernous sockets. He went to sit up straighter, but a spasm of pain wracked his body and he gave up. Bellina and Elvgren waited while his rapid, torturous breathing settled back down to slow, shallow heaves.

'I … I would speak with you as well, Your Majesties … but I cannot,' he finally said.

'What do you mean? What does he mean?' Elvgren spluttered, his head swivelling between the injured Burkeshi and Waltus.

It was Kurkeshi who answered. 'Marmossa he … he has done something to my mind. I would gladly tell you of his plans, no, his madness, but it is like a door closes in my mind when I try.'

'He's telling the truth,' Waltus added, breathing out a stream of dirty yellow smoke. 'I thought you might be able to do something, Your Majesty.'

'Me?' Bellina said. 'But if it's Marmossa who's done this, I might not be able to …'

'It's worth a try isn't it?' Elvgren said.

For a handful of moments, all was silence, the only sounds Kurkeshi's laboured breath and Waltus puffing his cigarette.

'Fine,' Bellina said, at last. 'I will try, but I promise nothing. Do you consent to me entering your mind?'

'If it removes the poison I can feel sitting in there, I welcome it,' the Grand Multan replied.

'Very well,' Bellina replied, pressing a button on her control conduit.

'I shall begin now.' She closed her eyes, focused her will and felt the pop as she established a cognopathic connection.

*

She found herself in a desert, the sky above her black and pitted with a million baleful stars, each one emitting a sickly smear of yellow light. They began to wink out one by one. The ground began first to shift and slip then vibrate hard enough to shake her bones. Desperately, she tried to establish her own psychic landscape, but with panic choking her throat, she could not. A crack formed in the sand ahead of her, growing and growing, seeming to swallow all around it. Then the tentacles appeared.

The arms slithered out, glassy, obsidian. Bellina had never seen anything so black in her life. It was as if the thing had been constructed out of the darkest corner of the universe, a place that had never seen the light of life. As the tentacles gripped the ground with a sucking squelch, a body began to crawl from the crack. It had the form of a mutated squid, its elongated core covered in luminous, green eyes. *This is one of the hells,* she thought. *Marmossa laid some trap, I know not how, and he's pulled me into a hell.*

No, a quiet but sensible voice spoke back, *this isn't a hell. It's nothing more than one of the decrepit old bastard's tricks. Stay calm and see through it.*

She knew the voice spoke true, felt it was true, and she took a deep breath. It drew a cover over her fear … but only a thin one, the type that could be torn with one rough yank. Heart pounding, she forced herself to look at the monstrosity.

'Do you like what you see, Bellina Ressa,' a voice called from the direction of the abnormality. 'Do you like my true form? The form that was old when the universe was young?'

'Marmossa,' Bellina hissed. 'I think the form reflects the filth and poison that you truly are.'

Laughter filled the air, and the creature shook with a hideous, rippling force that stopped as abruptly as it began. 'You are prying here, Bellina Ressa, prying, my little cog. You would know of my plans, of my secrets, but I cannot allow that.'

The tentacles lashed out at her, making a sound like a thousand whips snapping in chorus. She used her powers to soar out of their reach.

'Do not defy me, my little cog — you will only make it worse,' the Marmossa-thing said.

Bellina ignored him, her mind whirring as she tried to come up with a plan of attack. She tried to form a sand warrior as she had once done in the mind of Alcastus, put the landscape was dead to her powers, to her will. Looking down at the thrashing arms of the Marmossa-thing, her chin trembling a fraction, her stomach a ball of leaden ice, she felt as if all hope was going to desert her.

But then she saw something. It was a small point of light buried beneath the monstrosity's body, shimmering, faltering like the flame of a candle caught in a draught.

Help me, the light called to her in the voice of a child. *Use me — you'll need me to beat him — but please help me.*

Then, not really understanding fully what she was doing, Bellina stretched out her hand towards the trembling point of brightness and willed it towards her.

'Stop that! Stop that at once!' the Marmossa-thing cried.

But his voice had now become far away and unimportant. All that mattered was drawing the light towards her. And it was coming, coming in a thin strand like the finest thread of web ever spun. Then it was in her grasp, and she was giving it a form, the form of a weapon, the form of Barboza's spear, and with a mighty heave, she sent it plunging into one of the creature's twitching, scum-crusted eyes. With a single shriek of outraged pain, the creature shrivelled back into the crack from whence it came, the fissure sealing itself shut behind it. The spear lay on the sand, and Bellina drifted down towards it. She bent to retrieve it.

Your job is not done yet, it said. *You have cleansed most of Marmossa's poison but not all. He scarred me first when I was young and that scar runs deep and long. Help me, Bellina Ressa; save the man I will grow up to be.*

With that the spear shattered into a million glittering pieces, pieces that caught on the breeze for a moment then were gone. Bellina looked up and gave a start. The desert was empty no more. A building stood in front of her, one she recognised. It may have been a lot smaller, but the core building was the same. She was now looking at the Multanial palace.

Walking towards it, she saw a square fountain, its base picked out in a mosaic of dazzling, turquoise pieces. It was a beautiful feature except that no water ran within it. As Bellina drew closer still, she heard the sound of children giggling, a sound as soft and pure as fresh, dawn light on a summer's morn. Inside the dry, sand-filled fountain, she saw a boy and girl no older than six.

'There,' the boy said. 'Cook will never think to look for his favourite ladle here!'

'Keshi, don't,' the girl said, holding her hand over her mouth in a futile attempt to stop her laughter.

'He should have thought of that before he whacked your hand with it, Jeela,' Keshi said.

'We *were* trying to steal cake,' Jeela replied.

'That's not the point—' the boy began.

'Jeela!' a serving woman called from the palace door. 'Come and help your poor mother. Prince Kurkeshi, your lessons are due to start. Come now, the pair of you, chop-chop!'

Prince Kurkeshi let out a long groan. 'Not lessons.'

'You could switch with me if you like,' Jeela said, standing and brushing the sand from her knees. 'I'm to help mother scour the ovens today.'

'Really, Jeela? You would do this?' Kurkeshi asked.

Jeela laughed. 'No. You must learn, become clever and be Multan one day. You need your lessons.'

'I don't want to be Multan,' Kurkeshi whined.

'Stop being silly. If you don't become Multan, who will look after everybody when we grow up?' Jeela gave him a peck on his cheek then ran to her mother's side, leaving Kurkeshi in the sand. After a moment, he too stood, dusted himself down then walked towards the palace.

Bellina trailed behind him, an unseen spectre as they entered the building. She followed him through the shaded corridors of the palace, wondering at its lack of splendour. When they came to the throne room, she heard voices. The young prince heard too and came to a stop, peeking into the room beyond. Within it, a haggard-looking man was addressing another sat upon a throne.

'Your Majesty, the reservoirs are at their lowest in living memory; we must act,' the haggard man said.

'And what would you have me do, Ehmed?' the Multan replied.

'Enter the tomb, open the vault and use the power of the black gem,' Ehmed replied, setting his shoulders back despite the tremor in his voice.

'No,' the Multan replied. 'That I will never do.'

Ehmed emitted a frustrated squawk, turned sharply on his heel and headed for the door. Kurkeshi pressed himself against the wall. Even though she could not be seen, Bellina did the same. The haggard man stalked past them without a second look, all the while muttering under his breath. The prince let out a sigh and was about to walk off when a voice hailed him.

'I know you are listening, son, come in and let me see your face,' the Multan called.

Kurkeshi licked his lips then entered the throne room. 'Forgive me,

Father,' he said, 'I did not mean to pry.'

'But pry you did,' the Multan replied. He rubbed his hands over his face. 'Never mind, come, sit upon your father's knee before you grow too big for it.'

Smiling, Kurkeshi ran to his father and leapt into his lap.

'Is what Vizier Ehmed said true?' the boy asked. 'Could the black gem make it rain?'

The Multan looked towards the ceiling stroking his beard. 'Perhaps,' he said. 'But artefacts such as that are fragments of a forgotten world, and it is best that they stay just that — forgotten. Our family was not entrusted with the gem to use it; we are the guardians who stop those foolish enough to try. Does that slake some of your curiosity?'

'Yes, Father,' Kurkeshi replied.

'Then give me a kiss and be on your way. You're already late for your lessons.'

The young prince did as he was told and ran from the room. Bellina went to follow him, but as she did, the world around her turned into billowing smoke. The plumes danced, curling, sinuous, before returning to something solid.

To her surprise, she was still in the throne room, though Kurkeshi's father had changed, shrunken inwards as if some vital part of him had died.

'You wanted to see me, Father?' Kurkeshi called from the door. He too was older, perhaps ten or eleven.

'I-I have some bad news, son,' the Multan said.

'What is it, Father?' the boy asked, moving towards the throne.

'Jeela … she … she drank tainted water and … and has died.'

'No,' Kurkeshi said, chin trembling, 'This cannot be.'

'I'm sorry, son, there was nothing anyone could have—'

'Don't lie!' Kurkeshi bellowed. 'There is something you could have done, and the key to it lies round your neck! Jeela is dead, dead! All because you are a coward!'

Once more, the young prince sprinted from the room, and once more, the world shifted in gusts of smoke. The scene that formed showed a bedroom. Upon a canopied bed lay what looked like a skeleton, skin the thickness of paper stretched over its bones. Kneeling, with one withered hand in his grasp, was Kurkeshi, now a man of about twenty. On the other side of the bed, stood a kaffar feeling for a pulse.

'He has returned to the Mother's embrace,' the kaffar said, laying the hand gently upon the covers.

'Yes,' Kurkeshi said, his voice thick. 'He has.'

'I will leave for now but return for the funeral preparations,' the kaffar said, crossing to a door.

'Thank you, honoured grandfather,' Kurkeshi replied. Even when the door closed and the kaffar left, he never took his eyes from the dead Multan. 'I love you, Father, love you from the depths of my heart, but I will not repeat your mistakes, I will not see my people suffer.'

He stood. Then bent over his father. Kurkeshi planted a single kiss on the man's brow before reaching for a chain about the corpse's neck. It came away with a sigh, and Bellina saw there was a small key hanging from the end of it. She turned to follow the new Multan, and the scene blew apart in a whirl of smoke.

When things pulled themselves together once more, Bellina found herself in a cave. Behind her rose a series of steps hewn from the rock itself. In front of her was a vast metal door, swirling letters and glyphs played upon its surface. Kurkeshi stood at the centre of it, the key outstretched in his hand. A feeling of deep foreboding filled her then, and she wanted to cry out, to stop whatever madness was about to take place. But she knew her voice would go unheard. From the look of focused obsession on Kurkeshi's face, she was certain she would have had no power to stop him even if she had *really* been there. Without so much as a pause, he slipped the key into the lock. The sound of countless unseen gears and bolts filled the air with a tinny chatter. The doors opened and he advanced.

The space beyond was nothing more than a bare cavern of reddish stone. In its centre, upon a pedestal of marble, sat the largest gemstone Bellina had ever seen. The light from Kurkeshi's torch fell full on it, but there was no flash, no glimmer. It was as if the stone sucked the light into it, and she knew then what was contained within the rock — Marmossa.

'Come closer, boy,' Marmossa's disembodied voice called. 'Let me see the one brave enough to use my strength.'

'I am Multan Kurkeshi, thirty-fourth of my line,' Kurkeshi said, stepping forwards.

'Yes, yes … I see now. And what would you ask of me, Multan Kurkeshi, thirty-fourth of his line.'

Kurkeshi replied with a single word, 'Rain.'

'Hmm, a tricky proposition but not one outside of my powers. But what will you give in return, Multan Kurkeshi?'

'Anything I have to give is yours,' he said, not so much as a tremor in his voice. Despite herself, Bellina admired his determination.

'Then come, lay your brow against my prison and release me.'

Kurkeshi walked towards the pedestal and placed his forehead against the stone. While Bellina watched, it looked to her as if the gem was sucking something out of Kurkeshi. But whatever was happening, it was over in an instant. A loud splintering sound tore through the air as the stone cracked and what looked like a floating handful of black sand came out.

'You have done well, Multan Kurkeshi, thirty-fourth of his line. Look for my coming two moons hence. I shall wear the body of an old kaffar, and I shall bring the rain.'

With that both Kurkeshi and the essence of Marmossa vanished, and Bellina found herself alone. Why the hells was she still here? A faint noise came to her then. She furrowed her brow. Was she imagining things? No, there it was again. Focusing all her attention upon her ears, Bellina listened. The breath caught in her throat. It was a scream, and it was coming from the stone.

She crossed towards it and peered into the massive gem. For a long time, all she saw was darkness, then deep within its rotten heart, she saw a face, the face of Kurkeshi screaming. Without thinking, she grabbed the stone — even as just a memory it felt sick and alive — and dashed it against the cavern wall. When it shattered an anguished howl filled the air.

'No!' the voice of Marmossa screamed. 'He is mine! Mine!'

'Not anymore he's not,' Bellina replied, grinding a piece of the stone beneath her heel.

The psychic world came apart then, and she was pushed back to reality.

*

Bellina came back to herself with the pop of psychic disconnection ringing in her ears. She looked at Kurkeshi and saw tears streaming down his face.

'Thank you,' he whispered.

'You're welcome,' Bellina replied. 'Now, I think it's time that you talked. That we all talked, so we can put the pieces together. It's time we held a quorum.'

***

Elvgren looked around the Palace of Administration's assembly room and felt a swooping loss course through him. The furnishings were still the same. The long, rectangular ministers' table backed by three large latticed windows. The semi-circular delegates' table, its surface scuffed and scratched by thumping fists in the heat of debate. Yes, the physical things were the same, but something intangible had been lost, as if the soul of the Empire had been sucked out.

He was sat, in pride of place, next to Bellina in the middle of the ministers' table. Gestaffen sat on Bellina's left while Barboza was on Elvgren's right. A pale and sunken Kurkeshi made up the last at their table. Across from them, occupying the delegates' table was Torkwill, Yevad, Holger, Melek, Cirona, Dofri, Waltus, Khasal and Dargo. Spaces had also been left for Whist, Fontaine and Jeremias.

The thought of his brother stirred a stew of emotions in Elvgren's stomach. A part of him he didn't want to recognise felt a dumb joy at Jeremias' return, like a dog who sees its absentee master walk through the front door. A larger part of him was desperate to know where his brother had been and what he had been doing, but the largest part felt a red, seething anger — how could he have left, left him alone with mother and father, left him to bear the weight of their expectations? The doors to the room opened. Jeremias led in Whist and Fontaine, and Elvgren pushed the feelings as far down as he could crush them.

'I thought your brother would be in his thirties,' Bellina whispered into Elvgren's ear.

'He should be, yes,' Elvgren replied

'Then why does he look closer to fifty?'

Even though the sunlight streaming through the windows was weak, Elvgren managed to get his best look at Jeremias since his brother's arrival. To his surprise, he found what Bellina said to be true — his brother *did* look much older than he should.

'Buggered if I know,' he said eventually. 'Maybe it will become clear when he tells his tale.'

Bellina nodded but continued to gaze thoughtfully at Jeremias. When everyone was seated, she got up and said, 'Friends, before we begin properly, I would like to make a few announcements. Firstly, I have appointed Minister Gestaffen as Lord Chancellor. He is free to appoint his ministers as he sees fit, though I have recommended Bert Allgood and Whist Dashell to him. Melek will be elevated to the new role of Lord Engineer and supervise the reconstruction of the Empire. Torkwill is now the School of Cognometry's Master and will help to lead the remaining cognopaths.

'Khasal has asked to take the surviving mages back to the Shattered Land, despite our offer of sanctuary within the Empire. I wish him all the best in restoring his ancestral home to life.

'Finally, Yevad has decided to head home to Burkesh to continue his role as a kaffar. He goes with our love and blessing.

'At last, we reach the true meat of our meeting. I have called this quorum so we can all combine our knowledge and, hopefully, put our individual pieces of this puzzle together. As such, I would like to call upon the Grand Multan to begin our talks. I have been privy to his mind and fear he is as much a victim of Marmossa as the rest of us.'

'Thank you, Your Majesty, for your kind words. Your generosity and forgiveness are a balm for my troubled soul. However, I must accept responsibility for the state of things — I was the one who loosed Marmossa from his prison.'

There was a murmured ripple of shock at his words.

'I beg your understanding. I did it out of love, love for my country and my people. I did it for the rains, may the Mother forgive me. But even as I speak, what I say sounds like the puling excuses of a schoolboy. Instead of crying for your forgiveness and stating my own pitiful case, I shall tell you what I know.

'After I released Marmossa from his prison, he appeared to me in the form of an ancient kaffar. With him came the rain, with the rain came prosperity, with prosperity came a happy people and a healthy army and with that came the expansion of Burkesh's territories. I and my army were cold and ruthless, qualities Marmossa's poisonous aura seemed to stoke into raging fires. Part of me knew something was wrong, but I pushed that aside, squeezed my conscience till it was nothing more than a small voice coming from the bottom of a deep well.

'But the conquest of the Eastern Continent wasn't enough for him. He wanted the relics, and he had a plan to get them. He pulled the strings like the master of a shadow play. He orchestrated the terrible event that left thousands dead in Kurgobad. To my eternal shame, I agreed to these plans.

'His ultimate aim was to destabilise Estria and bring down the Lord Chancellor, a man he feared and hated to the core of his rotten being. With the help of the Duke of Tremore and the purgistas, he finally achieved his aim. Still, I believed in him. Still, I thought he would use the relics to bring rain to the empire we had created.

'Marmossa had won the duke over by telling him he would make him a god. I thought this was a lie to get the man on side, but it turned out to be the truth. Marmossa plans to use the relics he has gathered in a ritual. A ritual where he needs people, vast numbers of them. He is strong now, and his powers are beyond any magic I have heard of. I watched as he turned the population of this city and others like it into birds.'

'Hang on a damned second,' Elvgren said. 'Do you expect me to believe he turned hundreds of thousands of people into pigeons?'

'With the utmost respect, Your Majesty, you can believe what you want. I know what I saw. And it was because of this and the boy that I came to my senses.'

'Boy?' Bellina asked. 'What boy?'

'The boy, the Heir to Excellus, though you know him as Midge.'

Elvgren felt the breath catch in his throat. It was clear that others in the room felt the shock even more keenly. To his left, Bellina looked as if she was about to be sick, while on his right, Barboza had shot to his feet, the tip of his spear pressing against the soft flesh of Kurkeshi's neck.

'You will tell us where he is,' Barboza commanded. 'And you will tell us now.'

'I will tell you gladly, though it's hard to talk with a weapon at one's throat,' Kurkeshi said.

For a moment, Barboza did not move, only stood there, muscles taut, nostrils flaring. At last, he resumed his seat.

'Thank you,' Kurkeshi said. 'As I was saying, the boy, Midge, when he captured him, Marmossa discovered he was able to draw from the boy's vast power. Marmossa's plans came on at a pace. He abandoned his plans to collect the other relics; he no longer had need for them. Marmossa keeps the boy drugged and pliable. Midge … he … he is in a pitiful state. Seeing him so, seeing row upon row of transformed people, shook me out of my stupor.

'I did not let my disgust and hate show. Instead, I bided my time, waited for Marmossa to feel comfortable, to let his guard down. And I thought my chance had come as he prepared to leave Victory, as he wallowed in his self-satisfaction. But the duke surprised me, shot me. They left me for dead and went to the Scorched Earth.'

'But … this … that is impossible. There *is* no way to reach the Scorched Earth. The seas are unassailable and a constant storm rages around its coast,' Elvgren said in the tone of voice someone might use to explain to an idiot that the sky is blue and grass is green.

'There is a way,' a new, gruff voice said. Elvgren looked to its source and saw that it was his brother. 'A secret way long forgotten, though it is not the way Marmossa went. Am I right, Your Majesty?'

'Yes,' Kurkeshi replied. 'Marmossa can soothe the storm and quiet the churning sea. But what he plans there …'

'I … er … I think I might be able to pick it up from here,' Fontaine said. 'If that's alright with everyone?'

Elvgren nodded along with the rest.

'Well then …yes …' The scholar cleared his throat. 'With the help of young Master Dargo, I have been able to break the *Radiana*'s final secret A … um … secret written down by Amlith himself, though not literally, it's a copy of his words, but it is a copy made by none other than—'

'Damn it, man — stick to the point!' Elvgren cried.

'Yes … my apologies, Your Majesty. The book speaks of how Amlith Castria and the rest of his fellowship stopped the Old Terrors from completing a ritual that would open a gateway to other worlds. They managed, with the help of the relics, to turn their machine against the Terrors and trapped them in what we call the twelve hells. We believe that Marmossa is intending to reopen this gateway and bring the Terrors, his brothers and sisters, back.'

'And what does this have to do with the people he's taken?' Bellina said.

'An excellent question, Your Majesty. For the ritual to work, a sacrifice is needed, a rather large one. The device to open the gate will gain its power by sucking the life force from those nearby.'

A deep silence fell over the room at these words, each person lost in their own thoughts.

'I suppose the question now is — how do we stop him?' Cirona said.

'This is where I come in,' Jeremias said, climbing to his feet. 'You all know of the prophesy, and you all know how strongly the Lord Chancellor believed in it. Well, he didn't just believe it, he was doing something about it. For years, he has been sending mages he managed to rescue to a haven he established on the Scorched Earth.'

An excited babble broke out at this. Elvgren watched Waltus and Khasal both jerk up in their seats as though there was a fire under their arses.

Jeremias frowned and waved the noise away. 'Yeah, yeah, save it,' he said. 'The sanctuary wasn't just a safe place for mages. We've been busy up there, busy finding the weapon that helped Amlith breach the City of the Dead and bring the Terrors down. We've been digging up Leviathan.' This time, Jeremias allowed the shocked chatter to peter out before he continued. 'We will need Leviathan again, cos we won't be able to rely on armies, boats or even these flying air things I've heard about. The only people going will be the ones Her Majesty was told of in her vision, maybe a couple more.'

'I beg your pardon?' Elvgren heard himself say.

'You heard me — only the ones mentioned in the vision.'

'Then we must leave at once,' Bellina said, her jaw firm.

'I'm afraid it's not so easy,' Jeremias replied. 'The Leviathan needs huge amounts of power to run. In short, it needs three of the relics, and we only have two.'

'I'm sorry, brother of mine, but I only see one,' Elvgren said, pointing to Barboza's spear.

Smiling, Jeremias pulled out a short sword from a scabbard beneath his coat. 'We found this alongside Leviathan. That leaves four of the five relics accounted for. After meeting with Whist and the scholar, we are more than certain that the last relic is in Sylucia.'

'That's all very well and good, but how do we get it?' Elvgren said.

'Finally, a good question, brother,' Jeremias replied. 'You, Her Majesty and Cirona shall go. As you know, Sylucia is a small country with an inferiority complex. This relic is part of the king's ceremonial garb, a small dagger, which compared to the jewelled crown and sceptre, they view as a piece of little value. In exchange for the relic, you will offer them arms and designs for weapons and the like.'

'What if they will not accept our deal?' Bellina said.

'Then you must steal it,' Jeremias replied flatly. 'Use whatever force you deem necessary. Time is short.'

'What do you mean?' Cirona asked.

'By our … erm … calculations,' Fontaine said. 'There are around thirty days until the City of the Dead is covered by an eclipse.'

'And that's important why?' Elvgren said.

'It is a-another requirement of the ritual,' Fontaine replied.

'Just know that time is short and against us,' Jeremias said, drumming his fingers on the table. 'You will leave tomorrow. The engineer, Malak—'

'Melek,' Melek interrupted

'Yes, yes, Melek has found an almost complete airship, and men have been working round the clock to get it going. This is how you will enter. I will come and get you. Look for my coming by the statue of the first king at midnight in two days' time. With me will be the other members of our party. Is everyone agreed?'

Like everyone else, Elvgren was too stunned to argue and simply nodded along with the rest. While his head still spun with all the information he had just received, Jeremias stood and left the room without so much as a backwards glance. He felt Bellina squeeze his hand.

'Looks like we're getting to the end now,' she said. 'Are you ready?'

'I … well, yes, I suppose so,' Elvgren lied.

CHAPTER FOURTEEN

Cirona felt a warmth upon her face. Lashes fluttering, her eyes opened, and she saw, to her surprise, sunlight pouring in through the window. The clouds hadn't completely gone, but the ones remaining sailed cheerfully across a blue sky. And there was no rain! *Maybe it's a good omen*, she thought.

She looked to her left, at the gently snoring form of Dofri. They had slept together a half dozen times now, had fallen into each other with a mad passion, a passion she long thought had gone out in her. Cirona watched the sunlight wash over him catching the hair on his arms and chest, turning them into curling wisps of gold.

You should be ashamed of yourself! a shrill voice in her head cried. *He's half your age.*

With a shake of her head, she banished the thought. Cirona almost marvelled at her mind's capacity to attack itself, at that dark snake of self-hatred that coiled around her. Besides, it wasn't as if she had dragged him to her bed. Oh no, he had come willingly enough and no mistake. And why shouldn't she enjoy a small piece of happiness?

But what about Trafford? the shrill voice sneered. *What would he have thought about another man sharing your bed?*

For a moment, she contemplated the question. She searched deep inside herself, probing her feelings like someone choosing the ripest vegetables, giving them a thorough once over. To her surprise, she found she didn't care; she wasn't going to let the memory of her dead love dictate what she did in the present. A shaky laugh escaped her lips, a feeling of giddiness stealing through her body. Yes, she didn't care. For the first time since he had died, the ghost of Trafford lay quiet.

With a full and content heart, she leaned over and kissed Dofri's brow. 'Thank you,' she said.

Not wanting to wake him, Cirona swung her legs to the floor and picked up her trousers. She had just finished buckling her belt when she heard Dofri stirring.

'Trying to sneak off, eh?' he said, yawning and stretching as he sat up in the bed.

'Wouldn't dream of it,' Cirona replied, sitting down to haul on her boots.

Dofri kissed the base of her neck, and a shiver of pleasure passed through her. 'I should be coming with you,' he said.

'Don't think I can look after myself?' Cirona said, smiling and raising an eyebrow.

He laughed. 'Alright, alright. I just … don't want this to stop I s'pose.'

'All things come to an end,' she said. Her voice managed to stay light, but a lump had formed in her throat. This was why she had wanted to creep away. By the gods, she hadn't thought it would be this hard.

'Just have to wait here till you get back from saving the world,' he said.

'What?'

'I said I'll just have to wait here till you get back. I offered my services to the new Lord Chancellor, and he took me up on it I—'

Before he could say anymore, Cirona pounced on him, kissing him. 'Why didn't you say anything before?' she said, wiping at her eyes.

'Wanted it to be a surprise … Hey, what's the matter?'

The tears were now coursing down Cirona's cheeks. 'I-I … it's just that I've been on a lot of campaigns, always moving, always in motion, and for the first time in a long time, I've got something to come back to.'

She threw off her boots and climbed on top of him.

'You sure we've got time?' Dofri asked. 'What if you're late?'

'Fuck it,' she said.

***

Elvgren stood hunched over a travel bag frantically stuffing shirts, trousers and socks into it. He was late and, although he knew the airship would not leave without him, could not help but feel a small bubble of panic floating up from his stomach. He wasn't usually one for signs and omens, but he thought it would, at the very least, be a damned poor show if they didn't arrive in Sylucia on time.

A series of three loud knocks echoed on his door.

'Alright, Dargo, I know we're late just give me a couple more minutes and—'

He turned. Instead of Dargo he saw his brother. Elvgren's mouth fell open, and he clutched the pair of socks he was holding to his chest. For a handful of heartbeats, this is how they stood — Elvgren agape, Jeremias in the doorway chewing at his lip and frowning.

'I … thought I'd come and see you, you know, before you … leave,' Jeremias said, his voice so gruff it sounded like he was crushing rocks in his throat.

Elvgren continued to stand with his mouth flapping, the only sound coming out of it a faint squeak.

'I know it must have been a surprise for you when I turned up—' Jeremias began.

'Well only as much of a surprise as it would be to anyone who had a family member rise from the dead,' Elvgren interrupted, finding his voice. 'Did mother and father know?'

Jeremias closed the door behind him, took a deep breath and said, 'No, they didn't. The only person who knew I was alive was the Lord Chancellor. Fontaine and Whist knew of my existence, knew of my mission, but they had no idea who I was.'

'Do you know what it was like?' Elvgren replied, throwing the socks aside and balling his hands into fists. 'Can you even begin to imagine what it was like living in the shadow of Saint Jere-fucking-mias? By your age, your brother was writing; by your age; your brother was a master swordsman; by your age, your brother was already a captain.'

'How do you think I felt living up to those standards?' Jeremias growled, rubbing a hand over his face. 'They had me young, too young everyone said. I'm sure you know the inferiority complex they had because of the higher noble families. We had less land, a smaller mansion, lived closer to the bottom of the Olphant Hill than the top. They couldn't do anything about those things, but they could control me. I was their weapon, the talisman they wore to show off to the upper houses.'

'Oh, poor you,' Elvgren said. 'It must have been awful to be showered with love and attention.'

Jeremias gave a bark of laughter. 'Love? That pair of lizards wouldn't have known what love was if it bit them on the arse. And as for attention, yes, they paid a lot of attention — to everything I did wrong. If I could load and prime a ballisket in twenty seconds they wanted to know why I couldn't do it in nineteen.

'That's why I left. I couldn't keep up with their expectations. They had me trapped, were suffocating me. If it hadn't been for the Lord Chancellor, I think I might have killed myself. He took me under his wing, taught me about the prophesy and the grave threat facing the world. And when he said he needed someone he could trust to supervise the Leviathan dig site, I jumped at the chance.

'He was the one who arranged my fake death. Said a new type of ballisket had exploded in my face, so they couldn't identify me. I wanted to see them when they got the news, wanted to see how they would react. The Lord Chancellor arranged for a cognopath to hide me while he told them. And do you know what? There were no tears, no hair pulling or gnashing of teeth. They just sat there, sipping tea and nodding along as if they were being told how an investment they'd made was doing. I knew then there was nothing left for me in Estria.'

'There was nothing … What about me? I was there,' Elvgren said, tears doubling his vision.

'You have to understand — I was in my late teens; you were barely three. You were always with the nanny or the wet nurse. That coupled with my timetable meant I hardly ever saw you. I know it's a poor excuse—'

'A poor excuse is still just an excuse!' Elvgren roared. The tears were flowing freely down his face now. 'How … how could you leave me with them?'

Jeremias pinched the bridge of his nose. 'For what it's worth, I'm sorry,' he said. 'I didn't come here to argue with you.'

'What did you come here for then?' Elvgren asked.

'To do something our parents would never do,' he said before wrapping his arms around Elvgren. 'I love you brother, good luck on your mission.'

Despite himself, Elvgren returned the hug and buried his face in his brother's shoulder.

***

Hefting her bag to her shoulder, Bellina closed the door. She left her hand upon it, caressing the wood. Even though she had only occupied it for a little over two weeks, it had come to feel like home, her own private sanctuary. And here she was saying goodbye to it for the Father only knew how long. *You might never see it again. Have you considered that?* a voice said in the back of her mind.

She pushed the thought away and began to walk down the hallway. As she neared the stairs, she felt a pair of arms wrap around her.

'Guess who?' a voice whispered in her ear.

With a jerk, she tore herself away from the arms and spun round, chest heaving, to face who had grabbed her. Holger stood there with a dazed smile on his face, the kind of smile a practical joker has when their victim doesn't find it funny that they've swapped the sugar for salt.

'It's only me!' he said. 'What's the matter with you?'

'What's the matter with me?' Bellina hissed. 'What in the hells is the matter with you? What if you'd been seen?'

Holger waved her concerns away with a flap of his hand. 'Everyone's downstairs waiting,' he said. 'We've got this whole part of the Palace to ourselves.'

'And why, pray tell, would we need it?' Bellina said.

'I dunno, to say goodbye properly?' he said.

Taking a step forwards, Holger began to move in on her. She moved backwards, coming to a stop when her arse hit the wall. He leaned in, and she held him back by putting a hand on his chest.

'No,' she said. 'Holger, please don't.'

'What's wrong?' he said, pulling back, eyes growing wide beneath a furrowed brow. 'What about the other night?'

'The other night was a mistake. I … I was feeling low … and I … I used you,' she said.

'Used me? What are you talking about? What we have, between us, we both want it … so why won't you let yourself be happy?'

'We have nothing between us, just one moment of weakness, that's all. Now, I've got to go,' she said, beginning to move towards the stairs. She didn't get very far before Holger gripped her arm.

'It's because of him, isn't it? It's always because of fucking him.' Holger said, nostrils flaring, lips pulled back like a snarling jackal.

'Let go,' Bellina said. 'You're hurting me.'

The pressure of his grip increased. 'No. Not until you tell the truth. Not until you say you love me too,' he said, accompanying the last three words with sharp squeezes.

Bellina dropped her bag and brought her hand round in a vicious slap that connected with the sound of wood snapping. 'Get. Your. Hands. Off. Me,' she said, spitting each word.

For a moment, he stood there, dazed, holding a hand to his cheek. Then he looked down at his feet. 'I'm sorry, Bell, it's just—'

'Save your apologies. I'll forget this ever happened. I advise you do the same.'

With that she stormed down the stairs.

***

Fontaine stood watching as Empress Bellina boarded the airship. He made a feeble attempt at a cheery wave before tucking his trembling hand back into his pocket. His stomach pitched and rolled like a raft caught in a storm while his heart thumped. *They'll be fine*, he thought to himself. But if that was the case, why had a black shroud of dread fallen upon him?

He looked to his left at Jeremias. The man's face was set, all hard lines and angles. How could he be so calm? How, when so much was at stake? Their eyes met, Fontaine enthralled by the cold blue of the other's gaze, then the wanderer from the Scorched Earth gave him a nod and returned his gaze to the ship. The scholar did the same.

The airship was rising now, the weights holding it tethered cast off. Before long, it was nothing but a curiously shaped cloud taking refuge among its brothers. He could just hear the thrum of the propellers building up power, then the whole thing started moving away at speed. Fontaine stared after it, was still staring when it had become nothing more than a dot on the horizon. He felt a hand on his shoulder and turned to meet Jeremias' gaze once more.

'Come, scholar,' he said. 'We have work to do.'

'Yes,' Fontaine replied, his voice barely a whisper. 'I suppose we have.'

*

Cirona sat, boots up on the table in front of her, arms behind her head, surveying her companions. At the table next to her Dargo was throwing his dagger in the air, the blade making a series of small circles before he caught the handle. She winced each time he did it, half expecting the boy to lose a finger. Elvgren was pacing the cabin, sometimes pausing to look out of the small, round windows. Bellina sat on one of the bunks at the back, a book open but unread on her lap, her eyes gazing into space. The air in the cabin seemed heavy and expectant, like the moment before a storm.

'Dargo, will you please stop playing with that thing!' Elvgren said.

'Why should I?' Dargo replied. 'What else can I do anyway?'

'Something,' Elvgren said. 'Anything — just put that blasted dagger away.'

'Leave him alone,' Bellina added. 'What harm is he doing?'

'See?' Dargo sneered at Elvgren. 'Thanks, Belle.'

'Don't encourage him, woman — he's bad enough already. And you'd best remember it's, Your Majesty, and not Belle when we get to Sylucia.'

'*Me* encourage him?' Bellina spat. 'You're the one who let him keep that spider he found in Mandira, and I know it got loose in the Palace … I'm sure I saw the horrid thing dragging a rat under a stove.'

'Steve's only doing what comes natural to a spider,' Dargo said.

'Quite right, Dar. And for another thing—' Elvgren began.

'Enough!' Cirona cried, slamming her fists down on the table.

'We're all tense, but sniping and grousing ain't going to make anything better. We've used up our first day travelling, which means we've only got till tomorrow midnight to secure the relic. Hopefully, things will go according to plan, and we'll make it to our meeting with Jeremias on time. But we need to be ready for things to go wrong. Which means we need to rest. Therefore, I'm ordering everyone to their bunks.'

'You can't order me,' Elvgren said. 'I'm the Emperor.'

Cirona stared at him. For a moment, he kept his stubborn chin high … then it fell to his chest.

'Alright,' he said, 'but I'm only going because I was feeling sleepy anyway.'

'Whatever you say, Your Majesty, just get in the bed,' Cirona replied.

Dargo tucked his knife away and jumped onto a top bunk, Bellina placed her book under her pillow and Elvgren stomped to his cot and threw himself upon it.

'Aren't you coming, Rona?' Bellina asked.

'In a minute,' she replied. 'I had a nap earlier, so I'm good for a bit yet.'

Cirona put her feet back up and let out a contented sigh. Through the windows, she watched as the sun set and the night flowed in. She listened to the snores of her companions and drifted off thinking of Dofri.

*

'Cirona,' a voice hissed. 'Cirona!'

The General woke with a start and almost toppled out of her chair. She shook her head, rubbed her eyes and looked up into the face of Bellina.

'What is it?' Cirona said, stifling a yawn.

'I want to talk to you,' Bellina said, biting her lip. 'Gods I need to talk to someone.'

Worry was etched into the girl's face, plain as day; how had Cirona not seen it before? 'Go on,' she said.

Bellina cast a furtive glance at the snoring form of Elvgren then said, 'I-I … think I might be pregnant.'

Head snapping back as if she had been slapped, Cirona just manged to stop herself from tipping over her chair for the second time. 'Are you sure?' she said.

'My … my monthly flow has not appeared, and I'm usually very regular.'

'When did this happen? Does Elvgren know?'

'No, he doesn't. But there … there is a bigger problem than that — I don't know if it's his.'

Cirona felt her mouth go dry and swallowed hard. 'You're not telling me … Holger?'

Bellina nodded.

'How did you let this happen?' Cirona said.

'I don't know, I don't know,' Bellina groaned, rubbing a hand over her face. 'I was feeling down, depressed, sick of all the dying and pain, and I just … it just—'

'Happened?' Cirona finished for her.

'Happened … yes. What should I do now? Do I tell Elvgren? I feel like I should tell Elvgren.'

'No, no, no, no … we need everyone pulling together. This would just put a barrier between you. I know this must be shitty for you, and it's not every day the fate of the world could turn on who a young woman takes to her bed, but this is one of those days.'

'That's a bit overdramatic, isn't it?'

'Maybe, but it shouldn't have ever come to this. I knew it was a bad idea keeping that idiot around. Do you even love him? Do you love either of them? Wait, I don't care. You are the Empress because of your engagement to Elvgren; how the fuck could you piss all over that?'

'I didn't … I wouldn't …' Bellina said, tears filling her eyes.

'Stop that right now,' Cirona hissed at her. 'Crying isn't going to fix anything. Listen, I'm about to tell you what we're going to do; are you listening?'

Bellina nodded.

'You had a moment of weakness, happens to everybody, but you're going to forget it, push it right to the back of your mind and lock it up tight. Then you're going to get back in bed. Then I'm going to forget you ever told me about it. How does that sound?'

'I don't know if I can—' Bellina began.

'Well, you're going to have to try your damnedest,' Cirona interrupted. 'Now get to bed.'

Although her eyes still looked on the verge of tears, Bellina set her jaw firm and nodded before going back to her bunk. Cirona got up and walked to one of the windows. She looked out at the night sky, the first tinges of dawn tickling the horizon.

'What a fucking mess,' she whispered.

***

'Well, thanks for the lift, Melek,' Elvgren said, extending his hand.

'My pleasure, Your Majesty. I'm glad to play even a small part in a quest as vital as this,' Melek replied.

'I think you've played a major part,' Bellina said.

Elvgren watched as she pulled the inventor into a hug. Another hug came from Cirona and a further shake of the hand from Dargo.

'May the light of the Father guide you,' Melek said. 'I'm sorry that I won't be there to pick you up, but Jeremias is insistent that he will collect you, though by what means, I would love to know.'

'You're not the only one,' Elvgren said. 'Best be off, there's supposed to be a man waiting for us.'

With one last nod to Melek, Elvgren opened the cabin door and jumped the two feet or so to the ground. His feet landed with a squelch on a muddy scrap of field on a muddy scrap of land. They had seen the landing spot from above, just one more island in the huddled lagoon that made up the Sylucian capital.

Turning back towards the airship, he saw Bellina waiting in the doorway. Elvgren stretched out his hand, and she took it with a smile. Just as Bellina stepped out her right foot slipped, and she went tumbling into his arms. Their faces were inches apart, so close he could feel the heat from her flushed cheeks. Elvgren could feel his heart smashing against his breastbone, threatening to break through its cage and tear loose from his chest. Bellina's lips parted, and her head moved almost imperceptibly closer to his.

'Oi, love birds,' Dargo cried. 'Kiss or get out of the bloody way, some of us are still waiting to get off!'

'Wh … er … yes, yes, of course,' Elvgren said, lowering Bellina down and out of his arms.

Despite having let go of her, Elvgren's pulse continued to rise. All at once, the world seemed to come to vivid life, the smell of the damp earth, the soft sighing of the wind. Looking at the profile of Bellina's face, he could see every individual eyelash, each strand of hair. *There's a mole just below her ear,* he thought, *was that always there? Why didn't I notice it before?*

Because you weren't in love with her before, an alien voice sang from the back of his mind.

Gods … could it be true? He had always respected her, admired her even, but love? His throat had gone very dry, his legs weak and quivering. *By the Father … I am in love with her.*

'Sorry for ruining the moment,' Dargo said, a grin on his face.

'Don't be silly, Dar,' Bellina replied, looking haughty and close to divine in Elvgren's eyes.

'Where's this bloke then?' Cirona said.

As if in answer, a voice called out behind them. 'Hail, Your Majesties!'

Elvgren, along with everyone else, turned round to see a man walking towards them. He was tall and thin, a ceremonial robe of red and gold clinging to his body like a second skin. An angular face set with sharp glittering eyes sat atop his shoulders. There was a smile upon his thin lips, and at that moment, it looked to Elvgren to be the grin of a starving hound, one who has just spotted his first meal in weeks. When the man reached them, the light changed, and the look of hunger vanished.

'Your Majesties, honoured guests, welcome to Verradolla, the Floating City. I am Anrico Alazar, aide to His Highness King Omberto,' the man said.

'A pleasure,' Elvgren said, shaking Alazar's hand.

'Well met, Mr Alazar,' Bellina said, offering her own hand. When Anrico kissed it instead of shaking it, Elvgren was pleased to see a tiny shiver of disgust pass through her.

If the royal aide had noticed, he didn't show it. Instead, he said, 'Please, follow me; I have our carriage waiting.'

Alazar set off back along the path, a steep foot-worn track. 'I apologise that you must carry your own bags,' he said. 'But all the servants are busy, busy, busy at the palace making things just right for such — what is the word? — auspicious guests.'

'We'll manage, Mr Alazar,' Bellina replied. 'We're travelling light.'

It wasn't long before they reached the top of the small hill. As they did, Elvgren felt his breath catch. He had seen paintings of the Floating City, many of them considered masterpieces … but none of them did credit to what he was now looking at. Tall multi-storied buildings rose impossibly out of the lagoon's water. Row upon row of them stretched back to a central point where a series of levels rose up like a glided wedding cake. At the top of the cake the golden domes of the palace shone as if on fire in the early morning sun.

'It's beautiful,' Bellina said in a hushed voice.

'Yes,' Alazar sighed. 'From here, she is beautiful.'

'I hate to spoil the mood,' Cirona cut in, 'but we're on a bit of a tight schedule.'

'Of course. Let us go to the carriage,' the royal aide said.

They hurried down the other side of the hill towards a small jetty. What Elvgren saw waiting for them was a sight almost as awe-inspiring as Verradolla itself. A boat of white with gold trim was waiting for them. Attached to reins at the front were, what looked like, a pair of giant sea horses. Their skin was a translucent turquoise flecked with shimmering blobs of white. The bony rings that lined their bodies were the creamy white of ivory. Dargo ran forwards and stroked one of the beasts at the base of its neck. The creature flapped the fins behind its ears in appreciation.

'Are those equimars?' Bellina asked.

'Yes, Your Majesty,' Alazar answered. 'The nobility hand rear them to pull their boats. They are savage beasts in the wild. I have heard tales of them tearing a man to pieces in seconds.' He laughed as Dargo jumped back. 'Don't worry, these are quite tame. Now, shall we?'

He walked forwards and opened a door in the boat's side. Bellina went in first, accepting the hand Alazar offered her. Elvgren went next, followed by Cirona and Dargo. Alazar climbed in last, making his way to the front of the boat where he took the reins.

'Sit back and enjoy the ride,' he said. 'Take it … take it all in.'

Alazar clicked his tongue, flicked the reins, and they were off. It didn't take long for them to reach the outlying buildings of the city. They passed under what seemed to be innumerable bridges, some high, some so low they had to duck their heads, some connecting streets, some connecting houses.

As they made their way further in, Elvgren saw that the plaster on many of the buildings was rotting, falling away to reveal the water-ravaged brick underneath. A stench began to assault his nose, a mingling smell of rot and decay. The water around them that had seemed so pure and blue from a distance was choked with rubbish, and at one point, he saw a family of rats floating on the back of a dead dog, using it like a raft while they gnawed at its flesh. Stifling the urge to vomit, he turned away.

'I know,' Alazar said. 'The lower city is not what it was. The decay is spreading up to the middle city. Soon it will reach the top.'

'How did this come to be?' Bellina said.

'Once, we were rich. Our empire stretched far and wide, our navy was king of the sea. Then the Varashis took it from us, then you took it from the Varashis. It is the way of empires I think — they come; they go. You of all people should understand this,' he said with a sigh.

They sailed on in silence, the only sounds the odd shout of an argument. As they passed out of the crowded streets of the lower city, a massive statue came into view. It showed a rather rakish young man, hips tilted suggestively, a robe falling off his shoulder to reveal his naked body. In his mouth, he held a dagger. The whole thing rested upon a huge block of black marble veined with glowing blue lines.

'The First King of Sylucia,' Alazar said. 'Inburna. The base is said to be from the ruined temple of some unknown god. Some say the stone is haunted, that they have seen faces in it, the faces of people trying to get out.'

'Do all your kings go about with their dicks out?' Dargo asked.

'You little—' Elvgren began.

Alazar laughed. 'No, my young friend. I'm sure you will be pleased to know our monarch will be fully dressed when you meet.'

They travelled on, past the statue and towards the massive, circular wall. Drawing close, Elvgren saw that the wall wasn't flat as it had first appeared. Instead, it curved upwards in a series of sloping, water-filled paths. When they reached the base of the largest one, he felt the equimars strain to ascend the downward-flowing stream.

'Can they make it?' Bellina asked with concern.

'They will be fine. Coming up is a chore for them but they are strong enough to handle it. Coming down is much more exciting. In fact, we have annual races upon this waterway.'

The equimars *did* ease into their task, and they ascended the wall quicker than Elvgren would have expected. Following the waterway, they completely bypassed the middle city and came straight to the top. Here, he could see elaborate mansions, windowed islands resting on stilts of wood.

At the centre of it all was the king's palace. The front of the building was dominated be a series of high, vaulted arches, with a second set sat upon the first. Gilded domes and turrets wrestled for space on its roof. All of this sat upon a courtyard of slick, gleaming marble. A horde of jetties protruded out from it, many of which were occupied by boats as magnificent as the one they travelled in. Alazar found an empty berth and drew them to a stop.

The royal aide got out first and offered his hand to the others. Once they had all disembarked, a pair of guards, balliskets propped against their shoulders, came to meet them. They offered a salute then spun sharply on their heels and began to lead them across the gleaming marble.

'Bloody hells,' Elvgren muttered to Bellina. 'They've put out an actual red carpet! Can you believe that?'

'Yes, it's all very lovely,' Bellina hissed back. 'But I would like to point out we are being escorted under armed guard.'

'Pfft,' Elvgren replied, waving his hand. 'It's all part of the pomp and ceremony.'

'Well, I just hope you're right,' Bellina said through lips drawn into a tight line.

Before long, they reached the main entrance. In front of them stood a huge wooden door with a pair of silver rings for handles. Above it, a lion and an equimar were carved into the stone, each trying to look more regal than the other.

'Your Majesties,' one of the guards said as they took position on either side of the door. 'We have been instructed to ask that your group relinquish all weapons before entry.'

'Not bloody likely,' Elvgren heard Cirona say from behind him.

'Your Majesties, honoured guests,' Alazar said, stepping forwards with his hands raised. 'Over the years, there have been many assassination attempts, both successful and foiled, in the palace. As such, it was written into our law that none should enter with weapons upon their persons; we are not, how you say … picking on you.'

With a sigh of regret, Elvgren handed over his ancient weapon. As soon as it was away from his side, he felt naked, vulnerable. Cirona and Dargo followed suit.

'May we now enter?' Bellina said. Her voice was calm, but Elvgren could feel the icicles dangling from each word.

'I'm afraid there is one more matter,' Alazar said.

'And *what*, pray tell, may that be?' Bellina asked, her eyes narrowed.

'It … well it concerns you, Your Majesty … and your gifts. We would ask that you wear this,' Alazar said, taking out a thin bracelet of midnight black. As he held the thing it caught the sun, and Elvgren could see a misty, swirling pattern upon it.

'What is it?' Bellina said.

'It is a device that will nullify your powers.'

'And where would the King of Sylucia find such a bauble?' Bellina asked.

Alazar licked his lips. 'That … that you will have to ask His Highness.'

'Is this really necessary, old boy?' Elvgren cut in. 'I mean, for the Father's sake, we are here to discuss trade and diplomacy, not overthrow your king.'

'Please believe me,' Alazar said, clasping his hands together. 'The king, myself, we understand you mean no harm. But other members of the court were not so easily persuaded. With having never had many dealings with cognopaths, but the stories, *the rumours*, well … they have a way of playing on people's minds.'

Elvgren watched as Bellina closed her eyes and took a deep breath. 'Fine,' she said, holding out her left arm.

'Thank you, Your Majesty, you are most—'

'Just bloody well do it,' Bellina spat.

Alazar nodded, a greasy smile upon his face. He slid it over her wrist. A twinge of anger passed through Elvgren when he saw Alazar's greedy fingers stay a pause too long upon Bellina's flesh. Once it was on, the darkness of the bracelet contrasting vividly with the white of her skin, the aide muttered something under his breath. At this the bracelet shrunk until it was tight against her skin.

'What in the world!' Cirona cried.

'Now hang on, chap, what kind of devilry is this?' Elvgren said.

'I do not know. I was just told to place it upon Her Majesty's wrist then say words I do not understand beneath my breath. The answers you seek can only be given to you by His Highness.'

'Well, I suppose we'd better get inside and meet him then,' Bellina said, looking at the bracelet, cold fury burning in her eyes.

'Of course,' Alazar said with another subservient smile.

He turned to the guards and, face changing in an instant to one of stern command, clicked his fingers. The guards gave a sharp salute and pulled open the door.

'This way, if you please,' Alazar said, beckoning them.

They were led into a long corridor. The floor was covered in diagonal stripes of gold, light from the elaborate, mullioned windows bringing the colour to life in a swaying haze. Along the corridor were tall, white columns decorated with plaster reliefs of intertwining foliage. After climbing a flight of stairs, they reached another corridor.

This was painted a rich, azure blue, the tops of the columns here gilded with silver. In front of them was an arched recess. A mural upon its ceiling depicted the First King of Sylucia raising the capital from the mud of the lagoon as if by magic. Beneath this was a double door of lacquered wood, the colour of gleaming bronze. Above that, statues of a lion and equimar once more stood regarding each other.

Alazar rapped his knuckles on the doors, and they swung inwards almost at once. As Elvgren entered, he noticed two pairs of guards standing to either side of the opening. He frowned but continued forwards. The room itself was an elegant study. Leather couches and comfortable seats lay scattered upon a shining wooden floor. A vast harp stood to one side, a gorgeous globe to the other. At the back of the room was a huge bay window, the light streaming through it illuminating a small man sitting at a large desk.

'Your Highness,' Alazar said, bowing low. 'May I have the honour of introducing to you Her Majesty Bellina Ressa, His Majesty Elvgren Lovitz, General Cirona Bouchard and His Majesty's manservant.'

'Oi! I ain't—' Dargo began. Elvgren cut him off with a stamp to his foot.

'Marvellous, marvellous!' the tiny king squeaked. Throwing down a quill, he bounced from his seat and raced towards them.

Despite his shortness, King Omberto had a stocky frame enhanced by the plush robe — a rich violet colour — covering him. He had a round face with a weak chin that was slowly being lost beneath jowly cheeks. His nose had a squashed quality, as if it had been broken and not set properly. Above that, small gleaming eyes, the colour of smoke, stared out. Omberto extended a delicate hand to Elvgren. He shook it.

'Well met!' Omberto exclaimed. 'Well met indeed, cousins. I can call you cousins, can't I? I read somewhere that's what one does when a royal meets another of his kind, and I've always wanted to say it.'

'Yes, yes … of course,' Elvgren said as the king continued to pump his hand with relish.

He finally let go and turned to Bellina. Omberto took her hand and kissed it. 'Empress Ressa,' he said. 'The tales of your beauty do not do you justice.'

'I was unaware tales of my beauty existed,' she replied.

'Well, they should!' the king cried. 'A heavenly creature such as yourself deserves songs written in your honour. I'm a bit of a writer you know. Was working on my latest poem just as you walked in. Perhaps I should pen one for you?'

'That … that would be most gracious of you,' Bellina said, a confused look upon her face.

'General Bouchard,' Omberto said, turning to Cirona. 'Your reputation certainly precedes you.'

The king took her hand and tried to kiss it, but Cirona turned it into a handshake. Untroubled by this, he turned to Dargo. He leaned in, bushy eyebrows drawn together.

'I say — you bear the most striking resemblance to my late brother. Don't have any Sylucian blood in you by any chance?'

'As a matter of fact, I think me dad was. Me mum always used to say only a smooth talking Sylucian could have got her to drop her drawers and spread 'em.'

'Dargo!' Elvgren hissed.

The king threw back his head and gave a roar of laughter. 'Oh, very good, very good indeed! Perhaps you're a long-lost heir to the throne, eh? Anyway, let us sit.'

With a wave of Omberto's hand, a guard peeled away from the wall and lined up four chairs in front of the table. While the king climbed back into his own seat, Elvgren and the others took theirs.

'Your Highness,' Bellina began as soon as her arse touched the chair. 'We are here—'

'You are here,' Omberto said, cutting her off, 'For this.'

He fumbled at his side then produced an ivory dagger from a sheath at his hip. *No*, Elvgren thought, *not ivory but bone, the bone of a god.*

'How did you—' Cirona said.

Once more, Omberto interrupted. 'How did I know you might come for this? Well, I'm afraid one of Marmossa's representatives got here first, a purgista I believe, went by the name of Garand.'

At the name, Elvgren felt his hands ball into fists. 'Whatever that man told you is a lie,' he said.

'Oh, I'm sure some of it was lies … maybe all of it, but he did offer me an outstanding deal.'

'Whatever it is, we will better it,' Bellina said, leaning forwards and putting her hands on the table.

'I don't think so. Come. See.'

Rising out of his chair, Omberto took them to the massive window. For a moment, Elvgren stood, mouth slack, eyes agape. He couldn't be seeing this. Ice crept through his veins like a prowling cat, forcing him to accept that he was looking at an army of malovors. The creatures were penned in what looked like a hastily built compound of brick. Around the walls was evidence of the displaced, manicured garden that was once in its place.

'Your Highness,' Cirona said. 'Those … things are extremely dangerous and will only obey the orders of a mage.'

'Garand said you would say that. But as long as I have the dagger, I can control them too. And how I will control them. How I will lead them through the lands of Varash. How I will lead them straight to Yondapolis, bathe its streets in blood and make their king kneel before me,' Omberto said. Then he shook his head, eyes blinking like a man waking from a trance. 'Oh my, I got a bit carried away there, didn't I? Excuse me, cousins, excuse me, but a Sylucian's hate for a Varashi runs deep indeed.'

'So, you got an army of unstable abominations,' Elvgren said, somehow managing to find his tongue. 'What's your side of the deal? Are you going to kill us? Is that it? Because I tell you, weapons or not, I will fight to the damned death.'

'Cousin, please don't be so dramatic. I am not a barbarian. The deal was that I kept the dagger and kept you here as my guests for the next month.'

'And by guests you mean prisoners?' Bellina said, one eyebrow arched.

'No, no, no,' the king said waving his arms. 'You will be guests, truly. Only guests accompanied by guards. But other than that, I'm sure you will love it here. And the entertainments I have planned! It will be a month of merrymaking starting with a ball this evening. Now the guards will show you to your rooms.'

At this the four guards walked forwards and stood one behind each chair. Elvgren saw Cirona size up the man assigned to her. Catching her eye, Elvgren shook his head a fraction. The General scowled, then nodded. Bellina was shaking, many might have thought it fear, but Elvgren knew better — this was rage. Before she could explode, he took her by the arm and stood.

'Very well, *cousin*,' Elvgren said. 'We shall try our best to enjoy our time in your beautiful city. Come, my love, let's follow these fine chaps, eh?'

'What are you—' Bellina began.

'Now is not the time,' he whispered in her ear. 'We'll strike at the ball. Dargo will be able to steal the damned dagger without that old fool knowing, *and* we'll make our meeting with my brother. So for now, keep cool.' Bellina's eyes narrowed to slits, but in the end, she nodded and took his arm.

As the guards led them from the room, Elvgren felt his guts quiver. *We'll be cutting it bloody close, old boy*, he thought, *bloody close indeed.*

CHAPTER FIFTEEN

Cirona watched with dismay as the guards marched them off in different directions. *Gods*, she thought, *they're splitting us up. How the hells will we work out a plan now?* She trudged on, mind whirring, searching for an idea. Casting a look behind her, she saw that the man guiding her through the palace was not armed. It seemed the no-weapon policy extended to the guards too.

A thought came to her. Would it work? Who knew? But surely it was worth a try. Cirona licked her lips, drew a deep breath, then came to an abrupt halt. She bent down as if to tie her shoelace. *Alright, one backwards kick into his shins and he should fall right—*At that moment, she felt a sharp pain in the back of her neck like a bee sting. After that, she felt nothing — her body was paralysed.

'Please do not think,' the guard said behind her, 'that because we are without arms, we are weaponless. Those of us among the Palace Interior Guard are masters of hand-to-hand combat. This is a warning — if I was to move my grip half an inch you would never walk again. Do you promise to try no more nonsense?'

Cirona let out a strangled grunt in reply.

'Good,' the guard said. 'Let's move.'

Cheeks burning, she stood. To be overpowered so easily shamed her to her core. *Wait for your chance, girl*, she thought, *wait for your chance. And when it comes, knock that smug tone right out of the fucker's voice.* Allowing herself to be moved on, Cirona passed through gorgeous corridors and up marble stairs. The only other words the guard spoke to her were to give directions. Eventually, they came to a door.

'Open it,' the guard said.

Doing as she was bid, Cirona opened the door and entered a lavish bedroom. A canopied bed stood in one corner, hangings embroidered with golden thread stroking the floor. In the middle of the room was a table with a steaming teapot, cakes, a hunk of bread with meat and cheese and a pack of cards upon it. To the left of this was a bookcase stuffed with leather-bound volumes. The only clue that the room wasn't just for an honoured guest came from the barred windows.

Behind her, she heard the door close and a key turn. With a sigh, she crossed over to the table and sat down. She tore of a small piece of bread and toyed with it in her hands. A clock upon the wall said it was already two o'clock. That left eight hours, eight hours to somehow rob King Omberto of the relic and get the statue.

Dropping the chunk of bread, she stood. Placing her hands behind her back, she began to pace up and down, her boots sinking deep into the plush carpet. Cirona's throat grew tight, and her stomach felt as hard as granite. There had to be something they could do. Maybe they'd have to wait till the ball. But when would that start?

'Excuse me, guard?' Cirona said, walking over to the door.

'What?' the guard replied.

'When does the ball start? I wouldn't mind a scrub over before then.'

'The ball starts at eight, and you will not be needing a "scrub over" as you are not attending.'

Cirona stepped back in surprise. 'Why the fuck am I not allowed to go?'

'I don't know; it is one of the king's fancies. All we were told was to make sure you and the little oik stay confined to quarters.'

Absently, she walked back to the table, sat down and began to pull at her lower lip. Keeping her and Dargo away from the ball made sense. If only Elvgren and Bellina were going, that was only two people to keep an eye on. It was definitely what she would do if tasked with palace security. *Gotta do something, gotta do somethinggottadosomething.*

No inspiration came, and the hours began to tick by with remorseless speed. Three o' clock, five o' clock, seven. Time was devoured, their window of opportunity shrunk, and the sun sank below the horizon. From outside, she could hear the muted conversations of the arriving guests, and at eight exactly, a string quartet began to play.

When the clock rolled around to nine, she decided enough was enough. She had to get down there, and if that meant taking out whoever was guarding her, well, that was just too bad. *What if I can't take them out quietly? What if they raise an alarm?* No time to worry about that now. Their mission could no longer be accomplished by subtle means — it had turned into a smash and grab.

Her first job was getting them to open the door. But how? In a play once, she had seen a man pretend he was sick in order to lure his jailers to enter his cell. *That's not going to work!* a voice in her head cried. *No one would be stupid enough to fall for that.* But what else could she do? Her brain wasn't exactly serving up choice ideas. She lay upon the floor, assuming a position that she hoped would be taken for abject agony and opened her mouth to begin yelling.

Before she could, Cirona heard something. Shooting into an upright position, she strained her ears. Yes, there it was again, a faint tapping noise. She spun around on her arse and looked at the window. There, grinning from ear-to-ear, was Dargo. Climbing to her feet, she rushed over, but the boy motioned her to stay put.

'What are you going to do?' Cirona mouthed at him.

Dargo rolled up one trouser leg to expose his automaton limb and said, 'Watch.'

The windowsill outside was wide enough for him to stand on. He gripped one end of the bars covering the window and braced his metal foot against one in the middle. Then he began to push, and to Cirona's utter delight, the bar began to warp out of place. When he had enough room to get through, he knelt and picked the lock.

'Sorry, I'm late,' he said, hopping through the now opened window.

Cirona pulled him into a tight bear hug. 'Late? Late, you beautiful little bastard! I could kiss you!'

'Save that for Dofri, eh?' Dargo said, smiling. 'What time is it?'

'Ten past nine.'

'Shit. I would have been here sooner, but they had me chained up. Took me forever to get undone, then I had to find your room, and there's two ton of sodding windows in this place.'

'Did you see Elvgren or Bellina?' she asked.

'No such luck. But we know where they'll be now, don't we?' he said, grinning once more. 'And I've got a plan.'

***

Bellina sat on the edge of her bed, the corset round her middle making breathing difficult, excessive amounts of lace tickling her exposed flesh. A maid had come by a half hour before to help her into the ridiculous dress, but she had declined any attempt at conversation with a shy smile. Bellina had then been left alone to wait some more.

During the time she had spent locked away, she had tried to use her powers. It hadn't taken her long to give up. Every time she tried, her head had filled with a buzzing sound, as if a million flies had taken up residence between her ears.

She watched the minute hand of the clock in her room edge towards the hour mark. Eight o'clock, ball time, their sole chance to steal the relic and make their meeting with Elvgren's brother.

Even though she was expecting it, the knock on her door when the clock struck eight still made her jump. She climbed to her feet, brushing out the creases in her dress and smoothing her hair.

'Yes?' she said.

'Your Majesty,' a voice said. '*His* Majesty is waiting for you. Are you ready?'

Now that's a question, Bellina thought. 'I'm ready,' she replied.

There was the sound of a lock opening, and the door swung back. The guard outside gave her a stiff salute then stood aside so she could pass. Bellina entered the hallway and found Elvgren leaning against the wall. He straightened up as she approached.

'You look stunning,' he said.

'Thank you,' she said. 'You don't look too bad yourself.'

And he didn't. King Omberto had fitted Elvgren with a robe almost as extravagant as the one he himself had been wearing.

Elvgren smiled. 'I'm glad you approve.'

'Your Majesties, this way please,' the guard cut in. He extended his hand down the hallway and, once they started moving, fell in behind them.

As they walked on, Bellina put her arm through Elvgren's. At the end of the hallway was a massive mirror. She had to admit that they looked good together. There was a grace to them, a rightness, that she couldn't deny.

A girlish part of her — one she had thought long dead — was squealing with delight. *Look at you*, she thought, *you look amazing. And that's not to mention the handsome man on your arm. You've become a proper lady.* Maybe that was true, maybe it wasn't, but at that moment, she felt full of the dignity her title commanded. If an empress wasn't a lady, then who was?

The guard directed them down a sweeping staircase and to the doors of the ballroom. Despite herself, Bellina felt her breath catch a little. The room was long and narrow, the shining floor reflecting the light from the rows of chandeliers above until it seemed that they walked upon a sea of fire. Fluted columns painted blue and gold rose to a ceiling where gods and men frolicked in playful ecstasy. One side of the room was windowed and would have afforded a beautiful view of the gardens before the malovor pen had been put up.

'Good evening, cousins,' Omberto cried, gliding across the floor towards them, a large guard in tow. 'I do hope your wait wasn't too interminable?'

'With how graciously you furnished our suites, how could it have been?' Elvgren said with an elaborate bow.

'Please, Your Majesty, raise your head. Are we not equals?'

'If that is the case then I insist you call us Elvgren and Bellina,' Elvgren said.

'Done and done,' the king said, dusting off his hands before offering them, palm up, towards Elvgren. 'But you both must call me Omberto.'

'Agreed. Thank you, *Omberto*,' Elvgren replied.

The king tipped back his head and roared with laughter. 'Thank you, *Elvgren*,' he said.

'Your High … I mean, Omberto, where are the General and Dargo?'

Omberto's face froze, the only movement upon it was a slight twitching at his left eye. 'I have … arranged other entertainment for them. I thought young Deego especially would have found the ball a rather boring affair.'

He wouldn't be the only one, Bellina thought, but said, 'When will we see them? I have something to discuss with the General.'

'Soon, soon,' the king said, making an impatient gesture with his hands. 'But now, come — the guests will be arriving, and they're all positively thrilled about meeting you. We haven't had a gathering of noble blood like this in Verradolla for many a year.'

Omberto, too short to put an arm around Elvgren's shoulders, placed one around his waist. They moved off slightly ahead of Bellina, and she saw Elvgren's hand gently probing the section of robe around the king's middle. Even with her powers locked away, she could guess what her betrothed was up to. She saw the guard tailing Omberto scowl.

'You, man,' she said in an effort to distract him. 'What is your name, and why do you carry no weapon?'

'My name is Luca, Your Majesty,' he said, not once taking his eyes off Elvgren. 'And I carry no weapon as no one is allowed to bear arms inside the palace. Do not worry though, I am an expert in hand-to-hand combat. You are most safe.'

'That's … good to know,' she replied.

They were at the far end of the magnificent hall now, by the entrance. Coming to a stop, Omberto said, 'Everyone will be arriving shortly. I do hope you will honour me by greeting them?'

'Of course, old boy,' Elvgren said, removing his arm from the man. He wrapped it around Bellina, pulled her close and whispered, 'He's definitely wearing the damned thing. If one of us gets an opportunity to snatch it, we take it.'

Bellina nodded.

A cavalcade of nobility was paraded before them, each with strange, exotic names that floated out of Bellina's head as soon as she had heard them. From time to time she caught glimpses of the relic sheathed at the king's waist, tempting her. But the gaze of the guard, Luca, was upon them, and she dared not make a move. By the time all had arrived, she was terrified to see it was already half past nine.

'Balls to this,' Elvgren hissed at her. 'I'm making my move.'

'Wait a—' she began.

But it was too late. Elvgren took a step towards Omberto then tripped himself with his own foot. For all the tea in Chenta, it looked as if they would collide, but then, so fast she barely registered it, Luca swooped in and grabbed Elvgren. The guard whispered something in his ear then pulled him back up, dusting Elvgren off.

'Maybe that wasn't such a good idea,' Elvgren said, after walking back on legs that were wobbling like a set custard. 'Bastard pinched a nerve on my neck. Couldn't move. Damned sneaky way to fight if you ask me.'

'What are we supposed to do now?' Bellina asked.

'Wait. Hope for a miracle.'

'What miracle?' she replied.

Then the screaming started.

***

Cirona took one last look at the clock, twenty past nine, then squeezed through the gap in the bars Dargo had created. It was a tight fit, but she forced herself out and onto the windowsill. There was enough room on it for her to stand, and she sneaked a look down to where Dargo had already begun to descend the ivy and trellis.

A rush of vertigo made her head swim, and she gripped the bars to steady herself. *Come on, girl,* she thought, *if this is the worst thing you'll have to do between now and stopping Marmossa, you'll be more than lucky!* Her mouth had gone dry as a sun-bleached bone, and her tongue made a strange clicking sound in its search for some moisture.

Shuffling to her left, Cirona reached out towards the ivy. Her hand grabbed hold of it feeling the supple strength of the vines and leaves. Letting out a sigh, she stuck out her foot. For a heart-halting moment, it flailed in mid-air, then the toe of her boat found purchase. Next came the hardest part of all. Placing all her weight on the hand and foot attached to the ivy, she screwed up her courage and brought herself completely off the windowsill. Her sweat-slicked right hand groped then caught hold of the plant while her right foot did the same.

'For the Father's sake, Rona,' Dargo hissed from somewhere below, 'shift your arse!'

'I'm coming, I'm coming, you little shit,' she replied.

The descent she was making looked to be about seventy or so feet, but to her it felt as if she was climbing down a mountain. Dribbles of sweat chased down her face, creeping into the corners of her eyes and making them sting. Her hair, which she had allowed to grow long—mainly to please Dofri—was blowing in the breeze and tickling her nose. Despite all of this, she pressed on, gaze fixed firmly on a point in front of her, refusing to look up or down.

'That's it, Rona,' Dargo gently called. 'You've almost done it!'

Cirona turned her head to look and overbalanced herself. One of her hands slipped and her feet lost their grip. For a moment, her entire weight was supported by one hand. As she dangled there trying in vain to re-establish her hold, she heard a strange sound, like creaking and ripping combined. She had just registered that the trellis was coming away from the wall when she began to drop.

A good ten foot of the trellis gave way, and she went swinging into the wall. The air left her lungs in one whooping sigh. She swung her feet in desperation, trying to turn her body and grab at the ivy that was still attached to the wall. One of her fingers came free, then another, till she was hanging on by nothing but her index and middle digits.

'Shit,' she said.

She fell, the last fifteen feet of the drop whizzing past her. Cirona cannoned into a topiary swan then spun to her left coming to a stop in soft dirt, the rich smell of it filling her nostrils.

'That's one way to get down, I suppose,' Dargo said, crouching beside her. 'We better get a move on — someone's bound to have heard that racket.'

Trying her best to get her breath back, Cirona hauled herself up and followed Dargo round a corner. They kept low, using the manicured hedges that bordered the palace as cover. The sound of the ball was very close now, and she realised the party was on the other side of the windows just behind them.

'Over there,' Dargo said, coming to a stop. 'D'ya see it?'

Cirona's gaze followed his pointing finger, and she saw the gate to the malovor pen. It was guarded by two men. 'I see it, Dar, but do you think it's a good idea? Really?'

'No time for second thoughts now, General.'

'But they're ... they're monsters.'

'Look,' Dargo said. 'We need a diversion big enough for us to steal the relic and get the fuck out of 'ere. Letting the malovors loose is the only one I can think of. Unless you've come up with something?'

'No,' Cirona said with a sigh.

'Right then — I'll cause a distraction, and you take out those two guards.'

'Hey! Hang on a minute!' she called, but Dargo was already off. 'Gods dammit.'

In a crouched run, she crossed over the gravel path and into the shadow of the malovor pen. She began to inch closer to the unsuspecting guards. Just as she was wondering what kind of distraction Dargo had planned, she heard him.

'Oi! Shit for brains! I got out of your fucking room, what d'ya think about that, eh?' The boy practically sang his words, making obscene gestures the whole time.

The guards started forwards away from the wall, and Cirona pounced at the nearest one. She chopped down at the base of his neck and watched with satisfaction as he collapsed without so much as a sigh. Despite Dargo's continued efforts, the other guard turned towards her. For a brief moment, panic flared in his eyes, then he opened his mouth to raise the alarm.

Cirona sprang at him and sent the man sprawling to the ground. Diving on top of him, she raised a fist, but the man was quicker, landing two jabs to her midsection which sent her rolling away. She watched as the guard's boot moved towards her, watched the man pull it back in a kick aimed at the centre of her face and just had time to spin round and take the blow in her back. The space between her shoulders lit up with a lightning strike of pain. Flopping to her back, she bit down to stop the howls of pain from escaping her lips.

'The infamous, Cirona Bouchard,' the guard said, standing over her. 'Beating you by myself will be a tale to tell my grandchildren.'

'Don't think you're gonna have any,' she said, driving her foot into the man's balls.

He collapsed to his knees, eyes bulging in comical surprise, a strange, high-pitched hissing sound emanating from his throat. Cirona climbed to her feet, panting, then smashed a vicious punch into the man's temple. Eyes rolling back to show their whites, he joined his comrade in unconsciousness.

'Good work, General!' Dargo said, running to Cirona's side. He gave her a crisp salute then began to rifle through the guard's pockets.

'What are you looking for?' Cirona asked.

'Keys,' Dargo replied. 'One of 'em has to … aha! Here we go!'

Following Dargo as he moved towards the gate, Cirona saw that its mechanism was clockwork, more than likely Gortrixian. The boy entered the key into the central lock and turned it. Around them the sound of a thousand cogs and gears spinning filled the air, before a final loud click told them the gate was open. They both grabbed handles on the gate, looked at each other then pulled.

The doors swung back without so much as a squeak, and there they were — the malovors. Cirona and Dargo moved back a way and watched them. They stood, knuckles scraping the ground, vacant eyes staring at nothing. In truth, they were pitiful things, creatures sent mad by isolation. But that didn't mean they were harmless, oh no, once a large number were whipped up, there was little that could stop them.

'What are they doing?' Dargo said. 'I thought they'd charge out as soon as the gate was open.'

'They usually need a command to fight. Other than that, you have to rile them up,' Cirona replied.

'Gotcha!' Dargo said, before picking up a stone and throwing it at the nearest malovor. 'Come on, you ugly bastards; over here!'

The struck creature blinked then rubbed at the point he was struck. Its gaze then turned to the taunting Dargo. Letting out a guttural snarl, it charged. The others began to follow him, first just a trickle then a full-on stream.

'Father, forgive us,' Cirona said, thinking of the unsuspecting guests.

'I'm sure he will!' Dargo yelled. 'Now run!'

***

Elvgren's head swivelled round towards the source of the screaming. For a moment, he didn't quite believe what his eyes were seeing. He rubbed them like a sleepy child, but the scene didn't change. At the other end of the ballroom, a malovor had sunk its teeth deep into the neck of a waiter. Somehow, the man was keeping his tray of drinks from slipping. Then the monster shook its head like a dog with a rat, and the glasses went tumbling to the floor with a laughing tinkle.

Everything seemed to happen at once. The ballroom windows burst inwards as more malovors leapt through them. From somewhere, an alarm bell began to sound, and guards poured into the room. Three of them clustered around the king while the others tried to deal with the unexpected attack.

'This is it,' Elvgren said. 'This is our chance to snatch the relic.'

'Are you insane?' Bellina cried. 'We need to get the hells out of here!'

'Just wait here; I'll be back in a second.'

'Elvgren. Elvgren! Wait!'

But it was too late. Elvgren moved across the ballroom like a man in a trance. Everything slowed down — to his left, he saw a malovor punch a fist through a woman's chest, her still-beating heart clasped in its clawed fingers; on his right, he watched a guard thrown into a crystal fountain, wine spraying outward, each droplet clearly visible as it seemed to hang in the air.

King Omberto was in front of him now. The guards were trying to clear an escape route, but their way was blocked. Eyes bulging in their sockets, the king gazed around the room with a look of mild incomprehension, like the mayhem was a joke he didn't quite get. Desperate not to miss his chance, Elvgren dived at Omberto, his outstretched fingers brushing the dagger's handle before he was seized by the scruff of his neck and hauled backwards. He flew through the air and landed hard on his back.

'You!' Luca said, grabbing Elvgren by the front of his shirt. 'You've done this, haven't you? Haven't you!'

With each word, Luca shook him back and forth. 'How fucking backwards are you?' Elvgren said. 'I've been here the whole time, you utter moron.'

Growling, Luca wrapped his hands around Elvgren's throat and lifted him into the air. Choking, he tried to kick out at the guard, but it had no effect, each attempt becoming more feeble than the last. Bright dots started to eat into the corners of his eyesight, and a high-pitched buzzing blocked his hearing.

'You Estrian bastard,' Luca hissed, 'I knew you could not be trusted, knew you must be after something. That's all you do, isn't it? Take, take, take, take, take. What's the matter? Don't have any more insults?'

'Dere su bing hind yoo,' Elvgren managed to wheeze, a faint smile on his lips.

'What?' Luca said.

That was his final word. Cirona grabbed the man's skull and yanked it back, his spine snapping with an audible crack. Luca's grip fell from Elvgren's throat, and he tumblied to the ground, pulling in great, chest-shuddering gasps of air.

'You alright?' Cirona asked, holding out her hand.

'Yes,' Elvgren replied in a hoarse croak, letting the General pull him to his feet. 'The relic—'

'Dargo's on it,' she replied, jerking a thumb over her shoulder.

And he certainly was. Elvgren watched the boy duck and dive from the grasps of malovors and guards alike. The men protecting the king had formed a tight circle, their eyes staring with horror at the carnage unfolding before them. Dargo slid through the legs of one of the men, causing great uproar when they realised what was going on. The guards drew in tight, and Elvgren and Cirona made a move towards them, but their help wasn't needed. A mechanical whine filled the air, and one of the king's men went flying. Dargo came through the newly made gap, grinning like an idiot.

'I've got it!' he called. 'Now let's get out of here.'

'Where's Bellina?' Cirona asked.

'Over there … argh, shit!' Elvgren answered.

Bellina was where he had left here, but now she had company. While most of the malovors were chasing the fleeing guests, one had homed in on her. She was standing, her back against a table brandishing a smashed wine bottle at the advancing creature. Elvgren began to run towards her, but Dargo outpaced him.

'You forgot; I'm the only one with a weapon,' he said, drawing the stolen dagger.

With a fresh burst of speed, Dargo closed in on the malovor. Still running, he jumped and landed on the thing's back, driving the point of the dagger home. The malovor roared, leaned backwards, then seemed to light up from within. A yellow light filled it, illuminating its veins and black, beating heart. The light grew brighter and brighter until the beast disintegrated.

'Fucking hells — this thing is amazing,' Dargo said.

'Good work, Dar,' Elvgren said before turning to Bellina. 'Are you alright?'

'I … think so,' she said.

'Good. Let's go.'

Elvgren and the others began to run towards the exit. The malovors still in the room were preoccupied with eating the people they had caught and paid little attention to their flight.

'Stop them!' the king cried. 'Stop them at once!'

Much to Elvgren's dismay, he saw three guards answer the command. They all picked up their speed and raced into a hall. Blood covered its walls, and body fragments littered the floor. Elvgren felt his stomach lurch. *Just ignore it*, he told himself, *block it out. You can't stop now!* Swallowing the sick rising at the back of his throat, he pressed on.

Outside, they met a scene of chaos. All across the tiled courtyard, guards and guests alike were battling with the malovors, a few were winning but the majority were not. Elvgren felt his feet slip as they sprinted towards the boats. When he looked down, he saw his feet were covered in blood. Ahead, he could see terrified nobles clambering into the last remaining boats, and he swore under his breath.

'Over there!' Bellina cried.

Elvgren followed her pointed finger and saw two boats remaining at the far left of the docking area. One of the boats was a simple vessel with two equimars to pull it, the other had a canopied roof of gilded gold and three of the giant seahorses. Elvgren moved towards the latter.

'Not that one,' Cirona said. 'It'll move too slow under the weight of all that crap. Get in this one.'

'But … it's so plain,' Elvgren said.

'Just get in!' Cirona bellowed at him.

'But this one has three equimars. Surely—'

He was cut short when a ballisket bullet whizzed past his head. Elvgren turned and saw the guards still in pursuit.

'On second thoughts, General, you might be right,' he said, joining the others in the simple craft.

'I thought they didn't have weapons!' Bellina said.

'Well, they've fucking well found some,' Cirona replied. 'Elvgren, you take the reins.'

'Why me?'

'Must you make everything into a fucking debate! You know how to drive a coach, don't you? This has got be practically the same.'

'It might seem that way on the surface—' Elvgren started to say before being interrupted by a second bullet, this one lodging itself into the side of the boat. 'Bollocks to it … give me the reins!'

Taking the straps of leather in his hands, he gave them a sharp crack, and the equimars lurched into life. Much to his surprise, Elvgren discovered that controlling them was almost indistinguishable from controlling horses, and he turned them with ease towards the sloped waterways that descended into the middle and lower parts of the city.

'Just saw those guards boarding that other boat back there!' Dargo called.

'They'll never catch us in that thing,' Elvgren replied.

The equimars were rocketing along now, there heads bobbing with natural grace, the water churning and bubbling as they ripped through it. With a sharp tug on the right rein Elvgren drew the boat round in a tight arc at the bottom of one waterway and into the next. As he did, he felt his stomach plummet. Ahead of them was a choked cluster of boats, the drivers hurling curses at each other, each trying to figure out what the hold-up was.

'Shit,' Elvgren said.

'What the hells is going on?' Bellina added.

'I don't know, but we're not getting through that,' Cirona replied.

'The fuckers are catching up!' Dargo said.

Elvgren looked over and saw it was true. He could clearly make the men out now … especially the one reloading the ballisket. Elvgren felt his mind whirring — there had to be something they could do?

'Quickly,' he said, dropping the reins. 'Follow me.'

'What are you doing?' Bellina asked.

'We'll use the boats as stepping stones. They're so close together we should be able to run to the front of them.'

'I can't think of anything better,' Cirona said. 'Let's go.'

Leaping to the nearest boat, Elvgren rushed past a shocked passenger and on to the next. On he led as fast as he could. Some of the occupants grabbed at him, but he shoved them away, most were too stunned at what they were doing to even complain and stood wide-eyed and slack-jawed.

When they reached the front of the tangle of boats, he could at last see what the problem was. A huge vessel pulled by ten equimars had become impaled on the metal bow of another craft; the passengers on both were trying to dislodge it but with little success. Elvgren jumped onto the smaller of the two and waited for the others to catch up.

'Now what?' Dargo said as Cirona used her impressive frame to push back the passengers.

'Try and cut it with that dagger,' Elvgren said.

'You what? That's impossible,' Dargo replied.

'That thing just turned a malovor into a pile of ash. Gods know what else it can do. Just try it.'

Dargo raised an eyebrow but moved to the ornate metal bow. He gave Elvgren another sceptical look then slashed the relic downwards, the bone colliding into the metal with a dull clang. Nothing happened.

'See, I told you—' Dargo began.

Before he could finish, a grinding screech filled the air. Elvgren watched the spot Dargo's relic had touched turn from red to white-hot then finally melt. The two boats came loose and Elvgren felt the deck rock beneath him. Steadying himself, he ran to the front.

'Sorry, old boy,' he said taking the reins from the driver.

'What the fuck do you think you're doing?' the man asked.

'Taking the ship. I would have thought that was obvious,' Elvgren replied.

'You can't—'

'Listen, chap, you just saw what the lad's dagger did, and unless you want to be a steaming mess on the floor, I suggest you get on the other boat post-haste. Looks like they have plenty of room.'

The driver's face turned purple, and his lips formed a thin white line. For a moment, it looked like he was going to argue, then he turned and boarded the other vessel.

'That's it, yer scurvy bastards! Aar!' Dargo called as he and Cirona got the passengers off the boat.

'What are you doing, Dar?' Elvgren asked.

'My pirate impression. Like it?'

'It could use a little work,' Elvgren replied.

Dargo blew a raspberry and said, 'Why don't you just concentrate on driving, eh?'

Not needing to be told twice, Elvgren grabbed the reins and got the boat moving. 'I'd like to see the faces on those guards about now,' he said as they raced into the city's lower district.

Just then there was a tremendous explosion of water behind them. Elvgren turned to see the guards' boat bobbing not a hundred feet behind them. *Why can't I keep my big mouth shut,* he thought.

'The crazy bastards have driven their boat off the waterway above,' Cirona whispered.

'Don't just stare at it like a moron,' Bellina said, whacking Elvgren on the shoulder. 'Go!'

Once more, he geed the equimars into life and led them through a city street. On they went, everyone ducking when they passed under a low bridge. At one point, they collided with a string of washing, and Elvgren was left temporarily blind while he pulled the semi-dry bloomers from his face. All the time, the guards were closing in, their boat going faster now that they had torn off the gilded canopy.

Turning a corner, they entered the lower city's market district. Dotted all along the waterway were rickety stands made of wood, some even stood out in the water, connected to solid ground by precarious plank paths. Elvgren pulled on the reins and dodged a stand in front of him. As he did so, the guards' boat pulled alongside.

From the corner of his eye, he could see the man with the ballisket lower it, taking aim. Elvgren felt cold sweat trickle down his brows, stinging at his eye. With a jerk, he turned his boat into the guards', the attacker flying backwards as his vessel cannoned into a stand, sending apples and lemons tumbling into the water.

'Good work, Gren, but the fuckers are still on us,' Dargo said.

Shit, Elvgren thought, spurring the equimars on. They twisted their way through street after street never managing to quite shake their pursuers.

'We're lost,' Bellina shouted at him.

'We are not lost,' Elvgren snapped back. 'We're just taking the scenic route.'

'We don't have time for the "scenic route", just get us to the bloody statue.'

'Thank you, my love, until now, I had no idea where we were going, I thought us on a merry cruise and … Aha! See, there it is,' Elvgren said.

At last, the statue of Inburna was in sight, and with the distance between them, they would beat the guards to it. Elvgren let out a small sigh and felt some of the tension leave his muscles. In the next instant, the retort of a ballisket crashed the still night air, echoing off the close-knit buildings that crowded them.

With dismay, Elvgren saw a gout of blood plume from the neck of one of the equimars. The creature thrashed for a heartbeat then lay still. Its live companion was still trying to pull forwards, but the added weight of its dead brother had slowed them to a crawl.

Somewhere in the city, a clock began to toll the hour.

Elvgren watched as they pulled closer to the statue, the clang of the bells somehow in sync with his heart. They were fifty feet away, then thirty, then twenty. All the time, the guards' boat was closing in on them. He looked back, expecting to see the ballisket aimed at him, but it seemed the guard had run out of shot and now stood ready with a sword. Ten feet now, and the dying note of the final bell disappeared into the night.

Both boats came to a stop against the small island's muddy bank. Elvgren jumped out, followed by the others, and instantly started to run for the statue. The guards, a tad slower to disembark, bellowed behind them. Keeping his focus on the likeness of Inburna, Elvgren drove on. He saw a portion of the strange stone base ripple like silk caught in the breeze then collapse inwards. What was left in its wake was a door. Jeremias stepped through it, took one look at what was happening and shot a guard dead.

'Hurry,' he called, reloading his ballistol. 'I can only sustain this portal for another thirty seconds.'

The two living guards had stopped to look at their fallen comrade. They screamed with rage and, using it as fuel, sped on. Elvgren slipped and saw the others overtake him.

'Go on!' he cried as he regained his feet.

He felt a hand grab at his robe, and he wriggled out of it, missing the searching hands by inches.

'Duck, brother!' Jeremias called.

Elvgren did as he was told and felt the bullet sear the top of his head before crashing into the guard's chest. Chest burning, lungs screaming, he came at last to the door, and he followed Jeremias through it. Before he could get a look at his surroundings, a hand gripped his collar and he was yanked backwards.

'Quickly,' his brother ordered. 'Get him back through to this side, the door will close any second!'

They got him back, but the man still had a hold. Elvgren was caught, dangling just off the ground when suddenly he fell hard on his arse.

'I thought the bastard would never let go,' Elvgren sighed.

'To be honest, Gren,' Dargo said, 'he didn't. Look.'

Elvgren looked and he saw a hand still gripping his collar, a hand connected to an arm the had been perfectly sliced off at the elbow when the door had closed. *If I had been caught in the middle of that when it closed …*

With that thought, Elvgren threw up.

CHAPTER SIXTEEN

'Are you sure we're going to make it?' Fontaine asked.

'For the thousandth time — yes, scholar,' Jeremias replied.

Fontaine fidgeted with the straps of his pack and bit his lower lip. He thought about asking Jeremias what made him so sure, but the man was already striding up the hill in front of them. The scholar gave a yelp as he felt a sharp slap on the cheeks of his arse. He turned round to see Waltus behind him.

'Get a move on, dopey, we ain't got all night,' the old mage said.

'I … er … yes, yes of course,' Fontaine replied.

Facing forwards once more, he looked up the steep hill they were ascending. At the very top, like an accusatory finger, was Amlith's Door — a monumental standing stone thirty minutes' carriage ride from Victory. Of course, he had been aware for a long time of the stone's true properties and the pathways it hid, had studied it, read about it, but he was finding that all the reading in the world couldn't prepare him for the real thing.

It was all so much easier to believe in when written, so much easier to grasp, to quantify. All the prophesies, obscure references and hidden knowledge had led him to this point — following a man who was about to open a magic portal, so the lot of them could save the world. The mere thought of it forced him to choke back a hysterical laugh.

'Stop,' Jeremias commanded as they neared Amlith's Door. 'Wait there.'

Coming to a stop some thirty paces from the stone, Fontaine stood with the others and waited. *This won't work, rocks don't turn into doorways. Then again, if a tree can do it then why not?* he thought, batting away a mad giggle. It was then he realised that a part of him, a part lurking in the darkest hole of his spirit, didn't want it to work, didn't want to be part of this whole crazy mess anymore. He reached out his hand in a silent plea, desperate to scream, to shout, to make sure everyone understood this was all some ghastly mistake.

'Be still, scholar,' Barboza said, placing a giant hand on Fontaine's shoulder. 'The fear you feel is not yours alone. We all feel it. This is the beginning of the end. We will either return as heroes or not return at all.

'Maybe the prophesies are true. Maybe all our lives have been building to this moment. Then again, maybe it's all bullshit. All I know is that someone I love is being held captive. That gives me the strength I need.

'This spear is in my hands thanks to you, scholar. You are braver and wiser than you know, and together, we accomplished something that had never been done, something that was a million to one chance. Do you hear me, scholar?'

Fontaine wiped at his eyes. 'Yes … I hear you.'

'Good. Now look to the stone — it's not every day you get to see such sights. In fact, it reminds me of a passage from the play *Wisaconda*: In times of—'

'Don't think there's time for that, Bar — look,' Crenshaw said, cutting Barboza off.

The scholar's eyes were drawn to the stone. Jeremias had produced the relic and was placing the tip of the short sword — *A sword made from the bone of a god*, Fontaine thought dizzily — against the centre of Amlith's Door. He watched as Jeremias placed his forehead to the gnarled stone and began to whisper. The area around the point of the weapon started to spin, faster and faster, revealing a circular patch of light that grew until it was the size of a cartwheel.

Jeremias stepped back from it. 'Let's go,' he said before entering the portal.

This is it, Fontaine thought, *no turning back now*. He stepped into the portal. Straight away he felt as if his body was being pulled mercilessly upwards, as if some vast creature was trying to suck him through a straw. Eyes closed tight, he sensed the pull on his bones and the air whizzing past him. The pain in his joints built to an agonising climax, and just when he thought he could take no more, he lurched out onto solid ground.

For a second, his head swam while it desperately attempted to make everything stop spinning. When he regained his equilibrium, Fontaine got his first look at what the ancients called *Lia-Atum*. Translated, it meant the In-Between. He was standing in a small courtyard of stone, the low walls only broken by the portal he had just come through and an arched entryway in front of him. At the top of the arch sat a gleaming, bronze scorpion with a human head. *A gatekeeper*, he thought with a shudder.

'Stop gawking, man, and move out of the way — the next one will be coming through soon,' Jeremias said, pulling Fontaine to the side.

No sooner had he done so, Waltus tumbled out, followed by Barboza, Crenshaw and Holger.

'All here?' Jeremias said. 'All limbs intact? No one got anyone else's leg?'

'That could have happened?' Fontaine cried.

Jeremias rubbed his neck. 'No … er … that was a joke.'

'Ha, ha, very bloody funny! Can we get this show rolling, none of us are getting any younger?' Waltus said.

'Fine, fine — follow me,' Jeremias replied. He walked to the arched doorway and pointed up at the bronze scorpion. 'This is a gatekeeper. To travel upon the roads of the In-Between a price must be paid.'

'What kind of price?' Crenshaw asked, frowning.

'Your life,' Jeremias answered. 'Or three months of it at least.'

'Hang on,' Holger said. 'Are you trying to tell us that … that thing is going to suck the life out of us?'

'Yes,' Jeremias said.

The group fell into silence as they each wrestled with what they had just heard. Three months didn't seem like a long time, but if they had to pass through multiple gates …

'For the love of … it's too late to turn back now,' Waltus said. 'We've got a job to do.' He strode towards the door.

Jeremias nodded, a faint smile playing at the corners of his lips. 'Good man. Stand there upon the stone marked with the blue cross.'

'Are you sure about this, old man?' Barboza said as Waltus took up position. 'What if you don't have three months to give? You … you could die.'

'I've still got a fair few years left in me, son, don't you worry about that!' the White Mage replied. He turned to Jeremias. 'What now?'

'Now you ask permission to pass.'

'Let me through, yer nasty looking thing,' Waltus said, giving the gatekeeper an obscene gesture.

Fontaine watched, eyes wide, as the blue cross on the stone began to glow. The light groped at Waltus like the tentacles of some blind squid, coiling round his limbs, climbing up his body. Next, the old mage's mouth snapped open like a ventriloquist's dummy and the icy blue tendrils snaked down his throat. The scholar felt his gorge rise at the sight of Waltus' chest lighting up, veins, arteries, his heart, all displayed in vivid detail.

Then the gatekeeper's eyes blazed scarlet, its tail rising. A thin beam of red shot from its stinger and hit the mage's heart. A deep thrumming sound filled the air accompanied by a horrible burning smell. Waltus' body grew taut, his chest pulled forwards, as a thin stream of white light trailed away from his heart and travelled up the beam of red. Fontaine rubbed at his eyes. This couldn't be real. In all the texts he'd read about the gatekeepers none of the descriptions had mentioned anything as disturbing as the scene he was witnessing now. Unable to do anything else, the scholar mouthed a silent prayer, begging for it to end. As if in answer, the lights faded, and Waltus collapsed to the floor.

'That … that is quite the toll to pay,' Barboza said, a tremor in his voice.

Waltus coughed. 'Fucking hells,' he said. 'I ain't felt like this since my five-year bender after the Mage Wars.'

Jeremias helped him to his feet. 'Go now. The path is open to you,' he said, pointing up at the gatekeeper, its eyes glowing a soft green.

'I'm going, I'm going,' Waltus said. He set of towards the arched entryway muttering, 'What the fuck have I got meself into this time? Bloody right mess …'

Jeremias waited till the White Mage had passed through then said, 'Who's next?'

Fontaine shared a worried look with his companions. 'I-I'll go,' he said, fearing that if he didn't act now, he would lose his nerve.

Trying to disguise his shaky legs, the scholar walked towards the marked stone. Head cocked, eyes narrowed, he regarded the blue cross. Exhaling, he placed one foot on the stone. For a breath, he thought his legs would betray him … then both feet were on the slab.

Looking up at the gatekeeper he said, 'I … er … beg your leave.'

Through the soles of his shoes, he could feel a thumping pulse, a bruising beat that made the bones of his legs vibrate like a struck bell. Without warning, the grasping blue light coiled around him. It felt like being stroked by a glacier. He tried to let out a cry and realised he was paralysed. His mouth snapped open unbidden, and the light was in him. He closed his eyes, not wanting to see his chest glowing, not wanting to have his own mortality on display. Something warm struck his heart, the gatekeeper's sting, then he felt the life leaving his body. In some ways it was like being winded but in some vital, necessary place. Then as quick as it had started, it was all over, and he too collapsed to the ground.

'Are you alright, scholar?' Jeremias asked.

'Yes … yes, I'll live,' Fontaine replied.

'Yeah, only three moths less than you would've done,' Crenshaw spat.

Jeremias scowled at Barboza's lover then said, 'Go on, the way is clear.'

Nodding, Fontaine walked to the doorway. As he passed under the arch, he cast a glance at the gatekeeper; if he hadn't known better, he would have sworn the bronze contraption was smiling. Stepping through the door's milky surface Fontaine felt a small resistance, then with a pop, he was on the other side.

He was standing on a wide road made from huge, dark slabs of stone. All around him, similar paths twisted and spun, reaching up into space like the branches of some ancient tree. Most of the roads led to more arched entries, but some simply came apart, ending abruptly in a tangle of broken stonework.

By the gods, he thought, *I'm actually in the In-Between — a space that shouldn't exist.* Try as he might, Fontaine couldn't stop a small squeak of excitement escaping his lips.

'It's something, ain't it?' Waltus said.

'Y-yes,' was all the scholar could reply.

'Have a look over the side.'

Following the mage's words, Fontaine moved towards the stone wall that bordered the road. It came to his middle, so he was able to peer over the edge with ease. What he saw made his head lurch from a bout of vertigo. The overcast clouds that hung overhead continued to billow below, as if he were caught in a glass bauble filled with smoke. Punctuating the clouds, extending down as far as the eye could see, were more of the paths, crossing and re-crossing each other in a dizzying scene.

Fontaine stumbled away from the wall, his head still spinning. 'I think I'll have a seat while we wait for the others,' he said.

It wasn't a long wait. Jeremias was the last to come through. Fontaine watched as the man proceeded to take out a silver object just longer than the span of his hand. Then he dug a key out of his pocket and wound the gizmo up. Once satisfied, he removed the key and threw the object into the air where it sprouted wings and hovered next to Jeremias' head.

'What is that?' Holger asked.

'This is a wayseeker,' Jeremias replied. 'The paths of the In-Between shift and move, and it's easy to lose your way. The wayseeker always finds the right road.'

'Amazing,' Barboza whispered, extending his finger for the silver bird to sit on. 'I had no idea Estria was capable of such sophisticated automatons.'

'W-we're not,' Fontaine said. 'The wayseekers were built by the First Ones. That machine is thousands of years old.'

'Bloody hells! They built things to last, didn't they!' Crenshaw added.

'Amazing as it is, the wayseeker is still a tool, a tool with a job to do. Take us to Sylucia,' Jeremias said.

Hearing those words, the bird took flight and zoomed to the end of the path. Fontaine and the others trudged after it. It led them to a crossroads, several paths branching out from it. The bird flew to the end of each one, seeming to consider them before finally choosing the way forwards. This happened three more times before they reached another arched entry, a gatekeeper perched on top.

'I'll go through and collect the others,' Jeremias said.

Watching as he paid the toll, Fontaine wondered just how much of his life Jeremias had sacrificed on his travels. His fare paid, Jeremias crossed through the door. The scholar looked on as one by one Bellina, Elvgren, Dargo and Cirona came staggering out of the gate. Holger and Barboza passed them their kitbags while they waited for Jeremias.

Once they were all accounted for, Jeremias called the wayseeker to him and said, 'Atvoria.'

'What the bloody hells is Atvoria?' Dargo asked.

'It was the … er … original name for the Scorched Earth,' Fontaine replied.

'You didn't think it was always called the Scorched Earth did you, Dar?' Elvgren said with a smile.

'Well, I don't bloody know, do I? Not exactly the type of information that comes up on the streets of Tavarar.' Dargo huffed.

'Enough chat,' Jeremias cut in. 'We've got a long way to go so save your breath for that.'

The group began to move, and Fontaine found himself straggling at the back. To his surprise, the person next to him was Bellina. She was moving gingerly, her face still green from crossing through the Sylucian door.

'A-are you alright, Your Majesty?' the scholar asked.

'What? Oh, yes, just feeling a bit sick. It's nothing really,' she replied.

Her hand went to her belly, and for a second, he could have sworn it looked swollen. *Her breasts look bigger too*, he thought, blushing fiercely. *But that would mean … surely, she wasn't …*

'Pick up the pace back there!' Jeremias hollered, shaking Fontaine from his thoughts.

Gritting his teeth, the scholar pressed on, closing the gap between him and the rest. Down twisting roads and paths they marched, all the while the wayseeker picking out the right route they should take. For hours, they pressed on, until at last, they stood before the gate to Atvoria. This time, the arched doorway was flanked by two towers of black marble.

'Almost done, people,' Jeremias said. 'Once we pay the toll here, all the gates to Atvoria will be open to us, though we only need one. Are you ready?'

Fontaine voiced his assent with the rest. Jeremias nodded and started to usher them forwards. The scholar's turn came, and once more, he passed through with a loud pop. Looking around, he saw that they were in a circular plaza. Three short paths radiated out around its circumference.

'Right,' Jeremias said, when they were all through, 'the path we want is—'

He was cut off by the darkening of the clouds that surrounded them. A rumble of thunder echoed around them, the sound so deep and close it made Fontaine's teeth chatter. Forks of lightning started to shoot from the clouds, javelins hurled by an angry god. Overhead, the scholar watched a cloud sag, a gigantic face appearing in it.

'Marmossa,' Bellina hissed.

Fontaine turned towards her and this time was sure that her stomach was bigger. He didn't have long to dwell on it though.

'So,' Marmossa said, 'this is how you rats intend to invade my kingdom. Well, you go no further!'

The face in the cloud opened its mouth. In the centre, cracks of lightning smashed together creating a giant, stuttering ball of galvanic energy. A high-pitched whine filled the air.

'Everybody back!' Jeremias screamed.

Turning round, Fontaine tripped over his feet and went sprawling to the ground. Panic surging through him, he scrabbled forwards on his hands and knees. The blast hit the road they were supposed to travel down, blowing the massive chunks of stone aside like a child toppling a tower of wooden bricks.

'To me!' Jeremias howled.

But the next blast of lightning split the plaza and the group in half. Fontaine turned and ran towards the gate closest to him, there were people around him, but he paid them no mind, pushing and shoving them aside. Only one thought filled his head — run! Moaning, whimpering he bolted to the doorway and threw himself into it.

The last thing he heard was the rolling thunder of Marmossa's laughter.

***

For a long moment, Bellina lay on her back coughing and spluttering, the grit-filled air choking her lungs. Her nose whistled as she took great, heaving gasps, desperate to catch her breath. After a while, her breathing returned to normal, and she opened her eyes. Above her stretched a sky of the purest blue uninterrupted by even the hint of cloud. *We made it,* she thought.

Yes, a dark voice at the back of her mind hissed, *but to where?*

Around her, she could hear the low groans of whoever else had come through with her, but they were not her primary concern. For a heartbeat, her fingers trembled as they stretched towards her swollen stomach, then she placed her hand upon the large bump. A tiny foot kicked out at her touch.

Bellina gasped and drew her hand away like she had been burned. Oh gods, this couldn't be happening; this couldn't be real. She had thought there would be more time, time to digest the idea of being pregnant, to come to terms with it, but the Guardians' toll had put paid to that notion. *What am I going to do? Father, help me — what am I going to do?* Her mind whirred. *I'm not ready for this, for, for… it.*

'Your Majesty?' a gruff voice called from next to her. 'Are you alright?'

Bellina turned her head and saw Jeremias stumbling towards her. She quickly brushed the tears from her eyes.

'Y-yes, I'm … fine,' she replied, wondering if she had ever told a bigger lie in her life.

'Allow me,' Jeremias said, extending a hand.

She took it and together they managed to get her back to her feet. Once she was up, Bellina saw the elder Lovitz's eyes flick to her belly. Her mouth opened, her mind searching for the words to fend off the questions that were surely coming. Instead, Jeremias pointed to her arm.

'How'd you get that?' he asked.

'This?' Bellina asked, looking at the bracelet. 'It was a welcome gift from King Omberto.'

Jeremias knelt to look at it more closely. 'An ancient power dampener, eh? He must have got it from Marmossa or his cronies. Give me a second, and I'll get rid of it.'

With that he began to whisper strange words at the bracelet. It loosened then slid to the ground with a dull thump. Jeremias picked it up and hurled it away.

'We won't be needing that anymore,' he said. 'Now, let's check on the others.'

Those others included Cirona, Waltus and Barboza. Bellina watched the new king of Timboko offer Cirona a shovel-sized hand and haul the General to her feet in one swift movement. Bellina took a breath, centring herself. *You're here, alive and with allies*, she told herself; *we can worry about this baby business later.*

Just who do you think you're kidding? the voice at the back of her mind said.

Pushing the voice and all her other thoughts away, Bellina took in her surroundings. What she saw made her breath catch. Behind her stood a vast city located upon an island of rock, its sand-coloured walls rearing up from the ground like an extension of the landscape. A bridge speared out, connecting the city to the world around it. Flat-topped buildings peeped over the wall while dizzying, spindle-like towers sought to pierce the sky. From the centre of it all, rising like a rotten tooth, was a monumental square structure made from black stone.

'What is this place?' Bellina whispered to herself.

'That is Imun Nir, city of Hisoth, though you know him as the Sixth Terror.'

Bellina whirled round, heart pummelling against her chest, in response to the unknown voice. Before her stood a woman made of transparent, blue light; the light projected from what looked like a metallic dragonfly. She was dressed in a tight corset, reams of crimped cloth dropping from it. A choker with a locket drew the eye towards the V of her cleavage. Elbow-length gloves graced her arms, and in her left hand, she held an open umbrella.

'Bellina, get back!' Cirona bellowed, pulling out a ballistol and firing. The bullet whizzed harmlessly through the woman's chest.

'What are you?' Jeremias demanded.

'Can't you see?' Barboza said. 'She's a ghost.'

'I am not a … Oh, for heaven's sake — I'm a hologram,' the woman said.

'A holo-what?' Waltus said.

'A hologram. A projection of a nexus hub, or as you might put it, a Fargazer. My name is Alari, and I have come to help not harm. You have spoken with one of my kind before, haven't you, my love?' This last remark was directed at Bellina.

'I … I have but you're quite a bit … different,' Bellina replied.

'Oh, we've all developed our quirks over the centuries, but our mission, given to us by our creator, Lokos Vistas, has always remained the same — to prevent the return of the Old Terrors,' Alari said.

'I don't trust it,' Cirona said.

Alari began to move, the metal dragonfly keeping step. She stopped before Cirona. 'My, my, you are a cynical old thing, aren't you? But if I had wanted you dead …' she clicked her fingers, and the dragonfly's tail turned into a blade. In a gleaming blur, it was at Cirona's throat. A bead of blood blossomed on its tip.

'Enough!' Bellina bellowed. 'We will gladly take whatever assistance you can offer us, Alari.'

'At least one of you has some manners,' the Fargazer said. With a swipe of her finger, the dragonfly retreated.

'How long is it until the eclipse?' Jeremias asked.

'Three days,' Alari replied with a twirl of her umbrella.

Bellina took a small step back, feeling as if she had been slapped. 'How can that be?' she said.

Jeremias rubbed a hand across his face. 'You can lose time travelling the In-Between. It would have been fine if we had made it to Sanctuary but … damn it all,' he said, kicking at the dirt. 'It's impossible now. We'll never make it.'

'That's not quite true, darling,' Alari said. 'There is a way, but we'll have to get you to Hisoth's palace. There is a device there that can get you to your destination instantly.'

'Go into Imun Nir?' Jeremias said. 'Are you mad?'

Alari flashed a dazzling smile. 'You will be fine, poppets. After all, I will be there to guide you.'

Bellina bit her lip. 'What choice do we have?' she said. 'Lead on, Alari.'

The Fargazer dropped her a curtsy then headed towards the bridge. Bellina and the others trailed in her wake.

'Are you sure about this?' Cirona whispered, catching up to Bellina.

'No. No, I'm not sure. I'm not sure about anything at the moment,' she replied.

'But Marmossa could have sent that … thing to—'

'As Alari said, General, she could have killed us on the spot.'

Cirona took a deep breath. 'Fine, but what about … you know … that,' she said, pointing a finger at Bellina's belly.

'There is no time to think about that now,' Bellina said. 'We … we must carry on.'

With that Bellina stalked ahead of Cirona, a hard task considering the added weight she was carrying. Before long she had caught up with the Fargazer. 'Alari,' she called.

'Yes, Your Majesty?' the hologram replied.

'What do you know about us?'

'Why everything, my dear. We have been monitoring you all quite closely. I must say you are a plucky little band, aren't you?'

Bellina licked her lips. 'Do you … do you know what happened to the rest of our group?'

'They live,' Alari said. 'They appeared on the other side of Atvoria. My … *sister* will be aiding them.'

Bellina felt a knot of worry unravel inside her. They were alive. Then another question left her lips. 'You know the way, don't you?'

'Why of course! My memory plates have an intricate knowledge of the … ah.'

They came to a stop. Bellina saw that a large chunk of the bridge had been destroyed. Her mouth grew sour as a tense weight settled in her chest. *Ah indeed*, she thought.

***

Elvgren opened his eye with a soft moan. His head thumped out an aching beat. What had happened? The last thing he remembered was diving through the collapsing portal, desperate to get away from the carnage Marmossa had unleashed. Slowly, his vision began to focus … what he saw forced him to take a small gasp.

In front of him lay an ocean of green. The tips of palms and gigantic daioba trees shifted in the slight breeze, plunging down as they followed the sloping ground, creating elongated V-shapes in the jungle landscape. A fine mist hung above it all, snaking its way through branch and leaf. Something nagged at Elvgren about the scene before him, something off. Then he realised … he was looking *down* on all of this.

He tried to move and felt his legs cycle in thin air. A cold sweat prickled at his skin while he swung back and forth. Screwing up his courage, he craned his neck back and saw that the only thing separating him from an untimely demise was the cloth of his travelling cloak snagged on a branch. *Father, help me*, he thought, *how the hells am I going to get down from here?*

As if in answer, he heard the creaking groan of the branch giving way. Elvgren scrunched his eye shut in anticipation of the fall to come. Instead, the tree limb swung down, slamming him into the massive trunk of the tree with bone-crunching force. Electric bolts of pain radiated out from his spine. Before he had time to fully appreciate the agony, his cloak tore, and he belly-flopped onto a collection of branches lower down.

The air shot from his lungs in a great whooping sigh. For a handful of breaths, he lay there, eye still closed, listening out for the sound of the branches giving way. When they didn't, he forced his good eye open. Through the branches of the tree, he could see the ground below him. *I must be at least a hundred feet up*, he thought. From somewhere close by a parrot called, its cry sounding like a harsh laugh.

Unable to tear his gaze away from the drop beneath him, Elvgren's brain swam with vertigo, the jungle floor seeming to stretch away. *Focus, man*, he told himself, *we've got to get down from up here.* With slow, deliberate movements, he edged his body back from his nest of branches. For a second, his feet kicked out in mid-air, then the toe of his boots found the branch below and he lowered himself onto it.

After a moment to compose himself, he continued in this way down the tree. As the ground grew closer, he began to breathe easier. Then, some thirty feet from his goal, his boots slipped on the branch below him, and he fell. In an act of desperation, he pulled his short sword free and drove it into the soft bark of the tree. His descent slowed a touch, but the earth still rose towards him at alarming speed. With a jolt, Elvgren's weapon hit a knot in the trunk, and he went sprawling the last ten feet to the ground, his sword clattering down mere inches from his head.

In spite of the pain flaring through every inch of his body, Elvgren breathed in the rich, heady scent of the dirt and had to stop himself from kissing the ground.

'You going to sit there all day?' a strange voice said behind him.

Body reacting on instinct, Elvgren leapt to his feet and spun round to see who was there. He found himself face-to-face with a woman made of stuttering blue light, her presence projected by what looked like a metal insect hovering over her head. She was dressed in a pair of baggy dungarees, a plain white work shirt underneath. Fingerless gloves of thick leather covered her hands. The woman was small with shrewd, dark eyes and an amused sneer on her lips.

'Who the hells are you?' Elvgren asked, his hand reaching towards his ballistol.

'I'm Veta, a nexus hub, or Fargazer,' she said, looking him up and down. 'I'm supposed to help you and whatever.'

Elvgren stepped forwards and waved an arm through her. 'How can you help? You're not even real!'

Veta rolled her eyes. 'Are the rest of you this stupid or are you a special case?'

'Me? Stupid? Do you have any idea who I am?' Elvgren spluttered.

'Yeah, yeah, I know who you are — Amlith's Heir and all that rubbish. Now, are we going to get moving or just stand here bickering all day?'

'Get going where?' Elvgren asked.

'Well to start with, to where the rest of you are,' Veta replied, pointing into the trees with a sigh that said she would rather be anywhere else.

Straightening himself up, Elvgren said, 'I don't trust you, and I don't need your help,' before walking straight through Veta in the direction she was pointing.

'If you don't need my help,' she called. 'Why are you going where I told you?'

'I was intending to go this way before *you* showed up.'

He stormed ahead along the lush jungle path. Behind him, he could hear the chittering of the metal insect's wings betraying the fact Veta was following him. Ignoring it, he pushed on. Overhead, unseen animals hooted to each other in soft voices, melding with the soft gurgle of a stream, while the sickly-sweet smell of overripe fruit assaulted his nose. It didn't take long for him to see the others' presence in the form of smoke rising from a fire. Racing towards it, he pushed aside a palm frond dripping with water to see Dargo, Holger, Crenshaw and the scholar sitting round the flames.

'There you are, Gren,' Dargo said, hurrying towards him. 'Thank fuck for that! We've been looking for you all morning.'

'I … er … got a bit caught up with something,' Elvgren replied.

'Who's that?' Dargo asked, looking past Elvgren's shoulder.

'She says she's called Veta, a Fargazer, or so she claims.'

'Like the one who spoke to Belle?' Dargo asked.

Elvgren gave a grunt of assent. 'That's if she's to be believed.'

'Goodness,' Fontaine said, almost running forwards. 'A genuine Fargazer, here, in front of me.'

Elvgren watched the scholar walk around Veta, inspecting every angle.

'Do you mind?' she said. 'I'm not a bloody zoological specimen.'

Fontaine jumped back. 'Yes … yes, of course. My apologies.'

Veta watched him skitter back through narrow eyes before speaking again. 'Look, I don't have time for idiots, so I'm just going to tell it to you straight. There are now three days till the eclipse.'

Elvgren felt his breath catch along with everyone else.

'Yeah, yeah, shock, horror. Listen, you have no way of making it without my help. I'm not fussed either way. So … I don't know, take a vote or something and tell me what you decide.'

'How do we know you weren't sent by Marmossa?' Crenshaw asked.

Veta sighed and pinched the bridge of her nose. 'You don't. All I can do is assure you I wasn't. That's my final say. Take it or leave it.'

'I don't see what other choice we have,' Holger said.

'You really think we should trust this … this thing?' Elvgren spluttered. 'And who asked *you* anyway?'

you anyway?'

'Well, do you know a way out of here?' Holger replied, sweeping his arm at the jungle.

'I-I'm afraid I agree, Your Majesty — we have no other option,' Fontaine said.

Elvgren blinked in astonishment. 'Dargo? What do you say?'

'Sorry, Gren.' Dargo shrugged.

Crenshaw held out for the longest before letting out a sigh and saying, 'Fuck it. Why not?'

'Have you all gone mad?' Elvgren cried.

'Sorry, One Eye, looks like you've been outvoted,' Veta said, a smug smile on her lips. 'Anyway, let's get going. Gods only know what's been attracted by that fire.'

Veta took off, and Elvgren fell in behind her, watching her back, wary. They progressed deeper into the jungle, the humidity sapping his energy and plastering a sweat-soaked shirt to his back. The soft hooting he'd heard earlier returned — this time louder, more urgent.

Veta paused. 'Fuck, so soon. Why did you idiots have to light a fire?'

'What's wrong?' Holger asked.

Elvgren saw a blur at the corner of his vision. His brain just had time to register it as man-shaped before something solid hit him in the gut and threw him over its shoulder. He caught one last glimpse of his startled companions before he was whisked away through the dense foliage.

CHAPTER SEVENTEEN

With deliberate care, Cirona walked to the edge of the gap. Beside her, great chunks of the stonework had been forced up like spear tips. Licking her lips, she kicked a loose chunk of rock and watched it bounce and spiral down the broken section of bridge. After what felt like a lifetime, she heard the faint plop of it falling into the raging river.

'Fuck,' she murmured. 'There's no way we're getting across here.'

Alari came floating back from the other side of the bridge wearing a frown.

'If only you could tie a rope to one of the rocks over there you would be able to make a path to monkey along,' she said.

'You've got to be joking,' Bellina snorted. 'That gap is a good thirty feet across, and even if we could fasten a rope on that side, I'm in no … condition to be monkeying along anything.'

'Is there no other way?' Jeremias asked.

Alari played with the choker around her neck. 'There is, but it's on the other side of the city. It would take a good day to get round there, and there's no saying that bridge will be in any better condition than this one.'

'Why were you not aware of this … this destruction,' Barboza said.

The Fargazer crossed her arms over her chest. 'I'll have you know, sir, that this damage was done incredibly recently, and my sub-routine is only scheduled to scan for new topographic data every thirty days.'

'Alright, alright, the lot of yer!' Waltus said, a fag hanging from his bottom lip. 'I can get over there and carry the lass. Only be able to do it the once mind; the rest of yer will have to use the rope.'

'What is it you plan to do?' Jeremias asked, looking the old mage up and down.

'Just you watch,' Waltus answered.

A smile stretched across Cirona's lips. She had seen the White Mage's magic before, but it never stopped being impressive. Waltus stood for a second in concentration then lifted the hem of his robe. As he touched the tips of his fingers to his legs they filled and expanded like balloons becoming taut with muscle. He then did the same to his arms.

'Up yer come girl,' he said, sweeping a stunned Bellina into his embrace.

'What in the twelve hells—' Barboza began.

'Just watch,' Cirona interrupted.

Beginning slow, Waltus walked towards the gap, picking up speed as he went. He broke into a full sprint then leapt. For a second he seemed to hang in mid-air, framed by the sun. Despite her faith in the mage's abilities, even Cirona had her heart in her mouth. Then he landed, safe on the other side. Barboza let out a congratulatory whoop, and Cirona was not ashamed to join him.

'Absolutely wonderful, darlings. Well done, that man,' Alari chirped. 'Now, one of you toss him the rope and we can get this cabaret moving again.'

Cirona took the rope from her kitbag, marvelling at the forethought that Jeremias and Whist had put into assembling their equipment. She walked to the lip of the gap, whirled the rope round her head like a lasso and threw it to the other side on her first try. She expected Waltus to make some kind of comment, but he simply nodded before tying his end to one of the broken snags of rock. *He's not made one lewd comment towards me yet,* she thought; *I wonder if he's ill.*

'Um, General? Yoo-hoo,' Alari said. 'Would you be so kind as to tie this end. That's it, there's a good dear. Now — who will be first?'

'I'll go,' Barboza said. 'If it can hold my weight, it will hold for everyone else.'

'Very good then, on you pop,' Alari replied.

With his spear and kitbag safely secured, Barboza moved to the rope. Lying on his back he locked his two trunk-like legs on top of the rope then began to shimmy along hand over hand. When the Timbokan king reached the middle, the rope sagged dramatically. Cirona held her breath, the only sound breaking the silence came from Barboza himself as her recited a passage from some play, clearly trying to keep his mind from panicking. Soon the worst was over though, and he reached the other side. The lighter Jeremias made short work of the trial. Now it was Cirona's turn.

With small, shallow steps, Cirona walked to the rope. With her hands trembling at her sides, she looked over the edge once more. *Fucking heights,* she thought, *I've been stuck up high more times in the past year than in the rest of my life put together. When this is over with, I'm going to buy myself a nice cottage in the flattest bit of field I can bloody well find and—*

'Are you coming, General!' Jeremias called.

'Y-yes, just … hold your horses, will you!' she called back.

Her breathing became uneven, her palms sweaty, as she lay on her back and wrapped her legs round the rope. She wiped her hands on her trousers then took hold. Slowly, Cirona edged her way along, each time she took a hand off the rope, her heart stopped. After what felt like forever, she reached the middle. The rope began to sag, a strong breeze picking up that made her sway to and fro.

Body trembling, rasping breaths filling her lungs, she came to a complete and utter halt. *I can't go on*, she thought, *I can't, I can't, I can't.* Somewhere, a million miles away, she could hear people yelling to her, but she had no idea what they were saying. Then one voice did cut through to her panic-stricken mind.

'Hurry, General,' Alari was shouting, 'the rope is coming loose!'

This time, her fear drove her into action, and Cirona began moving forwards as fast as she could. The rope started to bounce and sway even more as the knot she had tied loosened. Every inch she clawed towards the other side, every slight motion, made her think the line would break.

'Rona, look out!' Bellina screamed.

Cirona began to fall, fall through what felt like endless depths. With a jolt, the rope became taut, and she cannoned into the broken section of bridge beneath Bellina and the others. The air was battered out of her, and a sharp burning pain shot out from her side. *Cracked some fucking ribs. Fantastic!*

'Just hold tight, Rona; we're going to haul you up,' Bellina called down.

Cirona did just as she was told, and after several shuddering heaves, she was up. She rolled to her side, panting, each breath sending a sharp pain out from her cracked bones.

'What have you done to yerself?' Waltus asked, kneeling beside her.

'Ribs … cracked some,' she said.

Waltus nodded then placed his hands over the damaged area. After a minute or so, Cirona felt the pain subside and her breathing grow easier.

'Thank you, Waltus,' she said, sitting up and planting a kiss on the old man's cheek.

'It's like that now, is it?' Waltus replied. 'It's all niceness and kisses when your fancy man ain't around.'

Cirona leaned back, stunned. 'Waltus … are you jealous?'

'Just thought we 'ad something special is all. But I've had me heart broken before, I'll get over it,' he said, climbing to his feet.

Before Cirona could respond Alari said, 'Well that was all very exciting, but we really should be off.'

Once more, the Fargazer led the way, her projected umbrella spinning above her head. Soon, Cirona found herself passing under a massive square gate, the portcullis suspended overhead. *By the father,* she thought, *these walls must be ten feet thick.* At last, they entered the city proper, walking along a road that six carriages could have driven along abreast.

The main road ended in a large square, and Alari began to lead them through the winding back streets. On all sides, squat, flat-roofed buildings crowded them, and every so often, one of the twisting, spindly towers.

'I … I need to stop,' Bellina said.

'But it will only take us another hour to reach the palace,' Alari said.

'Please, my feet and back are aching,' Bellina replied.

'Oh, very well,' Alari sighed, rolling her eyes. 'One of these buildings was an inn.'

She led them to one of the bigger constructions, through an open door and into a large room filled with copper seats and tables.

'There's not one speck of tarnish on these,' Barboza proclaimed.

'The ancient ones knew a technique that made metal non-tarnishing. Like most of their knowledge the secret to that process is now lost; Amlith Castria made sure of that,' Alari answered.

'What happened to all the people?' Bellina asked, lowering herself into a chair with a sigh.

'Some died in the cataclysm. Others were led to their deaths in a battle against Hisoth. The small number of survivors fled Atvoria to other countries around the world,' Alari said, her bottom lip trembling.

While the others spoke, Cirona walked around the inn and past the counter that had once served so many. She found herself in a backroom, a storage area if the rotting barrels were anything to go by. At the back of this room was a cupboard with a metal grate. She tilted her head to the side and raised her eyebrows. *Now just what the hells is in there?* she wondered.

Curiosity overcoming her, she reached out and pulled back the grate. Its contents made her draw in a sharp breath. An automaton. The machine's bottom bulged out, the metal ruffled to give the impression of a skirt. Its midsection was a glass cylinder exposing the gears and cogs of its inner working. Atop this was a spherical head, the only features, a pair of massive, round, lamp-like eyes.

'Is something the matter back there, darling?' Alari called.

Startled, Cirona spun round, her elbow catching the machine. 'No,' she said. 'Everything is fine.'

Behind her came the hiss of pistons firing and the clank of levers turning. She turned to see the automaton come to life, its huge eyes glowing green.

'Please stand still for facial scanning,' the machine said.

'No … I … you see, there's been a mistake and—'

'Facial recognition failed,' the automaton said. 'Please remain here while the appropriate authorities are called.'

'Shit,' Cirona whispered.

***

Fontaine stood stunned as he watched Elvgren whisked away into the jungle foliage on the back of what he could only describe as a man-shaped blur. *What in the twelve hells was that?* he thought. It had been humanoid in shape but the speed with which it moved would be impossible for even the fittest of people.

'Shitting hells!' Crenshaw cried. 'We better get after them quick.'

'I do not see what the particular rush is about,' Holger said, looking darkly in the direction Elvgren was taken.

'Whatever has come over him?' Fontaine whispered to Dargo.

'They've got previous those two,' the boy muttered. Then, 'Let's move before we lose them!'

Fontaine watched horrified as Crenshaw, Holger and Dargo raced away brandishing their weapons. 'Hold on!' he called. 'We need to think before we go tearing off; none of us know the terrain or-or what other beasts are lurking out—'

'I guess people still choose swords and guns over intelligence,' Veta interrupted, her face a mask of disappointment.

'Fargazer,' Fontaine said. 'What was that … beast?'

'That was a sloman. A mix of a sloth and a human. They hunt in packs, so there's bound to be more of them lurking nearby. I could have explained that, if those idiots hadn't gone off like that,' she replied.

Fontaine chose to ignore the phrase "a mix of sloth and human" for the moment and asked, 'What should we do?'

'We'll follow, *cautiously*, and hope it was just one sloman working alone,' Veta answered.

'V-very w-well then,' he replied, wetting his lips.

'I'll take point,' Veta said.

'If that's what's best,' Fontaine said, letting out a small sigh of relief.

'Of course it's what's best — nothing here can do me any harm,' the Fargazer replied before looking him in the eye. 'Besides … it would be a shame if the only one of you with a lick of intelligence got killed.'

With Veta's praise coursing through him like a shot of brandy, Fontaine puffed his chest out and followed her. The trail was easy to read even for a man who had spent his whole life in the musty embrace of libraries and studies. All around were broken stems, crooked fronds and the print of boots in the soft dark earth.

'E-Excuse me, Fargazer?' Fontaine said.

'Please, call me Veta, scholar.'

'Alright then … Veta, what … what is this place?'

'This was a bio-engineering laboratory.'

Fontaine's head jerked back. 'Engineering? Biology? How in heaven's name was that accomplished?'

'By manipulating matter at the atomic level.'

The scholar gasped. 'Then that means Heidrich's atomic model is correct! My goodness to think that all of creation is made from such tiny parts. Oh, the things I could learn from you, Veta.'

Smiling, the Fargazer turned to face him. 'Oh, the things I could teach,' she said. A cry of pain sounded ahead of them. 'Quick, we'd better move.'

Panting, a stitch burning in his side, Fontaine chased after Veta. Before long, she came to a stop, and he skidded to a halt beside her. She placed a finger on her lips and pointed through a gap in the trees. The scholar peered ahead and could see the crumpled forms of his companions, six slomen standing nearby while rifling through their kitbags.

'Shit,' Veta hissed. 'It was an ambush.'

'How could they coordinate such an attack?' Fontaine asked.

'Some of the specimens here were given a heightened intelligence,' she replied. Then added, 'Damn it all — what do we do know?'

Fontaine crouched on his haunches and rested his back against the trunk of a tree. His brow creased in concentration while his right hand rubbed at the scraggy stubble on his chin. There had to be a solution, there had to be.

'Veta, do the slomen have any predators?' he asked.

'Yes, of course.'

'What are the closest to our current position?'

'The sword-tusked leoguar, the hydrabasilisk and the Dorovian spider,'

'Which of those is the slowest?'

'The Dorovian spider, but do you mind telling me what you're planning?'

'Well, once, long ago, I read that a predator will give up its prey to another predator in order to escape.'

'I hate to burst your bubble, scholar, but you would still need to get rid of the spider and let me tell you — they're big bastards.'

Fontaine chewed his bottom lip. 'There must have been a way for those running this place to control the specimens?'

'Well, they were controlled by dense concentrations of sortilenergy … the ones lacking intelligence that is.'

'Are the spiders possessing high or low intelligence?'

'Low.'

'Then I have the answer. Quickly, lead me to them.'

Veta frowned and shook her head. 'It's your funeral,' she said.

Her projected body floating through the physical hazards of the jungle, Veta led the scholar into a deep patch of trees. Strung between the branches were massive sheets of webbing. In one, Fontaine could see a collection of large birds struggling to break free. He peered up into the canopy but could see no sign of the spider. *Going to have to flush the bugger out yourself, old boy*, he thought before heading to a tree and beginning to climb.

'What the hells are you doing?' Veta hissed. 'Get down here at once.'

'I'm fine. Just keep an eye out for the spider,' he replied.

In his youth, Fontaine had been a great climber of trees … before his mother forbade him from such activities that is. But despite all the years in between, his hands and feet moved with assurance as he ascended the trunk. Before long, he reached his goal — one of the lower webs. For a moment, he studied it, marvelling at the silken strands, each one as thick as a ship's cable. Before he could lose his nerve, he pulled on the bottom of the web, setting the whole thing quivering.

With haste, he scrambled back to the ground and waited. Then he saw what he had been waiting for. From the dizzying heights, a massive arachnid — at least the size of a small carriage — descended to see what had set off its web. As it drew closer, Fontaine groped in the undergrowth, searching. Finally, his fingertips curled around what he was looking for. He took hold of the large stone, bounced it to gauge its weight, then threw it with all his might at the beast.

Missing the spider would have been a very hard thing to do, but the fact Fontaine's stone connected squarely between the creature's eyes was down to luck alone. The beast let out a horrific squeal and dropped to the ground. For a second, the scholar and the spider regarded each other. Then the arachnid pounced.

Legs pumping like pistons, Fontaine raced back towards where the others were captured. Looking back over his shoulder, he saw that the spider's huge, sagging middle did indeed make it slow — but nowhere near as slow as he would have liked. He could feel the ground vibrating as each of the eight massive legs thundered into the earth, could smell the creature's rank stench as it closed in.

Before he knew it, he was bursting into the clearing where his companions were held. The slomen tuned to look at him, a sharp, unnatural cunning to their stares. Then they saw the spider. With a harsh hoot of anger, they retreated.

'Right, that worked,' Veta bellowed. 'Now what do you do about him?'

Fontaine ignored her — he had work to do. Running towards the still-prone form of Dargo, the scholar began to rifle through the boy's pockets. *Come on, come on*, he thought, *he must have it somewhere*. Behind him, he could sense the beast closing in. Then, tucked in the lad's belt, he found it. The relic stolen from the Sylucian king.

He spun round, brandishing the dagger like a flaming torch. The spider hissed and reared up on its back legs. Heart crashing in his chest, Fontaine forced himself towards it. With one last scream, the creature scurried back from whence it came. Breathing in ragged bursts, body trembling, the scholar collapsed to the ground.

'I can't believe that worked,' Veta said.

Fontaine let out a crazed giggle. 'Neither can I,' he replied.

***

Bellina cocked her head to the side and listened to the sounds that had started to emanate from the back room Cirona had ventured into. First came a hiss of steam and the sound of pistons firing. This was followed by the sound of cogs spinning and a dreadful thrumming that made her back teeth ache. Last and worst of all came an alien voice that sounded like someone was trying to form words with a broken accordion.

'Facial recognition failed,' the unseen thing said. 'Please remain here while the appropriate authorities are called.'

'What in the Father's name was that?' Bellina said, her eyes growing wide.

'Oh, dash it all!' Alari said. 'Now she's gone and done it.'

'Done what?' Barboza asked.

'Woken up the batots, the metal folk, what we would call automatons,' Jeremias answered, his face white.

There was a crash and an oath, then Cirona walked backwards into the main room. The gleaming machine followed her, red, lamp-like eyes flashing.

'This is your second warning,' the automaton wheezed. 'Failure to comply will result in loss of limbs.'

'Screw you!' Cirona spat back, pulling out her ballistol.

The noise from the weapon's firing in the confined space almost deafened Bellina, and instinct forced her to duck. Smoke curled from the weapon, filling the air with the stink of cordite. When she looked back up again, she saw that the machine had stopped advancing, left eye a ruinous cavern, the right now stuttering.

'Thank fuck for—' Waltus began.

He was cut short by Cirona's cry when the automaton lurched forwards and grabbed her.

'Get that thing off her!' Bellina yelled, her mouth dry.

'Allow me,' Barboza said, readying his spear.

'Stand back, the lot of you,' Alari commanded. 'If the batot sustains any more damage, heaven only knows what it will do. I shall deal with the problem.'

The Fargazer's projected body vanished. The metal insect flew across the room and inserted its vicious-looking stinger into the automaton's neck. For a second, the machine shook and twitched like it was having a seizure. Then it slumped forwards, letting go of Cirona.

The insect flew back into the air, and Alari reappeared. 'And that, poppets,' she said, 'is why we don't touch things we don't understand.'

Bellina watched in amazed amusement as the General hung her head and offered an apology.

'Well, I don't think you've done any major—' Alari started to say.

From outside, Bellina could hear the sharp tramp of footsteps. From the metallic clang, she concluded that more of the machines were on their way. She gave a small shiver and unconsciously placed a hand on her stomach. Jeremias stalked to the door.

'What ... what's happening?' Bellina asked, annoyed at the slight tremor she heard within her voice.

'More of them are coming,' Jeremias replied, confirming her fears. 'Looks like the blasted city is waking up. This is why we avoid Imun Nir like the plague. Can't you turn them all off or something?' This last remark was addressed to Alari.

'I can perform manual shutdowns on individual batots, but to override them all, I would need access to the main command centre at the palace,' she said.

'What the hells are we going to do now?' Cirona said.

'Run for it,' Barboza replied. 'Alari herself said we are not far from the palace.'

'I'm in no condition to run anywhere,' Bellina said, feeling the baby stir within her.

'There is one other option,' Alari said. 'The underground railway. It would take us right to the palace's doorstep.'

'Why didn't you say so earlier. All this exertion ain't too good for my old bones either,' Waltus cried.

'I was worried that powering up the railway would inadvertently awaken the metal folk, but seeing as they're online anyway—'

'That's settled it then,' Jeremias cut in. 'Where is the nearest entrance?'

'Not far. If we leave through the back, we should be there in minutes,' Alari said.

'Very well,' Bellina said, clambering to her feet. 'Let's go.'

The Fargazer nodded then led them out the back door of the inn. They passed through choked alleyways, stopping at every intersection to check for the machines. At one corner, Alari warned them to stop, sending them back into the shadows. Here, Bellina caught her first glimpse of the automatons on their trail.

What she noticed first was the body — a massive, shining sphere of copper. In the middle of this was a large lens that worked as its eye, a sick yellow spilling out from it. Towards the back of the sphere, two antennae jutted out, pulses of galvanic energy shooting between them. From the core, extended the machines' limbs. The left arm was without a hand. Instead, it had been fitted with a weapon much like the ones they had discovered in Gortrix. The right arm finished in a claw. All this was supported by long thin legs that looked as though they should not be able to bear the weight of the top half. Five of these inventions were walking abreast, stopping every so often to scan a building or road.

They're looking for us, for you, she thought, *creatures with no concept of pain or mercy. They're a stone's throw away, and they're looking for us!* Her arms broke out in gooseflesh at the thought. She held her breath, expecting at any second for one of the vile creations to spot them. Then she heard their clanging footsteps retreating, and Alari led them on once again.

Bellina and the others were ushered down another thin strip of alleyway and came to a stop. They had reached a dead end, the wall in front of them made by the same mortarless, interlocking stones as the rest of the city.

'Why the hells have you brought us here?' Cirona asked.

'Hold on, my dear, all will become apparent soon,' Alari replied. Her hand hovered over the wall. With a creaking groan the wall sank into the ground, calling up great puffs of dust and grit, and revealed a set of descending stairs. 'Quickly, in you go now, that's it.'

Bellina began to walk down the stairs and discovered that they spiralled. Soon there was no light to guide her steps. She paused, putting her hand on the cool stone of the central pillar. Below, she could hear curses as the others got in the way of the ones behind. *I can't fall; I mustn't fall!* she told herself, trying to swallow past the boulder that had settled in her throat, noticing that the fear she felt was not solely for herself.

'Don't be scared, my love,' Alari said behind her. 'Let's have some light, shall we.' At the Fargazer's words, a beam of light illuminated the way, shooting out from the front of the metal insect's face.

'Thank you,' Bellina said, a warm wellspring of emotion for their guide rising within her.

'You are most welcome, little dove. Now let's be off.'

When Bellina reached the bottom of the steps, she heard a cry and the sound of someone falling over. She looked at Alari then rushed ahead as fast as her current circumstances would allow. The scene that the Fargazer's light revealed made Bellina take a shocked step backwards. Scattered all over the passageway were skeletons, scraps of cloth and dried flesh still clinging to some of the bones. Lying in the midst of this nightmare was Barboza. When he saw what surrounded him, he leapt to his feet, a look of revulsion on his face.

'What … what happened here?' Bellina asked.

'The entrance we used was for emergencies. When the … the cataclysm came, people fled down here to escape on the railway. There was, of course, not enough room for … for everyone. These people were left behind. I'm afraid these will not be the last bodies you shall encounter,' Alari replied with sigh.

'We're wasting time. Come on,' Jeremias said, beginning to gingerly pick a path through the bones.

Before long, the passageway opened onto a large platform. Alari entered a control booth in the corner, and in seconds, a carriage came rattling into view. The doors slid open for them, and they all clambered inside. With a jolt, the train started to move. Bellina collapsed into a cushioned seat. The baby kicked and wriggled. *Not* the *baby*, my *baby*, she thought, feeling sick and confused over the disassociation she felt towards her child. She didn't have long to ponder though — a crash sounded from the back of the carriage.

The door at the rear was ripped loose, crushed in the pitiless jaws of the automaton's hand. Everything seemed to happen in a mad rush. Barboza charged at the machine but was caught in the midsection by a blow from the claw. It advanced towards Bellina, its revolting yellow eye scanning every inch of her.

Clicking one of the gems that controlled her cognopathic powers, Bellina pushed against the oncoming automaton. The contraption slowed, and she heard its gears straining against her resistance. With slow ponderous steps it began to make headway again. A cold fear clutched Bellina's heart and sweat broke out upon her brow as she tried to put more power into her defence.

'Keep it at bay,' Alari yelled. 'I'll shut it off.'

The metal bug flew at the machine. To Bellina's horror, it too was batted aside. Copper limbs trembling, the automaton began to raise its weaponised arm, aiming it squarely at her stomach. A wild protective fury flooded through her, and with a scream, she hurled the invention out of a window where it smashed into a million sparking pieces on the rushing tunnel wall.

Alari flickered back into existence. 'Well done, precious, absolutely first rate,' she said. 'Now, let's hope we don't have any more unexpected guests.'

Thankfully, they didn't, and within minutes, they had reached their destination. The Fargazer led them out of the station up into the sunlight. Despite the fact she was sweating like a pig and breathing with heavy dog-like pants, Bellina couldn't help but be impressed with Hisoth's palace. Massive stepped buildings of the blackest colour rose up behind protective walls, all decorated in relief with white figures paying homage to a giant figure that could only be Hisoth himself. The monumental scale was crushing, infecting Bellina with a horrible sense of insignificance. How could they hope to tackle beings that were capable of such things?

'Almost like this Hisoth was overcompensating for something, eh?' Waltus said with a wicked smile. Bellina let out a snort of laughter, and the spell the palace had placed on her broke.

'Not much further now, poppets!' Alari called.

She led them through a gap in the walls and into the palace grounds. Bellina felt her stomach lurch as she saw what surrounded them. Corpse after corpse lay in the courtyard, the majority of them armed with sword and spear. The Fargazer had said they would see more bodies, but there were thousands here, maybe tens of thousands.

'Were these people more evacuees?' Barboza asked.

'No … no, these people attempted to take the palace by force in the last days. All led to their doom by Amlith Castria,' Alari replied.

The sight of so much death pressed in on Bellina, reminding her of their flight from Burkesh. Her head began to spin, darkness creeping into the corners of her vision. Then she felt a hand on her back, comforting, steadying her.

'Come on, girl, let's get inside that palace,' Cirona said.

With the General's help, Bellina made her way to the top of the gigantic ramp that led to the palace entrance. When they all reached the top, there was a massive explosion from the courtyard below. To her horror Bellina, saw a mass of their automaton hunters streaming through a hole they had blasted in the wall.

'We've got company,' Waltus said.

'Never fear. All that's left is getting these doors open. I shouldn't be a second,' Alari replied.

Down below, the machines had located them. Blue gouts of energy shot from the weapons on their arms, hitting the building around them and sending down a shower of masonry. Bellina turned towards the huge bronze doors. Alari was at the bottom of the door where the elaborately etched designs finished.

'Any time now would be good,' Bellina called to her.

'I … well, there seems to be a problem,' the Fargazer replied.

'What?' Bellina asked, her stomach sinking.

'Well, it's the strangest thing … I can't get the doors open.'

CHAPTER EIGHTEEN

'Ow!' Elvgren cried as his fingers touched a tender lump the size of an orange at the back of his head. 'I can't believe those bloody monkeys got the drop on us.'

'It does speak volumes about your collective intelligence,' Veta said, a corner of her mouth pulled up in a smirk. 'You're just lucky Fontaine was here.'

'Yes, yes — well done, scholar. We're all very grateful, I'm sure,' Elvgren said.

'Y-you are most welcome, Your Majesty,' Fontaine replied.

'We got lucky,' Crenshaw called out from in front of them, holding out a kitbag. 'They took most of the dried meat, but everything else looks intact.'

'Good,' Veta said before anyone else could speak. 'Back on your feet then. We still have a way to go before we reach the main compound.'

With a groan, Elvgren climbed back to his feet and collected his pack from Crenshaw. He hefted it onto his weary shoulders, wondering to himself if the slomen had stuffed it full of heavy rocks, and they were off, Veta once again leading the way.

'So,' Dargo said, coming up beside him. 'When did it happen, eh?'

Elvgren massaged his temples. 'When did what happen, Dar?'

'You know,' Dargo replied with a conspiratorial leer, 'when did you do the naked tango with Belle?'

'What?'

'Bump nether regions, have intimate relations — shag!'

'How the hells do you know that?' Elvgren cried.

'It's hard to miss when your missus looks like she has a watermelon stuffed up her shirt,' Dargo replied.

'Watermelon? Shirt?' Elvgren said, his mind humming with confusion.

'Belle's pregnant,' Dargo said. 'Don't tell me you didn't notice.'

Elvgren cast his mind back. Now that he thought about it, Bellina had seemed rounder than usual and her breasts had definitely looked bigger … Oh gods — she really was pregnant. He brought a shaking hand to his forehead, strength dribbling out of his legs. No, this couldn't be right, not at all. Him? A father?

'I think he should call me Uncle Dar. Of course, if anything happened to you and Belle, I'd raise 'im like he were me … Oi, are you alright? You look like a milk bottle.'

'I-I'm fine, Dargo, I just need some time to think is all,' Elvgren replied.

'Alright, I'll leave you alone. But later you'll have to listen to my suggestions for names, got some good ones,' Dargo said, falling back a fraction.

A father, Elvgren thought. *Me, Elvgren Maximilian Lovitz, a father!* How could she have got pregnant after one swing around the barn? He'd always reckoned he was virile, but this was a joke. What type of parent could he be? It wasn't as if he'd had the best examples to learn from. Elvgren felt his mind begin to spin.

Stow it, old boy, a calm voice reasoned from the back of his mind. *You're halfway to bloody hysterical. You can deal with this baby business later. Right now, we need to concentrate on getting through this jungle of murderous beasts.*

Mind just about under control, Elvgren continued on, following the path the Fargazer blazed up a steep incline. As the minutes dragged into torturous hours and the oppressive, almost physical, humidity of the jungle tapped dry his reserves of energy, Elvgren began praying that they would reach their destination before too long. He was desperate for a pause, but his pride wouldn't allow him to ask for one.

'I suppose you lot had better have a rest,' Veta said as they reached a small clearing.

Elvgren could have collapsed to the ground and kissed her projected feet. Instead, he said, 'If you insist.'

He slumped onto a fallen log and drained his water skein in one mighty gulp. Smacking the bottom to shake loose any remaining drops, he turned to Dargo eyeing the lad's water supply greedily.

'There's a lot less of you than there is of me, Dar. How about you give me a bit of yours,' he said, pointing to the skein in the boy's hands.

'Bugger off,' Dargo replied. 'You shouldn't have guzzled what you had. There's such a thing as self-restraint you know.'

'But I'm your emperor! One of you give me some of your water this bloody minute!' Elvgren huffed.

'Will you shut up!' Veta cried. 'There's a stream just to the north of here. Go and drink your fill. But be back in ten minutes.'

'That's more like it,' Elvgren said, jumping to his feet and hurrying off.

'Just be careful,' the Fargazer called after him. 'There's a nasty drop back—'

'Yes, yes, yes — stop nagging,' Elvgren called back.

It didn't take him long to locate the stream. The clear water came murmuring over a shallow bed before plummeting off a drop, creating a small waterfall. Elvgren knelt beside it and threw some of the cool liquid over his face and neck before cupping it in his hands and drinking. He was just about to fill his skein when he felt the point of a ballistol jammed into the small of his back.

'Don't make a sound,' he heard Holger say.

'What the hells is the meaning of this?' Elvgren spluttered.

'I just told you to keep quiet,' Holger replied.

'You cretinous, gutless coward,' Elvgren hissed. 'Finally showing your true colours, eh? I should have done away with you long ago.'

'That's unfortunate for you. But it's time you disappear. You've got between me and Belle too often. But now she's carrying my child I can suffer it no more.'

'Your child? Your child! You misguided idiot — it's my child!' Elvgren said.

'Bollocks, how can it be yours if … if you and Belle have never … never had relations,' Holger said.

'Of course we've slept together! It's you that hasn't. By the Father — just saying you've been with my betrothed is enough to see you hang!'

'Shut up, shut up, shut up!' Holger yelped, the ballistol shaking in his grasp. 'She's mine, mine alone — Belle belongs to me!'

Elvgren couldn't stop himself laughing. 'Belongs to you? Bellina doesn't belong to anyone, even I've managed to figure that out.'

'Stop laughing!' Holger spat. 'Move.'

He jammed the weapon hard into Elvgren's spine and got him moving. Holger forced him to where the stream turned into a waterfall and plunged to the lower portion of the jungle.

'You,' Holger said as they reached the edge, 'are going to have a little accident.'

Elvgren looked over the drop and licked his lips. There was no way he'd survive the fall. He could think of only one thing to do. 'Let me turn around,' he said. 'At least look me in the eye as you kill me.'

There was a pause. Then Holger said, 'Fine.'

Holger drew back the ballistol and Elvgren spun round in a blur grabbing Holger's shirt and throwing him to the ground. The weapon went flying into the undergrowth, the pair wrestling for supremacy, elbows, knees, fists smashing into each other, neither realising just how close they were to the drop. Elvgren managed to get on top and drew back his fist. In mad desperation, Holger pushed himself up towards Elvgren.

Clutching each other, they rolled into nothingness.

***

'What do you mean, you can't get the doors open?' Cirona said, spitting her words at the Fargazer.

'If certain people weren't so rude and let others finish,' Alari said, 'then I would have been able to say I can't get them open … from here. Give me a minute, and we'll be in.' Her projected body vanished, and the metal insect squeezed through a small gap at the top of the doors.

'We don't have a minute!' Cirona bellowed after her. 'Gods damn it. Everyone, listen up, we have the high ground, these bastards will only be able to come up the ramp a few at a time. We'll use it as a choke point, battle them back and pray to the Father that the doors open soon. Any questions?' She looked around; everyone nodded their approval. 'Good. Bellina, you get behind the rest of us. No. No, I don't want any arguing, just do it. Alright then, here they come!'

The automatons trudged up the ramp three abreast, the vast horde falling into an ordered file. They had stopped their wild firing now as their shots would have a greater chance of striking a fellow machine than Cirona and the others. The General was crouched low, sword in one hand, ballistol in the other, mouth dry.

'Wait for it,' she said, as much to herself as anyone else. 'Wait for it.'

Then they were upon her. In front of Cirona, the great rolling yellow eye of a machine fixed upon her. It raised its weaponised arm. She lowered her ballistol and shot point-blank into the vile, mustard lens. The automaton took one more step then toppled backwards into its brothers, sending a handful to the ground like skittles.

While Cirona fumbled in her ammo pouch, trying to reload, she saw the others fighting back their own opponents. Waltus, arms bulging like a strongman, threw a meaty punch at his opponent. The whole front half of the machine caved in, and it tottered over the side of the ramp. Barboza was swinging his spear like a man possessed, the ancient relic slicing through the top of an automaton like he was opening a boiled egg. Jeremias was unloading shots from one of Lokos Vistas' weapons. They weren't having the devastating effect she had seen before — the machines' metal must have been toughened to defend against such blasts — but the shots were still knocking them backwards. *Bloody hells,* she thought, *we might actually do this!*

The machines took that moment to pick up the pace, they began to run at their targets. Cirona's world shrank to a space of a few feet, unable to look to her left or right, knowing any such distraction would spell death. She blasted the first rushing automaton in the eye and sent it careening back down the ramp with a shove. There was no time to reload, so she threw her ballistol away and lunged with her sword. With the precision honed from a lifetime of warfare, she chopped into the gaps between the machines' limbs, severing arms and legs.

Despite her best efforts, the machines were pushing Cirona and her small band back. The automatons were now able to spread out at the top of the ramp, taking up the positions Cirona and the others had just held and allowing their comrades to gain a foothold too. They now pressed in on the defenders in a semicircle. The metal men raised their weaponised arms. Cirona forced herself not to flinch; if this was to be her death, then she would meet it with eyes open. She saw the weapons discharge, the blue bursts of energy race towards them … and bounce off a shimmering wall.

'To me, everyone. I can't keep a shield of this size up for long.'

Cirona spun round and saw Bellina, face contorted in concentration, sweat streaming from her brow. The General smiled and said, 'You heard the woman — everyone, to her!'

'Are you alright?' Jeremias asked as they came racing to Bellina's side.

'I … I think so,' she replied.

'Good girl. Alari shouldn't be long now,' Cirona said before thinking, *I hope.*

The shots were raining down on them, an azure storm bouncing off Bellina's shimmering shield. Some of the ricochets hit the automatons, taking them out but more soon filled their place. Cirona gripped her sword with a shaking hand, cursing the fact there was nothing she could do, biting her lips as she watched great cracks form in Bellina's barrier.

'I don't think I … I can hold on much longer,' Bellina said.

Cirona turned round and began to batter on the brass doors. 'Alari? Alari! Open this fucking thing right—' she began.

The General was cut off when the entrance swung inwards away from her fists.

'About fucking time!' Waltus cried as they rushed into the safety of the palace.

Cirona collapsed to the floor when the doors shut with a boom behind them. *Close,* she thought, *far too close.* Looking up, she saw they were in a large corridor, the walls covered in writhing, grotesque reliefs of unnameable figures merging then swirling apart. She jerked her eyes away, not wanting to see or understand.

'We must press on now, poppets. It's just a bit further, and those doors won't keep them out for long,' Alari said.

A spluttering, hissing sound sprung up behind them, accompanied by the smell of melting metal.

'Lead on,' Barboza said.

The Fargazer led them through the palace, Cirona battling to keep out the thought that one of the Terrors had actually dwelt there. They raced past vast rooms, half hidden in shadows that twisted into monsters in her imagination, down a sweeping staircase that led out into a dank passage.

The passage thrummed with some unseen power. Lengths of thick cable and bands of copper wire snaked along its wall towards a single door with a porthole window. Alari came to a stop before it. She held out her hand and the door swung inwards with a hiss.

'V-very well then … you go in first, Bellina, my sweet,' Alari said.

'Alright,' Bellina replied, stepping into the room beyond, accompanied by Alari.

Cirona stepped forwards to follow and the door swung shut in her face. Through the porthole, all she could see was the Fargazer's face. 'What the fuck are you doing?' she screamed, pounding on the door with her fists.

'I'm … sorry,' Alari replied.

***

Bellina had a moment to take in the room. She saw tubes and wires everywhere, huge metal spheres hanging from the ceiling shooting galvanic bolts to a cluster of glass and bronze pods. The smell of burned ozone assaulted her nose, while the small hairs on her neck and arms rose thanks to the thrumming weight of the power flowing around her. *How in the name of the gods did they build this?*

Hearing a banging behind her, Bellina turned to find the door to the room closed, and everyone but herself and Alari outside. Cirona was pounding her fist into the glass, her words barely audible.

'What's going on?' Bellina asked.

'N-nothing you need to concern yourself with, my little dove. You just pop into one of those pods and we can be on our way,' Alari answered.

Bellina's face grew tight. 'I'm not going anywhere without the others,' she said, crossing her arms.

Alari tilted her head to the side, looked directly into Bellina's eyes and reached a hand out to stroke her cheek. 'It must be so glorious to have a body,' she said, licking her lips. 'To feel, to taste, to smell … to love, to touch and be touched.

'Lokos Vistas, father of the nexus hubs, was a cruel man. He gave us consciousness, emotions and personalities; he gave us everything but a body. But you … you!' she said, pushing closer till there was only an inch between their faces. 'You get to have it all — youth, beauty, even the honour of carrying life within you. It's not fair, it's not fair, it's not fair!'

Bellina swallowed hard and took a step back. She placed one hand on her belly and held up the other, as if she could ward of the Fargazer. 'I'm … I'm sorry Alari. I truly am. But you need to let me and my friends go.'

Standing straighter, Alari seemed to regain some composure. 'That's not possible, I'm afraid,' she said. 'Lord Marmossa wants them dead.'

Taking another step back, Bellina said, 'You … you've had contact with Marmossa? Look, whatever deal you made with him, it can't be trusted.'

'Do not take me for a fool, Bellina Ressa; I know he can't be trusted. But he will honour this deal as it suits his purposes as well as mine — he will give me your body.'

'That's absurd … how in the world could he—' Bellina spluttered.

'Enough talk, we are expected in the City of the Dead. Please step into the pod.'

'I will not step into that … thing without my companions,' Bellina said.

'Oh yes, you will,' Alari hissed. She waved her hand and the metal insect shot out its blade and pointed at Bellina's stomach. 'Move!'

Bellina stepped back into the pod and watched as the bronze door sealed itself with a hiss of compressed air. She heard the click of some mechanism turning and then everything began to hum. It was gentle at first, almost undetectable, then increased until she felt it would pull her apart … which is precisely what it did.

She watched horror-struck as her hands disintegrated in front of her. She tried to scream, but she had no mouth to scream with. The last thing she saw before her eyeballs dissolved was Alari licking her lips, twisted hunger shining from the depths of her eyes.

***

'I can't believe the ancient Atvorians had such advanced technology,' Fontaine said to Veta as he watched Elvgren disappear from the corner of his eye.

'They didn't,' the Fargazer replied. 'The Terrors hoarded all the knowledge for themselves. They might have used Atvorians for manual labour, but they were never educated. In fact, it was only the badevs, children produced from the coupling of a Terror with a human, who were allowed to help with experiments or the running of government, badevs like Lokos Vistas, Amlith Castria and the rest.'

Fontaine jerked his head back, eyes blinking. 'Do you mean to say the ones who overthrew the Terrors were their own children?'

'Yes,' Veta replied.

'Astonishing,' the scholar whispered, just noticing Holger slipping away from the main group, closely followed by Dargo.

'Just astonishing?' Veta asked with a smile. 'Not unbelievable? I could be lying, you know.'

Looking up into her eyes, Fontaine said, 'It tallies up with a lot of research I've conducted. In fact, it makes a lot of stuff I thought odd make sense.' He paused, shuffling his foot in the dirt. 'Plus ... I don't think you're a liar.'

Veta opened her mouth to respond, but before she could, a shout tore through the air.

'Help! Come quick!'

'That was Dargo,' Crenshaw said.

'Let's go,' Fontaine replied.

Together they raced off in the direction of Dargo's cry. Soon, they reached the stream. Fontaine traced the path of the water along its shallow bed to the point where it took a glittering plunge. On the lip of the drop, he could see Dargo, flat on his stomach, reaching out for something.

'Over here!' Dargo said without changing position. 'Holger had a ballistol on Gren, and they got to fighting, and they just rolled right off the edge and—'

'Take a deep breath,' Fontaine said, kneeling down beside the boy.

Tentatively, he peeked over the edge. He could see Elvgren dangling from a thick tree root that was jutting out from the rocks. Around his waist, clinging like a scared child to its mother, was Holger.

'I'll go and grab a rope,' Crenshaw said.

'There's no time,' Elvgren called up. 'This bit of wood is giving way!'

'There's nothing for it — someone will have to lean over and reach out for them,' Veta said.

'Scholar, you're the tallest here,' Crenshaw said. 'You lean out, and I'll hold your legs.'

'M-me?' Fontaine replied. 'I hardly think I'm qualified to—'

'This is no time for a fucking debate!' Elvgren yelled. 'Someone, do something.'

Biting his lip, Fontaine tried to think of another solution. None came. He took a deep breath, lay on his stomach and eased the top half of his body over the edge, feeling Crenshaw clamp down on his legs. His head gave a sickening twirl when he looked down at the ground far below. Sweat snaked into his eyes, and he wiped it away with the back of his hand. *You can do this*, he told himself; *you can do this.*

Focusing his attention on Elvgren, he reached out, his shoulder screaming in protest as he tried to extend it past its limits. Despite this, he only just scraped the top of the root with his fingers.

'I … I need more reach,' Fontaine said. 'I'm going to shuffle forwards a bit more.'

'You sure?' Crenshaw asked.

'Th-there's no other way,' the scholar answered.

He wriggled forwards, feeling the scrape of the rough ground scratch against his stomach and the fizzing drizzle of the stream as it plunged to oblivion. Now just over three quarters of his body was dangling over the drop, battling against gravity. Swaying back and forth, ribs crunching against the stony cliff, Fontaine made a grab … and missed.

'Gods damn it, scholar, what the hells are you playing at!' Elvgren yelled, the root making a horrible splitting sound.

Getting the motion of his body under control, Fontaine looked straight down at the Emperor once more. The root had developed a deep, vicious-looking crack. *There will only be one chance at this,* he thought. He stretched out his sweat-drenched hand, past the root, fingertips brushing over Elvgren's knuckles, until he wrapped his hand around the young ruler's wrist.

'Thank the gods,' Elvgren said. 'I'm going to let go of the root, so be—'

He was cut off by the dull, cracking cough of the root breaking. Without warning, Fontaine had the weight of two young men dangling from his left arm. He could feel the grating yawn of his bones threatening to dislocate. In desperation, he threw his right arm out too, and Elvgren seized it with his hand. With the weight divided just that touch more equally, the scholar was able to cling on while Dargo and Crenshaw worked to haul them up.

Fontaine rolled onto his back with a soft groan. His left shoulder howled with pain, his body was battered and bruised, yet he couldn't help but smile — he'd done it. From the corner of his eye, he saw Elvgren stagger to his feet and rummage around in the undergrowth. Seconds later, he was back, a ballistol cocked and ready to fire in his hand.

'I'm going to do what I should have done the second I clapped eyes on you, you Narvglandic barbarian,' he said.

The scholar hauled himself to his feet and watched Holger, jaw set firm, stare down the barrel of the weapon.

'Do it,' he hissed. 'Because I'll tell you right now, the second I get a chance to do away with you, I will.'

'Your Majesty, please,' Fontaine said. 'I know he has committed a grave crime against you, but he is part of the prophesy. To kill him now would weaken us even more.'

'He's right, Gren,' Dargo said, stepping in front of the ballistol. 'We can't kill him.'

Elvgren stared around at them, eyes bulging out of their sockets. 'Have you all lost your bloody minds? He tried to kill me.'

'And you will be able to properly punish him once you've dealt with Marmossa,' Veta said.

'I … Can't you see … he …'Elvgren spluttered.

'We know, Gren, but let's be having that ballistol, eh? I promise, if he tries anything again, I'll kill him myself,' Dargo said.

Fontaine watched the Emperor visibly deflate. The weapon hung limply in his hands and was retrieved by Crenshaw who then pulled Holger to his feet and lodged the weapon at the base of the boy's spine.

'Move,' he said.

In this fashion, they made it back to their resting spot. Holger's hands were bound and then they were on the march again. Fontaine took up his position just behind Veta who was leading them. His gaze lingered on the sway of her hips. Feeling a burning in his cheeks, he turned his eyes to the ground. There he noticed something strange. The area from the Fargazer's boot to her lower shin had turned black, shot through with pulsating red veins.

'I … um … Excuse me, Veta? Are you alright?' he asked, pointing at the affected area.

She looked down, her expression changing from curiosity to one of abject fear. 'No,' she said. 'No, no — this can't be happening.'

'Whatever's the matter?' Fontaine said.

'I'm being attacked by a bastard virus. May the Elder Ones damn that runt Marmossa's eyes.'

'You can get sick?' Fontaine said.

'Oh yes. And if we don't get to the compound in the next hour, I won't be able to fix myself or get you where you need to be.'

'What should we do?'

'Run.'

With each pounding step, Fontaine felt a lance of white pain shoot up his body. More than once, he tripped on a treacherous root or had his face torn at by branches. Just when he thought his lungs would explode, he burst out of the jungle and into a clearing. In front of him, he saw a squat building covered with an arching roof. Trees and bushes shot from its windows, and its walls were bent and bowed out of shape.

'This is the compound,' Veta said. Fontaine noted how the infection had spread up her spine. 'Quickly, everyone inside.'

She led them into the building, down a corridor of hissing pipes towards a door with a wheel lock. Fontaine grabbed it, ignoring the protest from his body, and opened the door. On one side of the room, he could see four bronze and glass pods. On the other, a mess of levers, pulleys, pedals and pressure gauges. As they entered, Veta collapsed to her knees.

'Are you alright?' he asked.

'Yes … but you're going to have to help me.'

'Of course.'

Together, they herded the others into the pods, and under Veta's instructions, Fontaine managed to get the machines to work, watching awestruck as, one by one, they disappeared.

'Now you, scholar,' she said. 'I have just enough power left to control the pod automatically.'

Fontaine looked at her. Her body was now completely black, the red tendrils threading their way up her neck and onto her cheeks. 'You're not going to make it … are you?'

'No,' she replied. 'As soon as you pointed the virus out to me, I knew it would … it would kill me.'

'There must be something … anything!' Fontaine said.

Veta pushed a projected finger onto his lips. 'There isn't, not if I'm to send you to Sanctuary.'

'I-I can't let you sacrifice yourself for me.'

'You need to live. There are far too many men who swing their swords first and regret it later. Intellect always wins out in the end,' she said. 'Oh, and before I forget, take that.'

Following her gaze, Fontaine saw a small collection of metal plates covered in punch marks. 'What are they?'

'They're called memory cards and contain all the information I could find on Marmossa, the *real* Marmossa. The people at Sanctuary should have a computational device that can read it. Now get in the pod.'

The scholar stepped in and the glass door sealed itself shut with a hiss.

'I'm glad I met you,' she said. 'You remind me of Lokos … and that's about the highest compliment I can think of.'

'I-I'm glad I met you too,' Fontaine replied.

Veta smiled. She was still smiling when the world around him turned to white, and she vanished from his gaze.

***

Cirona watched Bellina's body break apart like foam on the crest of a wave, watched the atoms, pearly white, dance then disappear. Through the porthole window, she saw the metal insect that projected Alari jerk, twitch then explode in a shower of tiny sparks. A surge of nausea poured out from her gut. Her head was spinning, turning, trying its hardest to find some equilibrium.

'No,' she said, her voice a hoarse sob. 'No, no, no! Give her back, you bitch, give her fucking back!'

'Here,' Waltus said, grabbing her hands and stopping them pounding on the door. 'Carry on like that, and you'll turn yer mitts into mincemeat.'

Cirona looked down, uncomprehending, at her bruised and bloody knuckles. 'I … we … we need to get in there; we need to bring Bellina back,' she said.

'I know,' Waltus replied. 'But your fists ain't gonna beat through that much steel. You, try the handle,' he said, pointing at Jeremias.

'No good,' he said. 'The thing's shut tight.'

In the distance, Cirona could hear the stomp of the automatons growing closer. *We need to get in there*, she thought, *before it's too late for us* and *Bellina. Think, woman, think!* She grabbed for the ancient blaster, plucking it from Jeremias' grip. Levelling it at the handle, she fired. The shot ricocheted off the door and just missed the tops of their heads as it whizzed by.

'What is that thing made of?' Cirona said.

'Here, let me try,' Barboza said.

He stepped forwards and placed the tip of his spear against the metal. Cirona watched his face draw tight with concentration. A humming filled the air, and she realised it was coming from the spear vibrating at tremendous speed. Awestruck, she watched the weapon sink into the door as if it were cutting a cake. Barboza moved it in a circle around the handle which fell to the floor. With that the entrance unsealed itself. Even after seeing the relics used, Cirona still couldn't get over their monumental power.

'Quickly, inside,' Jeremias said. 'The metal men will be on us soon.'

They all hurried into the room, Barboza using the spear once more, this time to weld the edges of the door to the walls, sealing them all in. Jeremias walked over to a complicated-looking control panel and began studying the dials and gauges. Cirona noticed his body tense at what he saw.

'Where did she send her?' the General asked.

Jeremias ran a hand over his face. 'She was sent to the Tower of Parlay. It's at the heart of the City of the Dead, and more than likely, where Marmossa has set up base.'

Cirona took a step back, stunned. Then she set her jaw firm and said, 'Alright. Get these machines ready to take us to her.'

Jeremias' eyes grew wide, and he gave a slow shake of his head. 'Are you mad, woman?'

'No. I am perfectly sane. Now take us to Bellina.'

'I understand how you feel, but you must understand that we'd be walking into the leoguar's mouth. I think I can re-programme this machine to take us to Sanctuary and that's what I'm going to do,' Jeremias said.

'But Marmossa could be killing her as we speak!' Barboza cried.

'For the love of … Am I the only one thinking straight in here? If Marmossa wanted her dead, the Fargazer could have done it. He needs her for something, which means she is still alive. And if that's the case, our best option to rescue her is with the Leviathan. Now, are we going to stand here arguing all—'

A massive explosion shook the room. Cirona spun around to see that the door, though still in place, was buckled and melting.

'Those doors won't take another blast like that. Everyone, in the pods now,' Jeremias commanded.

Cirona felt her chest tighten and swallowed hard. Her hands balled into fists at her side. She took a faltering step towards the pod and stepped inside. *I'll get you back, Bellina*, she thought, *I swear by all the gods, I'll get you back.*

Then the world turned white.

CHAPTER NINETEEN

Elvgren came round with a massive, chest-heaving, breath. To start with, all he could see was a wall of white. Slowly, this gave way to dancing dots of light which collided together till his vision had returned. He found himself looking out at a room similar to the one he had just left. The only difference being a small bespectacled man sitting behind a control console. Their gazes met.

'You came by the pods!' he said, running towards Elvgren and putting his hands on the glass door. 'Sweet Father, no one has ever used the pods. What should I do?'

Elvgren tried to say, 'Get me out of here, you cretin,' but all that came out was a wet sigh.

The little man bit his lips then said, 'I'll get Calsie. Yeah, she'll know what to do.'

He ran from the room, leaving Elvgren still stuck in the pod. Elvgren took the opportunity to pull himself together. His tongue felt thick and heavy in his mouth, his mind whirling. He attempted to move his arms, but it was like they belonged to someone else and had been merely sewn onto his torso. Wiggling his foot, he discovered his legs were no better. *Guess I'll just have to wait for Calsie — whoever the hells she is,* he thought.

A few minutes later, the small man returned accompanied by a woman. She looked as if she was in her fifties. Her body was thickset with muscled forearms jutting from the rolled-up sleeves of her shirt. Apart from the stained shirt, she was wearing a pair of trousers tucked into heavy work boots, all of this was partially covered by a grease-smeared apron. Her face was round and ruddy, auburn hair piled atop her head crowning a pair of steely blue eyes.

'This is them, Calsie,' the man said.

'So, these are the Children of Prophesy, huh, our saviours,' she said, hands on hips. 'Well, I can't say they're much to look at … Ah well, let's get 'em out.'

The woman strode towards Elvgren and reached out to press something hidden from his line of sight. With a whoosh, the pod doors swung open. Taking a step forwards, Elvgren almost fell. Calsie caught him under the arm and heaved him upright.

'Here,' she said, taking out a dented hip flask, 'take a sip of this; it'll see you right.'

Without warning, Calsie shoved the flask past Elvgren's lips and poured a shot of bitter tasting liquid down his throat. He coughed and spluttered as the drink set his insides on fire.

'What the hells was that,' he said, wheezing.

'Sanctuary's finest beverage — Golden Shine. It tastes like galvanic donkey piss, but there's nothing like a nip of it to set you right,' Calsie replied.

Elvgren was about to remonstrate more when he realised she was telling the truth — he did feel a lot more steady.

'Seeing as you've got only one good peeper left, I'm guessing that you're Jeremias' brother,' she said.

'That … ahem … that's right. I am Elvgren Lovitz, Emperor of Estria and first of his name.'

Calsie raised an eyebrow, the spectre of a smile playing at the corners of her mouth. 'Sure thing, honey,' she said. 'How 'bout you introduce me to your friends.'

Deciding to ignore the barely concealed humour in the woman's voice, Elvgren said, 'The small shifty-looking one is Dargo.'

'Nice to meet yer,' Dargo responded with a wink.

'The nervous-looking chap is Scholar Fontaine.'

'H-how do you do,' the scholar said.

'The bland-looking chap is Crenshaw.'

'You cheeky bastard!' Crenshaw said to Elvgren, then, 'Pleased to meet you, madam.'

'And finally, the one tied up is a cretinous piece of worm's vomit that goes by the name of Holger. If you have any manacles, he needs to be placed in them immediately. He made an attempt on my life.'

'First thing's first — it's nice to meet you all. Secondly, we don't believe in manacles here in Sanctuary. Lot of the folks who've wound up here were freed from sortilenergy plants. We've got a small cell — most it's ever been used for is giving someone who's taken a bit too much shine a place to cool their heads. But I think it'll suit your needs,' she said.

'That's it? Well, I can't say I'm very comforted. As well as being a treacherous piece of slime, he's a fire mage,' Elvgren said.

Cocking her head to the side, Calsie said, 'Honey, most of the folks here are *full* mages. We'll keep him under watch, and if he tries anything, they'll be able to burn, freeze or blow his head clean off his shoulders.

Does that make you feel "comforted"?'

Elvgren's mouth twisted into a pout, but he eventually nodded under Calsie's iron glare.

'Good,' she said. 'Hurz, you take that one to the cell then get your arse back here in case the rest of 'em show up via the pods. I'll give this lot the tour while we've still got a bit of light.'

'Got it, boss,' Hurz said before leading Holger away.

Once he was gone, Calsie led them out of the building. Elvgren saw a mess of squat, mud-brick buildings crowding a narrow street of hard-packed dirt. The setting sun was catching the tops of the structures and making them blaze with orange fire. Alongside the street, in a little channel, beautiful clear water ran. Poking out here and there were massive palm trees, the fronds waving in the slight breeze like a sigh made flesh.

'It might seem a touch unsophisticated to you folks, but we've done our best to make it home,' Calsie said, patting a wall.

'It's … amazing,' Crenshaw said.

Calsie laughed. 'If you think this is something, just you wait,' she said.

On they walked, the sound of life and laughter ringing around them. They turned a corner, and Elvgren drew in a breath. He could see a large body of water, only slightly smaller than a lake, the water an impossible shade of blue. The fat trunks of more palms surrounded its edges, while ditches carrying the water back into town ran away from it like the threads of a spiderweb.

'Beautiful,' he murmured.

'Why thank you very much, Your Majesty.' Calsie laughed. 'Sanctuary is an oasis town, always has been, always will be. Things are pretty much how we found them when Calvin ferried the first of us over, though we have improved the sewerage systems.'

'Magnificent,' Fontaine breathed.

Calsie clapped her hands together. 'Well, I got one more thing of wonder to show you before we sort out some beds for yer. Follow me.'

She began to lead them away from the village, and as she did, Elvgren noticed a curious thing. Here and there, painted on doors or crudely constructed flags was the symbol of a white boot on a black background, its heel dyed red.

'That's the symbol of the Tooms gang,' he said.

'The what?' Dargo asked.

'The Tooms gang were a bunch of criminals or freedom fighters depending upon your opinion,' Crenshaw answered. 'They ran riot about forty years back now. Me mum used to tell me they'd get me if I didn't behave.'

'Yes. Yes, thank you for the history lesson, Mr Crenshaw, but why is it here?' Elvgren said, furrowing his brow. 'Hang on a minute, you can't be—'

'Calsie Tooms,' she said. 'Guilty as charged. Those flags ain't flying out of my vanity. Over the years, the newcomers kinda adopted it for themselves.'

Elvgren couldn't be sure if the others felt the same twisting anxiety as him at being led around by the leader of a bunch of infamous cutthroat mages. He decided not to pursue the matter and carry on — Calsie certainly seemed cheery enough. Night had set in, and their guide produced a small stick of wood, snapped her fingers and created a large globe of fire that hovered over her head.

It seemed as if they were walking towards a large, dark hill. Drawing closer, Elvgren noticed the moonlight glinting off it. A strange thrill passed through him. *That is no hill*, he thought. Rearing up out of the sand was the top half of a monumental automaton. Its head looked like a bullet sat upright, a huge bubble of glass for an eye. Massive arms attached to the trunk of the body, each as thick and long as a locomotron carriage, ended in dense, claw-like fingers. Sticking out of its back like a copper volcano was the machine's steam vent.

'This,' Calsie said. 'Is Leviathan.'

'Fucking hells!' Dargo said with a whistle. 'It's gigantic.'

'Oh, this is only the top half,' Calsie said. 'Come closer, but be careful, there's a drop.'

Shuffling forwards, Elvgren came to the edge of what could only be described as a crater. The Leviathan sat in the middle of it, its body trailing down to the depths where it was connected to, what looked like, an upside-down ship, from the bottom of that protruded a line of metal, crab-like legs.

'She's something, isn't she,' Calsie said. 'We dug her out, piece by piece, and got her working again. I can't wait for my boy to see it.'

'Your boy?' Elvgren asked.

'Castros,' she answered. 'He's travelling with you, isn't he?'

Silence fell upon the group. Elvgren felt Dargo and Crenshaw's gaze upon him. He cleared his throat and said, 'I-I'm afraid Castros is … is dead. He … he gave his life to save all of us and Victory.'

For a second, he saw the woman's eyes glisten. Then she lifted her head, pushed back her shoulders and said, 'Well … then he died a good death.'

She turned on her heel, beckoned them to follow and headed back into town. Elvgren's mind whirred. *If she is Castros' mother then that means she's Bellina's grandmother ... by the gods, talk about a strange way to meet the family,* he thought.

They soon arrived in a wide thoroughfare, a small fountain in its middle. Calsie stopped before a large building.

'You can all bed—' she began.

She was interrupted by the sound of someone calling her name. The man, Hurz, was rushing up to meet them. He came to a sliding halt beside them and tried to catch his breath.

'The ... others,' he said, panting. 'They're ... here ... thought ... should ... know, boss.'

'S'pose we better go greet them,' Calsie said.

They all marched back to the building where Elvgren saw Cirona, his brother, Barboza and Waltus looking like they had been worked through a mangle.

'Where's Bellina?' Elvgren asked.

'Gone,' Cirona said, looking at the ground. 'A Fargazer tricked us ... sent her to Marmossa.'

'Then we need to get after her,' Dargo said. 'Get that flaming great lump of metal back there moving.'

'I know how you feel, honey,' Calsie said, kneeling beside Dargo. 'Bellina's my kin, and I want her back as much as you do, but the Leviathan ain't ready.'

'How soon can you get it operational?' Jeremias asked.

'Midday tomorrow,' Calsie replied.

'That will leave us only six hours before the eclipse. It'll be a damned close call to reach the City of the Dead in that time,' Jeremias said.

'She'll make it in half that if our most recent engine tests are accurate,' Calsie replied.

'Let's hope that's right,' Jeremias said. 'Well, I think we should try and get some rest. Tomorrow we ... well, I suppose we try to save the world.'

***

The first thing Bellina noticed was the sound of her own breathing. Everything around her was black. It took her a moment to realise this was because her eyes were shut. The inside of her head felt like it was stuffed with cotton, the thoughts and commands she was sending to her body getting stuck. Each eyelid weighed heavy as a drawbridge, but eventually, she got them open.

A dim light shone from somewhere overhead, revealing row upon row of terraced seating in front of Bellina. Looking down, she could see the length of her body. Her feet were strapped to a marble table by thick leather belts. She tried to move her hands and found them bound as well. There was a chemical smell to the air, and somewhere beneath that, the scent of blood.

Feeling came back to her in a slow trickle. She tested each limb one by one, struggling against her bonds … but it was no use. Bellina laid her head back and tried to get her breathing under control. Once, in what seemed like another lifetime, she had begged her grandfather to take her to a live dissection being performed by a renowned medificer and the room it was performed in had looked a lot like the one she now occupied. *What if they want to take the baby?*

The baby she hadn't sensed, not once since she came round. Bellina's chin began to tremble, and a cold sweat broke out across her brow. She tried to calm her breathing, but it was hard. Searching, probing, she attempted to sense some sign of life coming from her child. Nothing. Her body began to shiver, and she had to stifle a scream. *Please, gods, please … don't take the child.* Then, there it was, a tiny fist or foot pushing against her stomach. Bellina let out a bark of laughter, hot tears running down her cheeks.

A dull clunk sounded followed by the groan of machinery coming to life. Overhead, a halo of intense lights flared, burning Bellina's eyes and making her wince. Slow, deliberate footsteps clicked against the hard floor. The next moment, a man appeared before her. He was tall, coffee-coloured skin almost glowing bronze in the light. There was a muscularity to him despite his leanness. Thick, black hair — so dark it appeared blue — was slicked back atop his head. If it wasn't for the staff and cloak of ravens' feathers Bellina might not have been able to place him.

'Marmossa,' she hissed.

'Empress,' Marmossa replied with a smirk. 'It's lovely to see you again. Wait, where are my manners! I never did thank you properly for helping in the downfall of the Lord Chancellor.'

'Shut your filthy, fucking mouth,' she spat. 'Do whatever it is you're going to do to me, just spare me the two-bit monologue.'

'Really? Are you not interested to know the fate of your companions? Somehow, they have made it to Sanctuary. Though I have sent a little welcoming present their way.'

'Gods, why do psychopaths love the sound of their own voices so much. Just do whatever it is you're going to do, you misbegotten fuckwit.'

Marmossa moved, lightning fast. Fingers wrapped round her neck, squeezing, choking. 'Ah, your infamous tongue. It is lucky for you that I need it, otherwise I would take great pleasure in ripping it from your head.'

She tried to spit, but the saliva barely trickled from her mouth. Air not able to pass down to her lungs, Bellina twitched and struggled, black dots appearing at the edge of her vision.

'You promised me the body unharmed,' a voice called out.

Releasing his hold, Marmossa stepped back to reveal Alari behind him. 'Yes,' he said. 'I suppose I owe you that much.'

'And more if I complete the other task you have set me,' Alari replied.

'*If* you can convince the boy to give his power willingly, I would give anything that is in my power to provide.'

'So that's why you brought me here? To mislead a scared child into doing your bidding?' Bellina said. 'You may well take my body you … you machine, but if you do this, you will never be human.'

Alari stared at the ground, wringing the umbrella in her hands. 'The … the preparations are complete,' she said, avoiding Bellina's glare. 'We can begin the transfer at once.'

'Good,' Marmossa said. 'I'm hoping it's as painful as it looks.' He turned and walked behind Bellina, the Fargazer in tow.

'Cowards!' Bellina raged. 'Sneaky, rabbit-hearted cunts!'

A rumbling groan of gears, pistons and cogs coming to life filled her ears. Her breath came to her in tattered gasps, her pulse galloping wildly. From above her head came a whirring noise. She tried to tilt her head back to see what it was but couldn't. It grew louder and louder till something was dropped over her skull, blotting out her vision. Bellina clenched her jaw. *I won't scream, I won't scream*, she told herself.

Then the pain started, and she couldn't be sure if she was screaming or not.

***

Fontaine rubbed at his weary eyes and hid a yawn behind his hand. Unable to sleep, he had examined the Leviathan and the preparations to get it ready to move. He had seen the relics slotted into a plinth and felt the beat as their power was syphoned off. Fascinated, he had watched teams of mages take it in turns to charge up massive blocks of sparkling black stone that made up the rest of the machine's fuel source. They had also shown him the squadron of automaton warriors that came with the main machine, each one gleaming, menacing in their vacuousness.

Eventually, he had asked if there was a place where he could look at the memory cards Veta had given him. He had been led to a building, at the back of which was a mass of machinery. The various pieces of apparatus covered the whole back wall — dials, gauges and buttons all crowding around a tiny glass screen. After an hour's search, he had located where to insert the cards. Almost instantly, the machine had begun to translate the information into words that appeared on the screen, and he sat down to read them.

And now, the first feeble rays of dawn light crawling through the window, a part of him regretted not at least trying to get some rest, though another part of him was astonished by what he'd just read. If it was true, then that would mean—

A grinding roar resounded through the air accompanied by the ground rumbling. Coughing as dust and mortar rained from the ceiling, Fontaine went to the door and looked out. The inhabitants of Sanctuary were running with purpose to the city walls. Once more, the floor rocked with bone-jarring ferocity, and when the scholar looked up next, he saw what the problem was.

Rearing up over the walls by hundreds of feet was a gargantuan worm-like being. Its mouth was spread wide in a thunderous howl, a perfect circle lined with needle teeth the size of obelisks. It gave off another reverberating groan, and Fontaine saw three more monstrosities answer its call. By now, the mages were throwing everything they had at the worms, but they were having little to no effect.

'Scholar! There you are.' Fontaine turned to see Hurz coming to a stop behind him. 'We have to go. Now.'

'What the hells is going on? What are those things?' Fontaine asked.

'Dustworms. They usually keep to the wastes, never come as close as this before; something must've gotten them riled up good,' Hurz answered. 'Now, come on.'

Fontaine grabbed his kit bag and ran after Hurz. The air quivered with the movement and cries of the dustworms. People fled past, away from what they were doing, joining the fight. The scholar and his guide ran against their flow, pushing, shoving. They turned a corner, and the building next to them exploded. Thrown backwards into a wall, Fontaine released a sigh, air exiting his lungs, pain blistering along his spine.

'Up!' Hurz cried.

Gibbering, Fontaine pointed an arm past the mage. Hurz turned and saw it too, the cavernous maw of the worm rising above them.

'Move!' the mage said.

Feeling a hand under his armpit, Fontaine was hauled to his feet. Hurz pulled him down another alleyway as the creature dived underground once more. Running, ground quaking beneath his feet, loose bricks showering around his head, they weaved a path towards Leviathan. They reached the outskirts of the village, saw the immense machine, purple-blue steam billowing from its back.

The ground surged upwards underfoot. *It's beneath us*, Fontaine thought with dismay. Willing his legs to move, he ran, stumbling, scrambling as the earth rippled. The land rose up in a ramp. With no time to think, the scholar dashed up it, Hurz just behind. Arriving at the edge, he jumped. Time slowed, his arms and legs flailing, the sand below rising up to meet them.

He landed on his shoulder; the sand took some of the impact, but pain still blossomed throughout his body. On his feet once more, body shrieking in complaint, he sprinted for Leviathan. A door at the back of the machine was open, Calsie leaning out and beckoning to him. Fontaine scrambled in and lay panting on the floor.

'Can you see the others?' he heard Jeremias ask.

'They're coming,' Calsie replied. 'I just hope we've got enough juice in the tank to get away *and* reach the City of the Dead.'

'There's nothing we can do now. We'll just have to try to get manablock five fully charged as we go,' Jeremias snapped. 'Hurz, you get on that now.'

'Yes, sir,' Hurz said.

'I-is there anything I can do?' Fontaine asked, getting to his feet.

'Help us get the others on board,' Calsie said.

With a slight limp, Fontaine walked to the door. The dustworm that had been chasing him had stopped on the edge of Sanctuary, its brothers close by. Beneath the Leviathan, the mages were doing their best to keep the dustworms at bay. Closer, he could see his companions. Waltus came first, running like a man a fraction of his age, then Cirona, Dargo and Holger. Elvgren was last. There was a lurch and Leviathan began to advance.

'Who gave the order to move out?' Jeremias bellowed.

'Goddamn Dafel's at the helm. Idiot must've got spooked and started her up early,' Calsie said.

'Come on!' Fontaine called.

One by one, he helped them aboard. As he reached out his arm to Elvgren, Holger shoved him aside and closed the door.

'What the fuck are you doing, boy?' Calsie demanded.

'He can't come,' Holger raged, eyes bulging in his head. 'He has to die so things can be right.'

'I-I begged mercy for you,' Fontaine said. His voice starting as a whisper and rising. 'I … we all begged mercy for you, and he gave it, that man, our Emperor. Open that door!'

'No.'

Hands fumbling Fontaine fished out his ballistol. 'I told you to open it, you … you cowardly sneak.'

'Never,' Holger said, making a grab for the weapon.

They began to wrestle, and Fontaine wasn't quite sure what happened next. All that could be certain was that the ballistol went off, taking the top half of Holger's head with it and showering him with gore.

'By the Father,' Fontaine murmured. 'What have I done?'

'What needed to be done,' Jeremias said, opening the door and hauling his brother through it.

CHAPTER TWENTY

Bellina's teeth ground together as she tried to ride out the wave of agony making her body convulse. It felt like a ring of white-hot needles was trying to bore through her skull. The greasy reek of burning hair and flesh invaded her nostrils, threatening to send the churning bile in her stomach out past her lips.

Make it stop, make it stop, makeitstop, she prayed, but it kept on. Time bent and warped till it was like the pain had always been a part of her, an undeniable truth of her being. She could sense her sanity beginning to unravel. No. She was not going to let this happen, there was one last card she could play, and she was desperate enough to put it on the table — she could retreat into her own psychic landscape.

The technique, Alcastus had said, enabled a cognopath to hide from and blot out physical pain but it came with the risk of becoming stuck there permanently. The risk of it was irrelevant to Bellina; she had found a way out, and she was taking it. Fighting against the torture with every fragment of her being, she imagined an arched doorway filled with light and herself stepping through it.

With a faint pop, Bellina found herself upon the manicured lawns of her psychic landscape. The pain had now subsided to a faint throb, little more than a minor headache. *Thank the gods*, she thought, *now I've got some time to think. There has to be a way for me to get out of this, there just has—*

Something was wrong. Bellina scanned around her — lawn, hedge maze, flowerbeds, night sky … night sky? Her landscape had always been filled with the first light of dawn — her favourite time of day — but now everything was surrounded by an ocean of darkness, a darkness that was firmly eroding her creation.

No! No, this couldn't be happening. She imagined a giant bubble around herself and pushed back, but the terrible geography of Alari's coding crept in, remorseless, relentless, churning over everything in its path. Through her shrinking sphere, she saw a vista of blocks, all different shapes and sizes, all marked with elaborate, orange geometric patterns.

Soon, all she had left was a tiny orb of herself, stubbornly hanging on. She saw a swirl of small, turquoise squares coil in on upon themselves until the Fargazer appeared. Bellina took some small satisfaction in the fact Alari emerged looking just as haggard as she felt. Alari marched towards Bellina, her face a mask of fury.

'Let go!' she screeched. 'This is my body now, mine, mine, mine!'

'I'm *sorry*, is my refusing to die bothering you?' Bellina said, noting the rough, uneven breaths the Fargazer was drawing in.

'Stop this at once! I have waited a thousand years for this, and I won't be denied.'

'You'll have to destroy me first,' Bellina replied, 'if you think you've got the strength for it that is.'

Alari's nostrils flared. 'I'll show you strength,' she said.

An immense pressure bore down upon Bellina's bubble, a grinding, bruising weight. A moan escaped her lips, pain seared her chest, but she kept pushing back. She could see Alari had to be close to her limit too. It was just a question of who had the stronger will.

'Arghhghghhh!' the Fargazer screamed.

Bellina collapsed to her knees, smiling in triumph.

'Fine, stay in there then for what good it will do you,' Alari hissed.

With a wave of her hand, the floor rose up around Bellina's orb, encasing her in a tiny cell with a small window.

'No!' she wailed, pounding upon the walls.

'I'll deal with you later. His lordship is calling.'

Thereupon, Alari vanished, leaving Bellina alone in the stark landscape. She lay down, exhaustion and exasperation overcoming her. *So what if you're trapped?* she told herself. *You're still alive, aren't you? And where there is life there is hope. We'll find a way to turn this round and take that bitch down.*

***

Jaw set firm, eyes alert, Cirona watched as the City of the Dead materialised on the horizon. So far away, it looked like a dark indistinct blob, only the shaft of a colossal tower definite among the mass, but with each of the Leviathan's ponderous steps, it drew closer. *Hang on, Bellina,* she thought, *just you hang on, girl. I'm coming for you, we all are, and woe betide that fucker Marmossa when we get there.*

She tore her gaze away and swept her eyes around the control room. It was a remarkable space. They were at the very top of the Leviathan's bullet-shaped head tucked behind the huge glass bubble that looked like an eye. Behind the eye was a bank of terminals. Calsie sat at its centre working a series of levers and foot pedals. On either side of her sat two other mages, each totally absorbed by the instruments in front of them.

And behind all of that were her companions. Some stood, some sat in awkward metal chairs bolted to the floor, but they all had the same look on their faces — concern. Each seemed to have retreated into a small, mental realm of their own. She was most concerned about the scholar. His face was a sickly white, eyes unblinking within it. He was biting the nail of his left index finger, apparently unaware he was drawing blood. For an instant, she thought about trying to comfort him again … but in the end, coming to terms with taking another's life was a battle you faced alone.

Somewhere, deep down, she felt a small flicker of sorrow at Holger's death — gods only knew it had been ignominious enough. But that sadness was for the boy she had first met, the person he was before the broken splinters of his love had twisted and morphed into insanity. She had seen men lose it before while on campaign, seen their eyes turn dull, seen their souls split. And those men, well, they either went looking for death or had to be … ended.

'What's our arrival time?' Jeremias asked, snapping Cirona from her thoughts.

'We should make it, but it'll be tight,' Calsie replied.

'Gods damn it, can't we go any faster?'

'Our guys are working their arses off down there, Jerry; what more can we do?' Calsie said.

With a sudden lurch, the Leviathan ground to a halt. Cirona stumbled forwards.

'What the hells is going on?' Elvgren demanded.

'I don't know,' Calsie said. 'Situation report.'

'Unknown boss,' one of the mages to her side answered. 'There's no reason I can see for this, but the problem is coming from the aft.'

'By the fiery pit of … Aft crew? Aft crew! Can you hear me? Over,' Calsie called into a pipe with a mouthpiece. 'Shit, there's no response. Somebody needs to get down there.'

'I'll go,' Cirona said, desperate to do something, to not feel so powerless.

'Fine,' Calsie said. 'Once you get there let me know just what the fuck is going on.'

Cirona nodded and made for the door at the back of the room. It opened onto the steel platform of a lift. Pulling on a lever, she began to descend. With a small jolt, she came to a stop. Sprinting onwards, she rushed past dozens of confused mages — many still picking themselves up after the violent stop they had come to — towards the back of the Leviathan. She found the aft door buckled, the glass busted out from its porthole window.

Spinning the wheel lock round, she pulled. With the door now out of shape it took all of her strength to haul it open, the sudden release flinging her backwards. Cirona picked herself up and passed through the door. Upon the riveted metal floor lay five mages. Some were groaning, but two unfortunate souls had hit the floor with such force their heads had caved in.

What the fuck happened here? Cirona thought. Looking upwards, she saw five massive holes punched through the frame of Leviathan. Protruding from these ragged puncture marks were what looked like vast, metallic knuckles. She began to walk towards them but slid downwards as the knuckle flexed.

Skidding into the wall, she hit her head hard. Looking up through star-filled eyes, Cirona saw the knuckles disappear. The squealing crunch of metal grinding against metal filled the air as the roof was ripped away like the lid of a sardine tin. For a second, she couldn't quite believe what she was seeing, her mouth falling open.

There, looking down at her, the sands of the wastes trickling from their bodies were two enormous automatons.

***

Looking out through the gap in her cell, Bellina was astonished to see a projection of what was happening in the real world. She could see Marmossa staring down at her, brows furrowed.

'Alari? Alari!' he said. 'Are you there? Was the transfer a success?'

'Yesh lor Marmosha,' Alari slurred.

'Are you sure? There weren't any … complications?'

'No.'

'Very well. I will give you a moment to grow accustomed to your new body, then I want you to join me in the royal suite.'

'Yesh.'

Marmossa tilted his head and narrowed his eyes. He made a "hmm" noise at the back of his throat and left. Once he was gone, she saw Alari try to bring her hand up to her face. It quivered, twitched then fell back to her side.

I … I can't move! the Fargazer's voice rang out.

'Oh dear! What a terrible shame,' Bellina said.

You have to help me, Alari demanded.

'Why the fuck should I?' Bellina said, giving a harsh bark of laughter.

Because if Marmossa finds out about you, he'll kill us … including the baby.

Bellina felt her hands ball into fists. 'Fine. But I don't know what I can do from in here.'

Hang on a moment.

Bellina watched awestruck as Alari began to change the layout of the psychic landscape. First, the front wall of Bellina's prison vanished. Next, banks of computational engines popped up below the projection. Finally, manacles materialised upon her wrists and ankles, thick chains leading away to the back wall of her cell.

Taking a few tentative steps forwards, Bellina noticed that the chains extended as she moved. *Alright*, she thought, *let's see how far this bit of freedom goes.* She tried to alter the landscape. Nothing. Then she attempted to break her bonds. Nothing. Focusing all of her will, she tried to conjure a weapon, a simple dagger. Nothing. But then the vague shape of it started to emerge. If she could just—

Get a move on! Alari cried. *He'll be wondering where I am.*

Cursing under her breath, Bellina said, 'Alright, alright, I'm coming.'

Going as slow as she dared, Bellina moved towards the computational engines. Up close, she realised that they were clustered together in three main groups. Before her, and directly beneath the projection, was the largest collection of devices. Thick, snaking bands of wire trailed out to the left. Despite the amount of them, only a few actually connected to the machines in that corner and none at all reached the ones on the right.

The left side is sensory function, the Fargazer said, *the right is motor function. I've made some connections on the sensory side, so you should be able to connect that quickly.*

Not bothering to answer, Bellina moved towards the left bank of contraptions. She picked up a wire and saw that it ended in a metal-tipped point that fit precisely into the engines. As she plugged the wires in, she began to think. The psychic landscape Alari had been forced to create was crude, devoid of deception or protection. And that meant somewhere close to hand would be her psychic core, and if she could get to that—

Hurry up!

'Oh, shut up! There's an absolute million of these things to … There you go, all done.'

Good. Now move on to motor function.

Bellina trekked to the middle rank of engines to collect the wires.

*Where the hells would she put the core? It must be some—*Then she had it. The machines in the centre were Alari. That meant she had to be right on top of it. Her eyes glanced from device to device. Where was it? What form would it take? Her gaze locked on to a dragonfly embossed on a small metal box that all the wires surged back to. That was it. It *had* to be it.

'Where are you woman?' Marmossa's voice thundered, seeming to come from everywhere at once.

'I-I'm c-coming, my lord. Adjusting to a physical form has b-been a tad more … troublesome than I had anticipated,' Alari stammered.

'I gave you that body because I have a use for it, but there are many ways to flay a pig. If you are not up here in the next five minutes, I will kill you where you stand.'

P-please, you heard what he said. Hurry up!

Again, Bellina didn't answer. Instead, she made a move towards the dragonfly box. She stretched out an arm, her fingers almost touching it. Her chains snapped taut.

Where are you going? That's the wrong way.

Swearing, Bellina grabbed the wires and moved towards the machines for motor function. She rammed each one home with a curse. The perspective of the room changed as Alari stood up. A door came into view, then they were past it. Bellina wracked her brain. She needed to distract the Fargazer long enough to get to the box. But how?

'Why did you even want a body? Surely, it wasn't just so you could serve the monster you're running to now?' Bellina asked, searching for, well, she wasn't sure what but maybe something she would catch Alari off-guard.

Of course not! I … I have my reasons.

'What?' Bellina said taking a few steps forwards.

I … I want to love and … and be loved in return.

Laughing, Bellina moved closer to the box and said, 'Love? What the hells would a machine know about love.'

I know about love! Alari boomed. *I was in love. In love with the ancestor of your betrothed.*

'By the Father! You think you can use Elvgren as a proxy for Amlith, don't you?' Bellina said, the box only a short distance away.

Yes … no … maybe … I don't know. Stop asking me questions … I … I can't think.

'Let me tell you about love,' Bellina called, reaching out her hand. 'I love that little boy you're about to sacrifice. I love him, because he is kind and innocent and never hurt anybody in his life. You would destroy *him,* a person worthy of love, for what? In fact—'

Shut up shut up shut up! Alari screamed.

With a sound like a whip cracking, Bellina's chains pulled tight, and she went flying back into her cell. She tried to scream, but a piece of metal came flying out of nowhere, attaching itself to her mouth. *So close,* she thought, *I was so, so close.*

The despair she had been fending off flooded through her as the tears coursed down her cheeks.

***

Elvgren gripped the edge of his seat, knuckles turning pale. They were still stuck, Leviathan's metal shell groaning, vibrating around him as it struggled to break free. *Where the hells is Cirona?* he thought. *She's been gone too long.* An alarm began to blare, a red warning light radiating in time with each burst of noise.

'Turn that godsforsaken thing off!' Calsie roared. 'We already know we're in trouble, all that thing'll do is give us a headache.'

'Sure thing, boss,' the mage to her right said. As soon as it was off, a tinny voice could be heard.

Calsie grabbed the communication device she had attempted use earlier. 'Hello?' she called into it. 'Is that you, General?'

'Y-yes, it's me,' Cirona replied. Elvgren felt his chest loosen at the sound of her voice … until she spoke again. 'We've got a major problem down here. I'm … I'm not really sure how to … Well, two massive automatons have grasped the back of the Leviathan. So far, all they've tried to do is hold it in place. Not really sure how to proceed.'

It can't be, Elvgren thought. *How would they have been able to transport them all the way out here?*

'They … they're not automatons,' he said. 'They're one of the duke's creations. He calls them Gomech Warriors — enormous mechanised suits of armour for want of a better term — and they're piloted by a person.'

'So, if we kill the drivers they'll let go?' Calsie asked.

'Yes, I suppose,' Elvgren replied. 'But how would we get to them through all that metal?'

'You leave that to us,' Calsie said. 'We've can—'

'Er, boss? You might want to see this,' one of her mage assistants said.

Along with everyone else, Elvgren moved to the front of the cockpit. He peered out into the desert wastes. At first, he thought his eyes were playing tricks, so he rubbed them and looked again. There was no mistaking it this time. Moving at an impossible speed across the desolation was the Estrian army, the blue of their uniforms making their identity undeniable. To make matters worse, he could see at least twenty uresh, the giant monsters he had fought in Victory, at the rear of the charge.

'This is ridiculous,' Elvgren heard himself whisper.

'Ridiculous?' Jeremias said. 'Ridiculous? This is a fucking catastrophe. The eclipse isn't far off and we are not close to reaching the city.'

'We're doomed!' Barboza bellowed, smashing the butt of his staff onto the floor.

'Not yet we ain't,' Calsie said. She leaned over and called into the communication device. 'General? General! You still there?'

'Yes,' Cirona called back.

'Good. Get your arse to Leviathan's engine and grab the relics; you folks are gonna need those. After that, head to the midsection.'

'But without the relics, you won't be able to move,' Cirona replied.

'You just bring 'em back when you're finished dealing with Marmossa; we'll still be here. Now enough chat, you got that?'

'Understood,' Cirona said.

Jumping to her feet, Calsie pointed to her assistants. 'You two hold down the fort. As for the rest of you, follow me!'

She strode forwards, away from the cockpit and towards the lift. Elvgren matched her pace. They all crowded onto the steel platform. Calsie cranked the lever, and they dropped down the levels till they reached the middle of Leviathan's colossal frame.

Elvgren looked around the new room they found themselves in. It was a sparse space dominated by a huge silver orb divided vertically down its middle by metal teeth. Ringing the portion of the sphere that he could see was a curious series of pipes with flared ends. Stretching out from the bottom of the orb was a narrow groove that ended at a guardrail.

'What the fuck is all this when it's at home?' Waltus said.

'This is the escape capsule,' Calsie replied.

'I beg your pardon?' Elvgren said.

'It's an escape capsule. A capsule to help you escape. I don't really think I can put it any simpler,' Calsie said.

There was a clanking sound behind them, and Elvgren turned to see Cirona, with a nasty gash on the side of her face, come running into the room.

'What the hells is that?' she said, handing the relics to their respective owners.

'An escape capsule apparently,' Crenshaw replied, a confused look on his face.

'I didn't know you had managed to fix this,' Jeremias said.

'Well we did … sort of,' Calsie said.

'Sort of? You expect us to go sailing through the air in a device you "sort of" fixed?' Jeremias said.

Calsie narrowed her eyes. 'You know, Jerry, when you get stressed, you're a bit of a prick. Besides, the capsule's the only chance you've got.'

Jeremias sighed. 'You're right. I'm sorry. Get it into position … please.'

'I don't mean to be a naysaying ninny,' Elvgren said, holding up his hands, 'but how are you going to launch anything with no power?'

'There's bound to be at least a few minutes of residual energy left in the old girl's tank,' Calsie replied, patting the walls of the Leviathan. 'Enough to get you where you need to go…well it should do anyway.'

Elvgren swallowed hard and watched as Calsie walked to the left wall and pulled on a lever. The orb began to roll back along the groove, its teeth keeping it in place, till it clanged against the guardrail. With the sphere out of the way, Elvgren could see a long, narrow tunnel stretching ahead of him ending in a circle of light.

'It's almost like looking out from the inside of a cannon,' he said.

'That's exactly what it's like, because that's what it essentially is…and I'm about to fire you out of it,' Calsie said.

'You're what?' Elvgren asked.

'I'm gonna fire *you*' she said, pointing at Elvgren then at the tunnel. 'Out *there*.'

'This is incredible! Everyone stop talking — I wanna go now!' Dargo cried, running towards the orb.

Elvgren grabbed him by the collar. 'Hang on, Dar,' he said. 'I'm not sure—'

An immense rumble shook the Leviathan. 'Look, there ain't no more time to argue,' Calsie said. 'All of you in now!'

'Will you be alright?' Jeremias asked.

'We'll be fine, Jerry. We've still got a few tricks up our sleeves,' she said.

Elvgren watched his brother give a sharp nod then hug the female mage. 'Alright, everyone in,' he said.

They walked round to the front of the orb and were confronted by a door with a wheel-lock mechanism. Elvgren helped his brother get it open, and they all marched in. Once inside the sphere, he saw three banks of chairs, enough to seat twenty people. Barboza closed the door behind them.

'Is that locked as tight as you can get it?' Jeremias asked. The king of Timboko nodded. 'Everyone, take a seat … and make sure you strap yourselves in.'

Picking a seat at random, Elvgren sat down and heaved the weighty leather straps into place. The only view was through the tiny porthole in the door, and that merely showed the dark expanse of tunnel. His breath was coming in sharp, irregular bursts, his throat dry and tight. *What the hells am I doing?* he thought. *I'm strapped into a giant metal ball about to be shot towards a city from the stomach of a mythical machine by a mage!*

'Good luck, people,' Calsie's voice called through a speaker. 'Here we go — three … two … one!'

A thundering blast sounded, and the sphere began to shiver like an old man's hands. All at once, they began to shoot forwards. Elvgren could hear Dargo whooping and cheering. If he could have reached the lad, he would have clouted him round the back of his head. As it was, he was using every bit of his will trying not to pass out.

Forwards and up they went, the pressure building to the point Elvgren thought his head would pop like an overripe grape. He didn't dare think how high they were in the air. The pressure on his body eased, and for one brief moment, everything was still.

Then they began to plummet towards the ground.

***

Eyes dull, body numb, Bellina watched the projection jog up and down as her stolen body hurried to Marmossa. Her footfalls made a blunt slapping sound against the stone floor, and a forest of needle-like black columns extending to the ceiling flew past. Soon, they reached a series of curious round stones set into the floor. Alari stepped onto one and thin bands of glowing red lines appeared on it. With a quiet grating sound, it lifted them into the air.

They arrived in a narrow hallway, the floor glistening as though it were wet. Advancing, they passed doorways, the stonework surrounding them covered in carvings of obscene, writhing, blasphemous creatures. At last, they reached the final door and Marmossa emerged from the shadows.

'You are late,' he hissed.

'Forgive me, my lord,' Alari said. 'There were—'

'Enough! I don't have time for further excuses. The boy is coming round. Gain his trust then bring him to the top of the tower.'

With a swish of his cloak, Marmossa stormed off. Alari grasped the door handle and let herself into the room. The space was devoid of comfort, like it had been created for creatures who took no pleasure in luxury. Upon a stone slab, the light from a small, arched window illuminating his face, was Midge. Bellina felt a whimper leave her lips. He was stirring, fretting to and fro as if he was trying to escape from a nightmare.

'Midge? Midge, darling, are you awake? It's me, Bellina,' Alari said.

'Belle? Is it really you?' Midge said, snapping awake and gripping her arm. 'They've kept telling me you were coming, but you didn't, and then they'd give me another drink and it'd make me go to sleep and I was having the most terrible nightmares—'

'Shh … shh,' Alari said, pulling the boy into a tight hug. 'It's alright. I'm here now. But I need your help. Will you help me, Midge?'

'Of course, Belle … anything,' Midge said, his bright-eyed eagerness bringing fresh tears to Bellina's eyes.

'Excellent. You see, Midge, you are a very special boy. You have powers newly awakened in you that can change the world for good … or bad. Things might seem scary where we are going but what we will do there will … will make the world a … a … better place.'

'Will it help the captain and everyone else too? I've dreamed so much about everyone, and they always seemed angry or hurt and it made me angry and hurt that I couldn't help.'

'It certainly will help them. But enough chattering — we'd best be on our way,' Alari said.

The look of hope and blind trust in Midge's eyes was more than Bellina could bear. Screaming, she pulled against her chains. She had to get out. There was no way she could let these monsters abuse such a child. *You're better than this*, she told herself; *you're stronger that this!* With every scrap of her being, Bellina pulled. The taut chains snapped loose, and she was free.

Alari, in her haste, had forgotten to replace the front of Bellina's cell. Bellina was going to make full use of this oversight. She crept forwards, expecting the Fargazer to appear with every step she took. Each inch she gained felt like a mile crossed in enemy territory. The box with the embossed dragonfly came into view.

Dashing across the final few feet, she dived forwards and ripped the lid off the box. Inside was a large, glowing crystal, wires coiling into it like veins.

'What are you doing?' a voice screamed behind her.

Bellina looked round to see Alari rushing towards her. With a vicious yank she hauled the gem free.

'Stop right fucking there,' Bellina said.

The Fargazer stopped in her tracks. She licked her lips. 'Now, now … let's be reasonable. I did let you live after all.'

'And that,' Bellina cried, 'was a massive mistake!'

With all her force, Bellina dashed the gem against the floor. It shattered into a million sparkling pieces. Alari howled. Her chest began to exude light, expanding, growing till it covered every inch of her body. A final scream passed her lips, then she erupted into a fine mist that evaporated into nothingness.

Bellina fell to her knees. She had done it. She had won. *Careful now,* she warned herself, *we are nowhere near out of the woods yet.* That was definitely true. Should she take Midge and run? But where to? She had no knowledge of her whereabouts. Were the others on their way? Did she just need to buy time till they arrived?

'Belle? Belle! Are you alright?' she heard Midge call.

Pushing her questions aside, she waved her arms, restoring her psychic landscape, imagined a doorway and returned to reality. Looking through her own eyes once more, she saw Midge gazing up at her.

'I'm alright, Midge,' she said, ruffling the boy's hair. 'I didn't feel myself for a moment, but I'm back now.'

There was a knock at the door. Bellina turned as it opened and saw Dahlia walk in. Immediately, she felt the blood begin to pound in her ears. Her first thought was to rush across the floor and rip her fellow cognopath's face off. Somehow, she managed to quell the storm of anger building within her, realising her best bet for the time being was to play along.

'Yes,' she said. 'What is it?'

'We need to get up to Lord Marmossa. Things are coming off the rails. We managed to stop the Leviathan outside the city, but they fired some kind of ball out of it that's crashed within the walls,' Dahlia said.

Bellina allowed a small flicker of hope to catch fire inside her. 'I see,' she said, fighting a smile from her lips.

Dahlia cocked her head and looked at her. 'Are you alright?' she asked. 'You seem strange.'

'I'm absolutely fine,' Bellina answered. 'Don't you worry about me. Now let's go see what his lordship wants.'

Dahlia frowned and Bellina kicked herself for not speaking with proper deference. Eventually her fellow cognopath said, 'Alright. Oh, and before I forget, take this.'

For a moment, Bellina thought she wouldn't be able to stop herself laughing. There in Dahlia's hand was the control conduit for Bellina's powers. 'Thank you,' she said, taking it from Dahlia's grasp. Her first instinct was to activate her abilities and smash Dahlia's head into a bloody pulp. *Patience,* she cautioned herself; *there are bigger fish to catch here. If we can scupper, or even stall, Marmossa then that should be our primary aim.*

'I don't know if you have gained access to her powers yet, but Marmossa wants you to have the controls just in case we need to fight,' Dahlia said.

'Our lord is so wise, is he not?' Bellina said.

'He's definitely not an idiot,' Dahlia replied. 'Now, come on.'

Taking Midge's hand, Bellina followed Dahlia back into the hallway. She was led towards a set of doors she hadn't noticed on her arrival. Beyond them was a circular space with more of the floating platforms. Bellina set off towards one, but Dahlia grabbed her arm. Bellina wrenched herself free with just a touch too much force.

'What's wrong with you?' Dahlia said. 'You were about to take the wrong one.'

'Oh, I'm … I'm just a touch disorientated is all,' Bellina replied.

'Well, I'd snap out of it quick.'

Dahlia directed them onto the correct platform, and they rushed upwards. Floor after floor shot past till they came out in the open air. The platform came to a stop behind a row of titanic thrones. Walking past these, Bellina discovered they were on top of a tower. The floor in front of her was a large stretched oval. Thick cables criss-crossed the ground like arteries converging at a massive altar. Atop it lay the relics in Marmossa's possession. From the altar more cables snaked towards a giant glass sphere, the same as one would find in a sortilenergy plant, then to a circular archway. Visible in the centre of the arch, an edge just being nibbled by the start of the eclipse, was the sun.

'Bring the boy here,' Marmossa said, emerging from behind the altar, Garand and the duke next to him.

Unsure of what else to do, Bellina did as she was told, all the while looking for some destruction she could cause. As she walked, her left hand reached out to her control conduit … then froze. She tried again, but it was like an invisible hand was holding her back.

'I knew it!' Dahlia crowed. 'I knew something was off here. Lord Marmossa, Bellina has somehow retaken control of her body.'

'What?' Marmossa hissed, levelling his staff at her.

'No!' Midge bellowed. 'You won't hurt, Belle!'

A wall of energy erupted from the boy sending all but himself flying. Bellina praised the gods that she had landed on her back. With great effort, she climbed to her feet, noting how close she was to the edge of the tower's roof. Across from her, she saw Dahlia struggle upwards, a thin trickle of blood leaking from her nose.

'I've got you now,' Dahlia said. 'There's nowhere left for you to go.'

'Oh really?' Bellina replied, then leapt backwards into thin air.

***

Fontaine squeezed his eyes shut, insides lurching, as the escape capsule plummeted towards the ground. If not for the enormous forces pushing on him, he was sure he would have been sick. He was dimly aware of someone screaming behind him. Down and down they fell. In his mind, racing past in snatches, Fontaine imagined the state his body would be in seconds after they hit the ground — it was not a pretty picture.

Just as he was sure that death was imminent, the capsule jolted to a stop, the scholar's head snapping back brutally. They drifted down at a serene pace. There was a collective sigh of relief in the capsule. Coming to a stop, Fontaine and the others began to unbuckle themselves.

With a jarring screech, they fell once again. When they hit the ground this time, Fontaine was thrown forwards, bruising his ribs on the chair in front. They wobbled back and forth for a second then came to a complete stop.

'Th-this way,' Jeremias wheezed, staggering towards the door.

It took both him and Barboza to undo the wheel lock and push the door open. Filing into a line, they exited the orb. At once, Fontaine was struck by a coughing fit caused by a fine cloud of dust entering his lungs. Covering his mouth and getting his body under control, he looked around. They were in a simple mud-brick building. The capsule had clearly landed on the roof, been too heavy, and fallen through, exposing not just the top floor bur also the flat, idiot blue of the sky. At the back of the sphere, he could see where a hatch had blown. From it trailed a series of cords that connected to a massive amount of billowing silk. *So that's what slowed us down*, he thought. *Fascinating.*

By now, the others had found the building's exit and had moved into the street. Fontaine followed them and came to a sudden stop. Filling the thoroughfare they had walked into, packing it from side to side, were people — green, translucent people. They walked through and around the scholar and his companions, eyes dull, looking like they were searching for something.

'What are these people?' Barboza asked.

'Echoes,' Fontaine heard himself answer. 'Each of these houses was designated to a specific family. They would inter their dead here and the power of the manastream would create these … these shadows for people to visit — though I must say I never expected them to be so lifelike.'

'Are these ones dead?' Dargo asked, peering through a window.

The scholar hurried over. Inside the house Dargo was next to lay a body atop a flat, stone sarcophagus. The room was full of more such people. Fontaine watched them intently and, yes, he could just see the rise and fall of their chests.

'They're not dead,' he said. 'I believe these are the people kidnapped from Victory and … elsewhere.'

'Can't we help them?' Cirona said.

The scholar shook his head. 'Marmossa turned them into crows to fly them here. No doubt he's used similarly powerful magic to put them into a false sleep.'

'We should at least try!' Barboza called.

'No,' Jeremias cut in. 'Look ahead of you.'

Following the instruction, Fontaine looked out, over the heads of the echoes, towards a titanic tower. The stonework was mixed with twisting steel, merging together in a repulsive dance. Beyond that was the sun, nearly a full half of it eaten as the moon passed across its face.

'We're running out of time,' Elvgren said.

'We make straight for the tower,' Jeremias said. 'The echoes aren't corporeal so run—'

He was brought up short by an ululating cackle. Glancing upwards, Fontaine saw nine massive black birds circling, their wings wavering like the last twists of a dying flame. *This can't be good*, he thought.

'Everyone, split up,' Cirona ordered. 'If those … things attack together we won't stand a chance. We'll regroup at the tower.'

Brow creasing, Fontaine glanced at his companions as they dispersed down different avenues. His mind ran through the multiple possibilities each street might offer, desperate to work out what might be the shortest and the safest route. *I don't know what … where should I … how …* Paralysed by his own reason, all he could do was watch, stunned, as one of the birds plunged towards him.

The creature landed with a blast of air that sent the scholar sprawling onto his back. The thing looked down at him, cocking its head to regard him with both of its tiny, malevolent eyes. Its head resembled a cockerel's with the addition of a ridge of bones protruding from the skull. Two massive black wings bulged from the fiend's back, while its legs and arms, scabrous, rot-ridden, extended from the front, both ending in brutal talons. Opening its beak, it let out a caw, sending a horrific odour of tomb-like decay washing over Fontaine.

As the creature bore down on him, the scholar scuttled backwards, just eluding the pecking beak. He came to a stop against a stone wall, and the fiend seemed to sense its impending victory, letting out another cry. Before it could make its move, one of its brothers landed atop it, pinning it to the ground. This new attacker — probably summoned by the crowing from its associate — lunged for Fontaine only to be thrown backwards by the one underneath. The pair began to roll around the ground, fighting. Grasping the small reprieve the gods had thrown him, Fontaine ran.

Dashing, running, narrow alleys flying past him, he made his way onwards, the flap of the demons' wings appallingly close. Their talons tore at him, ripping through his clothes, gouging the skin underneath. Ahead of him, a narrow alley. He turned sideways to force himself through, the coarse brickwork aggravating his cuts and wounds, claws probing from above.

With a push, he burst out onto the main road. The buildings ended here, the tower close, but the last stretch of ground to it was utterly without cover. Ahead of him, he could see the others making a mad dash for their goal. Adrenaline speeding through him, Fontaine let out a wild scream and began to run.

He ran faster than he ever had in his life. Never before had he felt so keenly the interlocking of bone and muscle, of finding the perfect balance therein and transferring that into beautiful, fluid motion. At the tower's entrance, those who had reached it first were laying down suppressing fire. Howls of anguish and pain filled the air when the flying monstrosities were hit.

Despite his speed, Fontaine was the last left in the open. The sounds of the others urging him on were lost in the wild thrashing of blood in his ears. From above the gigantic arched gateway, a portcullis began to descend. It was moving fast … too fast. With a mad dive, he came skidding into the tower just as the portcullis dropped behind him.

'Didn't think you was gonna make it for a second there, son,' Waltus said, helping him to his feet.

'N-neither did I,' the scholar said, panting.

Behind him, the dark creatures thrashed against the gate. He and his companions all took up arms, slashing and stabbing at the probing talons till the monstrosities flew away in fear and frustration.

'We're here,' Dargo said. 'We actually made it.'

Fontaine turned round to look at the tower's door. The way to it was lined with ribbed columns that rose up to a ceiling of interlocking stone. All around were niches filled with carvings of grotesque, unspeakable forms. The scholar felt a shiver pass through him. For a second, they all stood, contemplating what was beyond.

'Everyone, forwards,' Cirona commanded. 'We've got a job to do here.'

Barboza took the lead and began to push against the immense door. Fontaine joined him, and they were all soon engaged in getting it open. With a protracted groan, it finally opened.

'At least it wasn't locked, eh?' Elvgren said.

'Yeah, but why?' Crenshaw asked.

'Do you think he's goading us … inviting us in?' Fontaine added.

'That or he didn't expect us to get this far,' Cirona said.

'It doesn't matter,' Jeremias said. 'We can speculate all we want, but it doesn't change what we came here to do.'

With the next breath, he led them inside the tower. They were met with more columns, these made of a black metal moulded into thin strips that corkscrewed up to an unseen ceiling. They headed across the marble floor, Fontaine trying his best to rapidly decode the blunt, geometric signs carved into it.

'What're these?' Dargo said, pointing at a ring of circular, glowing platforms.

'We can ride these to the top of the tower where the ritual will take place,' Jeremias said, 'Everyone—'

'Wait!' Fontaine called. 'No one step on anything.'

'What's the matter?' Cirona said.

The scholar retrieved his notebook and stood comparing his notes with the markings on the floor. 'Aha! So that's how it works.'

'Could you fill the rest of us in?' Elvgren said.

'Ah, yes, yes, of course. Only some of these platforms will lead us in the right direction. The other platforms would bring us to floors filled with traps,' he said.

'So which ones will take us to the top?' Dargo said.

'The ones we must take are inscribed with a vulture, a snake, a scorpion and a shark,' Fontaine replied, pointing the symbols out to his companions. 'They might not take us straight to the top, but if we keep following the correct symbols, we should make it.'

'Problem is,' Crenshaw said. 'I reckon only about two people can get on one of these platforms.'

'He's right,' Jeremias said. 'We need to pair up. Crenshaw and Barboza will go together as will Elvgren and Dargo. Cirona you go with Waltus. That leaves you and me, scholar. Let's go.'

Fontaine followed behind Jeremias onto the snake platform and watched the others take up their positions. They were grim-faced, determined, and the scholar felt an immense rush of pride to be fighting alongside them. Then the platforms began to move. He took a deep breath and tried to convince himself he was ready for whatever fate awaited him.

CHAPTER TWENTY-ONE

Bellina fell through the atmosphere, clothes billowing, limbs flailing. With a savage jerk, she managed to flip herself over so she was facing the ground. *Eyes open*, she told herself, *keep your eyes open!* The buildings below were nothing more than vague hints, the buttresses and pinnacles of the tower just blurs flashing past. Then she spotted what she was after — a balcony.

Imagining a cushion of air to land on, Bellina came to rest on the platform. She stood, legs wobbling, and fought to slow the frantic thrashing of her heart before moving as fast as she could into the room leading off the balcony. Bellina found herself in a banquet hall. Fluted pillars of ebony-coloured wood strained up, criss-crossing the ceiling and lending their support to three vast chandeliers. Along the length of the walls were huge, moth-eaten tapestries. They seemed to show a hunting scene. The Terrors — easily identifiable as they were depicted much larger than anyone else — were there, but she couldn't spot the prey. Bile churning in her stomach, she realised her mistake — the Terrors were hunting humans.

She turned away in disgust and began walking the length of the extensive dining table, past elaborately carved chairs covered in a thick layer of dust. Shortly, she found the tall, iron-bound doors. Grabbing a round handle, icy cold to her touch, she pulled.

Nothing happened.

'You won't get away that easily,' a soft voice cooed behind her.

Bellina turned round to see her fellow cognopath calmly descending onto the balcony, and for a second, she could have sworn she saw a dark pair of wings.

'Dahlia,' she spat, nostrils flaring. Without a pause, she launched an attack on her pursuer's mind. Bellina was met by a wall of darkness that pushed her back both physically and mentally.

Laughing, Dahlia said, 'Surprise! Bet you weren't expecting that?'

'Wh-what have you done?' Bellina asked

Dahlia ran her fingers over the top of a chair. 'Oh, just a few improvements courtesy of yaksit. My father and Garand have also been enhanced.'

'Then you're nothing more than Marmossa's puppets,' Bellina said.

'Shut your mouth!' Dahlia screeched. 'What do you know anyway? Nothing! Even now, you're still fighting for an empire, no, a world that has run its course, a world that will be cleansed by the Deivars, a world where Marmossa's chosen will be gods!'

'Like fuck it will,' Bellina said, before using her powers to launch a chair at Dahlia.

From nowhere, a giant black hand appeared, caught the chair and crushed it to splinters. 'See?' Dahlia said. 'See the strength I've been granted!'

The hand accelerated towards Bellina, a dark blur. She focused her mind, lifting four chairs, aiming one at the hand and the rest at her opponent. To her dismay, she saw a further three hands materialise, stopping the projectiles and protecting Dahlia. Desperate, a cold sweat running down her back, she strained to lift the dining table. With a yell, she launched it at her foe. A second later, her heart sank when she saw the four hands brush it aside like a cobweb.

'Are you finished now?' Dahlia said, walking forwards. 'Is it my turn?' Without waiting for an answer, the four hands shot out, throwing Bellina backwards and pinning her legs and arms to the wall. 'So,' Dahlia continued. 'What will the Empire's *former* strongest cognopath do now?'

***

Cirona came to a stop. She could see nothing, a shroud of darkness so absolute it seemed to engulf her entire being. Taking a faltering step forwards, she banged into Waltus. As she muttered an apology, there was a soft clunk, and from above, a halo of galvanic lights came on one by one. For a moment, she was dazzled by the sudden illumination, then her sight began to adjust.

The room was round, the floor made from sparkling blue marble, concentric bands of gold cutting through it. Golden pillars lined the walls, between which were niches containing statues of amorphous, alien creatures, blasphemous beings that sent a shiver of primordial fear though her body. At the centre of all this was a large, flat altar.

'Fuck me with a feather,' Waltus said, walking up to one of the statues. 'This one's an ugly bastard, ain't he?'

'Show some respect, old man,' a voice said before Cirona had a chance to respond. 'That is Shu'Egal, one of the ancient gods, worshipped by the

Deivars and now by me.'

From behind the altar rose Garand, his former purgista's robe cast aside for one of jet-black, small stars of silver thread stitched along its length. If Cirona had thought he looked mad before, it had been small change compared to the man who now stood before her, wild eyes bulging from his gaunt face, hair an unkempt mass of tangles.

'So, you've even turned against the god that protected yer for so long,' Waltus said. 'I'd say I was surprised, but what can you expect from a ruzmagi?'

Garand sneered. 'Do not speak to me of treachery, old man. I know who you are and what you did in your youth.'

'I think you had better keep that mouth of yours shut, sunshine, or I'll shut it for yer,' Waltus said, eyebrows bristling.

'As much as I'd like to hear you two banter all day,' Cirona said. 'We have somewhere to be, so either get out of our way or come at us.'

'Dodge anything he throws,' Waltus said.

'Throw? Throw! I need not rely on such petty weapons now. Marmossa has remade me, and now I am a weapon, an indestructible weapon!'

Upon that, Garand drew a bar of metal from his pocket and gripped it tight in his left hand. Along the tips of his fingers, spreading up his arm, was a covering of grey. Soon it swarmed over the entirety of his body.

'What's he done?' Cirona asked.

'I think the mad fucker's turned himself to metal,' Waltus answered.

With a roar, Garand lurched forwards, throwing a punch at Cirona. Despite now being made of metal, he was moving at impressive speed, and she only just dodged. The blow hit a pillar behind her, leaving a crater. Howling, the former purgista swivelled round to face Cirona. She drew her sword, already certain that it would do no good.

A blur streaked in front of her vision and there was a dull metallic thunk. Garand stumbled back a few paces while Waltus, muscles rippling, stood in front of him. Looking closer, Cirona was stunned to see an imprint of the old mage's knuckles upon Garand's chest.

'If we can land one more blow, I reckon we've got him,' Waltus said. 'Just gotta get past that armour.'

'Armour? I thought he had turned himself into metal?' Cirona replied.

'Don't be thick, girl. He can't have turned his insides to metal, or he'd be dead. We just have blast past that new skin of his and get to the squishy bits.'

'What do you want me to do?'

'Keep him distracted. I'll need to focus all me power in me fists, so I won't be as quick as I normally am.'

'Got it,' she said.

Garand let out another scream of rage and charged at Waltus. Cirona dashed forwards her shoulder connecting with his chest in a bone rattling collision. She staggered back, somehow managing to keep her feet. Garand pinned her arms to her sides and lifted her into the air. It felt like she was caught between two colliding locomotron carriages, bones shrieking in protest, breath not reaching her lungs. Then he spun her round, hugging her as if she was his favourite toy.

'What will you do now, old man?' Garand crowed. 'To get me you'll have to go through her.'

'Do … it …' Cirona rasped.

'I … I can't, girl … it'd kill yer,' Waltus said.

'Don't … care … some … of us … have … to … stop … Marmossa,' she managed to pant.

'I can't,' Waltus said.

'Of course you can't! You're weak. Weak and old. A hangover from another time,' Garand said.

'For the Father's sake, do—' Cirona began.

She was cut off when a stream of blood erupted from her mouth. Looking down, she saw Waltus' arm penetrating her gut. Their eyes met.

'Well … done,' she gasped.

Then everything went dark.

***

'What do you reckon this place was?' Dargo asked.

Elvgren looked along a hallway lit with flaming torches. Suits of armour and weapons dangled from the walls.

'An armoury of some sort … or maybe the Terrors just like looking at pointy things,' he replied.

'I think the latter is more likely,' a silky voice said. From the back of the hall, Elvgren saw the duke appear. 'Well met, Lord Elvgren,' he continued. 'We did not expect you to get this far.'

'Well, here I am,' Elvgren said, walking forwards. 'Now, I expect you've got a lot of nonsense you want to say to me, Tobért, but I'm afraid I just don't have time.'

At that he raced forwards, drew his sword and plunged it straight into the duke's middle. The duke fell to his knees. Elvgren walked past.

'Come on, Dar, one of these platforms should—' he began to say.

'It would seem your manners have taken a turn for the worst, your lordship,' Tobért said.

Turning round, eyebrows creased, Elvgren saw the duke climb back to his feet. 'How in the … that was a killing blow,' he said.

'It would have been,' the duke said, turning around to show his wound knitting itself back together. 'If Marmossa had not made me unkillable.'

With a roar, Dargo charged. The duke drew his sword and swiped but the boy was too quick, diving underneath the strike and slicing the arm off at the elbow. Almost instantly black threads grew out of the wound, spinning themselves into an exact replica of the stolen limb.

'You see, it is useless,' Tobért said, grabbing Dargo round the neck then throwing him against the wall. 'Submit now, and in the new world to come, I may let you keep the throne you so shamelessly took.'

'Bugger that,' Elvgren said.

He leapt forwards, the duke sighing as he took a sword off the wall, their weapons clashing against each other. Elvgren thrust, cut, slashed and jabbed, utilising every trick he knew. But the duke was equal to all of them.

'I must say you're not bad,' Tobért said, parrying another powerful slash with a flick of his wrist.

'Fuck … you!' Elvgren hissed through gritted teeth.

He ducked low and aimed a jab at the duke's midsection. His attack hit home, and he brought his blade up in a vicious slice that cut his adversary apart to the collarbone. As he did, for one brief instant, he saw something red and glittering in Tobért's chest.

'That's it,' he said. 'Dargo I know what we have to—'

Elvgren was interrupted by the sighing sound of a blade cutting through the air. Time slowed to a crawl, and with dim, uncomprehending eyes he watched his sword arm go flying through the air in a trail of blood.

***

Bellina twisted, turned, kicked and spat, but no matter how much she struggled, the hands pinning her to the wall would not give an inch. She watched Dahlia saunter towards her, a sneer of amusement contorting her lips. Hate, visceral, hot, all-consuming hate surged through Bellina's body. Chest heaving, her eyes glanced left, right, down and up, seeking a way to attack, to escape. *Maybe*, she thought, *just maybe that could work.* But she would need to keep her foe distracted.

'Ah, the great Bellina Ressa, once more at my mercy,' Dahlia said.

'Damn you to the Void,' Bellina spat back.

'The Void is not something I fear, not anymore.' Dahlia replied, placing a hand on her captive's swollen stomach. 'My, my! Pregnant, eh? You have been a naughty girl.'

'Get your rotten hands off my baby!' Bellina roared.

'Whose is it? That grubby, besotted Narvglander or that vacuous idiot you're betrothed to? Wait … you don't know, do you? You've slept with both of them. What would your father, excuse me, *grandfather*, make of you spreading your legs for all and sundry like a common, two-bit dockside whore?'

Nostrils flaring, Bellina said, 'You have no right to speak of him.'

Dahlia tilted her head. 'Why now, I think I've got every right, seeing as it was me — oh, and you, of course — who brought the great Lord Chancellor to his knees. To think he spent his entire life obsessed by prophecy, desperate to stop what is about to happen. It makes me wish he wasn't dead just so he could see all he planned for come to nothing.'

A smile spread across Bellina's face, then she began to laugh.

'What?' Dahlia hissed, pulling out a knife. 'What the fuck is so funny?'

'Look up, bitch,' Bellina said.

Dahlia looked up just in time to see a massive chandelier come loose from the ceiling. The light fitting came crashing down upon her, the massive weight of the crystal and iron banding skewering her to the floor with a laughing roar. The hands holding Bellina vanished, and she stumbled to one knee before gaining her feet.

With slow, deliberate steps she made her way towards Dahlia, picking up the knife that had come free of her foe's grip. She bent down, savouring the look of agony on her fellow cognopath's face.

'Please,' Dahlia wheezed. 'Please … mercy.'

'I don't do mercy,' Bellina hissed, before drawing the blade across Dahlia's throat.

She watched her nemesis thrash and jerk, lifeblood gushing out of her. Bellina waited for the final convulsion to end then headed towards the door. *You're next, Marmossa,* she thought.

***

Elvgren fell to the ground, screaming in agony. He clasped a hand over his wound, feeling the hot, sticky flow of his blood pouring out of it. His vision began to swim, the room shattering and piecing itself back together again and again. The pain was horrendous. He was dimly aware of his own hoarse screams filling the air.

His consciousness flickering, he saw Dargo leap in front of the duke. He opened his mouth to tell lad to move, to run … but all that came out was a faint gurgling sound. Now the boy was glowing, the dagger, his relic, creating a shimmering aura around him. The aura began to take the shape of a man.

Dargo swayed out of the way of the duke's swipe. He ducked as the blade came back at him, plunging forwards, the dagger aimed squarely at his enemy's heart. The relic bit deep, sinking into Tobért's chest like it were cream. Looking down at the dagger with a confused stare, the duke gave a rueful smile.

'Well fought. Maybe we should have grabbed the rest of those relics after all?' he said before exploding into a million, tiny particles.

'Good … work … Dar,' Elvgren said, a smile on his lips as his vision grew black.

'Gren? Gren! Stay with me,' Dargo was calling from a million miles away, some of the words lost. 'Don't you … I'm gonna … gotta stop the bleeding.'

Elvgren was brought round by a searing pain in his wounded arm. The greasy, unmistakable scent of burned flesh filled the air. He turned his head and saw Dargo a torch in one hand a blade in the other. The boy was heating the sword in the flame getting it to glow the—

'Argh! Fucking hells!' Elvgren howled as the metal touched his wound. 'Can't you let a man die in peace!'

'Not you,' Dargo replied. 'Not today. Now grit yer teeth one last time for me.'

Again, the blistering kiss of the heated metal touched his wound. Again, he screamed.

'Will you stop being such a baby. How d'ya think I felt when me leg was done?'

'I don't care what you felt then. I care about how I feel now, and that's fucking awful,' Elvgren spat.

Dargo twisted his mouth and raised his eyebrows. 'How about a little gratitude for the bloke who, you know, just saved you from bleeding out all over the floor.'

'Alright, alright — thank you, Dargo. Now, could you help me up?'

Dargo offered his hand, and Elvgren went to take it with his amputated limb. He looked at the raw, cauterised stump and felt his stomach wheel round in a sick, churning motion. It was gone. His left arm, his sword arm, a fundamental piece of his being had been chopped off like it was a piece of meat. *That's all you are though, in the end,* he thought, *just a piece of meat for the worms to devour.*

'You alright,' Dargo asked, his hand still outstretched.

'I think I'm having an existential crisis,' Elvgren replied, using his right arm to accept Dargo's hand.

'A what?'

'Well, it's a new branch of philosophy that—'

'You lost me at philosophy,' Dargo cut in. 'You sure you're alright? You look a bit grey.'

Elvgren raised an eyebrow. 'Really? I look a bit grey … really?'

'Alright, alright, smart-arse, excuse me for caring. You ready to go?'

'As ready as a one-armed, one-eyed man ever is,' Elvgren replied.

'Don't forget his one-legged partner.'

'Quite right, Dar, quite right. Now, let's go and stop a maniac from summoning a horde of demons from the hells they were banished to.'

***

With a sickening squelch, Cirona heard Waltus pull his arm back. She slid to the floor, her lungs fighting for breath. Her mouth opened, and as she tried to speak, more blood poured over her lips. Through eyes greying at the corners, she saw the old mage kneeling over her. He was saying something, but she had no idea what it was.

Then he leaned forwards and planted a kiss on her mouth. She could feel something rushing into her, something strong and vital. The White Mage's breath seemed to fill her with enormous energy. She could feel her decimated organs heal themselves. Her stomach tightened, skin itching madly as it stitched itself back together. All at once, she felt whole again, her breathing normal.

Then Waltus collapsed.

She sat up, head spinning from the sudden movement and looked down at the old man. His scrawny chest was rising and falling in shallow crests, his skin had gone the colour of winter clouds.

'Waltus? Waltus!' she cried, grabbing his hand. 'What have you done, you silly old git?'

'Played me last card,' he said. 'Put all me life force into you.'

She squeezed his hand tighter. 'Why? Why would … why?'

He gave a small chuckle. 'My time's up, girl. Has been for a long while. Meeting you all, standing on the grand stage one last time … well, it was brilliant.'

Cirona watched as his eyes closed. 'Waltus?' she cried. 'Don't you leave me … don't you leave us. We need you!'

'Nah … I reckon you young'uns have got it covered. I've given it all. My life is a gift to you, girl, a statement of my faith. Don't let me down, eh?'

Brushing tears from her cheeks she said, 'I … I won't … I promise.'

'Good girl,' he said. 'Good girl.' Then he took his last breath.

Planting a kiss on his still warm brow, Cirona climbed to her feet. She turned away, hands balled into quivering fists at her side, nostrils flaring. *It's time to end this*, she thought.

CHAPTER TWENTY-TWO

Day was turning into premature night as the moon crossed the path of the sun leaving only a rind of light. Fontaine peeked out from behind the vast throne in front of him. He could see Marmossa in front of an altar chanting and prostrating himself. Behind the altar was a glass sphere occupied by a small boy he assumed was Midge. He was wild-eyed and thrashing, clearly under the effects of ether, the orb full of his forcefully extracted sortilenergy. And finally, he could see the portal through which Marmossa intended to summon his kin.

'Gods damn it!' Jeremias exclaimed. 'Where are the others?'

'I-I don't … maybe they ran into some trouble?' Fontaine offered weakly.

Jeremias bit his lip. 'We'll give it five more minutes then—'

He was interrupted by a soft whooshing noise. The scholar looked round to see a battered and bruised Barboza holding up Crenshaw. A heartbeat later, Bellina appeared followed by Dargo, Elvgren and Cirona. Jeremias gestured for them to stay low and quiet then beckoned them forwards.

'By the Father,' Jeremias said, looking at his brother. 'What happened to your arm?'

'Had a little run in with the duke,' Elvgren replied. His face was ashen and his attempt at a smile morphed into a grimace.

'Where's Waltus?' Fontaine asked. 'Surely, he could do something about this?'

'He's … he's gone,' Cirona said, her chin trembling. 'He gave his life for mine.'

There was a moment of silence while the group digested this new information. Finally, Jeremias said, 'I'd ask if you were all alright to carry on, but we don't have that luxury — we have to be alright. Now, we've been observing the situation for a while and reckon the best course of action is to sever the portal's power—'

'Little rats? Oh, little rats,' a sing-song voice called. 'Won't you come out from there? I must say you're very good at cowering; I almost didn't notice you. Going to stay hidden? Very well, I shall fetch you myself.'

Before Fontaine had time to draw another breath, he felt his arms pinned to his sides as something grabbed him around the middle. He had no need to guess what the "something" was because he could see the shadowy beings that had the rest of his companions in their grasp. They were hauled in front of Marmossa who had a massive grin on his face.

'Ah,' he said, spreading his arms towards them. 'The heirs of prophesy. Those destined to oppose me. Descendants of the mythic heroes who banished my brothers and sisters. It's enough to make you laugh. To think you vermin, you ill-bred aberrations with only a few atoms in common with your ancestors could stop me.'

'Oh, would you shut your fucking noise!' Dargo said. 'If you're gonna kill us, do it — at least we won't have to listen to you talk anymore.'

'Why would I kill you?' Marmossa said. 'The time has almost come. Things have taken a touch longer than I would have liked, thanks to you, Miss Ressa. If the boy had given his power willingly, it would have been easier.' He gestured to the glass sphere. 'So much energy is lost like this. But no matter; it has sufficed in the end.'

Fontaine who had been kicking and squirming grew still. In the centre of the portal, the moon slid over the last remnant of the sun. They had to do something … but what? His overworked brain scoured itself for an answer, but none came. He gritted his teeth. The thought of having to watch, helpless, was too much to bear. It was then that he noticed Jeremias working a ballistol out of the waist of his trousers. If they could just buy him some time …

'And now,' Marmossa crowed. 'The end has arrived.' He lifted a hand over the altar, ready to bring it down on what looked like the activation node for the portal.

'Esmanon!' Fontaine heard himself cry.

Marmossa's hand paused. '*What* did you say?' he said.

Fontaine swallowed hard under the full glare of the enemy. His throat grew tight, and for a moment, he thought he wouldn't be able to continue. He took a deep breath and bellowed. 'I call you by your true name! Esmanon — meaning shrivelled fig, given to you by your brothers and sisters. You were a joke to them, the runt who trailed in their wake.

'But then you cost them the battle of Arnok, and the joke wasn't funny anymore. It was they who locked you in that stone, they who imprisoned their greatest embarrassment.'

'How did you find … shut up! They … they imprisoned me to keep me safe. You know nothing,' Marmossa raged, aiming his staff at the scholar.

At that moment, a shot rang out. Fontaine watched Marmossa's face fill with surprise as he jerked out of the way.

'You missed,' Marmossa said. 'Not that bullets would affect me now.'

Jeremias smiled. 'I wasn't aiming for you,' he said.

Marmossa whirled round. Fontaine watched a web of cracks spread across the glass sphere. Under pressure from the swirling sortilenergy within, it burst apart in a cascade of jangling glass. Midge stumbled out, howling, eyes white and unseeing from the ether ... and began to attack.

***

Midge howled then let loose a barrage of fireballs. Cirona felt the grip of the shadow creature vanish, and she dropped to the ground. She could see Marmossa desperately fighting off the boy's magical attacks. This was it. This was their chance. Without a second thought, she charged.

Marmossa's back was towards her, and she aimed the point of her blade at the base of his spine. She lunged, but the tip of her blade quivered half an inch from her enemy's back like he was covered by an invisible shield. Thrown back, she landed hard on her arse.

Marmossa had Midge by the throat, his arm on fire from the boy's attack. Cirona leapt to her feet and attempted another vicious strike, this time between his shoulder blades. Again, her assault rebounded, but this time, she had got his attention. Marmossa swivelled, throwing Midge to the side. He aimed his staff at her face.

Light shot from the end of it, and she froze. Her throat was being crushed by an unseen hand, her vision filling with dancing dots of light, her lungs burning. Then she heard a cry and saw Barboza driving his spear at Marmossa's guts. The pressure on her throat released, and she gulped down grateful gasps of air.

Barboza was also meeting resistance, but the point of his spear was edging closer and closer to the flesh of their foe. Cirona staggered forwards and added her strength to his weapon. Just as it looked like they might break through, an errant gout of flame rocketed towards them, singeing the hair on her head and forcing them both back.

'Swine!' Marmossa hissed, readying to attack.

Before he could, he was swamped. Dargo jumped onto his back, dagger aimed at Marmossa's neck, Elvgren — sword in his wrong hand — sliced at his side, Crenshaw and Fontaine made a grab for his staff while Jeremias fired blasts from the ancient weapon. Suddenly, their opponent let out a howl that froze the marrow in her bones.

They were sent flying backwards. She could see Bellina had taken hold of Midge and was trying to bring him round. Her attention returned to Marmossa, grabbed by his screams of rage. His staff began to glow, and it came apart, scattering into a thousand sparkling pieces which pierced his skin, merging with him. He began to grow, muscles bulging, skeleton stretching till he stood at close to ten feet tall.

'We need to wake him up,' Jeremias shouted, pointing at Midge. 'We need him to focus his attacks.'

'I'm trying!' Bellina cried, the boy twitching in her embrace.

'Die!' Marmossa bellowed.

He charged forwards and sent a gigantic fist into Barboza's gut. The Timbokan was hurled back, his back smashing into one of the thrones. Cirona swallowed her fear and hurled herself into the fray. She ducked beneath Marmossa's outstretched arms and sliced into his flank. There was no resistance this time, but her strike had left little more than a scratch.

Dargo ran at their assailant, slid between his legs and climbed his back, driving the dagger into the base of his neck. Marmossa roared and tried to grab hold of the boy, but Dargo was out of reach. Cirona saw the others rushing forwards but so did the Thirteenth Terror. He tried to dash ahead to intercept them, but he couldn't move, his feet locked to the floor by blocks of ice.

Cirona looked behind her and spied a shaken but conscious Midge. Bellina with her hand on his shoulder was urging him to use his powers, guiding him. Cirona wasn't about to let the opportunity slip by and neither were any of the others. They barraged Marmossa with savage blows, each leaving their weapons buried in his flesh.

Black blood flowed from his wounds, and he sank to one knee. *We've almost got him*, Cirona thought; *we can win this.*

Then Marmossa began to laugh.

His body bent, twisted, then snapped back to his original form. The weapons that had been embedded in him fell to the ground with a clatter, and he casually picked up the relics.

'Why thank you for the lovely presents,' he said.

***

Stomach churning, Elvgren scrunched his eyes shut. *We've played right into his hands*, he thought. In front of him, Marmossa began to radiate with a dark light. He raised his hands up then threw them downward. In that instant, it felt as if a huge block of stone had landed on Elvgren's back, pinning him to the ground. Looking sideways, he could see the others were in the same predicament.

'Enough!' Marmossa hissed. 'Now you will watch the rebirth of this world.'

He walked to the altar and placed his hand upon it. Behind him, the portal began to crackle and spark, tongues of electric fire dancing across its surface. The hole in its middle began to warp and bend like water coming to the boil, and within it, he could see shapes, hideous, unspeakable shapes.

Is this how you're going to let it end? an echoing voice called.

Elvgren didn't have to search far for the voice's owner. In front of him stood the spectral, blue form of a man, robe billowing around him in a phantom breeze.

'Who are you?' Elvgren asked.

It is a sorry world when a child does not recognise his forebears.

'Amlith?' Elvgren said.

So, you're not completely ignorant, he said, kneeling down. *Now come, we must stop this runt from undoing the work I sacrificed so much to accomplish.*

'I … I can't … I haven't got the strength.'

Stop being dull, boy; you have my strength.

The ghost of Amlith placed his hand upon Elvgren's head. He felt a surge of energy course through him. Suddenly the weight holding him down was laughable in its insignificance. He climbed to his feet.

'What … what are you doing?' Marmossa cried. 'How can you be standing?'

'Because I am Amlith's Heir,' Elvgren said, his voice booming. 'You said we only had a few atoms of our ancestors' blood in us. That may be true, but those few atoms are more than enough to deal with you.'

As he walked towards the altar a wraith-like arm appeared where his own used to be. He reached out and plucked Amlith's sword, the relic that was rightfully his, from its resting place.

'No,' Marmossa babbled, stepping backwards. 'This can't be happening, it just can't.'

'I'm afraid it is, old boy,' Elvgren replied and plunged the blade into his gut.

***

Bellina watched, stunned. Elvgren rushed forwards, Marmossa impaled on his sword, a sword he was holding with a phantom arm. He raced towards the portal, stopped before it and pulled his sword back with a flourish. With a savage kick, he sent the Terror plunging into the portal. For a moment, he stood there, head cocked, as if he was listening to some unseen person. He turned to face her.

'I am reliably informed,' he said. 'That the only way to shut this thing off is if I go through it.'

'Don't you dare!' Bellina cried, struggling up as the pressure on her was released. 'There has to be another way.'

'Afraid not. The portal's apparently like a runaway locomotron now. It'll spread, devouring everything in its path. But if I pass through holding the sword, it'll overload it, force it to collapse in on itself,' he said.

Bellina could feel hot tears streaking down her cheeks. 'Please … please don't.'

Elvgren gave a small smile. 'I … have to. I've been a bit of a prick really. Let me have this one chance to be noble.'

'Gren!' Dargo screamed. 'Gren, don't you leave me!'

'Look after her, Dar. My child too. Same goes for all of you,' Elvgren said, addressing his companions. 'Look after her … look after each other.' He walked towards the expanding portal. He paused, turned to Bellina once more and said, 'Goodbye, Bellina, I … well, I've grown rather fond of you. Be a dear and try to work out how to get me back.'

With that he stepped into the portal's waiting maw. As it swallowed him it cracked like a cheap mirror, lightning erupting round its rim. With a deafening boom, it exploded.

'I can't believe he did it,' Cirona said. 'The stupid, pigheaded idiot.'

Jeremias offered Bellina his arm and helped her stand. Dargo was kneeling by a piece of the portal's wreckage, his body wracked with sobs.

'Bastard!' he said, slamming his fist onto the stone. 'Bastard, bastard, bastard. How could he leave us?'

'I know it's hard,' Jeremias said, putting a hand on the boy's shoulder. 'But what he did was the right thing to do, the heroic thing to do.'

'We'll honour his memory,' Bellina said, wiping her eyes. 'We'll make sure everyone knows the sacrifice he made today.'

'And I'll devote my life to getting him back,' Fontaine said.

For a long while they stood there, each lost in the ocean of their own thoughts, the sun gradually reappearing.

Taking a deep shuddering breath, Bellina said, 'Well then, let's get out of here.'

CHAPTER TWENTY-THREE

Adjusting the crown on her head, Bellina looked into the full-length mirror. She gave herself a thorough inspection. Her dress was jet-black, with delicate lace sleeves and a furred collar. Around her neck was a silver choker, a teardrop-shaped opal dangling from it. She looked entirely befitting of a woman still officially in mourning and undeniably regal. *How did this happen?* she thought. *I never thought I was destined for this.* There was a pull on the hem of her skirt, and she looked into the face of her son, five years old and eyes wide with curiosity.

'Mummy,' he said. 'What's happening? Why are so many people here?'

Bellina scooped him up in her arms and planted a kiss on the tip of his nose. 'Don't you remember from last year, bunny? It's daddy's day, remember.'

'The one with the feast and the fireworks?' he asked.

'That's the one,' Bellina said, placing him back on the floor where he yelled with joy. There was a knock at the door. 'Enter.'

Two servants opened the door and Jeremias walked into the room.

'Uncle Jerry!' her son squealed, running to hug the man's leg.

'Prince Calvin,' he said, ruffling the boy's hair. He looked at Bellina. 'You look radiant, Your Majesty.'

'Thank you, Lord Exchequer,' Bellina replied.

'The others have arrived and are waiting in the receiving room.'

'Excellent. Shall we?' Bellina said, offering Jeremias her arm.

They walked the short distance to the reception room. She could feel the excited babble of the crowd coming through the walls from outside the Palace. It hadn't been easy transporting the stolen people home after they were freed from Marmossa's spell, but by marshalling every boat in the Empire, they had done it. From closer to hand, she could hear laughter as everyone swapped stories about Elvgren. Jeremias strode ahead and opened the door for her.

'What about that time in New Ledi when he ran out of that cathouse in nothing but a towel?'

'I don't think that story's suitable right now,' Bellina said.

'Sorry, Belle,' Dargo said, jumping to his feet, knocking the drink in Fontaine's hand. 'Didn't see little Cal down there.'

'Uncle Dar!' Calvin said, holding his arms out to be picked up.

Dargo obliged. He had grown tall and handsome, in a distinctly roguish way, and was now a top operative in the Estrian Secret Service — Bellina's blade in the dark. He gave a whistle. 'Don't your mummy look lovely, eh?' he said.

'She certainly does,' Barboza added. The Timbokan king was dressed in a dark suit over which he wore a charcoal greatcoat covered in golden embroidery. Crenshaw was to his side, equally attired.

'Boo ee ful,' a small voice said.

Turning her head, Bellina saw Cirona and Dofri, their three-year-old daughter Agneta between them. Another shot at motherhood for the General after the loss of her first daughter.

'Beau*ti*ful, darling,' Cirona said.

'Isn't Nana gonna get a smooch,' Calsie said. She was standing with Midge, now the king of the mages, and Khasal. Prince Calvin sprung from Dargo's arms and ran to his grandmother, who along with Khasal was one of Midge's main advisers. Much of the populace was still fearful of the mages but strides were being made and persecution of them had been banned by law, a law Bellina had signed with a ready hand.

Jeremias coughed. 'It's time, Your Majesty,' he said.

'Is everyone ready?' Bellina asked. The room gave their assent. 'Let's go.'

Heels clacking against the marble floor, they made their way to the grand balcony. The doors were already pulled back and a surge of noise was coming from outside. The square in front of the Imperial Palace was choked with people. Bunting was draped in copious amounts in all directions.

'He would'a loved this,' Dargo said.

Bellina smiled. 'Yes. Yes, he would.'

EPILOGUE

The sky overhead was filled with stars. Elvgren was no astronomer, but even he recognised the stars were in the wrong place. The scent of wet dirt filled his nostrils and the ground beneath him felt damp. He sat up, shivering, and looked about.

'Where the fucking hells am I?' he said.